Praise for the novels of Sasha Summers

"Buzzing with charm and as sweet as a honey-comb. I was captivated."
—*USA TODAY* bestselling author Teri Wilson on *The Sweetest Thing*

"Sasha Summers is simply a mesmerizing talent."
—Stephanie Dray, *New York Times* bestselling author

"Delicious reading! Sasha Summers writes books brimming with warmth, humor, and the kind of love that lasts a lifetime."
—*New York Times* bestselling author Cathy Maxwell

"Sasha Summers writes sweet, charming tales that are certain to warm your heart."
—*New York Times* bestselling author Lorraine Heath

"A delightful summer, small town read, full of family love and drama. One that will leave you wanting to visit over and over."
—*USA TODAY* bestselling author Nicole Flockton on *The Sweetest Thing*

"Sasha Summers offers us romance to treasure."
—Elizabeth Essex, *USA TODAY* bestselling author

Also by Sasha Summers

The Sweetest Thing

Look for Sasha Summers's next novel
available soon from Canary Street Press.

SASHA SUMMERS

Must Love
Bees

CANARY STREET PRESS

CANARY
STREET
PRESS™

Recycling programs
for this product may
not exist in your area.

ISBN-13: 978-1-335-45256-6

Must Love Bees
Copyright © 2024 by Sasha Best

Honey Ever After
First published in December 2023
This edition published in January 2024
Copyright © 2023 by Sasha Best

For questions and comments about the quality of this book,
please contact us at CustomerService@Harlequin.com.

Canary Street Press
22 Adelaide St. West, 41st Floor
Toronto, Ontario M5H 4E3, Canada
CanaryStPress.com

Printed in U.S.A.

CONTENTS

To my own amazing Bee Girls: Johanna Raisanen,
Teri Wilson, Allison Collins, Patricia Fisher,
Janine Smith, McKenna Lee and Julia London.

A special thanks to Bee Girl Jolene Navarro,
who came over and sat at my dining table
until I stopped panicking and got to work.

I am so grateful for you!
I love you all to the moon and back!

MUST LOVE BEES

CHAPTER ONE

"WHAT'S ALL THAT?" Astrid Hill eyed the large stack of mail Abner Jones, Honey's mail carrier, held in his arms.

"Supply and equipment catalogs, bills and flyers, and the usual." He paused and slid the stack on top of the counter. He riffled through the pile and pulled out a glossy magazine. "And this. Bet you get all puffed up with pride." He sighed, shaking his head.

Pride and awe, certainly. And yet, even though she was looking at a picture of her family on the cover of *Beekeeping Monthly* with the heading, "Female Bee-keeping Family Success Story," there was an air of disbelief to the whole thing. All of it.

"I bet winning the top honey prize was like winning the lottery." Abner was inspecting the magazine cover. "Not that I've ever won the lottery, even if I do buy a ticket every week." He chuckled and handed her the magazine.

"You never know, Abner. If you don't buy a ticket, there's zero chance of winning." Astrid took the magazine and set it aside. It felt wrong to flip through it without her sister Tansy and her aunts present. Every time their honey or family was featured in a newspaper or magazine article, television interview or commercial for Wholesome Foods, they'd ooh and aah and get excited all over again—together.

"Ain't that the truth?" Abner tipped his blue-and-white cap forward. "Give your aunts my best, won't you?"

"Will do." Astrid pulled a cold bottle of water from the small fridge under the counter. "You stay hydrated out in this heat." She offered him the bottle.

His weathered face crinkled up in a smile as he took her offering. "Thank you. This will help."

Astrid waved him goodbye, then leaned forward to prop one elbow atop the antique glass case—full of equally antique beekeeping supplies—and sifted through all the mail. As much as she enjoyed working in her family's Main Street boutique, no customers with hours to go had her fidgeting. She sighed, peering out the large picture window. The bright summer sun shone down, and the trees lining Main Street cast long swaying shadows along the sidewalk. Breeze or no breeze, she wasn't fooled. The temperature was nearing triple digits—the norm for the Texas Hill Country in mid-July. But, even with the heat, her favorite place in the world was being outdoors with her bees.

Her aunt Camellia was humming off-key as she worked in the jam-packed stockroom. Every time her pitch broke or she hit a note that made any nearby dogs howl, Astrid smiled. This was part of Aunt Camellia's "process." Humming and mumbling as she sorted through all the bee-centric bric-a-brac, beeswax lip balm and candle-making kits, and anything else that struck either aunts' fancy enough to stock. Their little shop, a mere six hundred square feet, had become quite a tourist draw since her family's honey farm, Honey Hill Farms, won the Best in Honey contest two months ago. The win hadn't been about the blue ribbon or bragging rights. The win had come with a large cash prize and a distribution deal with Wholesome Foods—meaning Astrid's family no longer had to worry over losing their ancestral family home or beloved bees.

Thanks to the win, Astrid's family, honey farm and tiny shop had been featured in all the local papers, magazines, two commercials for Wholesome Foods—as well as being listed on their store website. Just yesterday, Astrid had taken a message for her sister Tansy to call *Wake Up America* for an interview. It seems a family of all female beekeepers was newsworthy.

Of course, the win had been *huge*. If they hadn't won, who knew where she and her aunts and her sisters, Tansy and Rosemary, would be now? It wasn't that she wasn't eternally grateful that their home and future were no longer in jeopardy—she was. *But* all the attention from photo-taking tourists and reporters, podcasters and news crews were a little much for her. She preferred a quiet life.

She was braiding a long strand of her hair when she caught sight of two adorable girls walking past the shop. They appeared on the left side of the picture window, hand in hand, in deep conversation. She didn't recognize them. Tourists, perhaps?

Both of them had a riot of dark brown curly hair. Curls upon curls. The older girl was tall and slim and wore a bright blue headband to keep her curls from her face. The younger girl's curls had been pulled back and secured into a severely cockeyed ponytail. The older girl was holding the younger girl's hand as if it was something she did regularly, steering the smaller girl. The younger girl's free arm held a worn stuffed blue toy against her chest. How many times had her older sister,

Tansy, dragged her and her younger sister, Rosemary, about as if they were just another appendage? While the older girl looked to be years older than the younger, they were definitely sisters. *No doubt about it.* When the older girl pushed open the door of Hill Honey Boutique, Astrid's curiosity was piqued.

New people in a town the size of Honey were a welcome curiosity to Astrid. She had no desire to leave Honey, ever, but she loved hearing about other places and people's lives beyond the flowers and bees and family that made up her whole world. According to her aunt Camellia, that's why Astrid had never met a stranger: her insatiable curiosity and gentle spirit. *Everyone likes Astrid.* She'd grown up hearing that from just about everyone she knew. Which was a good thing—at least, Astrid thought so. Her aunt Magnolia, who was far more reserved than her sister, Camellia, said Astrid was entirely too nice for her own good.

Either way, Astrid liked people. That these two were young and adorable and reminded her of herself and Tansy only added to her delight.

The older girl peered around the shop. She looked equal parts interested and confused. She adjusted her headband and pushed her curls from her shoulders, continuing to pull her younger sister along behind her while wearing a dubious expression.

Likely not honey folk, then. If you weren't "in honey," the supplies and equipment taking up a good portion of shelf space might look a little suspect.

Suddenly, the older girl stopped, her eyes going wide when they landed on Astrid. "Um…hi. We're looking for Astrid Hill."

Which was the last thing she'd expected to hear. "You've found her. I'm Astrid."

"You *are*?" She blinked, exchanging a long look with her sister. "Wow. Okay. Well…"

"You're supposed to be an ol' lady." The little girl seemed shocked. "And you're not an ol' lady."

Supposed to be an old lady? "Oh…" Astrid shook her head. "Not really." But there were times she felt a good deal older than she was.

"My aunt Rebecca—well, our great-aunt—said you were the nicest person in this whole town and we had to meet if we visited." The older girl stepped forward, dragging the younger girl with her. "So, we wanted to meet you."

Great-Aunt Rebecca? The only Rebecca in Honey, Texas, was… *Rebecca Wallace.* The eccentric old lady had been the Hills' neighbor. She'd passed away a couple of months now and Astrid missed their frequent chats and visits with Rebecca's bees. "Your great-aunt Rebecca was a wonderful lady and dear friend."

"We never met her in person," the older girl said. "But Mom read us her letters. Charlie, too."

"She wrote long letters." The younger girl dragged out the word *long* for emphasis, making Astrid smile. "Pages and pages." She hugged her stuffed toy tightly.

"Rebecca did love to write letters." Many a time, Astrid had helped Rebecca snap peas or shell pecans or with whatever odd job needed doing while Rebecca had read aloud from the letters her beloved nephew Charlie—these precious girls' stepfather—sent her. "And she loved telling me all about you two." She held out her hand. "It's very nice to meet you."

The elder girl shook Astrid's hand. "Halley." Her

smile was shy and hesitant. "And this is Nova, my little sister." She wiggled Nova's arm.

"This is Scorpio." Nova held out her stuffed star-shaped toy. A star with arms and legs and a very happy expression on its star face. "Scorpio says your store is nice."

Halley sighed, shook her head and rolled her eyes—something Tansy would have done.

"Well, it's nice to meet you, Halley, Nova *and* Scorpio. And I agree with Scorpio. I'm rather fond of our shop." Astrid couldn't help but like them right away. "What brings you into town?"

"Charlie has to work." Halley shrugged. "He told us to occupy ourselves."

"He works lots." Nova nodded in earnest. "Lots and lots and lots."

"That's a lot of lots." Astrid grinned at the little girl. *Absolutely adorable.*

"Charlie is our stepdad," Halley explained.

Astrid nodded. She knew all about Rebecca's nephew, Charlie. Mr. Charlie Adam Driver, to be exact. Rebecca had painted him as quite the gentleman. He'd sent weekly letters without fail. While Rebecca had doted on her only nephew, he'd ruffled more than a few feathers since his arrival in Honey. Astrid had yet to meet him but she'd heard plenty about the man. Mainly, that he was not very...*neighborly.*

Rude. Abrupt. Short. Dismissive. Those were the most frequently used descriptors. Having so recently lost his aunt, and his wife not long before that, Astrid couldn't think ill of him. He was dealing with grief. The poor man probably wanted to be left in peace. Rebecca had mentioned on more than one occasion that her Charlie was slow to warm up to people. It was likely that he simply needed time to do just that.

"Is your stepdad with you?" Astrid peered out the window. She'd like to meet him and offer her condolences.

Halley looked panicked as she gazed over her shoulder. "Uh…no. I rode Charlie's bike. It has a seat on it for Nova. She can't ride without training wheels yet." Halley glanced at Nova. "We're working on that, though." Nova's nod was determined. "Charlie says the exercise will do us some good. Staying fit and healthy is important." It sounded like she was repeating something she'd heard more than once.

"Don't wanna get fat *or* lazy," Nova added, shaking her head. "That is *bad* for your body." She patted her stomach.

"Oh." Astrid wasn't sure what the appropriate response was for that. Neither girl had any extra meat on them and, even if they had, that seemed a tad harsh. More troubling was the idea of these two riding along the county road into town. Exercise was good—but not when it put two children in the path of a speeding vehicle or 18-wheeler.

"Charlie likes it when we essercise." Nova was peering around the shop with wide eyes.

"Exercise," Halley murmured.

"Me and Scorpio do sit-ups and push-ups and eat *all* our vegetables. Sometimes Charlie even smiles some." Nova rocked up and down on her toes.

"Oh." Astrid repeated. Smiling was a rarity? This didn't sound a thing like the man who'd written weekly, albeit dry, letters to Rebecca.

"What's this?" Halley asked, cautiously holding up a frame grip.

"It's a beekeeper's tool." Astrid showed Halley how to use the handle to release the pincher-like tool. "A frame grip. When you open a beehive to check on the bees and honey, you use this to very gently grip the edge of a frame and pull it free from the hive box to inspect the bees and…" She got the feeling they had no idea what she was talking about. "Everything."

Both girls were frowning at the slightly ominous-looking tool.

"You don't have to use it, though. Your hands work just fine—as long as you're careful." This eased their alarmed expressions somewhat. She tended to get excited and chatter away over bees. Working here, she'd learned it was best to presume a person knew nothing about beekeeping or bees in the beginning. If they did have some knowledge, a refresher couldn't hurt them. If they didn't, then they might learn something new. Of course, there were those that wanted to come in, put on the beekeeper's netted hat for a few pictures and leave, but Astrid never missed an opportunity to be a bee ambassador. "Have you ever seen a beehive?"

Both girls shook their heads.

Bee novices were her favorite. It meant she had the chance to turn them into bee lovers—something the world needed more of. She accepted that just because she was ridiculously enthusiastic about her love of bees didn't mean others would feel the same way. "Would you like to? Do you have any interest in bees?"

"Bee's sting." Nova hugged her slightly dingy star toy close. "That hurts."

"I don't know." Halley shrugged, eyeing one of the

long L hive tools hanging on the rack with open skepticism. "Some of this stuff looks like it could be in a scary movie."

"Halley likes hairy movies." Nova lowered her voice and leaned closer.

"Scary and horror," Halley translated.

Which makes perfect sense.

Nova kept going. "I watched one, too." She held up one finger. "I wasn't supposed to but I hid. It was so icky." She hugged her toy closer. "I don't like those hairy movies."

"I admit, I've only seen one or two myself." Astrid couldn't stop smiling. "The tools all have a practical use. And none of them are scary, I promise." She thought she saw a glimmer of interest on Nova's face. "What if I told you I could show you a beehive *and* bees without you getting stung?" Astrid waited, hoping they'd say yes.

"On TV?" Nova shook her head. "Charlie says too much TV will give you headaches. Or make your eyes go bad. Or rot your brains out."

Astrid stopped herself from saying another "Oh." This time she said, "I see." Then hurried on to say, "Not on the television. On an observation deck. You stand behind a screen wall to see the bees but they can't sting you."

"I guess that sounds okay." Halley shrugged. Clearly, she wasn't sold on the idea.

"Can you see the stars there, too?" Nova asked, holding up her toy. "Momma says obversation decks are the best place to lay and stare up at *all* the stars in the sky."

"Observation," Halley murmured.

"Obversation." Nova nodded. "That's what I said."

"It's a different sort of observation deck. But I can lie

on a blanket and stare up at the stars for hours and hours. Especially on a clear night. There's no bigger night sky than the one here in Honey."

"It's the same sky all over." Nova frowned. "Isn't it?"

Astrid giggled. "It is, you're right. I mean it feels bigger. There aren't any lights to dim their sparkle. Like there are in the city." Not that she had any personal experience with city night skies.

"I *miss* the city." Halley sounded downright mournful. "There is *nothing* to do here. Nothing. And there's no one to talk to. I miss my friends, you know?" She swallowed.

Astrid understood exactly how Halley felt. Her best friends had always been her sisters. When Rosemary had moved to the other side of the country for school, she and Tansy had missed her desperately—but they still had each other. It took effort to resist hugging the girl. "How long are you staying?"

"Until Charlie sells Aunt Rebecca's house." Halley shrugged.

"I like the house. I like that it's purple. And crooked. And I love all the flowers. Except for the rat monster, I like it." Nova's little nose crinkled up. "It could be in a hairy movie."

"Rat monster?" Astrid paused.

Halley shook her head. "Nova has invisible friends."

"He's real." Nova pushed back. "I won't miss *it* when we go back home."

Astrid was heartsick to hear the property would be sold. Things were just getting settled with the neighbor on the other side of Honey Hill Farms. Settled as in her sister Tansy and the owner of the neighboring farm, Dane Knudson, were officially in love and making all sorts of plans—the sort of plans a couple makes when they know their future is together.

Now the Wallace place was going to be sold? Rebecca would be so sad to know her little "slice of heaven," as she'd called it, would no longer belong to the family. She and Clyde Wallace had met and married later in life and spent eight joy-filled years together. When he died and left the place to her, she'd had it another twenty-six years on her own. In that time, she'd come to savor the quiet and peace of her gardens and the bees she'd let Astrid keep there.

Rebecca had said some of her happiest memories were Charlie's boyhood visits. Long before Rebecca had become friends with Astrid or her aunts, Charlie had spent time working in the garden, catching fireflies, studying the bugs and birds that resided on his aunt's property. Rebecca had always been a big proponent for the outdoors.

When Astrid and Tansy had agreed to co-sponsor the Junior Beekeepers, Rebecca had eagerly invited the group out to care for her bees. In fact, the club's upcoming summer service project was to build several new hive boxes to replace the existing ones on Rebecca's property.

Oh, no.

A tiny bubble formed in her stomach. Tiny but nausea inducing all the same... Did Charlie Driver know about the project? Would he care? She knew Rebecca had told him about it in one of her letters, but that had been before the place was his responsibility so he might have forgotten. The Junior Beekeepers were counting on these service hours. Especially Benji and Kerrielynn— they were so close to leveling up their beekeepers' status. There was no time to find another qualifying project before next month's testing.

Don't panic. She'd simply explain and plead their case. It wouldn't affect him and she'd make sure they stayed out of his way. Surely, he'd be on board. Rebecca always said he had a good, practical head on his shoulders. Astrid would count on that.

"Well, who do we have here?" Aunt Camellia came out of the stockroom, her arms loaded with boxes of buttons, decorative bee-print ribbons, honey pots and other sundries they carried at the boutique.

"Let me help you, Aunt Camellia." Astrid hurried around the glass-front display cabinet. "These delightful young ladies are Rebecca Wallace's great-nieces. Halley and Nova, this is my aunt Camellia."

"And this is Scorpio." Nova held out her star. "He's my bestest friend."

"It's so very nice to meet you all." Aunt Camellia adored children—almost as much as she adored her pets, cooking and her sweetheart, Van Kettner. "I'm delighted to know Rebecca's kin have come to stay."

Nova shook her head. "For a visit."

"Until Charlie sells the place." Halley picked up one of the bee buttons. "These are so cute."

"They're some of our best sellers." Aunt Camellia looked as entranced by the girls as Astrid felt. "I don't suppose either of you like candy? I have some honey drops that are melt-in-your-mouth delicious."

"I do, I do." Nova let go of Halley's hand for the first time, her whole face lighting up. "But…" She sighed. "Charlie says candy is bad for you. It can give you cavities and give you diabebes."

"Diabetes," Halley corrected.

"That." Nova nodded.

Astrid wasn't one for jumping to conclusions but... she was beginning to wonder if Rebecca's opinion of her nephew hadn't exactly been objective.

"I don't think one piece would hurt you." Aunt Camellia chuckled. "It's only bad for you if you eat the whole bag."

"Can we, Halley?" Nova stared up at her sister. "Please. Just one." She held up her pointer finger and squished up her face, like she was waiting for bad news.

Halley considered her answer far too long. So long, Astrid began to worry this candy would lead to more trouble than it was worth.

"One, maybe." Halley eyed the clear canister. "But, maybe, we won't tell Charlie."

"Deal." Nova hooked pinkies with her sister. "One, please."

Aunt Camellia shot Astrid a pointed look—one that said she was thinking exactly what Astrid was—before handing each of the girls a piece of candy. "I hope you like them."

Astrid watched them as they both removed the cellophane, popped the candy into their mouths, and smiled.

"Here." Astrid held out her hand. "I'll throw the wrappers away."

Halley handed the wrappers over. "Good thinking."

For a moment, Astrid felt a teensy bit guilty keeping something from the girls'... Charlie. But really, it was one candy. One candy couldn't hurt a thing.

The door opened, the welcome bell jingled and Astrid turned to greet a new customer.

At well over six feet, the man was broad and fit. He wore casual business attire, a pale blue pressed button-down, brown slacks and polished leather shoes. At first glance, he looked like a businessman on a lunch break.

Until the tension rolling off the man flooded the room. He was struggling. Not only was the overlong hair mussed—a contradiction from his put-together appearance—but his jaw was clenched so tight it looked painful. He looked tormented. Conflicted. His hooded eyes were fixed on the girls.

The man drew in a deep breath and a visible shudder shook his large frame.

"May I help you?" Astrid's words broke the awkward silence.

He didn't even glance her way. "I was looking for my daughters. And now I've found them."

This was Charlie Driver?

"We only had one." Nova's eyes went so large they took up her entire face.

Halley elbowed her but didn't say a word.

"Halley…" It was a hoarse whisper. He pressed his eyes shut, and took a deep breath—his jaw still clenched—before he ground out, "How about we get the bike into the car and head home." He held the door open for them, the doorbell jingling again.

"Bye, Astrid. Bye, Miss Camellia." Nova waved and walked to the door. "I would like to meet your bees, Astrid. If Charlie says it's okay." She looked up at the thundercloud of a man standing, silent, in the doorway and winced.

"I hope so." Astrid smiled at the little girl. "It was very nice to meet you and Scorpio."

"Scorpio says it's nice to meet you, too." She offered a parting smile, then walked outside to where Halley was waiting.

When Astrid glanced back at Charlie Driver, he seemed to be evaluating her. And he didn't look the least bit happy. Then again, he didn't look unhappy—or angry. In fact, Astrid had no idea what to make of the completely blank expression on the man's face.

He left without a word, pulling the door shut behind him.

"What on earth was that about?" Aunt Camellia hurried to the front window. She didn't bother to hide the fact that she was watching Charlie Driver carry the bike to Rebecca Wallace's 1970 Buick Electra. He set the bike down, pulled open the back door, ran his fingers through his hair and attempted—rather forcefully—to wedge the bike into the back seat.

Astrid was certain there was no way that bike was fitting in that car. Charlie Driver, however, wasn't ready to admit defeat. He pulled the bike out and tried again, from a different angle, and with an increased vigor that couldn't be good for the bike. Or Charlie Driver.

"I can understand why people are saying he's short on charm. I might even agree with Corliss Ogden's assessment of downright rude." Aunt Camellia shook her head. "*He* didn't even bother with introductions."

Astrid didn't argue. One look at the girls' faces and she wished there was something she could do. After all, Halley and Nova had come here looking for her because of Rebecca's letters.

Charlie Driver doggedly continued to try with the bike.

"Poor little things. I should have filled their pockets with candy for later," Aunt Camellia murmured, turning back to the stack of mail. "Astrid, look. Oh, my word, did you see this?" Camellia held the magazine out at arm's length. "This will be going in the scrapbook."

"I did." But her focus remained on Charlie Driver, the bike and the two girls watching. She winced at one especially hard shove of bike against car door—and the way both girls jumped from the action.

The man was drawn so tight, there was a good chance he'd pop right here on Main Street. She could feel it, in her bones. She winced as he pulled his hand away, shaking it and flexing his fingers.

To Astrid, the entire exchange felt like a sign. He and his girls needed help. They were in a new place, knowing no one, and it would be hard to enjoy all that Honey had to offer. She could help with that. She'd take him some of Aunt Camellia's delectable treats and see if there was anything she could do for the family. He might resist her offer, he seemed a proud sort, but she wasn't one to give up easily.

CHARLIE WAS AT a loss for words. He'd looked up from his computer to see the girls sitting on the front porch swing and talking. They hadn't exactly looked thrilled, but he could see them and knew they were safe. Safety, for Charlie, was a big thing.

Ten minutes later, they were gone. The only thing that had prevented him from going into a full-blown panic was noticing his bicycle was missing. He and the girls had discovered a series of paths across his aunt's four-hundred-acre property a few days ago. He'd convinced himself they were probably riding one and would be back shortly. Except they weren't back. The longer they were gone, the more anxious he'd become. After running every path on the property, he'd climbed into his aunt's metal tank of a car and driven into town.

Seeing his bike, with both bike helmets swinging off the handlebars, allowed his lungs to fully inflate and his heart to resume a sort-of normal rhythm. He'd parked in front of the shop where the bike sat, waited until his agitation wasn't so obvious and collected the girls. The thrum in his temple had yet to subside.

Now he was dripping sweat, trying to wedge his damn bike into the damn back seat of the awful mustard gold car. He'd yet to find a place to recharge his electric car so he was having to make do with this monstrosity. The bike didn't want to fit but, dammit, he was going to keep trying. He bent over, turning the handlebar so the wheels would fit behind the front seat.

"Are you mad?" Nova stood on the sidewalk behind him. "About the candy?"

Her wobbly voice made him pause, rub the back of his forearm across his brow and will himself to stay calm. He slumped to rest his forehead on his arm. From this angle, Charlie could see Scorpio dangling from one of Nova's little hands.

"Are you, Charlie?" Nova's voice quivered a little. "It was one teeny-tiny-teeny piece."

He sighed and pulled the bike from the back seat. He looked down at her, forcing himself to smile as he ran his fingers through his hair. "No."

"He didn't even know about the candy, Nova." Halley sighed. "I did something to make him mad. Like always." She crossed her arms over her chest, her gaze fixed on the sidewalk at her feet.

He and Halley's relationship had grown more fragile since they'd arrived in Honey. She barely looked at him. She had every right to be angry with him, but she didn't get *angry*. She cried. A lot. Tears rendered him absolutely useless. He didn't know what to do about it. What was he supposed to do? What was he supposed to say? Their mom would know. Yasmina should be here to handle this whole teen thing. He wasn't equipped for this. Not in the least.

"Prolly. You always do *something*." Nova nodded, imitating Halley's long-suffering sigh to perfection.

Great.

"What did Halley do, Charlie?" Nova whispered loudly—so loudly there was no doubt Halley heard.

Charlie swallowed. *Be careful with your words.* Yasmina's warning echoed in his head—over and over. It took effort, a lot of effort. He wasn't the talker. Words always tripped him up.

"Something really bad?" Nova asked.

"I didn't know you two were planning to ride into town." He eyed the bike, then the car, and wanted to throw something. Throwing the bike sounded pretty damn tempting. "It's a long ride. On a road with traffic…" A dangerous road. *Calm, stay calm.*

"Halley wrote a note." Nova hugged Scorpio close. "I saw it. She did."

Halley was staring at her nails. "After I tried to tell you and you did your one-minute thing." She held up her index finger—what he did when he was in the middle of something and just needed a few more seconds to finish the line of code.

"It took a little longer than I'd anticipated," he murmured.

Halley went back to staring at the sidewalk but her

voice wobbled when she said, "It was on the kitchen table."

He hadn't been looking for a note. He'd been too worried about all the horrible things that could have happened to them. They could've gotten lost or hurt or, he swallowed hard… The bottom line was, bad things happened all the time. He knew that. The girls knew that.

Not so long ago, a very bad thing took Yasmina away from them. Since then, worry had been constant. Protecting the girls had him by the throat every second of every moment of every damn day. As long as he could see them, he could keep the fear at bay. But that wasn't the sort of thing he could admit to a thirteen-year-old.

"If my phone was working, I could have texted you," Halley said.

"You're *always* on your phone, Charlie." Nova said in singsong, making Scorpio dance, completely oblivious to the underlying tension between him and Halley.

They might be spending their summer in Honey, but he wasn't on vacation. He still had to work.

Halley's phone was another source of conflict. In Fort Worth, she'd obsessed over friends' constant texting and social media posts and parties and teen drama. Instead of doing her homework or her extracurriculars, she'd close herself in her room with her phone—especially after Yasmina's death. That had been concerning. When he'd walked in on Halley cuddled up with some boy with patchy facial hair and a car, he'd been more than concerned. There was no way, *no way*, he was prepared for that. Halley and boys? No. Hell, no.

His reaction? Getting out of Fort Worth. He could have handled the sale of his aunt's place from home or he could take the girls and attempt to reset everything.

Plus, he'd hoped being in Honey would make life a little easier for him. Nova was Nova, she had Scorpio and was happy enough. Halley had yet to forgive him. If she knew her phone was acting up because he'd limited her data and turned on parental controls, she'd *never* forgive him.

Work was the only thing he had a handle on. His office had been amazingly accommodating since Yasmina's death, but he knew better than to take advantage of that. There was no wiggle room with his work, none. It had always been that way. Now that Yasmina was gone... Well, that hadn't changed. He took a slow, steady breath. If he couldn't get the job done, they'd find someone else. He might be the best in his field but that wouldn't matter if he couldn't deliver.

"I have to work." It was that simple.

"You work a lot, Charlie." Nova hugged Scorpio close. "All the time. Even when it's dark outside."

Charlie didn't respond. Other than worrying about the girls, work consumed him. If he stopped or let his mind wander, he'd get lost in this reality without Yasmina and that sent him into a tailspin. After almost twelve months, the realization that he was parenting alone still sent him into a panic attack. It made no sense. He wasn't wired for this. He would—he *was* screwing this up. But he was all they had left.

"My job is important, Nova." Charlie smiled at her—at least, he tried to. "But nothing is more important than you two."

Nova smiled at him.

Halley continued to stare at the sidewalk.

Charlie wanted to get home, out of the sun, and away from the too-prying eyes of Honey, Texas. He wouldn't be surprised if the occupants of every shop were watching them from their storefront windows. What else would they be doing? It was a quiet Wednesday, not that he'd ever seen Honey bustling with activity.

Everything moved at a snail's pace. Everything. Even business. It was what he wanted, initially, but he hadn't considered just how glacial Honey's pacing was. From arranging the property appraisal to finding a real estate agent to list the property, no one appreciated his sense of urgency. Due to a health crisis, the earliest the lawyer could schedule Aunt Rebecca's will reading was in two weeks—even though she'd been gone for months. With luck, his sisters would continue to stay disinterested in all things concerning their "weird aunt" and her "bug-infested" property. If they did, he'd sell, divide the profits amongst the three of them and go back to Fort Worth, their condo, a tightly scheduled week for the girls and real life—minus Halley's stubble-faced boyfriend, that is. He hadn't exactly worked that part out, but he would.

The faster this was done and over with, the better. He set the bike down and looked at his swelling knuckles.

"You can leave the bike here, if you like." A woman stood under a store awning, shielding her eyes against the bright sun.

He'd been too wound up to care about anything beyond the girls. But now… He swiped the back of his arm across his head. The woman from the shop. Hazel-green eyes. Long strawberry-blond hair. Watching and waiting with a smile on her face.

It wasn't a happy smile, though. It was sympathetic. Almost pitying. Too much. Which was akin to rubbing salt into his wounded pride. He didn't like it. Then again, he didn't do well with people. Especially those he didn't know. He wasn't exactly a people person.

"It will be safe." The woman looked less certain now, glancing from him to the bike and back to him. "The bike, I mean."

He frowned.

"Charlie," Nova whispered, too loudly. "You look grumpy."

Right. His gaze fell from the woman. According to Nova and Halley, he tended to look grumpy most of the time.

"That's Astrid." Halley managed to actually whisper.

Nova's attempt at a whisper was a little quieter this time. "Aunt Rebecca's friend?"

This was Astrid Hill? His aunt's letters had painted Astrid as her peer. An older, eccentric, free spirit of a woman with a penchant for gardening, walking barefoot, and tending to and talking with bees. He glanced at Astrid's feet. She was wearing sandals. For some reason, that was reassuring.

If he calmed down and cleared his mind, he might be able to acknowledge that he needed help. *Fine.* With a deep breath, he carried the bike back onto the sidewalk and leaned it against the shop next to her. "I'll come back for it." He forced himself to make eye contact.

"There's no rush." She was studying him, her green eyes unsettling this close.

Studying and judging, no doubt. He nodded, his mouth too dry to speak, and tore his gaze from her. Making eye contact was hard for him—maintaining eye contact was a nightmare. He took a deep breath and let it out slowly. After all the years of therapy and self-help books, the eye-contact thing was still a huge issue for him. That, and touch.

"I'm Astrid Hill." She held her hand out. "I suppose we will be neighbors for a bit?"

Great. He shook her hand, horrified by how sweaty and grimy he was. He wiped his hand against his leg—and realized his mistake. Now he'd made an even greater ass out of himself by wiping his hand off after they'd shaken hands. "Yes."

She blinked.

"Neighbors?" He tripped over his words, but didn't look at her. "Temporarily."

"If there's anything I can do, I'm right on the other side of the fence." She sounded sincere.

He nodded, his gaze shifting her way as she tucked a long thin braid of hair behind her ear.

"Well, on the other side of the fence, down the trail past the little creek and beeyard. You can't miss the trail. Rebecca and I dug up the rocks and made the path together. Follow it all the way and I'm right there. Rather, our house is right there." She moved her hands, pointing one way and then the other. "Not me, just standing there. That would be weird. But I guess that's obvious?"

Charlie went through her words again. Even if he didn't struggle with conversation, he wasn't sure he'd know what to say to that. He didn't spend much time with people—other than Nova and Halley. His work was entirely remote so he didn't have to worry about these types of uncomfortable interactions. Astrid Hill's lively sort of rambling left Charlie…baffled. "Right." It was a neutral response.

Astrid blinked again, looking a bit baffled herself.

"We should go." And yet, Charlie found himself staying put—watching Astrid Hill's expressive face.

"I'm sure you have things to do." Astrid's smile gave off an almost tangible warmth.

He swallowed against the lump in his throat and went back to frowning. "Yes, I do."

"Charlie." Nova's impatience was clear. "It's hot. Are we going?"

Yes. Now. He nodded, turned and opened the back door of the car. Once Nova and Halley were safely inside, he climbed into the driver's seat and pulled away from the curb. He thought he saw Astrid Hill wave. He didn't wave back.

"You are so weird," Halley murmured, staring out the window.

Charlie glanced in his rearview mirror. "I'm not."

Halley was wearing her *yeah right* expression. "You were *way* harsh to Astrid. She didn't do anything."

"She's pretty—fairy princess pretty, even. I like her hair. It was so long. Like Rapunzel." Nova sighed, hugging Scorpio. "We made friends."

Halley's sigh wavered. "She was probably just being nice."

Charlie agreed with Halley, but stayed quiet. The idea that Astrid Hill, an adult, would want to be friends with children was far-fetched. Especially children she wasn't related to. Even then, there were no guarantees. He knew this because of the home he'd grown up in. Now that he was a stepfather, he wasn't sure how to be their friend *or* their parent. He was failing on all fronts.

"She was *so* pretty. I liked her flowy dress." Nova wasn't the least bit fazed by her sister's statement. "And Miss Hill was nice. Like Mrs. Claus. Only with colored hair." Her big brown eyes met his in the rearview mirror. "She did give us each one piece of candy."

Nova was incapable of keeping a secret. Charlie hoped this was a permanent trait—it would make her teenage years much easier for him. "That was nice of her."

Nova relaxed against the car seat and yawned. She'd been having bad dreams and a rough time sleeping since they'd moved into Rebecca's house. "We said thank you."

The girls had impeccable manners. Yasmina had been a stickler about that.

"I did try to tell you." Halley continued looking out the window. "But you're still mad."

Charlie took a minute. He had to. He spent all day writing and thinking in code. Words didn't come easy to him. "I was worried." *Worried sick.* "I'm not angry." He was too relieved to be angry. He glanced at her in the rearview mirror. "We need to work on...communicating."

She glanced at him, her lips pressed tight—like she was holding something back.

Don't ask. He'd handled himself well, so far. But he wasn't sure that would continue if Halley dissolved into tears. He wasn't trying to make her life miserable, he was...*trying.*

Halley didn't see it that way. She'd start with everything that was wrong today before eventually circling around to them being here, him ruining her social life, and how Steve or Sam or Scott was the love of her life and she might lose him now that she wasn't there. Because of him. It was easier not to say anything else until they'd turned off the farm-to-market road and onto the gravel drive leading to Rebecca's house.

"You have to work?" Nova glanced up at him as they walked to the front porch.

Yes, he had to work. He'd lost the better part of the day looking for them. Dammit, he'd also missed a call that he shouldn't have missed. But... He slowed, took a deep breath and really looked at Nova. Her curly pony-tail was crooked, her shoes didn't match and she was staring up at him, focused on his answer. "I can take a break."

"You can?" Nova bounced up and down, gleeful. "Can we play a game? Please."

Halley sighed. "Not Monopoly."

"Agreed." Charlie could take a break, not the after-noon. "How about Clue or Sorry?"

"Sorry." Nova went running into the house.

Charlie glanced at Halley from the corner of his eye. There were times, like now, when she looked so much like her mother.

Every time he tried to fix things, he wound up mak-ing a bigger mess. Yasmina's girls were counting on him.

My girls, now. It should be the three of them against the world. But, most of the time, it felt like the two of them against him.

"What do you think of the town?" he asked, picking as neutral a topic as possible.

"The Hill Honey Boutique was okay." Halley waited until they were inside to murmur, "That and the grocery store is all we've seen. I know you're too busy to take us to look around."

Charlie swallowed back his immediate *My job is im-portant* response. The girls were important, too. He had to make time. "No. We'll do it. This weekend."

Halley didn't look convinced but she gave him a slight nod before following Nova into the family room.

Most of his memories of Honey revolved around Rebecca and her place. In a world full of judgment and criticism, this was a sanctuary. If only he could tap into that now—the peace and freedom he'd had when he'd been a boy here.

Instead, he'd find something to do with the girls. Fishing or hiking or swimming at the lake, there'd be something they could enjoy together. He'd look over his schedule, move things around and make a day of it. But first, he had to play Sorry, get his bike home and try to reschedule the call he missed.

CHAPTER TWO

"ARE YOU SURE this is a good idea?" Aunt Camellia paused in tallying the day's sales to choose her next words carefully. "He didn't strike me as the most... sociable of fellows."

Astrid made a noncommittal sound as she flipped the Open sign to Closed.

Tansy shifted on the honeycomb-print tufted chair and smoothed her jean overalls down. "Has anything ever been stolen in Honey? Like, ever?" Tansy always wore something with a bee on it. Today it was her boots, covered with embroidered bees.

"Cute boots," Astrid murmured, before turning back to the matter at hand. "It's not about that. You have a truck." For her, delivering the bike seemed the neighborly thing to do. Plus, it wasn't like it would inconvenience them. They had to drive right past Rebecca's place on the way home. "He doesn't have a truck." She remembered his multiple failed attempts to shove the bike into Rebecca's old car and the frustration rolling off him when he'd set the bike back against the shop. Astrid couldn't shake the feeling that Charlie Driver, in all his grumpiness, needed a break.

Tansy was watching her. "Aunt Camellia said he was a real charmer."

Astrid shrugged. "The girls are precious."

"They were." Aunt Camellia nodded. "There's no arguing that."

"And they were interested in bees." *Sort of.* Still, a spark of interest could easily grow. "I thought I could bring them by the observation deck when it's ready?"

"Of course you can," Tansy gushed—she always gushed about her project. "Too bad you hadn't turned them into bee lovers a few weeks ago. We would have had two more sets of hands for the honey flow."

Astrid laughed. Honey flow—or harvest—usually happened around the first week of July. "I'm honored you have that much faith in me."

Tansy rolled her eyes. "If anyone can get someone excited about bees fast, it's you." She pushed off the chair, her gaze wandering to the shop's front door. "You want me to go with you?" She sounded a tad distracted.

Because Dane Knudson, Tansy's sweetheart, was heading for the door. Dane's teen brother, Leif, walked along beside him. They were laughing at something and Tansy was grinning like the lovesick woman she was. It made Astrid happy when her sisters were happy. Tansy and Dane were blissful together and had all sorts of plans for the future. Her other sister, Rosemary, was off following her dreams participating in an important bee genetics study in California. They were happy. In turn, Astrid was. No matter what, the three of them had each other's backs and always picked up right where they left off.

"I think I can drop off the bike by myself." Astrid and Aunt Camellia exchanged a smile.

"I'll head home and get dinner started. Mags and Shelby won't be back from their museum excursion until tomorrow. So, who should I expect around the dinner table?" Aunt Camellia picked up a pen and tablet, waiting. "The three of us."

The jingle of the doorbell rang out and Dane and Leif walked in.

"Good afternoon, you two." Aunt Camellia smiled. "You guys are eating with us."

"Isn't that a thing now? Dinner and lunch and...food, with y'all." Leif adored Aunt Camellia—and her cooking.

Dane chuckled, tearing his rather intense gaze from Tansy before the kissing could begin. "Thank you, Camellia, we will both be there—if you can stand to have us?"

"Of course." Aunt Camellia waved her hand dismissively. "As Leif said, it's a thing now." She smiled at Leif, who grinned back at her.

"Good." Dane's hands were already pulling Tansy close. "Can we bring anything?"

"No, no, just yourselves." She scribbled something on her tablet. "Plus, Van, of course—"

"Of course." All four of them said in unison.

"Behave." But Aunt Camellia was grinning.

Van Kettner was a well-respected Honey resident, the local butcher—and, recently, Aunt Camellia's beau. As far as Astrid was concerned, he was also one of the sweetest men to ever walk the planet. Once he'd finally got up the nerve to express his longtime adoration to her aunt, the two of them were inseparable. Now it was hard to imagine a time when they hadn't been together.

"Looks like we're the singletons again." Astrid nudged Leif.

"Speak for yourself." Leif grinned.

"Oh?" Astrid stared at the boy with wide eyes.

"I'm taking Kerrielynn on a date tonight." Leif's cheeks were red-tinged and he was all puffed up with pride. "Now that I've got my driver's license, I'm driving." Kerrielynn was older and had been driving them around so this was a big deal.

Dane groaned, holding Tansy against his side. "Which is why I'm getting more gray hair every day."

Tansy reached up to tug on Dane's long blond ponytail. "Don't believe it, Leif. I don't see a one."

"No?" Dane only had eyes for Tansy now. "I'm pretty sure there's a few with your name on them, too."

Tansy laughed. "I'm pretty sure the *majority* of mine have your name on them."

"Whatever." Dane kissed Tansy then.

Compared to some of the kisses she'd seen them exchange, Astrid thought it was almost a socially acceptable kiss.

"Ugh." Leif didn't agree. He made a gagging sound before asking, "Anything new here?"

"We got another one of those cards from that real estate company." Camellia shook her head.

"Another one?" Dane frowned. "This is bordering on harassment. Want me to call them and set them straight?"

"Maybe if we get another one." Camellia chuckled. "Or we could set Mags loose on them?"

Astrid's aunt Magnolia was a force to be reckoned with. She'd set these overly persistent land developers on their ear.

"Oh, we also met the new neighbors." Aunt Camellia finished writing on her tablet. "That Charlie Driver character? And his two precious daughters."

"'That Charlie Driver character'?" Dane asked. "That doesn't sound good."

"I have to say, I don't know what to make of him." Aunt Camellia ripped off the top sheet of paper. "But if you help Astrid take his bicycle out to him, you can see what you think."

"People have been saying he's a real ass—er, jerk. Was he rude to you?" Leif asked, fiercely protective of them.

"No." Astrid patted his arm. "He was…abrupt. Honestly, Aunt Camellia, can you blame him? He'd been looking for his daughters. From his reaction, I get the feeling he didn't know that Halley and Nova had ridden into town. If he was a bit out of sorts, I'd say it's a reasonable enough explanation."

Once Astrid and her sisters had come to live with her Poppa Tom, Granna Hazel, and two aunts, they'd been allowed many freedoms. It was a small town and people looked out for one another. But, even then, they hadn't been allowed to ride their bikes along the county road. "If Tansy, Rosemary and I had ever done something like that, Poppa Tom would have been—"

"Terrified? And, once you were safe, he would have been relieved—overwhelmingly so." Aunt Camellia nodded, tapping her chin with her pencil. "I suppose you're right." She reached out to take Astrid's hand. "You're right to point that out, too." She gave her hand a squeeze. "I imagine he was scared to death."

"Yeah, that would do it." Dane gave Leif a playful shove. Dane was Leif's big brother but, in many ways, he was more father than their actual father. "That road is too dangerous for bike riding."

"We'll go with you," Tansy volunteered.

Dane took Tansy's hand. "Let's go meet Charlie Driver."

Which was a great idea. Most people liked Dane.

Leif's phone pinged. The growing smile on his face told everyone who was texting him. "Kerrielynn's free now. But I'll get the bike into the truck before I go." He gave Aunt Camellia a quick hug and headed for the door. "I'll be home at eleven." He pushed through the front door without a backward glance.

Dane shook his head, watching Leif.

"He'll be okay." Tansy tugged on Dane's arm.

"I know." He sighed.

Not too long ago, Leif had been determined to stir up trouble. If Dane told him to go left, Leif would go right just to spite him. But that was then. The brothers were on a different path now, together.

"He's doing great." Dane captured Tansy's hand.

"Of course he is." Aunt Camellia grabbed her massive tapestry purse, tucked the list inside and grabbed her keys. "Are we all ready?"

Five minutes later, Aunt Camellia was headed to the grocery store and Astrid, Tansy and Dane were heading to Rebecca Wallace's place to return Charlie Driver's bicycle.

"I think we should go swimming Sunday." Tansy was wedged between Dane and Astrid, making it easy for her to rest her head on Dane's shoulder. "See if Leif and some of his friends want to go? It's hot and the water will be ice-cold and refreshing."

"Sounds good to me," he agreed.

Astrid couldn't help but smile at the exchange. Now that the two of them weren't at each other's throats all the time, they were surprisingly like-minded. Both creative and driven, loving and thoughtful. Loyal and stubborn. Oh so stubborn.

"Why are you smiling like that?" Tansy was studying her.

"You two." Astrid left it at that.

"We're pretty much the perfect couple?" Dane didn't wait for an answer. "I think so, too."

"That's *exactly* what I was thinking." Astrid giggled.

They turned onto the gravel road that led to Rebecca Wallace's cottage. It had been a plain white house until Rebecca had moved in. That's when it got a fresh coat of pale lavender paint—Rebecca's favorite—and the place began its metamorphosis. Several windows had been replaced with stained glass, window boxes had been added all along the front of the house, and the snug covered porch had been leveled and adorned with blooming hanging plants. All because Mr. Wallace wanted to make Rebecca happy.

"Looks like he's taking care of the flowers." Astrid slipped from the passenger seat, pleased to see the plants and flowers in full bloom. "Rebecca loved her flowers almost as much as I love my bees."

"I don't think anyone loves the bees as much as you do, Astrid." Dane headed around to the rear of the truck and pulled the bike out.

"Aunt Camellia's calling. You two go ahead," Tansy said from inside the cab of the truck.

As soon as Astrid knocked on the front door, she was second-guessing her decision. After today's events, she suspected coming here—even with the best of intentions—might not be welcomed. Now that she'd knocked there was no going back, all she could do was wait and try not to get too flustered.

The front door swung wide and Charlie Driver stood inside. He was surprised to see them. At least, that's what it looked like until his expression went blank. Only the slightest V settled between his brows. Instead of smiling—something Astrid had yet to see—his heavy-lidded gaze shifted from the bike, to Dane, then her. "I was coming to get it."

Not exactly the response she'd expected. "I thought dropping it off might be more convenient for you... It was no bother. We drive by on the way home so... Here it is."

His dark brown eyes fell from hers.

"I'm Dane Knudson." Dane stepped forward, hand outstretched. "I own the honey farm on the other side of the Hills."

Charlie blinked, turned to Dane and shook his hand. "Charlie Driver."

"Charlie." Nova's little voice reached them. "It's your turn."

"Just a minute." Charlie glanced over his shoulder.

Rapid footfalls announced the little girl's imminent arrival.

"Astrid?" Nova smiled up at her. "Hi." She turned to look up at Dane. "Who are you?" She cocked her head to one side. "You look like that superhero with the hammer. The one with the lightning eyes and fingers." She wiggled her fingers.

"Thor?" Charlie gave Dane a thorough assessment. "No, he doesn't."

Dane hated the constant Thor comparisons so Charlie's quick refusal won major brownie points with him. "I know." He shook his head. "I don't get it."

"Well, I think you do. And I think he's cool." Nova

rocked forward onto the balls of her feet, swinging Scorpio back and forth. "We're playing Sorry. And I'm winning."

More footsteps and Halley arrived. "Hey, Astrid." She glanced at Dane. "Hey. Are you Astrid's boyfriend?"

Astrid shook her head. "No. No. Dane's my sister's boyfriend." She pointed at the truck. "My sister. She's on the phone at the moment."

"Is she on the phone all the time, too?" Nova asked Dane in her not-so-soft-whisper voice. "Does she have important work to do, too?" She stared up at Charlie then, smiling.

Charlie didn't smile back but one dark brow did arch up. "Who is not on the phone but playing Sorry with you?"

"You are." Nova rocked forward again, still smiling. "And I'm winning."

"It's a big deal that she's winning." Halley rolled her eyes.

Astrid had to smile then. The eye-roll thing was a signature Tansy move. "Sorry is one of my favorite games. Monopoly, too."

"Monopoly takes too long." Halley shot a glance at Charlie—as if that explained everything.

It did. She glanced at him. Now both eyebrows were elevated and his lips were pressed into a thin line. Astrid wasn't sure what to make of the man's expression but she found herself saying, "Well, I like Monopoly. You and Halley are always welcome at Honey Hill Farms. If you'd like to play." As soon as the words were out, she regretted them.

Halley glanced at Charlie, silent but hopeful—it was written all over her face.

"I would like that lots and lots and lots." Nova clapped her hands, Scorpio bouncing around, as she sort of hopped up and down. "Can we, Charlie? Can we? Please?"

"We'll see," Charlie murmured. "We should get back to the game. I have a conference call in thirty minutes." The crease between his brows deepened and the corners of his mouth drooped as both the girls seemed to deflate.

Astrid wasn't sure who to feel sorriest for—Charlie or the girls.

"Maybe Astrid can come play with us here?" Nova asked. "Then you can work and not worry about us." She held up Scorpio to her ear. "Scorpio thinks that is the best idea."

"I'd like that," Astrid agreed, wanting to ease the awkwardness between the man and his stepdaughters. She had no idea what their circumstances were but, after listening to the girls and watching Charlie's interaction with them, she knew things were strained. "Sometime…" Agreeing to come visit wasn't quite as bad as inviting the girls over without consulting Charlie first, was it? Maybe it was. But how was she supposed to resist Nova when she was asking so nicely?

Charlie Driver looked at her then, really looked at her. It was almost as if he was seeing her for the first time. Was he upset that she'd invited herself over? She wasn't sure. Considering how reserved he was, this could be the equivalent of a death glare. But she couldn't shake the feeling that the somber, brooding man wasn't frigid so much as he was guarded.

But from what and why?

Astrid resisted the urge to reassure him she was a truly nice person with no ulterior motives. She'd been more than welcoming to him and the girls. Now it was up to him to accept her and any or all of her invitations. She hoped he would, for the girls' sake. If he didn't want to be her friend, so be it. But she could tell by the looks on their faces that the girls did. *And, since they're bored and lonely and precious, I should keep trying— for their sake.*

CHARLIE DIDN'T NEED Halley or Nova to tell him he was staring at Astrid. He knew. He was staring and he couldn't seem to stop. Here they'd been having a somewhat enjoyable game of Sorry and this woman showed up. With reinforcements. Why? What did they want?

Not only did he not appreciate them showing up without an invitation, he didn't like that she seemed clueless to the fact that her presence wasn't welcome. Did he need to explain it to her? That this set a bad precedent? Dropping by, unannounced and uninvited, might be what people did here in Honey but he would never dare to invade someone's home that way. And now Astrid had gone and offered to come visit them here—without talking to him first. He didn't like being manipulated or getting the girls' hopes up only to lead to disappointment.

"Sorry." Another woman joined them on the front porch. "Tansy, Astrid's sister." She shook Charlie's hand. "My aunt called. She's at the store so..." She broke off, glancing around the porch.

Probably because it's getting awkward as hell out here. He'd done it. He always did it. He didn't know how to do the conversing-with-strangers thing—them showing up like this only made it worse. If he'd had some kind of notice, he might have been prepared. No. He'd still be awkward and irritated.

Halley's sigh snapped him out of it. She had the disappointed sigh down.

"Charlie Driver," he mumbled.

Tansy nodded. "And I'm guessing you're Nova and you're Halley? Astrid has been talking about you two all afternoon."

"Really?" Nova was practically vibrating with excitement. "We've been talking about her, too. And her aunt. And the candy. And the grippy thing from the hairy movie."

Charlie did have some questions about the grippy thing the girls had seen in the shop.

"It's called a frame grip." Astrid was laughing softly. "It *does* sort of look like a big pincher." She met his gaze then. "It helps pull the frames out of each hive box."

Which didn't really clear up any of his questions. But questions would lead to more conversation and he was pretty sure everyone wanted this to end as soon as possible.

"Astrid also said you had lots of good questions about beekeepers, like us." Tansy pointed between herself and Astrid. "And that you two wanted to come to the bee observation deck? Get a safe look at the bees."

"Because bees sting and that hurts." Nova wasn't intentionally mimicking him. He had repeated the words to her, over and over again, once they'd discovered the old hives on his aunt's property. The last thing he needed was for one of them to get stung. For all he knew, they could be allergic. Honey, Texas, might have some sort of rudimentary medical facility but any real medical establishments would be a good forty-five minutes away—at least.

"Is it true bees don't want to sting us?" Halley frowned.

"If they sting you, they die." Dane crossed his arms over his chest. "Believe me, they don't want to sting you."

Charlie winced, waiting for the girls' reaction. They didn't talk about death or dying, not since Yasmina had passed. He'd purchased a whole library of books on healthy grieving and talking to kids about death but all that had done was guarantee that, without reading directly from the book, he wasn't equipped for that sort of deep and introspective discussion.

"They only sting when they absolutely have to." Astrid tucked a long strand of braided strawberry-blond hair behind her ear. "When they're protecting their hive or another bee has sent out a distress signal and wants backup. Just like any family, really. They rally to protect each other and their home."

"They *talk*?" Nova's eyes were round with astonishment.

"Not like we do, no." Astrid crouched. "But they communicate through scent and dancing."

"They do not." Halley laughed. "Dancing?"

Halley laughing? Charlie's chest tightened.

"It's true." Astrid was all smiles.

Her smile had Charlie's throat constricting to the point of discomfort.

"They have dances to tell the other bees where food is located and how much there is." Astrid shrugged. "It's a bee thing."

From the looks on the girls' faces, they were just as surprised by this information as he was. He was grudgingly interested. Not enough to carry on a conversation, however.

"Cool, right?" Astrid asked. "That's the thing about bees, they're surprising. I've grown up around them and I still learn from them—all the time."

"They can't sting up on the observation deck?" Halley asked.

"Nope," Tansy answered. "It's almost ready. You'll be one of our inaugural visitors." She looked up at Dane, who smiled back at her.

Charlie wasn't one for public affection—affection of any kind wasn't something he had much experience with. Watching the two of them reach for each other's hands and smiling at each other had him swallowing down a groan of impatience. Not only were they sticking their nose into his business, Halley was making that face that guaranteed he'd be forced to listen to her go on about Sam or Scott or whatever his name was and he'd have to remind her she was too young for a *relationship* and how love was only hormones firing and something that would fade. He could hardly wait.

He didn't like the Hills. Not Dane or Tansy. Especially not Astrid Hill. He didn't know why, but there was something about her that set his nerves on edge. They'd delivered the bike. Mission accomplished. He wasn't inviting them in, he wasn't pretending to be pleased over this visit so why weren't they getting the hint—and leaving?

But then his gaze met Dane's. Okay, Dane got the hint. The narrow-eyed look he was shooting Charlie's way was anything but friendly. Which was fine with Charlie. He had no interest in being friends with any of them. Making friends would only complicate things when he and the girls went back to their real lives. As soon as they met with the lawyer and he sold this place that could happen. Honey would only be a memory.

"You're welcome to come visit our observation deck, too, Charlie. It might be a nice break for you all." Tansy shrugged. "Honey, Texas, is all about the bees. And the honey."

"Word has it, you're planning on selling." Dane draped his arm across Tansy's shoulders. "I'm guessing you've got lots to do to get the place ready to put on the market."

Charlie nodded. *Not that it's any of your business.* "That's the plan." *The sooner the better.*

Dane nodded. "Eager to get home, I'm sure. Where is home?"

"Fort Worth." At the moment, it felt like a world away.

"Our aunt and cousin are there now. Visiting museums. Some limited modern exhibition. My cousin is into graphic arts and modern design so she was looking forward to it…" Astrid's words trailed off but she was still smiling. "I'm sure they're having all sorts of fun."

"We should probably get going." Dane's tone was cordial enough. "And you can get back to winning your game." He smiled at Nova.

"I will." Nova smiled back. "You do look like Thor," she whispered loudly. Nova didn't do anything quietly.

Tansy thought this was hilarious, her laughter ringing out until everyone—but Charlie—was smiling in return.

Astrid stood, smoothing her hair from her shoulders. And then, without realizing it, his gaze was tangled up with hers. Why was she smiling at him that way? Looking at him as if she…what? What did that look mean?

The porch was shrinking in. Too many people. Too many unknowns. His nerves stretched tight, pressure clamped down on his chest and lungs, making his ribs ache, and heat seared up his neck to his face. *Shit*. He ran both hands through his hair, tore his gaze from Astrid and drew in a slow, steady breath.

"Where do you want this?" Dane's voice pulled Charlie's attention back to the man. He still held the handlebars of Charlie's bike.

"I'll take it," Halley volunteered. "I got it out. I should put it away. See you, maybe, Astrid. Or not." Her sigh wavered. "And…and thanks for bringing the bike." With a long look between Dane and Tansy, she steered the bike down the steps and around the side of the house.

"What manners." Astrid crossed her arms over her chest.

"I'm impressed." Dane chuckled. "I could send Leif over here for lessons."

Not going to happen. He didn't know who Leif was or why they were having this conversation on his front porch. Sweat was trickling down Charlie's back now.

"Hey, Leif is getting better." Tansy nudged him in the ribs.

"Leif is Dane's teenage brother." Astrid glanced his way. "He's a great kid."

Charlie didn't care. All he really, really wanted was for them to leave. He'd also really like Astrid to stop looking at him in that sunshiny way. It wasn't doing a thing to help him keep it together.

"If you get to meet Leif, he can tell you all sorts of stuff about bees." Astrid turned those clear eyes on Nova now. "He's a little older than Halley and funny."

That told Charlie all he needed to know. Halley was too quick to get invested in boys. If this Leif kid looked anything like Dane, he suspected Halley would likely develop a sudden affection for bees. *Not going to happen.*

"I hope we get to meet your bees." Nova surprised him by hugging Astrid around the legs. "I hope we get to play Monopoly, too."

"Thank you for the hug," Astrid said, holding her close.

"It will be fun and we won't be bored anymore." Nova smiled up at her.

Dane managed to turn his laughter into coughs but Charlie felt the sting of truth to his daughter's words.

In Fort Worth, the girls had dance, swim, gymnastics and piano lessons to keep them busy. Yasmina had picked dance and the piano while Charlie had advocated for swim and gymnastics. He had always loved to swim. He'd hoped he and the girls would have a shared interest. So far, Nova was still scared to go into the deep end without her floaties and Halley had no interest in anything other than the boys that hung out around the pool. That was where Scott or Sean or Sam had popped up—he'd been on swim team, too. Which led to Charlie walking in on them, in her room, when he'd gotten home from work. Not what he needed to think about at the moment.

"I want to see the bees dance." Nova shook her head, her curls bouncing.

"Maybe, if we're lucky, they'll dance for you." Astrid glanced his way again.

She'd put him in a no-win situation. If he said no, he was the bad guy—again. She'd offered up fun and he'd be the one to take that away from his girls. If he said yes... Why would he say yes? He knew nothing about these people. For all he knew, they could belong to some sort of radical bee cult or something. No. He didn't want to know these people. "We'll see." Charlie tried not to snap, he really did. But he wasn't sure he was successful. "I wouldn't want to inconvenience you again."

"It's no inconvenience," Astrid assured him.

"Astrid loves kids." Tansy's expression was more shuttered now.

Charlie nodded, but refused to change his answer.

"All right." Dane shook his head, his disbelief bordering on scorn. "We'll get out of your hair."

Tansy and Dane headed down the porch steps and toward the truck without another word. Astrid hesitated. She rested one hand on the porch railing and glanced back at him. "We can be a lot, I suppose. Too much?"

"A bit." Charlie hadn't planned on answering so his reply surprised them both.

"I thought so. Dane is big all around and Tansy, well she's a force of nature, too. But they're wonderful, I promise. I'm not so bad, either, as neighbors go." She shrugged. "It was my idea. The bike, I mean. I didn't know how you'd planned to bring it back and I thought this would help. I was trying to help. I'm very good at helping."

In theory, it sounded nice. In reality, it felt suspect and invasive. He didn't know who his neighbors were back home and he liked it that way. His business was his business.

"You did help." Nova nodded. "And I got to see you."

"And Scorpio, too." Astrid waved at the toy Nova refused to let go of. "Bye, for now."

Charlie ran his fingers through his hair and watched Nova waving wildly until the truck was out of view. The farther away the truck went, the more the pressure in his chest eased and he could breathe.

"You *always* do that. Freak out. Why don't you like… people?" Halley's voice came from behind him.

He turned to find her leaning against the doorframe, her usual frown in place. "I like people."

"Name two. And you can't say me and Nova." She crossed her arms over her chest, waiting. "Or Mom."

Charlie couldn't do it.

Halley pushed off the doorframe. "Mom always said getting out and spending time with friends was good."

Good for the soul. That's what Yasmina would say when she'd go to her monthly book club. She hadn't been an extrovert but she had made sure to spend time with the friends she valued. And she'd constantly poked at him to do the same.

"How about we finish our game?" Charlie steered them inside, closed the door against the sweltering heat, and headed for the family room and their to-be-completed game.

Nova dropped onto her knees on the pillow on the floor, leaning over the game board on the coffee table. "Is it because you miss Mommy?"

Charlie swallowed, hard.

"That you don't want to make friends." Nova cradled Scorpio close. "Because you're too sad?"

"I miss her." She'd been his best friend. *I miss her no-nonsense nature and practical advice.* If she were here, he'd know how to handle this. If she were here, he wouldn't have to.

"It's my turn." Halley rolled the dice and tossed them on the ancient board.

He was thankful for the distraction. He'd stayed strong for the girls, and he wasn't going to break now.

"You don't have to like any of them." Halley moved

her yellow game piece. "Except Astrid." She glanced at him. "She is supercool. It'd be nice to know someone here. Someone other than you and Nova, that is."

"Please, Charlie." Nova leaned forward, her curls bouncing. "Please like her."

"We don't *know* her." He rolled the dice, mentally scrambling for reasons to not like Astrid Hill.

"Yet." Halley propped herself up on her elbow. "It was cool of her to bring the bike. She didn't have to, you know. Maybe she wants to be friends. Is that such a bad thing?"

"Aunt Rebecca said she was nice and her friend. She said everyone liked Astrid—so we should, too." Nova shook the dice in her hands, scrunching her little nose up as she tossed them onto the game board. "Yay!" She moved even farther ahead.

Maybe that was part of it. When Rebecca had described Astrid, he'd pictured someone different. Someone less… Or more… Someone *not* Astrid. He understood why the girls were intrigued. Astrid was interesting. He couldn't quite pinpoint why, exactly, only that she stood out. There was *something* about her—he wouldn't deny it.

"You might just win after all, Super Nova." Halley grinned at her little sister, collecting the dice for her turn. "If Aunt Rebecca said Astrid was nice then Astrid is nice."

Enough about Astrid. "I said we'll see, Halley." Charlie sat back in his chair. "You know I'm busy—"

"She said we could go there, Charlie, *or* she'd come here." Halley held the dice in her hand, pleading. "She's basically offering to babysit us so you can work."

Charlie really wanted to end this conversation. "If she's babysitting, then I have to pay her."

Halley sniffed. "Well, she didn't ask you to pay her so that means she wants to be friends."

"People don't show up at your house, uninvited, wanting to spend time with your children." Charlie tried to appeal to reason. "If that happened in Fort Worth, I'd call the police."

"So, your *we'll see* is a no." Halley slouched back in her chair, her chin wobbling. "You're so…so…" She broke off, dragging in a ragged breath before saying, "If you've already decided, why not just say no, then?" She threw the dice on the table. "I don't want to play anymore." She stood, ran up the stairs and slammed her bedroom door.

Nova stared at the game board, her eyes going round and filling with tears. "But… I—I was winning." She hugged Scorpio tight. "I was. I never win." She jumped up, ran up the stairs and slammed her bedroom door, too.

Charlie pinched the bridge of his nose and stared up at the ceiling overhead. His limited experience made constructive parenting a challenge. His family sure as hell hadn't provided any frame of reference. His two older sisters hated each other. His father, Dr. Jack Driver, was a judgmental, pompous ass who thought money and power were everything. He'd encouraged his daughters' rivalry because it would make them work that much harder to win. His mother was all smiles but disengaged due to her personal pharmacy of mood-altering drugs— thanks to her husband, the very important surgeon.

He didn't know how to make the girls understand where he was coming from. He didn't want to punish them, he wanted to protect them. He had to. He'd failed to protect Yasmina. And each second of that nightmare of a morning was etched into his brain in crisp detail.

Halley had spent the night with a friend so she hadn't been there—thankfully. She'd always ridden alongside Yasmina. Saturday mornings had been coffee, a pancake breakfast, laughter and getting ready for their family ride. Nova was buckled into her seat on his bike when he'd pulled onto the shoulder of the road to take a business call. Nova had kept saying, "Go, Charlie, go." Yasmina had ridden ahead—to the bend in the road... The noise had been deafening. Screeching brakes. A crash...

He stared at the brightly colored game pieces on the board, keeping a tight grasp on his emotions.

He ran his hand over his face.

Charlie's goal remained the same: hear the stipulations in Aunt Rebecca's will and dispose of the property. The only change was getting back to the city as quickly as possible. Coming here was a mistake. He knew that now. He'd warn off Halley's crush and find activities to keep the girls busy for the remainder of the summer. That made sense. That, he could do.

He'd always been the deliberate sort—surprises were overrated and often led to upheaval. He and the girls had had enough upheaval, adding someone like Astrid Hill to the mix wasn't an option. Whether or not she was well-meaning, making friends with the woman didn't make any sense.

NOVA LAY ON her bed crying, Scorpio crushed close. It wasn't fair. She never won anything. She sniffed.

Next door, Halley was crying, too. Nova could hear. *Why is she crying? She ruined our game.*

Halley was right. She did mess up a lot and make Charlie upset.

"I want to be friends with Astrid, too," Nova whispered to Scorpio. But Charlie didn't want them to be friends and Mommy always said Charlie was super-duper smart. Charlie did know lots of stuff. He knew eating candy and watching TV and playing video games were bad for her brain. Which made Nova wonder, "Is Astrid bad for my brain?" But Scorpio didn't answer her. "I'll ask Charlie."

She peered around Scorpio at the window in the roof. Charlie said she'd like this room because she could see the stars in the window. Watching the stars made her think of Mommy. Mommy used to love watching the stars with her gigantical telescope and now she was up with the stars watching over her and Halley and Charlie, too.

It was daytime so there weren't any stars now. Big fluffy clouds floated across the blue sky. "That cloud looks like a flower," she told Scorpio.

Charlie called the window a skylight but Nova called it a monster hole. Especially at night. That's when the rat monster came. When it was dark. "Mommy wouldn't like the rat monster."

Halley didn't believe there was a rat monster. She'd had a sleepover in Nova's room but she'd fallen asleep before the scratching started.

Charlie said she was having bad dreams.

"But we've seen it, haven't we, Scorpio?" she whispered. "Maybe we could try to trap it?" Then she could show them it was real. "And creepy." But trapping it was scarier than it screeching and hissing and scratching at the skylight monster hole each night.

Another cloud floated across the sky—this one looked like a bug. "A beetle." She shook her head. "No, Scorpio, look. It's a bee. Like Astrid's bees." She stared at the cloud. Would it dance like Astrid's bees? That was one thing Nova really wanted to see—dancing bees. She and Halley took dance classes so maybe they could dance with the bees. If she did get to see Astrid again, she'd have to ask her about dancing with bees. And what kind of dance did bees dance? Did they wear ballet shoes? Or tap shoes? And where did the tiny shoes come from? Did other bees play music? The more she thought about Astrid and her bees, the more questions she had. "I guess I can ask Charlie." She held Scorpio up, making the star dance and wobble. "But I'd rather ask Astrid. If she's not bad for my brain, I guess."

CHAPTER THREE

"You two *must* behave." Astrid adjusted the basket she carried. Both Oatmeal and Pudding, two of Aunt Camellia's sizable canine collection, wagged their tails at her. "I don't know how Charlie feels about dogs." She hoped Halley and Nova would be dog enthusiasts. "No jumping or barking... Or drooling, Oatmeal." She patted the large St. Bernard mix on the head. "I know you can't help it, but try the best you can."

She'd waited until Saturday to visit the Driver family again—hoping Charlie wouldn't mind her visit as much on a non-workday. She walked the path from Honey Hill Farms to Rebecca's cottage, armed with a basket of baked goods, some flowers from their gardens and the Nova-sized bike helmet they'd found in the bed of Dane's pickup truck. Dane had offered to return it but Astrid took it as a sign to deliver the helmet herself. Tansy had told her to stop wasting her time, Aunt Camellia told her not to get her hopes up, and Dane had outright called Charlie a condescending ass but Astrid was determined. Besides, she had to get the whole Junior Beekeepers discussion out of the way.

It was only when the cottage came into view that Astrid slowed.

Charlie had been displeased by her last unplanned visit, why had she thought this would go any better?

Maybe she should write a note, leave the basket on the porch and go?

"That would have made sense." She peered down at the dogs trotting alongside her. "Don't you think?" But the dogs' tails only kept wagging. "I'll take that as a yes."

She tiptoed onto the porch, her stomach a jumble of nerves, and rummaged through her bag for a pen and paper—when the front door opened.

"Astrid!" Nova squealed, opening the screen door. "Hi. Whatcha got?" She stared beyond Astrid. "Are those your dogs?" There were soapsuds in Nova's hair and her shirt and shorts were dripping wet.

"Good morning." Astrid couldn't resist the little girl's enthusiasm. "Treats." She patted the basket and glanced back to find Oatmeal and Pudding sitting on the top step, looking hopeful. "They are my aunt's dogs. And they're very well-behaved and will stay." She held her hand out. "That's right, you heard me. Stay."

Oatmeal and Pudding didn't look very happy about this development.

"Hey, Astrid." Halley came onto the porch. "I thought Charlie scared you off forever." She ran her hand over her wet hair and shook soapsuds from her leg and foot.

Astrid wasn't sure what to make of both girls' mildly sodden appearances. "It takes a lot to scare me off." She held out the basket. "I thought I'd return Nova's helmet and leave some yummies my aunt Camellia made."

"You want to come in?" Halley waved her inside.

"Oh, no." She shook her head; she didn't want to push her luck. At the same time, the soapsuds had piqued her curiosity.

"Son of a monkey!" The exclamation was like a gunshot, so loud Astrid winced. It was Charlie. He was *not* happy.

"It's the washing machine," Nova whispered in her not-so-whispery voice. "It attacked Charlie. And Halley. And me and Scorpio, too."

Which would explain the soap bubbles and dripping.

"The door keeps flying open. There's soap and water all over the laundry room floor." Halley was trying not to laugh.

She'd been a victim of Rebecca's temperamental washing machine a time or two and had learned a few tricks to ensure the machine behaved. Apparently, Charlie had not been informed of the broken latch or the need to balance the finicky machine. "Did he put the frog on top of the washer door?"

Both Nova and Halley gave her an odd look.

"Maybe I should come inside." Astrid grinned, took a deep breath, and walked through the living room and into the kitchen. There was a constant stream of muttering coming from behind the pale blue café doors that separated the laundry room from the kitchen.

She placed the basket on the kitchen table, smiled at the girls—who were following her—and peered over one of the café doors, into the laundry room. She wasn't sure what she'd expected but finding a red-faced, soaking wet Charlie Driver sprawling across the lid of the machine as it bounced and shook wasn't it. She shouldn't have been surprised that his white button-up clung to him like a second skin—a very tight, very see-through second skin. From the looks of it, the washing machine was winning *and* dumping water all over the tile floor.

Astrid was on the verge of announcing her presence when his hold tightened and the muscles in his arms and back flexed. Charlie was fit. Not big muscles like Dane, but lean and strong all the same. Astrid hadn't stopped to consider how much was too much in the muscle department before, but seeing Charlie's impressively carved torso, she decided Charlie's build was exactly right.

Now that she'd made this unexpected realization, she was having a hard time ignoring the rather insistent fluttering in her stomach. Oh so much fluttering. Which would have been fine, if her brain hadn't suddenly become a confused and jumbled mess. If she was going to have any sort of productive conversation with this man, being confused and jumbled would not do. Better to steady herself before announcing her presence and defeating the washing machine. Then he'd be in a better mood? Even grateful? Perhaps?

"Close… Just. Stay. Closed." The frustration in his voice suggested poor Charlie was at his wit's end.

"Astrid's here, Charlie." Nova announced this with great enthusiasm—and volume.

"H-hello." She waved, stepping back as he let go of the lid and turned to face her. The lid flew back and soapsuds rained down, the spin cycle flinging water everywhere.

Charlie frowned, his hooded eyes narrowing a fraction of an inch. A large pile of iridescent soap bubbles perched atop his head—wiggling in time with his harsh, uneven breathing.

She smiled, refusing to be distracted by the water-soaked shirt glued to Charlie's chest. "Laundry day?" Apparently, her attempt at a joke wasn't funny. She cleared her throat.

If he kept making that face, he'd have a permanent crease between his dark brows—making his handsome face perpetually grumpy. An errant spray of water squirted him in the eye, prompting the muscle in his jaw to bulge and setting her into action.

"May I?" She nodded at the washing machine. "Rebecca had a trick for it. She was very good at that—coming up with all sorts of Band-Aids. She didn't trust anyone to do repairs without charging her an arm and a leg." Talking, when nervous, was what she did. "And she hated spending money when she didn't have to. She wouldn't hear of replacing a perfectly good—albeit temperamental—washing machine. Excuse me."

Charlie pushed his thick hair from his forehead, his expression going blank as he moved aside. The bubbles on the top of his head shimmied, but remained as they were.

"Lovely." Astrid stepped into the room, her sandals slipping out from under her, thanks to the soap-bubble-covered floor.

"Careful." Charlie caught her by the upper arms. His deep brown eyes raked over her face, his scowl worse than ever, all impatience and disapproval.

"She's just trying to help." Nova tugged on his pants leg.

This reminder didn't seem to do a thing for Charlie's frame of mind. He continued to glare as he held her upright with surprisingly warm hands.

Astrid gripped his strong, solid arms until she'd regained her footing—fully aware that all the touching and staring was only increasing her jumbled-ness. "Thank you." With a wiggle of each foot, her sandals were off and she let go of Charlie. "There." She scanned the room, her eyes settling on Rebecca's washing machine fix. "Found it." She held her hands up as she stepped past the washing machine and lifted the concrete frog garden sculpture.

"What are you doing?" Charlie sounded just as impatient and disapproving as he looked.

Astrid hefted the frog sculpture, closed the lid and rested the frog on the exact right spot on the lid. "Your laundry." She brushed off her hands and smiled at him. The machine continued to jiggle, but the machine was no longer shaking the entire house and the lid stayed shut. "Rebecca almost took the frog to the town swap meet. She said it didn't fit in the garden—she was very particular about her garden. Well, I don't need to tell you, you know that." She paused, aware of the man's ability to remain absolutely still. It was unnerving. "Then the washing machine shifted, along with the foundation, and she said it was meant to be. The frog fixed the machine, without her having to spend money on the foundation or the machine. Easy-peasy."

Charlie eyed the frog, his jaw clenched tight.

"Does it go anywhere on the lid?" Halley asked, sloshing across the floor to peer at the washing machine.

"Right here." She pointed. "On that purple sticker— preferably before you start the machine." Astrid shrugged. "It works."

"Yay. I like his silly face, too." Nova stuck her tongue out and crossed her eyes like the frog statue.

Halley laughed. "Dork."

The teensiest corner of Charlie's mouth curved up. "You look just like him."

"Can we name him Hero?" Nova was very serious about this. "Since he made the water and soap and clothes stop flying all over the place."

That was when Astrid noticed a pair of red shorts

hanging off one of the fan blades overhead. There was a sudsy sock atop Rebecca's craft boxes stacked on the laundry room's shelves. And several other items on the floor or stuck to the wall. She couldn't keep a straight face, no matter how hard she tried. She giggled. "A hero, indeed."

"You, too, Astrid." Nova clapped her hands. "Look, Charlie. She brought my bike helmet back and treats from her aunt and her aunt's dogs, too. And showed us how to do laundry."

Charlie's hooded gaze darted her way before sweeping over his girls, the frog and washing machine. He sighed, both hands raking through his hair.

It wasn't the first time he'd done that—the hair thing. "I didn't want Nova to miss her helmet." Astrid shifted from foot to foot and stared down at the water. "And my aunt is an amazing baker. She's on the traditional side. New neighbors are always welcomed with food and a smile." She smiled at Charlie.

"That wasn't necessary." Charlie glanced her way again, but he didn't smile.

Halley's sigh was even more disappointed than the last one.

"And her dogs are really cute." Nova paused. "One of them is huge."

"Oatmeal. He's harmless." Astrid's gaze caught on the very blue spot on the pocket of Charlie's all-but-see-through shirt and his rather distracting chest. While he might be fine staring at her, she was not okay with staring at him or the drastic surge of her stomach flutters that resulted. "Your shirt. There's a spot."

Charlie stared down at his shirt, scowled again, and tugged the garment up and over his head. He sprayed the shirt with spot cleaner and moved aside the frog statue, added his shirt to the wash, closed the lid and put the frog back in place.

Astrid watched the whole thing, speechless. Besides his chest being…well, impressive, his barely repressed frustration was obvious by the force he used to throw his shirt into the washer. Astrid had never met anyone so…so mad. He seemed angry with the world. She'd hoped showing him the frog trick would somehow ease the tension but, clearly, that wasn't the case.

"Can we have some treats?" Nova asked.

"What sort of treats?" Charlie asked.

"Honey apple muffins." Astrid glanced his way, his dark gaze briefly meeting hers. "A spiced honey pear pie and a loaf of buttermilk honey bread."

"She made all of that?" Charlie's confusion was a vast improvement over his scowl. He bent forward, opened the dryer and sighed. "I need to clean up first."

"Don't mind me." Astrid nodded. "I can give the girls a muffin—if that's all right with you, of course?"

Charlie glanced at the girls, then the basket, and nodded. "One."

"Yay!" Nova clapped her hands.

Charlie sighed as he brushed past Astrid and headed for the stairs, taking all the tension in the room with him.

Astrid took a deep breath and turned to the girls. "What have you been up to this morning?" She stepped into the kitchen and wiped her feet on the braided rug. "Besides watching Charlie fight the washing machine."

"Oh, man, I wish my phone was working." Halley laughed. "It was epic. *All* of it. Charlie doesn't cuss, Mom told him he couldn't, so he says all this dorky stuff instead."

"Like 'son of a monkey'?" Astrid asked. It had been the last thing she'd ever expected to hear from Charlie Driver.

"And fish stick and son of a biscuit." Nova leaned forward, using her not-whisper voice. "But, I'm not supposed to know them…"

"Asp. Spit-head. Ditch." Halley ticked them off on her fingers. "Like we can't figure out what he's *not* saying?"

"I don't know." Nova shot her sister a bewildered expression. "I do know an asp is a snake and snakes are really bad." She wrinkled up her nose and shuddered. "Calling someone an asp is *really* bad."

Astrid laughed as she pulled plates from the kitchen cabinet and carried them to the table. Nova's rationale made sense. "I don't want to be called an asp, that's for sure." She set four plates around the table. "He's been fighting with the washing machine all morning?" Which would be reason enough for his temper.

"We got up. I read. Nova did a puzzle. Charlie had a phone call and then the washing machine exploded." Halley started picking at the black nail polish on her pointer fingernail.

Charlie was taking business calls on a Saturday? "What sort of puzzle?" Astrid asked.

"Animals." Nova watched, wide-eyed with excitement, as Astrid put one of the oversize muffins on her plate. "Wow. That's enormous-ful-big."

Astrid grinned. "*And* it tastes good." She set a plated muffin in front of Halley.

"Thanks, Astrid." Halley slowly pealed the wrapper back. "For the frog—"

"Hero." Nova was turning her plate, sizing up the muffin.

Halley rolled her eyes. "Thanks for showing us the whole Hero the frog thing." She paused to watch her sister. "Just take a *big* bite."

"It's gigantical." Nova propped her elbows on the table, then rested her chin and stared at the muffin. "Maybe I'm too tired to eat. The rat monster was scratching *all* night."

Astrid carried two forks to the table. "Maybe this will help with the muffin. Do you want to tell me about this rat monster?"

Nova glanced at Halley, who groaned and rolled her eyes. "No, thank you."

"If you don't eat it, I will." Halley nodded at the muffin.

Nova grabbed the muffin and took a huge bite.

Astrid laughed and patted Nova's shoulder. "Napkins." She looked in the spot where Rebecca had stored her paper products. As far as she could tell, everything was just as Rebecca left it—making it that much easier for her to find the mop to clean up the laundry room floor once the girls were settled with their muffins and juice.

"You don't have to do that." Charlie came into the kitchen with slightly damp hair and a dry shirt. A shirt that was in no way, shape or form see-through.

"It's no trouble. Almost done, anyway," Astrid assured him. "I like to stay busy." She nodded at the table. "There's a muffin for you, too."

"You didn't have to do that, either." Charlie eyed the muffin but didn't sit with the girls. Instead, he leaned against the kitchen counter and shoved his hands into his pockets.

"I didn't. My aunt Camellia did." She winked at Nova,

who grinned. "She's the foodie in the family. It's her love language. If she likes you, she cooks for you. Or gives you a piece of candy or a muffin."

"She gave us candy. And muffins." Nova grinned. "She likes us."

Charlie's grunt was disapproving.

"What's not to like?" Astrid asked.

"These are big and de-li-cious." Nova rubbed her tummy. "Yummy."

"They are." Halley peered into the basket Astrid had placed on the table. "I can't wait to try the other stuff."

"It's too much." Charlie crossed his arms over his chest and shifted from one foot to the other.

"If I'd brought what my aunt had wanted me to bring, *that* would have been too much." Astrid carried the basket to the counter and pulled the plastic wrap from the kitchen drawer. "I'll cover the pie and put it in the refrigerator." But she paused, glancing his way. "I'm sorry. I showed up and started making myself at home—"

"It seems to be a habit." Charlie's gaze held hers for a few seconds, then fell away.

She didn't like it when he scowled, but at least she had some sort of clue as to what he was thinking. But this, the blank face, the intense eye contact, then the avoiding eye contact? She had no idea what to make of that. Her tongue felt a little thick as she started to ramble. "I've always thought of Rebecca's home as a second home. I'd come care for the bees that tended her garden and I'd stay to chat or share some lemonade or weed a flower bed. I think we got along so well because we had such similar interests. And we both like to do things and stay busy. And, for the most part, live a quiet life. *Quiet* is one word I wouldn't use to describe my home. Not to imply I don't love my home and my family, I do. I adore them…" She stopped before she could keep going.

"She was fond of you." His tone was equally hard to decipher.

"What will happen to the bees when Charlie sells this place?" Halley was picking up the remaining crumbs of her muffin.

"I imagine I'll take them to Honey Hill Farms." Astrid shrugged. "Maybe the new owners will want to keep them? Or I'll find someone else who will. She has very gentle bees."

"How do you know?" Nova was still working on her muffin. "Do they dance for that, too? To tell you they're nice?"

"No." Astrid smiled, wrapping the bread in plastic wrap as she spoke. "It's a beekeeper's job to manage the bees, to keep a healthy and strong queen, and protect them from pests. Rebecca's queens are all Italian— golden and gentle." She stored the pie and bread in the refrigerator.

"Do they buzz in Italian?" Nova asked.

"You mean, like do the bees have an Italian accent?" Halley was looking longingly at Nova's uneaten half of a muffin.

"That would be something, wouldn't it?" Astrid pulled one of the kitchen chairs out and sat at the table. She tapped her chin, then shrugged. "As far as I know, all bees speak bee. No accents—just buzzing."

"Are there French bees?" Nova asked.

"There are bees in France. Bees are all over the world. People need them, you see. For plants and food—they keep us healthy so we should help them." She resisted the urge to get Halley another muffin and kept talking.

"It's up to each beekeeper to try to find the best bees for them. Bees, like people, have different characteristics. Do they produce a lot of honey? Are they hygienic and resistant to pests? Gentle? There's a lot to think about when it comes to bees." Astrid couldn't help but smile when Charlie finally sat and broke off a piece of his muffin.

"What sort of pests?" Nova had stopped eating and had propped her elbows on the table once more, focused on Astrid. "Mosquitos? They are pests."

"They are." Astrid leaned forward. "They're even worse when you get one stuck in your bee suit."

Nova wrinkled up her nose. "Itchy."

"Very." From the corner of her eye, she saw Charlie's resistance fade—the muffin was gone in three bites. "But mosquitos don't bother bees. Wax moths, small hive beetles, varroa mites—they *do* bother bees. Keeping those critters out of the hives is one of the most important things a beekeeper can do." Something she could teach both the girls about when the Junior Beekeepers came over. She took a deep breath, trying to find a way to slip that into conversation. *Hey, Charlie, I hope you remember that you'll have eight-to-ten high school kids on the property in a week*, seemed a little too forthright.

"You really like bees?" Halley was smiling at her.

"I do. Deeply. They're…family." Astrid had always considered her bees part of her family. "Taking care of the bees is a part of who I am."

"Like Charlie loves to code and Mom loved the stars." Halley shrugged. "I guess everyone should have something they get excited about."

"Mommy loved the stars." Nova held up Scorpio,

making the toy dance. "That's why Halley is named Halley and I'm named Nova."

"Halley's Comet." Halley pointed at herself. "Nova is a bright new star." She pointed at Nova.

"That's lovely." Astrid sat back in her chair. "My parents named us after bee-friendly flowers. Astrid, Tansy and Rosemary. My aunts are Camellia and Magnolia. My dad was lucky—he was named James."

"Is your dad a beekeeper, too?" Nova asked. "And your mom?"

"No. Dad was a science teacher and my mother was a nurse." She hurried on. "But my grandparents were and their parents before them. Now, it's up to me, my sisters and my aunts to care for our bees."

"Can we meet the bees, Charlie?" Nova was one hundred percent adorableness when she turned wide, pleading eyes his way.

If Charlie noticed Nova's adorableness, he didn't let on. He was staring at Astrid, his brown eyes unguarded and pinned to hers. And this time, his face wasn't blank. For a minute—less than that—there was a flash of grief. It all seemed so clear to Astrid then. Charlie wasn't grumpy or mean or rude, though his manners might be lacking. Charlie was hurting. So much so that Astrid found it hard to breathe. He'd just lost his aunt. But he'd lost his wife, too. Rebecca had mentioned something about an accident… It hadn't been all that long ago.

Aunt Magnolia would tell her to mind her own business. Tansy and Dane had already made it abundantly clear that Charlie Driver wasn't worth her time. But this changed things. This wasn't just about Charlie, it was about Halley and Nova, too. Astrid knew the pain of losing a loved one. As deep as her grief had been, she'd had her aunts and sisters to comfort her. She was beginning to think Charlie and the girls only had one another and the three of them were chasms apart.

There were plenty of reasons to leave it alone. One, she didn't know them. Two, and this was a big one, Charlie would likely resist—and possibly resent—her interference. Three, she had no idea what she could do to help. Not to mention they'd be gone soon. She'd be wise to leave the basket and the baked goods, get the dreaded Junior Beekeeper conversation out of the way and wish them well.

But Astrid had always listened to her heart first, something Aunt Magnolia constantly warned her against. Her heart didn't give a fig about all the reasons she shouldn't get involved with the Driver family. Her heart wanted to help—all three of them—desperately.

CHARLIE WATCHED THE play of emotions on Astrid's face with mounting concern. Her features were fluid, shifting from one thought to the next. The initial droop to her mouth turned into the flat line of her full lips. From there, her jaw tightened and there was the slightest jut of her chin—as if she was making up her mind about something. And then, those green eyes of hers met his and her smile was so blindingly warm that Charlie's concern ratcheted up to very definite unease. He dropped his gaze immediately.

"Do you like dogs?" Astrid asked. "My aunt's dogs followed me. I should probably get them some water before I head back." She stood, crossed to the kitchen sink and opened the cabinet beneath. "They loved to visit Rebecca with me." She pulled an oversize metal bowl from the cabinet. "She kept treats for them."

That explains the large box of dog treats. He ran his fingers through his hair.

"Let's go meet them." Halley slipped from her chair. "Come on, Nova."

"I'm coming." Nova held out her hands. "Wait for me."

"They're right out front." Astrid nodded. "Oatmeal is the big one. He does drool a bit—it's the St. Bernard in him. Pudding is the brown shaggy one."

"Does he drool, too?" Nova asked, her nose wrinkling.

My thoughts exactly. Charlie frowned.

"No. But he does love a good tummy rub." Astrid filled the water bowl. "I'll be back."

"I'll get the door." Halley ran ahead, pulling the door open. "Oh, look. They're so cute."

"Wait. I'm coming, too." Nova jumped from her chair and ran after them, the front door closing with a thud.

Charlie didn't move. He sat, staring at the brightly painted cuckoo clock on the wall, enjoying the quiet. Quiet was a rare thing. His girls were joyfully loud—a constant stream of conversation and laughter. Thankfully, they didn't go at each other the way his sisters did. Sure, they'd argue from time to time, but it was nothing like the screaming and cut downs his sisters had delighted in hurling at one another over the course of any given day.

He didn't want to think about his childhood or his sisters. He should be grateful they had no interest in coming to Honey or the reading of Aunt Rebecca's will. At least, so far. They'd both agreed he'd been the only one that had a relationship with their aunt so he could handle it. But his sisters were known to change their minds—

especially when there was money involved. And, according to the property assessor's estimate, this property was worth far more than he could have imagined. The Texas Hill Country was prime real estate and Rebecca's place was, apparently, exactly what developers were looking for. If he were smart, he'd start preparing himself and the girls for the possibility of their arrival.

He pushed himself from his chair, finished off the rest of Nova's muffin—which was dangerously delicious—and made his way outside. Astrid was leaning against the porch railing, her long skirts brushing against her calves. She was barefoot this time.

Because she'd kicked off her shoes inside after she'd almost fallen. But he'd caught her, made sure she was fine, and had no problem with the contact. Why? As a rule, he didn't like touching people. He flexed his hands and shoved them back into his pockets. He waffled, standing just inside until he figured out what was wrong. People weren't nice without a reason. He'd learned that at an early age and had yet to have it proven otherwise. Astrid Hill must want something from him, he just needed to figure out what that something was.

And there was the other thing. She wasn't…predictable. He had no idea what was going to come out of her mouth or where she'd pop up next. Maybe he should pick up a dozen or so No Trespassing signs when he was in town next. Maybe he should tell her he didn't appreciate her coming into his house, taking over and fixing things—all with a gentle smile. He didn't appreciate it, even if she had fixed the damn washing machine and mopped up. But she had, as if she had every right to do just that.

She took up space and confused things—confused him. Deeply.

And yet, even with those concerns, the most perplexing thing about Astrid Hill inserting herself into this morning was… He didn't hate it. He wanted to. But he couldn't. Instead, he watched her, captivated. She was… fascinating in a peculiar way. From her fluttering skirts to her long hair and her bare feet, she rambled on in a way that should irritate him. Instead, it was quite the opposite.

Now, she was leaning against the porch railing with her hair blowing in the warm summer breeze and he found himself working through her visit. What did she want? Why was she here? And why did she seem to belong here? Once upon a time, he'd belonged here, too.

Rebecca's place had been a haven for him. Besides Yasmina, his aunt was the only one who'd accepted his anxiety and honest—often blunt—communication style. At home, his family didn't like hearing what he had to say. They never acknowledged the school counselor's suggested social anxiety disorder or recommendation to test him for autism. They certainly never tried to understand what those diagnoses might mean. His parents had believed they could fix him or *normalize* him by signing him up for every extracurricular activity, club or camp. It had never worked. He still wasn't normal. Even military school hadn't *straightened him out*.

Aunt Rebecca had said he was too honest. She'd warned him that people can't take the truth, especially when it's things they don't want to hear about themselves. She'd been the one to help him understand that he didn't have to say everything he was thinking out loud. After that, his parents and sisters stopped asking *What is wrong with you?*

Yasmina had said his family's idea of *normal* was anything but. She was the one who had convinced him he was better off without them. She'd been right. He'd felt more at ease in his own skin since he'd removed them from his life. It had been hard to tune out the constant judgment or ridicule that had been hard-wired into his brain but he'd managed. He was who he was. No apologies necessary. He thought differently. Spoke differently. But that didn't make him any less human.

"That's it." Astrid laughed. "Pudding is very happy. Look at that tail."

The shaggy dog was sprawled on his back, his wagging tail sending dust into the air.

"See, Charlie?" Nova crouched by the dog, giggling. "Isn't he funny?"

Charlie nodded, the smile on Nova's face easing the constant grip of tension compressing his chest. Nova should smile like this. Even Halley, who was throwing what appeared to be a log-sized stick, seemed less angst-ridden playing fetch with the massive dog bounding across the yard. "That's Oatmeal?"

Astrid turned those green eyes his way. "Yes. The biggest, sweetest lovebug of a dog you'll ever meet."

Charlie shook his head at that. *Lovebug?*

"It's true." Astrid smiled. "We have a small herd of dogs and cats—even donkeys, you name it, really. A scruffy, old, one-eyed Chihuahua named Butters is the alpha. He might only be eight pounds but he's rather ferocious. He keeps the other dogs in line."

Of course, Astrid Hill would own a one-eyed Chihuahua. "Are all your animals named after food?"

"All except Lord Byron the parrot. Aunt Camellia is the one that brings them home so she gets to name them. You met her at the boutique the other day. She loves to cook so I suppose it makes sense." He could hear the affection in Astrid's voice. "It's like all the dumped or stray animals know she'll welcome them home." Her gaze met his—and held tight. "Everyone and everything should have love and a home, don't you think?"

Fascinating wasn't the only word that suited Astrid. She was…bewildering. Rather, she bewildered him. The more he studied her, the more bewildered he felt. There was no reason for it. There was nothing exceptional about her. Except there was.

"Is something wrong?" Astrid's smile was fading.

He blinked, the words slipping out before he could stop them. "I don't know." He frowned, his gaze returning to the girls playing with the dogs.

"Oh." Astrid laughed softly. "I hate that feeling. That sense that you can't quite name what's lingering on the edge of your mind, bothering you?"

That's not exactly what he was feeling. But his feelings were his business—not hers. Especially since she was the cause of these *feelings*.

Halley's laughter rang out, grabbing Charlie's undivided attention.

"OMG, Astrid. He loves to play fetch." Halley threw the large stick again, patting her thighs and grinning as the pony-sized dog came barreling back her way.

Charlie held his breath, fearing the dog would slam into Halley and knock her over. At the last minute, it stopped and Halley gave the dog a scratch behind the ear.

"He's gentle." Astrid leaned forward, resting her elbows on the porch railing. "You looked worried Halley would get hurt. I wouldn't have let him come with me if there was even the slightest chance that would happen."

"I wasn't worried," he murmured.

"Good." Astrid stood. "I guess we should let you three enjoy the rest of your day."

He did look at her then. He hadn't wanted her here but, now that she was here, he was in no hurry to see her go. Halley was laughing. Nova was all giggles. He wasn't weighted down by fear and worry. All because of Astrid and her dogs. "No rush."

Astrid didn't shy away from his gaze; instead she seemed to be searching for something.

He didn't like it. "Unless, of course, you have responsibilities." He forced his attention away. "What are bee-keeping hours?"

"Oh, mornings are best. Especially when it's hot like this." She pushed off the railing.

Charlie was acutely aware of her walking around him to sit on the top porch step.

"Honey harvest just ended so there's a lull now. Which is good since it's so hot. Sweltering, really. But that's Texas in the summer, I guess. I've often thought someone would become a millionaire if they learned how to build an air conditioner into a bee suit. Then again, I imagine it would be too heavy and then you'd have that to worry about instead of the heat." She pushed her hair from her shoulders. "It's all part of the job, though. Lots of sweet and sticky work."

He stared down at her feet. Her toes wiggled.

"But the rewards are worth it. You and the girls are welcome to come see the bees, if you like? The Junior Beekeepers help out, plus some younger siblings. The girls could make some friends." Astrid glanced up at him. "I can make it worth your while and get you some fresh honeycomb. There is nothing more delicious in this world."

The longer he stared into her eyes, the harder it was to get words out. "Those muffins were good." Small talk was acutely uncomfortable.

"I'm glad you liked them." Her smile added an extra lightness to her. "I'll have to tell Aunt Camellia. She takes her baking very seriously."

"It shows." Fascinating. Bewildering. He swallowed, his mind racing. He did not like this.

"Lots of practice." Astrid laughed. "She's always baking."

Charlie said, "Practice makes—"

"Perfect." Both girls chimed in.

"That's one of Charlie's mantras." Halley threw the stick again.

"Practice. Practice." Nova was sitting on the ground beside the shaggy brown dog, carefully plucking tiny white flowers from the grass and tucking them into the dog's thick fur. "Practice."

Astrid made a face. "I've never been perfect at anything."

Charlie shrugged. "It's something to work toward."

"Is it?" She shrugged. "I prefer to set goals I can reach." She stood, shaking out her skirts. "If I was aiming for perfection all the time, I think I'd start to feel defeated after a while."

In a handful of words, she'd summarized his entire childhood. But he'd never stopped trying to achieve perfection. He kept right on staring at her. This time it had nothing to do with her clear green eyes and everything to do with what she said.

She disappeared inside the house and came back out, her sandals on her feet. When she stopped beside him, it was closer than before. "I wanted to tell you the board game offer still exists." Her voice was low. "Here or at Honey Hill Farms. My aunts would love them but, I confess, there will likely be more baked goods involved. I'm a nice person, Charlie. I promise. Your girls remind me of me and my sisters when we were younger. And I remember what it was like, being their age. Anyway, I put my number on the notepad stuck to the refrigerator door. In case…" She glanced his way, adding, "We could do something else. Maybe go bicycling along the city park path? I know the girls like cycling."

And, just like that, the pressure in his chest became crushing. The only biking they'd done since Yasmina's death was around the property here. He was a rational enough man to know that what happened to Yasmina was a fluke accident—but the fear was real. He didn't need to think about his answer. "We can't."

Astrid's expression dimmed. "I understand—"

"No. You don't." He cut her off. There was no reason to say more. "Their mother… Yasmina." He swallowed. It was none of her business but words kept coming. "She…died. You know what happened?" For the first time in his life, he hoped his aunt had told Astrid all the details. He wouldn't—he couldn't.

"Only that she had an accident." Her voice was barely a whisper.

He watched the girls, both of them too wrapped up in the dogs to worry about what he and Astrid were saying. "An accident…while cycling." He nodded, blowing out a slow breath. That was enough. It had to be. His gaze wandered to the flowers by Rebecca's birdbath, pushing back the images he couldn't scrub from his brain.

Astrid's breathing was unsteady but she didn't say anything.

He took a slow, deep, calming breath.

"I'm sorry, Charlie. I...I didn't know." She was quiet for a time. "Truly." Her hand rested on his forearm.

He shook his head. *Don't look at her.* He should say something. But the tightness of his throat wouldn't ease. Now she was touching him. Warm. Soft. Her hand gently squeezing his arm. Standing too close. Stealing the air. Sweat beaded along his upper lip.

"Losing someone like that—is something that never leaves you." The grief in her words startled him. "But you have to keep going." A long silence stretched out between them. Long enough for him to be acutely aware of her hand. Her nearness. The sound of her breath. A gust of hot wind blew one long strand of her hair along his forearm.

"I... I'll go." Her hand slipped from his arm. "I'm happy to have the girls visit, just so you know. You can work and I'd make certain to keep them safe." She broke off. "They could play with the dogs and help me in the garden? Have some fun? And give you a break? Maybe... Think about it, please." But she didn't leave. She leaned around, forcing him to look at her. With a sigh and sad smile, she left him standing there, speechless and beyond muddled.

The girls gave Astrid and the dogs goodbye hugs while his mind scrambled to process her parting words. His eyes stayed glued on the path long after Astrid and her flowing skirts were out of sight. Now that she was gone, he found himself adding to the list of words that described his neighbor. Fascinating. Bewildering. Warm. *Appealing.*

He frowned at the now empty path she'd taken. *Appealing?* That wasn't good. None of this was good. Their living situation was temporary, something he'd tried to make clear to Astrid Hill. But no, she kept coming back. Life was complicated enough without her dropping by or offering to "help out" and getting them worked up over two boisterous dogs. When she was here, he seemed to forget that Astrid was still a stranger. Rebecca had been old and lonely—she'd probably been glad for any company. *He* didn't need company. He had the girls and the girls had him. He gripped the railing, feeling more and more the fool. He ran his fingers through his hair and pushed off the railing.

In the yard, Halley was whacking at some tall grass with the stick she'd been playing fetch with. Nova was hopping along behind a grasshopper, her curls slipping free from another of his failed attempts at a ponytail.

Amid all the things Astrid had said, one thing needled him the most. He could be fun. He and the girls could have plenty of fun on their own. He'd told the girls they'd do something this weekend and they would. He didn't know how or where or what the hell they'd do but it would be fun, dammit. Loads of fun—without the appealing Astrid Hill tagging along.

CHAPTER FOUR

ASTRID MOVED SLOWLY. So far, the bees were behaving but she and Tansy had yet to start the removal process. "Good morning." She kept her voice low and soft. "Tansy and I are here to move you someplace safe." She peered inside the grill. "Looks like you ladies have been working very hard."

There was no finer architect in the natural world than the bee. Astrid had seen hundreds of different hives and combs in her life but it hadn't dampened her admiration for their work. Inside of Abner Jones's barrel grill was a highly productive colony. Row after row of deep U-shaped stalactite-like comb hung, the colors varying from gold to deep amber.

"It's a good thing Abner's grill is heavy-duty." She pointed inside the barrel with her gloved hand. "That's a lot of honey. We should have brought another bucket."

"Definitely should have brought another bucket." Tansy leaned forward over Astrid's shoulder. "I wonder how long it's been since Abner used this thing? Or if these little ladies are just super productive?"

Astrid went back to inspecting the comb. Hundreds of golden bees crawled across the hanging comb. Feeding baby bees. Attending to the hive's queen. Capping honey into the comb. Flying off to gather more pollen. Adding propolis to keep the combs securely in place. A bee was never still so a beehive was a very busy place. Bees were all about work.

Like Charlie Driver. Considering she was always one hundred percent focused when working with bees, the thought was surprising. *But not exactly wrong.*

"My smoker's about ready." Tansy pressed the bellows pump of her smoker. "Are we good to get started?"

She and Tansy were both fully suited—taking precautions since they didn't know the temperament of these bees. In her pockets, she had her hive tools, a frame brush and a queen catcher. Tansy had the same. Beside her sat an empty nuc box to move the frames of baby bees, called brood, and some honey into. The two five-gallon buckets were for the honeycomb only. But she held up her hand before Tansy could start pumping smoke into the barrel. "Did you say hello to the bees?"

Tansy gestured at the hive with her smoker. "You said hello—that's what matters. You're the one who *gets* the bees with that mind-meld thing you have going on. You're the bee whisperer."

Her grandfather, Poppa Tom, had been the first one to call her that. When she'd been a little girl, she'd trailed after Poppa Tom to learn everything she could. She'd spent hours in his shadow, sitting and watching and listening and talking to the bees. She still did. Poppa Tom said the bees were so delighted with her interest and dedication and hard work that they had decided to make her an honorary bee. That was the reason even the worst-tempered bees wouldn't sting her, he'd said. Whatever the reason, Astrid had developed a way of doing things. One of them was saying hello to the bees before working a hive. It was just good manners. "Tansy—"

"Hello, bees." Tansy leaned forward. "I'm here, too.

With Astrid. So, you know... Please don't sting us while we move you someplace safe."

Astrid gave her a thumbs-up. "Much better."

"There you go." Tansy pumped the bellows on the smoker and the buzz inside the metal grill grew softer. "It's like bee valium."

Astrid laughed as she reached inside the barrel grill. "I never thought of it that way before." The cement-like propolis holding things in place gave with a pop and crunch and Astrid freed the stalactite-like comb. With a few light sweeps, she brushed the bees into the barrel grill, and put the sticky structure into the bucket. "All honey." Astrid repeated the process. "You stay right here, safe and in the shade," she said to the bees. Removing a wild hive was hard work. Removing a wild hive in triple digits made it twice as hard.

"At least they're not aggressive." Tansy turned the long comb she held. "More honey."

"I can't wait to see the queen. She's got a high-producing team here. Honey *and* brood. Even though foraging is getting harder with no rain." Queen bees had always fascinated Astrid. Beyond their size and oftentimes interesting coloring, there was something regal about the queen. It wasn't just that she was the largest bee in the colony, it was the way the other bees parted and tended to her. Royalty, indeed.

It took a good forty minutes but she and Tansy managed to get the brood comb secured into frames and stored inside the nuc box and most of the combs of honey packed tightly into the five-gallon buckets.

"She's a shy queen, I think?" Astrid was leaning into the barrel, peering into every seam and divot of the old metal barrel. "Can you imagine? You're doing your bee thing and all of a sudden faceless white giants are puffing smoke into your house and taking things away. I'd be a little wary, too." Tansy didn't say anything so Astrid used her softest, most encouraging voice as she said, "I promise, we're not going to hurt you. We're going to give you a lovely new home. It's like…like a bee resort."

Tansy laughed. "It's true, our bees are living their best life."

Astrid agreed. Honey Hill Farms made sure their bees had everything they needed and more. Several of their original beeyards even had themes—a little something more than the traditional white bee boxes. From detailed and elegant castles and famous Impressionist re-creations to the boldly painted *Alice in Wonderland* apiary, the beeyards added a sense of quirkiness that made Hill Farms extra special. "You don't want to leave your hive. We don't want to have to find them a new queen. We both want the same thing. Plus, I'd really like to meet you."

Tansy's giggle was soft but her hand rested on Astrid's back. "You sweet-talker, you."

Astrid kept on murmuring encouragement until, finally, the unmistakable larger, oblong body of the bashful queen appeared. "Well, hello there. Aren't you lovely?" She pulled the queen clip from her pocket and carefully encased the tawny-brown queen inside. "We even have your very own transport, your majesty. You'll be safe. And so will your bees."

"You literally talked her into coming out." Tansy pointed at the nuc box. "I'm going to have to start carrying around my phone so I can record *that*." She started picking up the supplies. "You. Bee whispering. It's unbelievable. Instagram. TikTok. You'd get lots of followers—"

"No, thank you." That sounded awful. They had contractual obligations to do promotional stuff due to winning the Wholesome Foods partnership, that was one thing. Tansy and Dane might enjoy posting and sharing and talking with the strangers online that commented and liked and subscribed. Just thinking about it made Astrid shudder. "Why would I want that?" She slipped the queen clip between two of the hive frames.

"To meet people? New people. *Male* people." Tansy picked up the nuc lid. "It wasn't all that long ago you were telling me you wanted lots of babies. The conversation was basically burned into my brain so don't even try to deny it. A lot of babies normally requires a little help from, you know, *male* people."

Astrid giggled. "I won't deny it. I can still remember your face. And I do want babies. Eventually." Tansy was with her every day—she had an up-close-and-personal glimpse into Astrid's nonexistent personal life. But now was not the time to have this conversation. It was hot and only getting hotter. She did her best to move all the straggler bees into the nuc. "That should do it." She stepped aside as Tansy slipped the lid onto the nuc but stooped down to say, "We'll be back after the sun goes down."

She hefted the five-gallon buckets into their squeaking wagon and started tugging it to the Honey Hill Farms van parked under a tree on the far side of the unfenced yard. Between then and now, Astrid had to work the closing shift at the Hill Honey Boutique and babysit precious baby Beatrix while her cousin, Shelby, had an online meeting with her California client.

And there was that other thing. That thing she kept avoiding because she wasn't sure what to do.

It had been two days since she'd left Charlie's house and she was still processing what she'd learned. The word *accident* covered a broad range of things vague yet ominous. But Charlie's hint was enough to tell her all she needed to know and it gutted her. First the girls' mother, then Rebecca. She'd had no idea what that little family was dealing with. It had taken her years to come to terms with losing her mother, then her father. The Drivers' loss was still new and raw. And here she'd sauntered in with a basket of muffins and an offer to play Monopoly—as if that could do anything more than provide them a temporary distraction.

All the little bits and pieces she couldn't make sense of fell into place. Like how upset Charlie had been when he came into the shop that first day. And his frustration as he fought to shove the bike into Rebecca's car. Imagining Nova and Halley bicycling along the busy roads was enough to cause fear in any parent. But she couldn't begin to imagine how Charlie had felt. A busy road, his girls missing, the memory of his late wife and her accident. For Charlie, the whole incident would have been like a waking nightmare.

Then she, Tansy and Dane barged in unannounced to return the bike when the little family was playing a game. Because he'd needed to spend time with them, be with them, see that they were safe and sound after all that.

It didn't matter that they'd meant well, they'd invaded.

Tansy began unzipping and tugging off her vented bee suit so Astrid did the same, setting aside her concerns about Charlie and the girls for a bit longer.

"We're thinking about going to that bee farm in Navasota. Dane and I, that is." Tansy hung her suit on one of the hooks in the van, then reached for Astrid's. "They've really embraced the agritourism thing and are doing well. They're willing to share some secrets with us."

It wasn't all that long ago Tansy would have balked at the mention of agritourism as a potential revenue stream. Thanks to Dane's persistence and enthusiasm, Tansy was willing to consider it. It was nice to see how the two of them were growing together.

"Do you think people would talk if Dane and I went away for the weekend? The two of us? Alone." Tansy stretched her arms over her head.

"Why would people talk? Everyone knows the two of you are working together now. You're compromising. That's what you do in a healthy partnership, isn't it? We both know Dane would never do anything that would threaten—"

"No. Not that. It's just…" Tansy broke off. "Dane and I haven't gone away together. You know, the two of us. *Alone*." She rolled her eyes. "Will this set the tongues wagging and kick up more talk than it's worth? I mean Willadeene Svoboda is going to do and say whatever she wants but…" She glanced at Astrid from the corner of her eye. "But I don't want people thinking we're running off to have wild and vigorous sex all weekend."

"Wild and vigorous sex all weekend?" Astrid was so surprised, her laughter sort of erupted. Finally, she could breathe. "That is what I *immediately* thought when you said the two of you were going to a bee farm for the weekend. *Bee farm* is universal code for a weekend sexfest." She shook her head, still grinning as she said, "No,

Tansy, seriously? That, what you just said, is a *giant* leap from visiting a bee farm to take notes on agritourism."

"Is it really? Good." Tansy's smiled widened. "But… I hope Dane doesn't feel that way."

"I don't want to know that." Astrid was laughing again. "Go, enjoy your weekend away, learn how to make an environmentally friendly agritourism vacation, and have some time with your fella." She fanned herself, the sun already beating down on them. "How about we finish this in the AC?"

Tansy slammed the rear van doors. "I was going to use all that to transition into setting up your online dating profile. Nicole has already started it, I think."

"What?" She blinked, staring at her sister. Nicole had been her friend since they'd moved to Honey and Astrid loved her dearly. But Nicole was into risk-taking, painfully blunt, and not the person Astrid envisioned creating a dating profile for her—not that she'd ever imagined creating an online dating profile. "You need to seriously work on your openings. Why do I need an online dating profile? A profile Nicole is making? Um, how did you two imagine this would play out?" Astrid made a face at her sister, then walked down the side of the van and climbed into the passenger seat. This wasn't what she wanted. Once the AC was blowing, Astrid decided shutting down all talk of her dating life was the best sort of action. "It was one silly comment. Yes, eventually, I do want a big family. But I'm not going to force anything. It'll happen. Or it won't. Let's just leave it at that." She lifted her long hair up so the AC could cool her neck.

"It wasn't silly." Tansy turned to look at her. "And if it's what you want, then I want you to have it. But you do need to help it along, Astrid. There's not one man in Honey, except Everett Taggert, that's worth a fig."

And Everett Taggert had given his heart away at the tender age of ten, so he wasn't an option. "I don't want to pick some guy off the internet—like a mail-order groom."

Tansy stared at her. "Is that a thing? You're joking?"

"Yes, I was joking." She stared, open-mouthed, at her sister.

"*Try* the online option. Please. One, there are no options in Honey." Tansy ticked off one finger. "Two, at least you'll have options." She ticked off another finger. "Three, you'll have practice with men. I'm not saying you won't go through a lot—a whole lot—of frogs before you find a prince or a duke or a lord—heck, even a noble stable boy. I'm just saying you have to *start* somewhere."

"Options and practice and kissing all the frogs?" Astrid's good mood dimmed. "What a horribly depressing conversation, Tans. Really, talk about a pep talk." She twisted her hair up and tied it in a messy bun at the back of her head. "Maybe I'll follow Aunt Camellia's lead and collect strays?"

"You would be guaranteed unconditional love." Tansy put the van into gear and pulled out onto the gravel road leading out of Abner Jones's homestead. "Don't judge me but, deep down, I was sort of hoping Charlie Driver was the amazing man Rebecca had made him out to be. I mean, you'd already be ahead on the lots and lots of babies and, he might be an ass, but he's handsome and all that. Then you'd have what you want and I'd have what I want—you here forever with me." She held her hand out.

Astrid took her sister's hand. "It was a nice idea. And Charlie is handsome." He seemed to get more handsome every time she saw him. But she was nothing but a nuisance to him. "I haven't told him about the Junior Beekeeper project yet. Can you drop me off on the way home?" She'd put it off long enough.

"Can do." Tansy squeezed her hand, then let it go. "And if he is rude to you, Dane has offered to come and talk to him on your behalf."

"Thanks." Astrid could only imagine how that talk would go. Dane didn't need to be involved. She could do this. He'd seemed less prickly by the end of her last visit. While he might not be thrilled over the Junior Beekeepers invading his space, he'd honor Rebecca's wish. Astrid had to believe that.

FROM HIS DESK, Charlie could see out the large picture window that sat in the middle of the front wall of his aunt's home. He'd commandeered the formal dining room for his office because it was in the center of the house. He could hear every creak and pop in the wooden floors or squeaking older hinge and he could see anyone coming or going. Thankfully, there hadn't been much of either the last couple of days.

But it looked like all of that was about to change.

He sighed, crossed his arms over his chest and leaned back to watch his neighbor draw ever closer to his house. It was Astrid. Here. Again. Without notice. She pulled a wagon behind her. Her white veiled hood hung back between her shoulders so her long red-blond hair was visible. If he hadn't known she was a beekeeper, her getup might have been cause for alarm as the head-to-toe white suit looked a lot like a hazmat suit. But it was the determination on her reddened face that had him kicking into fight-or-flight mode. What was she after?

He could pretend they weren't home, turn her away or find out why she was here dressed like that—without giving him some sort of advanced notice.

"Charlie, Charlie!" Nova's voice was excited—followed by rapid footsteps descending the stairs. "Did you see?" She ran into the living room and sucked in a deep breath. "Did you see Astrid and what she's wearing?"

Now that Nova was in the mix, his choices vanished. He'd have to engage with the woman. He ran a hand over his face. "I did."

"She's dressed like a spaceman, sort of." She grabbed on to the arm of his chair, her wide eyes earnest. "For protection. Do you think she's here to do some bee fighting with Rebecca's bees?"

Charlie couldn't help but smile at the image of Astrid squaring off against a swarm of bees. Something told him she was more likely to charm the bees than fight them. Which was, for him, an odd thought to have.

"She's got lots of stuff." Nova stood on tiptoe. "Is she staying for a while?"

He hoped not. "She does have lots of stuff." He rolled his head, stretching his neck.

"Is that Astrid?" Halley appeared from the living room, her headphones around her neck and her phone in her hand. "She looks like some cool chick from an end-of-the-world or alien movie."

"I like her boots," Nova added.

Charlie felt certain nobody looked cool or chic in a bee suit but he didn't argue. Besides, there wasn't enough time. Astrid was climbing the steps and…knocking on the front door. Four knocks. Then silence. He didn't move.

"Are you going to let her in?" Halley took a couple of steps toward the door and stopped.

"What if she is here because there is a bee emergency?" Nova's little face crumpled into concern. "To warn us?"

"I'm not sure that's a thing, Nova." Halley wrapped her arm around her sister's shoulders. "Don't worry. If there is a bee emergency, Astrid will fix it."

The girls had spent less than eight hours with Astrid so how was it they both looked at her like she was some sort of superhero. Nova was into superheroes—which meant Charlie was into superheroes—and, apparently, a lot of them came from outer space. Astrid was not from outer space. She was not a superhero. She was a persistent nuisance he wasn't sure how to deal with.

Astrid knocked again, then stepped back. The problem was, she stepped back just enough so that she could see through the window. His window—the very window they were all staring through. He could only imagine how strange it would be to find the three of them inside not opening the door. First, she made eye contact with the girls, who waved wildly, then her gaze met his. She waved once, then stood there.

Manners dictated he answer the door, but he was sorely tempted to just close the curtains. If he did, maybe she'd get the hint. He'd had two blissfully normal days and now she'd popped up and whatever happened next would be anything but normal. Closing the curtains sounded good—

"Charlie?" Halley hissed.

"I can open the door if her outfit is scaring you." Nova offered, patting his arm. "It is a little scary."

Both girls were staring at him with round, expectant eyes.

"I'll get it." He stood, took a slow breath in, then out. As he crossed to the door, he did it again. He opened the door. "Miss Hill."

"Hi." She waved again. While her style was nothing like the business suits and pressed shirts required for all his virtual conferences and meetings, Astrid had her own version of presentable. Normally. But not at the moment. Her cheeks were flushed pink, there was a smudge of ash on her cheek, and her hair was a mess of braids slipping free from a knot at the back of her head. "I'd like to check on Rebecca's hives, if that's all right? It won't take long."

He nodded. She wasn't coming in. This could work.

"If you have a few minutes, you could come with me? I have something to discuss with you." Whatever it was, Astrid was the one having a hard time making eye contact.

But before he could call her out on it, Nova squeezed between him and the doorframe.

"Hi, Astrid." She was hugging Scorpio against her chest. "You're wearing your bee-fighting suit. Is there a bee emergency?"

"No." Astrid smiled down at Nova. "No emergency."

"Do you always wear that when you're working with the bees?" Halley stepped around Charlie and onto the porch.

"Hi, Halley." She smoothed her hair back, twisted it and tied it in a knot on the back of her head. "Not always. Tansy and I got a call this morning about an unwanted beehive and, since we don't know the bees or how friendly they were, we suited up." Her green eyes returned to Nova. "The bees had filled up our mailman's barbecue grill. I guess that could have been a bee emergency for the bees if Mr. Jones had started the grill without checking it first." She shuddered. "Poor little bees."

"But you and Tansy rescued them?" Nova asked, her worried face easing.

"We did." Astrid nodded. "We rescued them and will move them to our farm once the sun goes down."

Charlie found it all oddly fascinating. Tending bees sounded like herding cats—was there any control in either situation? Still, he listened to his girls' questions, having quite a few of his own answered in the process.

"Why when the sun goes down?" Halley asked.

"The bees will come home and go to bed and then we won't leave any behind." Astrid blew a strand of hair from her forehead. "We get everything set up in the morning, make sure the queen is secured, and come back when they're all asleep to move them and put them in their new home."

He wondered what "the queen is secured" meant, but Nova asked another question before he could get clarification.

"Is it hot?" Nova pointed at her suit.

"It is." Astrid patted the suit. "But this is a vented suit so it's not too bad. See all the little holes?" She held the suit out. "Air can go through but the bees can't."

"Can they sting you?" Halley was studying the fabric. "Through those holes?"

Astrid shook her head. "Nope. But I should go check on Rebecca's hives before the sun gets any higher."

"Can we go?" Nova jumped up and down, Scorpio swinging.

"I haven't visited them in a while, Nova. I'd want to

make sure they were on their very best behavior before I brought you or Halley with me." Astrid blew the same curl from her forehead.

He was so relieved she was the one to tell them no. There was a chance the girls wouldn't be mad at him for the rest of the day.

Nova wasn't ready to give up. "But—"

"Listen to Astrid, Nova. If she says you need to wait, you need to wait." He was quick to back Astrid up— but gently.

"Okay." Nova's shoulders slouched.

Astrid's smile was all sympathy. "I'm sorry to disappoint you, Nova."

"It's okay." But Nova's sigh told a different story.

"Could you stop by when you're done? And tell us about Rebecca's bees?" Did he want Astrid hanging around? No. Did he want Nova anywhere near an actual beehive? Absolutely not. But if Nova was interested in bees, Charlie didn't want to dampen her curiosity. Sitting safely around the kitchen table talking about bees with a beekeeper, even Astrid, seemed like an appropriate way to accomplish that.

Charlie had been married to Yasmina for almost a year when she'd had her accident. In that time, she'd done her best to help him parent. She'd called him a *dad in progress*. And while his parenting knowledge was limited, he had enough disappointing childhood memories to remind him of what not to do. Namely, ridicule or act disinterested in the girls' interests or try to shut down their inquisitiveness. Nova and Halley were both so smart—so full of life. He wanted them to pursue everything and anything their little hearts desired. *But* he knew he had a lot of work to do to get his overly protective instinct under control. "If you have time?"

"Oh…" Clearly, Astrid wasn't expecting his response. "Of course."

He wasn't the best at reading body language but she seemed to…perk up a little.

"Really?" Nova's smile was back. "Yay!"

"Nova and I will make some lemonade." Halley nodded. "We can. It's Aunt Rebecca's recipe."

"While you do that, I'm going with Astrid." Charlie shoved his hands into his slacks. Like it or not, he was curious to find out what Astrid wanted to discuss with him. "I won't be long."

"To the bees?" Nova was looking worried again. "But is it safe?"

"Yeah, you don't have a suit." Halley was frowning, too.

"Don't worry." Astrid pointed over her shoulder with her thumb. "I have an extra one, if you want it."

No, Charlie did not want it. In the time he'd had the door open, the heat had rolled into the house in waves.

"You have to, Charlie." Nova wasn't going to let up. "Please."

"Okay." How could he say no to that?

Astrid nodded. "Let's go."

"Be careful, Charlie." Nova hugged him around the knees.

"Come on, Nova." Halley guided her inside. "Let's go make lemonade."

Charlie pulled the door closed behind him and followed Astrid off the porch into the brilliant Texas sun. He drew in a breath, his lungs filling with thick, warm air. It wasn't unpleasant—it was familiar. Cycling, in

Texas heat, meant hot air and sweat—lots of it. But it had felt good. Riding for hours, going until his restlessness had subsided.

"Here you go." Astrid handed him the suit. "It might be a little short on you."

"It's fine." He shrugged into the suit and it felt like the temp shot up a good ten degrees. He pulled up the zipper and turned to face her.

Astrid circled around him, checking the suit zippers and cuffs before nodding. "Do you know where her hives are?" She pulled the wagon behind her.

He nodded. "They're your hives, aren't they?"

"Oh, no. These are Rebecca's bees." There was a smile in her voice. "She'd become quite a proficient beekeeper. She liked collecting pretty things and offering it to the bees to thank them for the honey."

His aunt had always taken pleasure in the "treasures" nature left around her property. "That would explain all the shells and rocks and tiny statues around."

"Yes. She was one of a kind." There was a hint of grief in Astrid's voice.

"You miss her." It wasn't a question. Until now, he'd believed he was the only one who'd missed his aunt.

"I do." Astrid glanced back at him. "But being here helps. This place will always hold a part of her."

He nodded, appreciating Astrid's take on things. Even though his aunt was his mother's sister, he'd never met two more different women. Rebecca had been affectionate and communicative, she'd loved visiting with friends, gardening and hunting for snails and pretty rocks on long walks. His mother wasn't a hugger, she was silent and withdrawn, and she didn't like dirt, animals or bugs, and very few people. As far as he knew, his parents had a gardener and if his mother worked out, it was inside with her personal trainer daily.

Astrid stepped in front of him as the path narrowed. "Rebecca and I were of like mind there. Adding a bit of whimsy—for the pure joy of it."

Whimsy. It wasn't a word he'd ever use, but it could also apply to Astrid. Her hair had slipped free to pile in the hood of her bee suit. It was an unusual color. Not quite red, not quite blond. A few braids. Whimsical, maybe. With the sunlight filtering through the branches overhead, there were hints of gold and copper threads, too. It was when he realized he'd been pondering the color of Astrid Hill's hair for at least a solid minute that he stopped, ran his fingers through his tangled mop and stared up at the sky overhead. When he dared look ahead of him, he realized she'd left him behind.

Which was fine until he heard Astrid sounding very un-Astrid-like, saying, "Who are you... Be careful. Please. Stop! No, don't move—" Her cry had Charlie running down the path after her, cold fear gripping him by the throat.

CHAPTER FIVE

ASTRID WAS IN SHOCK. Not only were two strangers in the clearing, she'd arrived in time to see Rebecca's beehive topple onto its side. Time seemed to slow as the well-established colony slammed into the ground. Two of the five hive boxes split wide, spilling honey and brood-heavy frames all over the river rock Rebecca had used for ground cover. Before she could determine the extent of the damage, the bees were swarming.

The men were dressed in reflective vests and helmets and armed with clipboards. The taller of the two was using his clipboard to swat bees while trying to shake off what looked like crushed propolis and honeycomb from his work boots.

The bees weren't happy and they were going to let these men know it.

The two men cursed and waved their arms in the air while Astrid watched in horror. If they kept flailing about, the bees would keep defending their homes. She moved quickly, pushing one of the men back onto the path. "Go that way. Don't make sudden, large movements or yell—they don't like that." She headed back to the hive, where the other man was stomping the ground. Stomping on bees and comb and doing nothing to diffuse the situation.

"Please listen to me." She tapped against his clipboard. "You are aggravating them." She tried to steer him, one hand gripping one of the man's arms. "Move slowly—"

"I've got a job to do, lady. How about you get out of my way so I can do it." A bee stung the man beside his eye but he stood his ground.

She wasn't quick to anger—normally. "Fine. I won't worry about you—" which wasn't exactly true as the bees were attacking him with glee "—but I am worried about my bees." She tried to tug him after her, digging in with all her might. "If you stay here, you'll continue to be stung and, if that happens enough, you won't fare so well." He yanked his arm away from her. "Also, you have no right to be on this private property so I'm going to ask you to leave nicely. Then I'm calling the sheriff." The air was a deafening roar and the bees kept bumping off her suit.

Astrid blinked, startled by the appearance of Charlie. The bee suit was too small, his ankles exposed, but he'd been smart enough to don her spare gloves.

"Let's go." Charlie's voice was so intimidating, the man actually held up both of his hands and walked along the path.

Astrid followed, the buzzing fading but still audible. It wouldn't be a quick cleanup. She'd need some new deep hive boxes and waxed frames to replace the ones that had been damaged or broken. Once she got to the house, she'd text Tansy.

The minute they reached a small break in the trees, Charlie unzipped his bee hood and pushed it back. "Who are you and why are you here?"

"We were hired to do a full commercial survey by Stinson Properties," the first man said.

Charlie's physical response was hard to miss. He jerked back, his eyes shifting to the blue sky overhead, before he drew in a deep breath.

Was he counting? Astrid unzipped her hood to get a better look. Yep, he was counting. And angry. Like, really angry. He was beet red and his hands were clenched into tight fists. His breath powered out of him, ragged.

Finally, Charlie flexed his hands. "Do either of you have a card?"

The man who had far too many bee stings offered a card.

Charlie read the card and muttered something under his breath. "The invoice you will receive for the damages needs to be paid in full or law enforcement will become involved." Charlie tucked the card into one of the bee suit's pockets without bothering to look at it.

The two men exchanged looks.

"This is some sort of misunderstanding," the less stung man said. "Is this Rebecca Wallace's property?"

Astrid felt a lump form in her throat. Her instinct was usually spot-on. Right now, her instinct was telling her Charlie knew more than he was letting on.

"It is." Charlie nodded. "But Stinson Properties has no claim to this property and you two are officially trespassing. You need to leave. Now."

The two men exchanged another look.

"If you've got a long drive, you might want to go to the medical clinic." Astrid was growing more concerned about the man covered in stings. "Ten stings per pound of bodyweight is generally safe, but more than that can be dangerous to an adult." She gave him a meaningful once-over. "It's up to you, of course, but the Lewis County Medical Center has an ER. I'd suggest going there."

"I'm fine," the bee-stung man grumbled, his gaze dismissive.

He really wasn't. If she'd had her phone, she would have called an ambulance.

"Maybe she's right, Trey?" The other man was assessing the red welts on Trey's face. Thankfully, he seemed to understand his coworker's predicament was cause for alarm.

"I'm not wasting money on an ER visit," Trey ground out. "Damn bees. Call pest control and spray the damn things until they can't hurt no one. Shouldn't there be signs out? Warning people?"

"The No Trespassing signs should suffice." Charlie was still grumbling and more than a little threatening.

"It was an accident. Trey tripped—fell into those things—"

"You don't need to explain." Trey cut the other man off.

Astrid didn't want to waste time with pointless arguing. The sting close to Trey's eye was looking angrier and angrier. "A bee sting on the eye can blind you." She nodded at him. "I'll repeat, I strongly encourage you to go to the ER." She hoped Trey would listen.

Trey's jaw jutted forward and he turned on her with open hostility, making her step back. His color was blotchy and his face was already swelling. "Oh, you encourage me? Maybe I should sue you—it was your damn bees that did this to me."

"She saved you. While you were trespassing. If she says you need medical help, you do." Charlie stepped closer to her. "Say thank you and walk away." He drew a deep breath. "This is the last time I'm asking you to go." His hands clenched tight and his narrow-eyed gaze shifted between the two men.

"Come on, Lyle." Trey waved the other man to follow. "Let's hit the road."

"Take that trail—it'll keep you out of the bees' way." Astrid pointed at the secondary path. "And go to the Lewis Medical Center. Please."

Trey's smile was hard, his head-to-toe appraisal of her downright insulting. "I guess we know who wears the pants in the family." He sneered at Charlie.

"Walk." Charlie was upset. Very upset. "Now."

For a minute, no one moved. There was a shift in the air that doubled the size of the lump in her throat *and* made breathing difficult. Trey was sizing Charlie up. Charlie was sort of staring straight ahead, not bothering to return Trey's goading stare but undeniably at the ready. Astrid held her breath, scrambling for a way to defuse the situation—until Trey and Lyle turned and headed down the trail she'd indicated.

They were out of sight, but Trey's grumbled invectives were plain to hear. The man spouted off more insults and curses than Astrid had ever heard strung together. Some new insults and curses, too. Aunt Magnolia said obscenities were the sign of a small mind. But Trey's brain couldn't be too small considering the way he was *still* verbally eviscerating Astrid's supposed superiority and mocking how whipped Charlie was.

Charlie. Charlie was as still as a statue. Tension rolled off him in waves. He was flexing his hands, over and over, while his jaw tightened until Astrid was wincing.

"Do you think I acted superior?" She waited, watching the muscle in his jaw.

His heavy-lidded gaze met hers and held. Slowly, his jaw muscle smoothed. "No."

She smiled up at him. "Are your ankles okay?"

Her question caught him off guard and his furrow deepened. "My ankles?"

"The suit is too short. I'm hoping the bees knew you were on their side and focused all their energy on Trey." She remembered the numerous red spots on the man's face and neck and glanced down the path the men had gone. "And I hope they go to the ER."

"My ankles are fine." Charlie closed his eyes and took a deep breath. "If they don't, that's on them." When he opened his deep brown eyes, he looked everywhere but at her.

"I suppose." She tugged off her gloves and reached up, running her fingers along a painful telltale bump. "They got me." She smoothed her hair back and used one of her braids to tie the rest into a knot. "My own fault for not making sure I'd zipped the hood all the way up."

Charlie lifted her knotted hair and leaned down. "Do you need medicine? Ice? What helps?"

The gentle probing of his fingers was too distracting for her to feel much pain. And his closeness, his breath along her ear… A shudder rolled over her. "No," she mumbled, turning to look at him. *Oh, my.* Whatever was happening, she liked it.

He let go of her hair and took two large steps back, wearing an expression of horror.

It was so sudden, and not in the least bit subtle, that Astrid found herself laughing. It was laugh or run away and cry. She was too tired and hot to run or cry or apologize for…whatever. "Did the girls say something about lemonade?"

He nodded, the blank mask he normally wore slipping back into place. "Didn't you have something to discuss with me?"

"I do." But how would he feel about letting the Junior Beekeepers handle these bees when he'd just seen them at their worst? No, that's not true. They were doing what any living creature would do when threatened. Just thinking about Trey knocking over the hive, which she felt certain he'd done, had her temper rising again.

"Is it bad?" He was watching her.

"No." She smiled. "It's good. Rebecca had an idea, a wonderful idea really. She'd put everything in place right before her passing." Her smile dimmed somewhat, missing the dear old lady. "I'm not sure you'll feel the same way as she did, though."

The furrow was back. "It sounds bad."

She took a deep breath, the words coming out in a rushed stream. "Well, it all depends on how you look at it. She'd volunteered her beeyard for the Junior Beekeepers' summer project—"

"No." It was firm.

She wasn't going to give up so easily. "It won't take too long. All of them know what they're doing and Rebecca worked so hard with the Junior Beekeepers—"

"No." No hesitancy or hint that he was listening.

"Charlie, please consider it. Please." She didn't want to beg but that was exactly what she was doing.

The furrow in his brow eased but his lips pressed into a thin line.

She swallowed, processing the not-so-blank expression on his handsome face. Not that she could get a read on what he was thinking... She added, "Rebecca said you two spent hours out here when you were younger.

That you made all sorts of special memories together. She wanted to share this place with kids." As soon as the words were out, she regretted them. "That sounded manipulative. I apologize."

Charlie's gaze shifted to the dirt path at their feet.

"It's just…well, it was something she wanted to do." She stopped then, knowing she'd said all she could. "So… I could use some lemonade before I start cleaning up that mess." She pressed her hand to the bump on the back of her neck.

His gaze came up and landed on her hand. "Does it hurt?"

"A minor irritation." She offered him a smile.

He went back to staring at the ground. "Lemonade." Without a backward glance, he headed toward the house.

As far as days went, today had been quite eventful. She wanted to ask about the men that were here. Charlie's reaction suggested he knew something about Stinson Properties. Did he know why they'd be surveying the place? A commercial survey, no less. Did Charlie have plans for the property he hadn't mentioned? If he did, would he tell her?

No. At the moment, all she should care about was ensuring the Junior Beekeepers got their service hours and doing damage control on Rebecca's almost destroyed hive. She'd give the bees a little time to calm down, get supplies from Tansy and set the colony's world to rights.

Her eyes swept over the tall, straight figure of Charlie Driver and his ankles peeking out between the bee suit cuffs and his well-worn oxford business shoes. "I'll bring over a larger suit next time."

"Next time?" He didn't look back or stop walking.

"It might come in handy if you have to rescue more

bees." She tucked a strand of wayward hair behind her ear. "I can't wait to tell the girls of your heroic efforts." She knew his girls would be proud of him. And, in turn, Charlie would be happy. There was a high probability that he wouldn't let on he was happy but Astrid held on to a sliver of hope that she might finally get to see Charlie Driver smile.

JUNIOR BEEKEEPERS? Why did such a thing exist? After what he'd just seen, the idea of putting bees and teenagers together was a surefire recipe for disaster. As far as he was concerned, the bees hadn't needed any help. One look at Trey's face and there was no doubt the bees were more than capable of taking care of themselves. So why was she still worrying over her battle-worthy bees? Especially when they'd repaid Astrid's efforts with a sting?

The truth was, he hadn't given a thought to the bees. He'd heard her yell and some as-yet-undiscovered instinct kicked in. Something had been wrong and he'd needed to get to her. The whole damn morning had been unsettling.

They reached the house to find both girls waiting on the back porch.

"Charlie." Nova came running down the steps. "You are in a bee-fighting suit."

It had been close. The fighting part, anyway. If there was one thing he'd learned today it was just how dangerous bees could be. Which made Astrid's request even more ridiculous.

"Beekeeping." Halley corrected her. "How'd it go?"

He was hot and tired and more irritated than he wanted to admit—none of which his girls would be interested in knowing. He was still trying to formulate an answer when Astrid spoke up.

"It was…different." Astrid glanced his way, then went on. "Every day with the bees is a new experience but I've never experienced anything like today. And I've been a beekeeper since I was your age." She winked at Nova—who instantly took Astrid's hand.

He watched the exchange, marveling at how free and easy the girls were with Astrid. Affection was still hard for him. Yasmina had been the hand-holder and bedtime-story-snuggler. He needed to try harder. He liked the idea of Nova looking up at him like that—like he was someone who made her day better.

"What happened?" Halley leaned forward on the porch railing.

"Charlie was amazing." Astrid wiggled Nova's arm. "A real hero."

Both girls were staring at him now. Halley, in disbelief, and Nova, in awe.

Yeah, yeah. He wasn't buying it, either.

"Charlie?" Halley asked dubiously, holding open the back door for them.

Charlie sighed but didn't defend himself. Apparently, Astrid was superhero material but he was…not.

"Yes, Charlie." Astrid nodded. "An appraisal crew wound up on Rebecca's property by mistake, found one of the hives, and, somehow, it was accidentally knocked over."

"Seriously? How did that happen? I bet the bees weren't happy." Halley followed them inside.

Nova clung to Astrid's hand. "Are the bees okay?"

Charlie shot a glance Astrid's way. Would his daughter be this concerned if they'd seen Trey's bee-stung face? He sure as hell hoped they listened to Astrid and went to the ER.

"Oh, the bees will be fine." Astrid sat in a kitchen chair and unzipped her bee suit. "I do need to call my sister for supplies." She bent forward to slip the elastic band from under her foot, unzipped the legs of the suit, then stood and shimmied free. She wore a thin T-shirt and snug-fit jeans. "Hopefully, we'll get them settled before nightfall and they'll forget all about today."

He'd never seen her in jeans before. She wore skirts or dresses—all flowy and loose and feminine. These clothes were too tight. And…and not at all Astrid-like. Her braids slipped loose and her hair fell down her back. It seemed he had some odd fascination with her hair, too. But he was not going to stand here and stare at her. Again. He tugged on the zipper at his throat, but it wouldn't budge. He tried again.

"Oh." Astrid was up and hurrying to him. "Hold on, this zipper snags sometimes." She reached up, gripping the zipper pull-tab with one hand and tugging the fabric tight with the other. "We need to order some new suits but Aunt Magnolia tends to hold off on new purchases until she deems it necessary. I suppose, other than the zippers this is still a good suit." Her green eyes bounced from his face to the zipper to his…mouth.

His throat tightened. So did his chest. The ache that hollowed out his stomach caught him off guard. Her gaze lowered and focused on the zipper but the ache remained.

Astrid's cheeks were a rosy pink. "She doesn't suit up anymore." She swallowed. "My aunt. I think that's why she's not quick to order more. I mean, every once in a blue moon she does… It's really stuck." She pulled the fabric tighter. "It's not an easy fix, either. The fabric is so thick you can't switch out the zippers unless you have a heavy-duty sewing machine. Even then, there's a chance you'll bend a needle." Finally, the zipper gave. Astrid's smile was pure relief. "There we go." She patted his chest before pulling her hand back as if the contact had burned her. "You should be able to take it from there." She stepped aside, braiding the curling strands that framed her face, then braiding those into larger braids to keep them up.

Charlie could see the red bump on the back of her neck from here. It had to hurt. It looked like it did.

"But they left? The men?" Halley asked, peering out the window. "You're sure?"

"There is another gate down the road. I'm not sure if there's any sort of lock on it." Astrid went to her suit, picked it up and carried it out the back door to drape it over the porch railing. When she came in, she pulled the door closed behind her. "But when I go back out, I'll make sure they're gone and the gate is secured."

It was unlikely that Trey was still hanging around but he didn't like the idea. He had no doubt Astrid would do as she said but this place wasn't her responsibility. "I'll take care of it."

"Deal." She smiled an all too sunny smile but didn't make eye contact with him. "I'll take care of the bees."

He swallowed.

"Astrid, why did you leave your honey bee-keeping suit thingy out there?" Nova asked.

"There's honey, wax and all sorts of stuff on it. If the bees smell the honey and come to investigate, I'd rather they stayed outside." Astrid turned to him and held out her hand. "I can take yours out."

Charlie handed over the suit, unable to ignore the spot on her neck as she carried his suit out to hang next to hers. The red stood out, almost angry, against her pale skin. There had to be something she could take? A cream she could use? One tiny sting didn't compare to Trey's face but, still, it bothered him.

"Charlie." Nova nudged him. "Staring."

He nodded. "Thanks," he murmured. It was time to change the subject. "It's hot out there. How about some lemonade."

"Yes." Nova clapped her hands and carried two tall glasses to the table. "You sit." She tugged on Charlie's hand until he sat. "You, too, Astrid."

"Yes, ma'am." She sat. "Thank you."

Halley carried the large pitcher to the table. "It's fresh." She set the pitcher down. "Ice." She carried the cups back to the freezer and scooped ice into them. "There."

Charlie poured Astrid and himself each a tall glass of lemonade.

"It looks delicious. Thank you." Astrid gave him a little salute and took a sip.

"Cookies." Halley disappeared into the pantry.

Astrid sipped her lemonade, cleared her throat, then set the glass down. Her face… She was warning him of something. She looked meaningfully at the lemonade.

He glared at her but she only shook her head. With raised brows, he took a sip—and promptly set his glass down. His tongue was stinging. He didn't drink lemonade often but he didn't remember it being so…salty. He peered into the perfectly normal-looking glass of lemonade, then looked at Astrid.

Astrid's look was one hundred percent *I told you so.*

"Here." Halley appeared with an unopened box of frosted oatmeal cookies. "Nova hid these in the bottom of the grocery cart so Charlie didn't see them."

"I saw them," he grumbled, reaching into the box for a cookie.

"Whatever." Halley got two smaller cups from the cabinet. "Here, Nova."

All four of them sat at the table, munching cookies and smiling at one another. Charlie watched as Astrid downed the majority of her lemonade before inhaling a cookie. He admired her efforts but there was no way he was going to follow her lead.

"You don't like it?" Nova was staring at his cup.

The earnestness on her face had him doing something he rarely did—lie. "I do."

"You're not drinking it." Nova tapped the glass.

Fine. If Astrid could do it, he could do it. As Charlie lifted his glass, Nova smiled.

"Wait." Halley grabbed his arm. "Oh, man, this is awful." She stuck her tongue out.

Nova picked up her cup and took a sip. Her face twisted up as her little body shuddered. "Nasty."

"How did you drink that?" Halley was staring at Astrid's nearly empty glass.

"Oh, well, I had a little sister. She was always so proud of her creations we didn't have the heart to tell her they weren't exactly tasty." Astrid shrugged. "But the cookies helped. I'm glad Charlie didn't see them in the grocery cart."

"I saw them," he repeated.

All three of them looked at him wearing exactly the same expression before laughing. Nova asked Astrid about how she'd fix the bee houses and that started the three of them on a rapid-fire, talking-over-one-another conversation that he couldn't quite keep up with. He took another cookie from the box and sat back. It looked so simple. There was laughing and talking with hand gestures. A happy, peaceful, animated conversation. Like they were pleased to be together and eager to hear what the other said. It wasn't forced.

Growing up, his family dinners had started with teasing and declined from there. Insults. Prodding at one another's insecurities or sneering ridicule. Then anger. Lots of it. This was nothing like that. It was hard to accept that this sort of camaraderie actually existed.

He and the girls had dinner together every night but they'd never had this sort of lively interaction. It was more than beekeeping, he knew it. It was Astrid. Astrid and her messy braided hair, distractingly tight clothing, and that warm and welcoming smile. That was another good Astrid word. *Warm.* She filled the kitchen with warmth and she wasn't even trying.

Of course, the girls would respond this way—it was a night-and-day difference from what he had to offer. What could he say to get this sort of response? He was who he was. It wasn't that he didn't care, he did. But caring and showing that he cared made him vulnerable. He couldn't afford to be vulnerable when he had the girls to protect.

He sat back in his chair and stared up at the overhead light fixture. There were cobwebs hanging off the old brass chandelier, dancing and swaying in the cold air blasting from the overhead vent.

His thoughts wandered back to the business card he'd gotten from Lyle. Stinson Properties. His sister was up to something. Lindsay Stinson, his sister. She and her husband were into land development and real estate. She'd reached out to him about the land before he'd left and he'd listened. He didn't want the land, he wanted to be rid of it. But the men showing up today meant they'd likely discovered how much Aunt Rebecca's place was worth and wanted to capitalize on it. That was why she'd hired those men to perform a commercial survey of the place. It wouldn't matter if their aunt had made provisions in her will for her property. Lindsay would dig and push and fight until she got her way. That's what she did. Big entrances, high drama and good—or bad— surprises were her thing.

Charlie expected Rebecca's will to reflect her unique quirkiness. All he could do was hope that her will was straightforward so he could sell to his sister without any of the drama. If Lindsay tried to pull something, maybe he'd call in the bees for backup. He paused.

If Rebecca's last wishes included this Junior Bee-keeping service thing, he'd have to honor that request as well, wouldn't he?

He slumped forward and propped his elbow on the table, exhaustion and defeat crowding in on him. He'd been treading water for the last year. He knew it, the girls probably knew it, too. He glanced their way. They were telling Astrid a story, back and forth and talking over one another. Astrid seemed thoroughly entranced—until she reached up to rub the back of her neck.

Charlie frowned, stood and headed for the downstairs bathroom. He rummaged through his toiletries bag until he'd found a tube of antihistamine cream and carried it back into the kitchen. He set the tube on the table in front of Astrid, ignored her blinding smile and whispered "thank you" and just how appealing she was at that moment, and carried his glass of salty lemonade to the counter.

He took a deep breath and poured the lemonade down the drain. He didn't know what was happening. Nothing felt as it should—as he should. Then a sudden chorus of laughter rang out, his girls and Astrid, and he was smiling. He had a call to make and hours of work to do but he found himself emptying all the glasses, washing the pitcher and finding things to keep him in the kitchen. Once the laughter ended and the real world crept in, he'd go. Until then, he'd stay and listen and smile.

NOVA CHOMPED ON another cookie. Two cookies. Even Charlie had two. Two.

And nobody was mad the lemonade was nasty. Astrid even drank it. Nova couldn't drink it—it was gross. Astrid had to be a superhero. She saved bees and fixed washing-machine attacks and drank salt-lemonade and had funny dogs and made Charlie smile, Nova saw it. If she had a cape, she'd definitely be a real-life superhero. If she was a superhero, she would know what to do about the rat monster.

Plus, Astrid was funny. And nice. And pretty. And Nova really liked her laugh.

She really hoped Charlie would let them be friends, because Nova liked Astrid. Lots.

"You got stung?" Halley made her owie face.

"It happens." Astrid put a glob of cream on her finger and rubbed it on her neck.

"You did?" Nova was shocked to hear this. "Why would the bees sting you?"

"They're bees, Nova." Even though Charlie said it, Nova didn't think it made sense.

"But you said they don't want to sting. And you're their friend. Why would they sting you when you were helping them?" Nova wasn't so sure she wanted to meet Astrid's bees now.

"They were scared." Astrid put the cap back on. "Once their bee alarm goes off, all the bees work together to protect their hive. One little bee on their own can't do much. But a whole hive, working together? They're pretty good at protecting their home."

"Bees have alarms?" Nova couldn't believe it. "Alarm clocks? Brooglar alarms?"

"Burglar." Halley always knew what Nova meant.

"Not an alarm like we have." Astrid had the prettiest smile. "Bees don't have words. They use their movements, their wings and their scent to send messages."

"They dance." Nova loved that most about the bees.

"They do. That's another way they talk to each other. A bee sends out an alarm signal, then another bee sends it and another and the whole hive gets the message." She shrugged. "When the message is 'Danger, time to defend our home,' the bees will swarm and protect."

"Okay." That all made sense. But still. "Don't they know you're a good guy?" Nova wasn't sure how to feel about this. "You're the bees' friends. Friends don't hurt each other."

"If I'd had my suit secure, they wouldn't have. And it's not so bad, Nova, I promise." Astrid patted her hand. "The poor bees were confused—what with their house falling over and people in their clearing. I'd probably have stung someone, too, if I was a bee."

Nova shook her head. "You're too nice."

"And she's not a bee," Charlie pointed out. "There were hundreds of bees, Nova. Hundreds." He frowned.

He was probably worried about the sting on Astrid's neck, too. "She was lucky." Charlie sat at the table and reached for another cookie.

Three. Charlie had three cookies.

"It's a miracle she only got stung once." Charlie finished munching on his cookie.

"You didn't get stung." Halley reached for another cookie—and Charlie didn't stop her.

Nova grabbed another one, too. They were really good cookies.

"He was working with the bees—chasing off those men and telling them to leave." Astrid was smiling her prettiest smile at him. She looked at Charlie and Charlie looked at Astrid.

Charlie didn't frown. He was staring but he wasn't grumpy.

Halley was staring at Charlie and Astrid, too. She was smiling. Which was good. Halley didn't smile all that much anymore.

Nova grabbed another cookie and sat back. Four cookies and no one had noticed. They were all too busy looking at each other. For a long, long time. Long enough for Nova to sneak one more cookie.

CHAPTER SIX

ASTRID SCANNED THE LIST. "Root beer."

"Since when do the aunts like root beer?" Tansy shot her a disbelieving look.

Growing up, sodas and sweetened drinks were occasional treats out and about—not a staple in the Hill home. "They don't. Van does." Astrid held out the grocery list. "See. You can tell Camellia was thinking of him by the extra loopy rolls."

Tansy rolled her eyes but she was smiling. "They are something else."

"They are one hundred percent adorable." Shelby, Aunt Mags's daughter and their cousin, shifted her baby daughter on her hip. "Mags thinks he's going to propose."

The Aunt Camellia and Van Kettner lovefest was only a couple of months old, but they acted like they'd been a couple forever. Astrid had never seen anyone as giddy as her aunt—except maybe Van Kettner. The two of them were pure romance and sweetness. Her aunt would go pink in the cheeks as soon as she laid eyes on her handsome, older beau. And Van? He adored Aunt Camellia. Anyone could see it, plain on his face. He was always bringing her flowers and chocolates or taking her on an evening hand-in-hand stroll or roping them into a marathon board game so he could stay a little longer. That he didn't bother to hide his adoration made it all the more precious. And since Aunt Camellia was blissfully happy, they were all pretty darn happy, too.

"Propose?" Tansy appeared legitimately surprised as she steered the grocery cart onto the next aisle. "Really?"

"Is it a bad thing?" Astrid liked the idea of Van officially joining their family.

"No. It's just… No offense, they both have lives and a home and getting married just seems…weird." Tansy's look was almost guilty. "I can't imagine not waking up to Aunt Camellia being there. You know? She's *always* been there. Like, always. But she wouldn't be, if they got married." She shook her head, as if she couldn't quite absorb the information.

To be fair, Astrid hadn't thought about that part. Now that Tansy had introduced the idea, her enthusiasm for a proposal and wedding was instantly dampened.

"Well, if it isn't the Hill girls." Willadeene Svoboda stood in the middle of the grocery aisle. When confronted with the gossip-loving instigator, escape was often the best option, but between her sizable hips and the grocery cart she'd angled just so, there was no escaping the older woman this time. "Why the long faces? Is everything all right?" Her gaze sharpened, bouncing between the sisters with far too much interest.

Oh, no. Willadeene was like a hyena scenting blood. Hopefully she hadn't heard the exchange about Van and Camellia or all of Honey would expect an invitation. Astrid smiled. "Good morning, Willadeene. We're trying to find the oyster crackers. They're never in the same place." She shrugged.

"It's a crisis," Tansy agreed, shooting her sister a look. "For Lord Byron, anyway."

"Dear me, is that overstuffed buzzard still alive?" Willadeene and Lord Byron did not get along—a fact that helped Aunt Mags tolerate the bird. "Well, now, I haven't seen the two of you out and about in ages."

Astrid could almost hear the theme song for *The Wizard of Oz*'s wicked witch playing. Dane hummed it every time he saw or heard the name Willadeene Svoboda so now, even when he wasn't around, Astrid could hear him humming—with gusto. Like now. It made it incredibly hard to keep a straight face.

"No?" Tansy was on the same page as her boyfriend—she wasn't fond of the gossipy older woman. "I suppose there hasn't been a festival in a bit. Then there was the honey harvest. And it's been so hot."

"It has." Willadeene nodded. "If we don't get some rain soon, everything will wither up and die. My poor garden's hurting."

Astrid scrambled for something to say. "Yes, we're lucky to have our own well on the property."

"Lucky, indeed. And you have one another. You girls know I live a lonely, quiet life. I imagine Honey Hill House is bursting at the seams, what with all the changes taking place." She turned her gaze on Shelby.

There was no help for it. "Have you two met before?" Willadeene's quick headshake meant Astrid was going to have to make introductions. "Shelby Dunholm, this is Willadeene Svoboda."

"The *new* Bee Girl? The one everyone is talking about?" Willadeene shook Shelby's hand. "A surprise for one and all?"

Astrid did try to give everyone the benefit of the doubt but it was extra challenging with Willadeene. She enjoyed sticking her nose into other people's lives—

like now. Shelby had tracked down Aunt Magnolia—her birth mother—a few short months ago, which made her a curiosity to the small town. It was clear the woman was fishing for something, but what? And who, exactly, was *one and all*?

Shelby wasn't the least fazed. It helped that she'd heard plenty of stories about Willadeene and her love of stirring the pot. "That's me. The surprise." She bounced Bea on her hip. "I suppose this is the mini-surprise. Two for the price of one—out and about and surprising at will."

If Willadeene picked up on Shelby's sarcasm, she didn't let on. "I've heard so much about you." She cooed at baby Bea. "I wasn't sure what to believe—since I know Magnolia so well, you see." She lowered her voice. "Mags? A mother? It never occurred to me that all the rumors were true. People will talk, of course, but it was such a shock… Still, here you are. In the flesh." There was nothing subtle about Willadeene's inspection. "And, oh, my, you look so much like… Magnolia."

Astrid could only stare at the woman, stunned. It had surprised them all to learn that Aunt Mags had a baby as a young teen and that she'd given the baby up for adoption. When that baby, Shelby, showed up, Aunt Mags's secret had come out. And the years of pain and regret Aunt Mags had endured. Willadeene had no right to go digging into something so personal.

"Mags *is* my biological mother." Shelby didn't just look like her mother, she shared her mother's sharp wit and intimidating nature. And her adoptive parents taught her to stand up for herself and what was right. She did not tolerate bullies.

"Yes, poor dear." Willadeene's face was all sympathy.

"Poor dear? Which poor dear are we referring to? Me or Magnolia?" Shelby made a silly face at Beatrix. "Though I'm not sure either one of us *is* a poor dear. I'd say things are pretty good at the moment." She turned her green eyes on Willadeene. "Who, exactly, do you mean?"

Willadeene blinked rapidly. "Well, I meant… I mean…" She cleared her throat. "I'm sure this was a surprise for—for everyone."

"My parents let me know I was adopted as soon as I was old enough to understand. It was all very out in the open and nurturing." She shrugged. "No surprises. And since Mags gave birth to me, I'm not really a surprise to her, either."

Willadeene wasn't about to let Shelby get the upper hand. The determination on the older woman's face was unsettling, to say the least. "I was referring to you showing up, out of nowhere, with no forewarning. I'm sure Mags was delighted, of course, regardless. It does *seem* to have turned into a happy reunion for all."

Which led to a long, awkward silence that made Astrid's chest heavy. If Willadeene was trying to imply Aunt Mags was unhappy about Shelby's appearance, nothing could be further from the truth.

"Wow. Okay." Shelby surprised them all by laughing. "Thank you so much for your concern and interest in things that have nothing to do with you." She held Willadeene's gaze. "This has been…*enlightening.*"

Willadeene was speechless.

"We should probably get back to shopping." Tansy started to back up.

"Dog food. Or, um, oyster crackers…" Did it really

matter? Astrid grabbed Shelby's hand and tugged her along, in awe of her cousin.

"Humph." Willadeene, thankfully, and her cart headed in the other direction.

Shelby glanced after the woman. "She's something."

"You were amazing." Astrid squeezed her arm. "I've never seen the table turned on Willadeene Svoboda before."

"It was cool. But you should still be careful around her." Tansy steered the cart. "She's all ears and mouth. In the ears, out the mouth."

After that exchange, Astrid wasn't overly worried about Shelby. "Oyster crackers." She stopped their cart and pointed to the bottom shelf.

Tansy crouched and picked up the large bag. "I'm pretty sure they're only in stock because of Aunt Camellia."

"She does love that bird." Shelby cooed to Bea. "And you do, too, don't you? When you're walking, Lord Byron will have to find himself a higher perch."

"Mags will love that." Tansy put the bag in the cart and giggled at the face Bea made. "What's next?"

"We forgot the dog treats." Astrid scanned the list. "I'll go get that. You can get the fruit and diapers. I'll take Bea?" Bea promptly reached for her, all smiles.

"I guess so." Shelby tapped her daughter's nose. "You two behave."

Astrid held the baby close and said, "It's okay, Bea. We won't tell Mom when we go bowling with cantaloupes."

Bea giggled and babbled most of the way to the dog food aisle.

"Goodness, you are such a fuss bucket." Astrid

teased, hugging Bea close. "If only everyone was as easygoing as you, little Bea, life would be nothing but giggles and sunshine and happiness." She gave the baby a bunny-nose rub, which made Bea laugh and grab hold of Astrid's face so she could give Astrid a kiss. Bea loved giving big, open-mouthed kisses. And Astrid loved receiving them. As much as she loved her bees, they couldn't give her hugs and giggles and open-mouthed kisses. And Astrid was beginning to ache for those things...

"Hey, Astrid. Hey, baby Bea." Nicole, Astrid's best friend, steered her grocery cart alongside them. "I just saw my mother circling the store and figured I should give you a heads-up before I bail. She's been in an especially bad mood—which means she's especially dangerous." Nicole's long hair was a mess of blond and green and black stripes on her head, poked through with chopsticks. "Grab what you need and make a run for it."

Astrid laughed. "Too late."

"Nooo." Nicole drooped forward onto her grocery cart. "Is everyone okay? No casualties?" Nicole and her mother were not close—to put it nicely. "It's too early in the morning for her crap."

"Interestingly enough, Shelby totally derailed her." Astrid nodded at the very skeptical look Nicole shot her. "Seriously. She has a whole lot of Aunt Mags in her."

"I guess I need lessons." Nicole scanned the grocery store. "I swear, Astrid, I don't know what to do with her. She's...she keeps pushing and pushing and I feel like I'm going to snap."

"What happened?" Astrid hurt for Nicole and the constant trials she endured at the hands of her mother.

"Where should I start?" Nicole sighed. "First, she

backs out of paying for Benji's Young Beekeeper Ambassador Clinic, now she won't stop pushing this offer some developer made on the salon. She can't sell since we're co-owners so she's laying it on thick. She said it will allow her to retire—*and* give her the cash to send Benji to the clinic. Classic mom manipulation, right there." She chewed on a green strand of hair. "Grandmother of the year, too."

"I'm sorry she's being…challenging."

"Challenging? I can't say the words I'd use—not with little Bea on your hip. I'd hate for her to repeat one of them. Not exactly the sort of thing Shelby would want to put in Bea's baby books." She smiled. "But I love how hard it is for you to be mean about anyone—even when they deserve it. You're a reminder that not all people suck." Nicole nudged Astrid. "Isn't that right, Bea?" she cooed, taking the baby.

Bea babbled something adorable that sounded like, *Wawa bow too tee.*

"You don't say?" Nicole asked. "Right back at you."

She watched Nicole with the baby. "How is Benji taking it?" She knew how much the teen had been looking forward to the weeklong conference in Houston.

"He's awesome. As usual." Nicole shrugged. "Seriously, I don't deserve that kid."

"You do, too. You're a fantastic mom, Nicole." She spied Tansy and Shelby and slowly headed their way. "Benji *is* so awesome because he has you for a mother."

"Sometimes I'm not sure who is parenting who." Nicole shrugged again, her voice tight. "I feel bad for him. He's only got me and we know I'm sort of…well, me." Her smile was tight and forced.

"Which makes him lucky." She draped an arm around

Nicole's shoulder. "Don't forget, you're an honorary Bee Girl. Meaning you've got the Hill women *and* all the ones attached to us on your side."

"All that?" Nicole took a deep breath and bounced Bea. "That's a lot."

Tansy and Shelby had been watching their approach so they both had questions ready by the time Astrid, Bea and Nicole reached them.

"What happened?" Tansy asked. "You're eating your hair. That's never a good sign."

"Was I?" Nicole stopped chewing on her hair. "Willadeene." She almost spat the name out. "I just...she can...ugh."

"This sounds like we need some coffee and comfort food," Tansy suggested. "Let's check out and go eat carbs."

Crackers, dog food and root beer acquired, they put their groceries in the van and headed down the block to the green awning of Delaney's. After they were seated in a booth, Bea was occupied with a teething biscuit and coffee was poured, Nicole let it all out. Benji's camp tuition, her mother backing out, the sudden pressure to sell the shop to this developer, as well as Willadeene's constant poking at Nicole's "questionable parenting style and stylist skills."

"And I've got my cousin's little girl, Ruthie, coming to stay." She shook her head and took a sip of coffee. "I can't believe I almost forgot about that."

"First, Benji." Shelby was pouring sugar packets into her coffee. "How much does this Young Beekeeper Ambassador Program cost? Is there a scholarship fund? Would there be someone in town who might sponsor him?"

Astrid smiled at her cousin. "That's a great idea."

Tansy and Nicole perked up, too.

Shelby glanced amongst the three of them. "It seems to me Willadeene shouldn't be the one to decide whether or not he can attend. He's not asking for a handout, he's asking for sponsorship. From everything I've heard, Benji is a good kid with a bright future. I imagine a local business would love to send him and have him wear a company shirt every day or something, you know?"

"Maybe we could even reach out to Wholesome Foods?" Astrid asked Tansy. "I bet they'd be all over it—since Benji volunteers on the farm?"

"I'll call." Tansy scribbled a note on the paper napkin.

"Next, you've received an offer on the salon? This might not be bad news." Shelby handed Bea another teething biscuit. "*Is* the offer too good to refuse?"

"I haven't read it," Nicole confessed, looking ashamed. "I couldn't. She was shoving it down my throat—heaped with how wrong it was that she even had to ask me to agree to it since the shop should have been hers, blah, blah, blah…" She leaned forward to cover her face with her hands. "I need strawberry pancakes. With extra strawberry syrup." She sighed. "And a mountain of whipped cream."

"Oh, that sounds good." Astrid waved over their waitress and everyone ordered.

"I think you should look at the offer." Shelby sipped her coffee, then added another packet of sugar. "If it's that good, you could sell and start your own shop without having to be partners with your mother. If it's not, don't sell. It's that easy."

"To be fair, Willadeene Svoboda never makes anything easy," Tansy murmured.

Shelby stared into her coffee, stirring it slowly with a spoon. "I'm so sorry you have to put up with all that, Nicole. I can't imagine. And from your mother, of all people. My parents thought I was the sun and moon and everything else. And Mags is like this together, badass, take-charge woman that I'm in awe of. And she likes me, too, so…" She frowned.

"Did you say Aunt Mags likes you?" Astrid laughed. "Mags adores you."

"I was about to say." Tansy rolled her eyes. "She *loves* you." She took a sip of coffee.

Shelby's smile lit up her whole face but conversation paused while the waitress slid plates of mile-high pancakes, whipped cream, fruit and little pitchers of syrup onto the table.

Shelby gave Bea a small bite of pancake, then glanced Nicole's way. "Did any of that help? I guess I came across sort of bossy—"

"Not bossy. I was wallowing and you offered solutions." Nicole cut up her pancakes, making sure each bite was covered in cream, berries and syrup. "Thanks, Shelby. Thanks for calming me down." Nicole smiled around the table at them all. "I don't know what I'd do without you guys."

"You'll have to do without me this weekend." Tansy pointed at her with her fork. "Dane and I are going to Weaver's farm to look at their agribusiness. Until then, Astrid and Shelby have your back."

"You're going? Wait." Nicole's eyes went round and her fork paused midway to her mouth. "You're legit considering Dane's idea of opening the farm to tourists? Are there pigs flying outside? Did… What… How… Words fail me."

Which was fair. Astrid had pretty much thought the same thing when Tansy had told her—not that she was going to offer that up. Instead, she ate her pancakes in silence.

"Maybe." Tansy's cheeks were reddening. "And thanks for not making it into a big deal."

Nicole was laughing then. "I'm not laughing *at* you. I love you two together—it gives me hope I might find someone someday." She hugged Tansy with one arm. "And, as far as I'm concerned, an extra revenue stream is never a bad idea." She rested her head on Tansy's shoulder. "I'm happy for you too, really."

"We all are happy for you two." Astrid took a sip of orange juice.

"I just wish he had an older brother." Shelby winked at Tansy and shared more of her pancake with Bea.

Bea's father was a mystery. In the time since Shelby's arrival, he'd never once come up in conversation. But, like Mags, Shelby kept those sorts of things to herself. They were a close-knit group but they also respected one another's privacy.

At times, it was hard for Astrid to believe it had *only* been six weeks—six weeks of life-altering events. Winning the honey competition and financial freedom for Honey Hill Farms. Tansy and Dane's relationship. Shelby and Bea's arrival. Van and Aunt Camellia's courtship. It looked like there was a plan for Nicole and Benji, too.

And her last visit with Charlie and the girls had gone well. He hadn't shied away from her gaze once—he had the most soulful eyes she'd ever stared into. And she'd done plenty of staring. He was the most handsome man she'd ever laid eyes on. It was true. It was also true that she liked being with him. Him and the girls, of course.

She couldn't be sure he felt the same but he'd been genuinely concerned about her neck. She'd like to think that was progress. And, for now, she'd take it. *For now.*

IT WAS TEN and Charlie had yet to have a cup of coffee. And that was only one of a half a dozen irritations he'd been greeted with this morning. Work was…work. Having coworkers who didn't pull their own weight but still wanted praise was hard. He'd been up most of the night, staying ahead of a super-aggressive computer virus that almost breached one of their biggest clients' firewalls. Nova had a bad dream, insisting the rat monster was trying to get in through the skylight, so he'd sat in the rocker by her bed. Instead of getting up and going back to work when she'd dozed off again, he'd fallen asleep in the rocker and woken up with a massive crick in his neck.

Then there was Halley. She wanted to invite her best friend up for a week because she was "so bored her brain was melting" and it was her best friend's birthday. But Halley's best friend was dramatic and hyper and loud. Charlie wasn't good with loud. Hyper or dramatic, either. Besides that, Nova would be left out of whatever the older girls did. Halley hadn't taken his "no" well.

There'd been no coffee, but he managed to choke down Nova's singed pieces of toast for breakfast with the orange juice he split between the three of them. Sadly, that didn't hold any of them for long. Around nine thirty, he stared into the empty pantry and accepted what was to come. They were going out to eat. In town. Surrounded by the nosy people of Honey, Texas. There was no one to blame but himself. If he'd stayed on top of things, this wouldn't have happened. But he hadn't. And now…

"Girls, get dressed." He sighed and ran a hand over his face. "Let's go into town for lunch and go to the grocery store after."

"Really?" Halley hopped up, the pout replaced by an excited smile. "Like, in town with people? At a restaurant?"

He managed not to sound deflated. "Yep."

"We're going on an adventure." Nova held up Scorpio so she was eye to eye with her stuffed toy. "Hurray." She ran to the steps. "Can I wear my space suit?"

The "no" had been on the tip of his tongue but when he'd seen the hope on Nova's face, he swallowed the word. "Yep."

"Charlie." Halley moaned. "Please, Nova. What if there are other kids there? Like, potential friends? What if there's a little girl, your age, who doesn't like outer space or dressing up? You might miss out on making a new friend."

"I don't wanna be friends with anyone like that." She looked at Halley as if her older sister was speaking a foreign language. "That's silly. Everyone likes space. It's cool."

Halley shot him a pleading look. "Come on, Charlie."

This was when he wished Yasmina was here. If he told Nova she couldn't wear the suit, he would upset Nova. If he told Nova she could wear the suit, he'd upset Halley. This wasn't going to end well. He looked back and forth between them. "I'm not sure I want to make this decision."

Halley seemed surprised by this answer. Nova looked confused.

"But you're the grown-up." Nova's matter-of-fact answer did sound irrefutable.

He nodded. "I am." He glanced back and forth between them. "How about we do a coin toss?" Then they could be mad at the coin, not him.

"Why can't you just decide?" Halley was watching him, eyes narrowed, head cocked.

"I don't like being the bad guy." He pulled a coin from his pocket. "Halley?"

"Okay." Halley took the coin from Charlie. "Which do you want, Nova? Heads or tails?"

"I don't even know what you're talking about." Nova's forehead was wrinkled and Scorpio was squished against her chest. "I don't want anyone's head or tail."

Halley was smiling as she bent forward. "Look." She held the coin out. "Heads." She flipped over the coin. "Tails."

"I don't see tails?" She stooped closer to the coin. "Where are they?"

"It's an expression." Charlie tended to be on the literal side so Nova's frustration over the coin had him smiling.

"I don't get it." Nova straightened.

"I'll call tails." Halley shook her head and flipped the coin up into the air.

"Do you have to call the tails to get them on the coin?" Nova was still trying to figure out the tail situation when the coin hit the floor.

Halley's posture was answer enough but she recovered with grace. "Go put on your suit, little astronaut."

Nova squealed and almost tripped over herself as she ran up the stairs.

"Good idea." Halley handed him the coin.

"Next time, you could ask for two out of three." He tucked the coin into his pocket.

"Nah, she was having a hard enough time with the

whole tails thing." She sort-of smiled at him and ran up the stairs.

Charlie stood there, giving himself a second to mentally prepare. He'd had enough therapy and taken enough classes to prevent his anxiety from crippling him. He might be a little rusty, but he'd use those tactics today.

On the road into town, Nova pointed. "Look, is that the school? It's not very big, is it? I wonder what they do at their school?"

"Probably what we do at our school." But Halley was curious enough to study the building.

"Did you go to a school like this, Charlie?" Nova wiggled Scorpio, making the stuffed toy dance.

"No." Charlie spared a passing glance at the building. "I went to a private school."

"You did?" Halley adjusted her headband. She had an extensive headband collection—one that helped tip him off about Halley's mood. Flowers were good. Solids were not. Her current headband was all geometric shapes. He was trying not to worry about it. "Did you like it?"

"It was…interesting." He shrugged. "I learned a lot." Not just in class, either. Charlie's lengthy and thorough bullying lessons lasted his entire military school career.

"Were you, like, the supersmart kid that everyone tried to get help from on their papers and stuff?" Halley smiled.

He nodded again. Those were the *do this or else* scenarios that he'd learned to hide from. Old storage closets. Dormer window crawl spaces. The attic over the kitchen. He'd become an expert at hiding in grade school. In time, he got too big to be bullied. By then, he'd learned the best place to hide was deep inside himself.

The green canopy of the Delaney Café barely fluttered in the hot Texas breeze as they walked from the car to the café. Once he'd pushed the door open, he wasn't sure which was nicer, the gust of air-conditioned air or the scent of coffee.

"Can we sit in a booth?" Nova stood in her space suit, staring around the restaurant.

"If there's one open." Charlie tried not to sweep the café goers or count the number of people enjoying their lunch.

"You and your astronaut are in luck." The waitress smiled. "Follow me to your very own booth."

"Yay!" Nova acted like this was the best news she'd ever had.

"Nova, please. You're wearing your suit. Can you try to act normal?" Halley fidgeted with her headband again.

Nova sighed but stayed quiet until they were in their booth.

Charlie hated going out to eat more than he hated in-person business meetings. At work, he had a title and authority and no one dared give him side-eye or openly judged him. Sitting in this new-to-him restaurant surrounded by strangers was something he avoided at all costs.

"Is everyone looking at us?" Halley looked around the restaurant, her cheeks going pink.

"Scorpio thinks they are." Nova was sitting on her knees, Scorpio on the table. "Is it 'cause they've never seen a real-life astronaut before?"

"Don't worry about them." Charlie didn't bother looking up. "Decide what you want to eat."

But then Halley said, "Astrid?" with such pure delight, the words on the menu blurred before Charlie's eyes.

Astrid was here? It was bad enough he'd found him-

self glancing out the window, looking for her. It was
worse when he found his thoughts turning to her for no
particular reason. Not just once, either. He closed his
eyes and drew in a deep breath. Apparently wanting a
peaceful meal was too much to ask for. He slowly forced
all the air from his lungs and started counting. The hollow ache was back, stronger than before.

"Oh, your baby is so cute." Halley's tone was soft
and awestruck.

Charlie's brain slammed to a halt over the "your baby
is so cute" comment. Astrid? She had a baby? She was
the mothering, nurturing type. It wasn't surprising. It
fit with what he knew of her but... The ache sharpened
and twisted. He had to start counting all over again.

"Hi, Astrid. I'm an astronaut." Nova's rather loud and
assertive announcement had Astrid laughing.

He liked the sound of Astrid's laugh. *Dammit*. What
was wrong with him? He barely knew the woman. If he
did, he'd know she had a baby. He swallowed against
the tightness of his throat.

"Are you going on a mission after your lunch?" There
was a smile in Astrid's voice.

"I don't know." Nova's not-whisper was muffled behind her space helmet. "Where are we going to after
we eat, Charlie?"

At that point, he realized he had to open his eyes
and engage.

Astrid. With a baby. A baby that had a hold of one
long thin braid in Astrid's hair—and was smiling at *him*.
The baby didn't look a thing like Astrid. He frowned.
The baby's lower lip quivered and Charlie's throat drew
so tight he couldn't breathe. The baby made a sad gur-

gling sound and sniffed. Had he done that? How did he make it stop? What was he supposed to do?

"Charlie, you're scaring her." Halley moved closer to the baby. "Don't pay attention to Mr. Grumpy Pants."

The *baby* was scared? How did they think he felt?

Halley reached over and tickled the baby's feet, ending the potential tears. "What's her name?"

"Petunia Snowflake?" Nova quickly offered suggestions. "Worcestershire? Or Queen Margaret?"

Astrid laughed again, making him glance her way. Instead, his gaze locked with the baby's—now waving her tiny hand at him. He plucked at the front of his shirt before looking beyond the baby, at Astrid.

"Her name is Beatrix, but we call her Bea." Astrid winked at Nova. "Though Petunia Snowflake has a lovely ring to it."

We? Meaning she and her husband? It was strange that her marital status had never come up in conversation. No, it wasn't. Her marital status wasn't relevant to any of the conversations they' had. *Her marital status isn't relevant, period.* At least, it shouldn't be.

"Does she walk? Or talk?" Nova asked. "She likes you, Charlie Grumpypants."

The baby did seem determined to get him to wave or smile back. Young babies made him anxious. They were unpredictable and loud and breakable and terrifying. When he and Yasmina married, Nova was already walking and talking, with a sweet disposition. "She's very…small." Which was a stupid thing to say.

"'Cause she's a baby, Charlie." Halley cooed and gushed. "A beautiful little baby."

"Was I a beautiful little baby?" Nova asked, watching her sister with Bea.

"Not when you were first born. You were all squished up and red and you screamed all the time." Halley looked at Nova. "But then you stopped squishing and screaming and you were a very beautiful little baby."

Nova hugged her sister tight, more like crushing her. "I'm sorry I screamed all the time."

"It's okay. It's what babies do." Halley hugged her back with just as much enthusiasm. "All babies scream."

Charlie loved it when the girls were like this. There was a sweetness between them that set his heart at ease. He didn't remember many times like this in his own family—hugging, as a whole, hadn't been a thing in his home. But his girls had a chance at a different upbringing and different memories. If he had anything to say about it, they'd look forward to family gatherings versus dreading them.

"I bet even Charlie screamed when he was a baby." Halley made a weird face. "What is that look?"

Nova's astronaut helmet was squished down over her face, but her impish grin was still visible. "I can't see. I can't see. What look?"

Halley adjusted her helmet. "That one."

"He's happy." Nova rose up onto her knees to see him. "His grumpy forehead line is gone. See?"

Charlie hadn't realized he had a grumpy forehead line—he'd have to work on that. "Yep." He was happy. It had been so long since he'd felt this way that he didn't care where he was or who might be watching. Until the high-pitched squeal by his right ear reminded him people were watching.

The baby clapped her hands and spewed an unintelligible stream of nonsense sounds and noises that had Charlie leaning away.

"You don't say, Bea? She likes to be part of the conversation." Astrid sighed, shooting a surprisingly hesitant look his way. "I don't want to interrupt your lunch but I did want to say hello. And, I have a question for you."

A question to do with the Junior Beekeepers, no doubt. All he could imagine was a group of kids running from a swarm of angry bees. It wasn't a pretty picture. "I haven't made up my mind about...*it*." He waved his hand, not wanting the girls to have any knowledge or input on the whole potential summer camp disaster.

"No, no. I was hoping tomorrow would be okay for me to stop by early and check on the hives?" She smiled at the baby. The baby squealed and clapped her hands. "You'll have to stay home with your mommy, Bea."

"She's not yours?" he asked, relief slamming into him with the force of a wrecking ball.

"No." She looked surprised by his question. "No baby and no significant other. I do like to borrow her from my cousin sometimes." She pointed at the booth where three other women sat—watching them.

The fact that Astrid was single didn't make sense. She was... She was... What? And why was he so relieved? His lungs were empty—as if he'd resurfaced from deep beneath the waves after holding his breath for too long. Tossed about and winded and very much adrift. He sipped from his water glass and plucked at his shirtfront again—hoping the thudding of his heart wasn't obvious.

Astrid was studying him. "Is tomorrow morning convenient?"

"Yes." The word was instantaneous. Breathe. Calm. He flexed his hands and reached for his glass, adding,

"That's fine." Normally, he used the person's earlobe as a focal point, to keep his anxiety at bay. It didn't work with Astrid. He'd start with her earlobe and wind up studying her hair and her braids. Recently, he'd moved on to her forehead and every facial feature until making eye contact with her was, almost, natural. Maybe it was because Astrid's green gaze was earnest and friendly and…appealing. There was that damn word again. Better not to look at her at all.

"And bring the dogs?" Nova pleaded.

"And some muffins?" Halley tickled the baby's foot again.

"I'll see what I can do." Astrid hesitated then, but he didn't look at her. "Well… Okay." She waved. "Say bye, Bea."

Halley and Nova both chimed in, "Bye, Bea."

And then it was back to the three of them. He didn't have to look up to know Nova and Halley were disappointed in him.

"Charlie." Nova pushed her astronaut helmet back on her head and sat up on her knees, leaning across the table toward him. "Are you okay?"

"You did act way weirder than normal." Halley was watching him. "Nova and I really like her. And she's, like, the only friend-ish person we have here. Can you try to like her? I mean try *really* hard?"

Luckily, Charlie was saved by the arrival of the waitress. Menus were passed out and the girls debated their options while his traitorous gaze sought out Astrid. She was talking with her sister and two other women, her smile and laughter free-flowing. Could he really blame his girls for wanting her to visit or to spend time with her? If he was being honest with himself, he wanted to spend more time with her, too. *That* was the reason he didn't want her around.

That—the way he reacted to her—was unlike him. He wasn't a people person. He liked his privacy. He liked maintaining control of his environment. But Astrid… Well, there was nothing controlled about her. She was comfortable around people, barged in without apology and usurped him without trying. Nova thought she was superhero worthy. Halley thought she was cool. Even he had a long list of mostly complimentary words that suited Astrid. Her continued presence would complicate the uncomplicated summer he needed. So why was he already looking forward to tomorrow morning's visit?

CHAPTER SEVEN

"Triple digits all week. Looks like we'll be breaking records on Friday. Lovely." Aunt Mags shook out her newspaper. "And not a single drop of rain on the horizon."

Astrid rinsed her coffee cup in the sink, her gaze fixed on the long, brittle grasses waving in the distance. Without rain, they'd be looking at another drought. No water meant no flowers or blooms and no pollen. Without pollen they'd need to up the supplement feed for the bees.

"Wait an hour, the weather will change." Aunt Camellia sipped her tea. "Isn't that what Poppa used to say?"

"Let's hope he's right." Aunt Mags turned to look out the window. "We need a torrential downpour that gives the ground a good soaking."

"We'll need to check all the water sources now." Astrid sniffed the strawberry-honey galette on the wire cooling rack. Tonight's dessert was mighty tempting.

"I'm on it." Leif inhaled another slice of honey streusel coffee cake into his mouth.

"Thank you." She smiled, ever impressed with the amount of food the teen packed away. "I've got a feeling we'll need to do more than feed them syrup."

"Pollen patties?" Aunt Camellia sipped her tea. "I'll do a shop and make sure we have enough sugar." She scribbled something on the tablet at her side.

"You sure?" Dane asked, scanning Aunt Camellia's note before turning to look at her.

"If Astrid says we need pollen patties, we need pollen patties." Tansy offered him a bite of her toast. "She is the bee whisperer."

Dane took a bite. "Got it."

"What is a pollen patty?" Shelby flipped her spiral notebook full of bee notes. "And when you say syrup, do you mean syrup-syrup?" She ran her finger over the page. "How did I not know we feed the bees?"

Astrid pushed off the counter, stepping over the pile of sleeping dogs, and grabbed a basket. "We like to do as little as possible—and let bees be bees. But we don't want all the bees to go off in search of greener pastures, so we make sure they're not starving and give them enough to thrive."

"Why are you putting cookies into a basket?" Tansy watched as Astrid put two more freshly-baked cookies into the basket. "Are you still trying to win them over?"

"For your information, I've won the girls over just fine." Astrid hesitated, then added a couple more honey-lemon sugar cookies.

"Fine. Are you still trying to win *him* over?" Tansy asked.

Astrid was fully aware that every eye—even Lord Byron the parrot—was now focused on her. "No. I'm checking in on the bees. The bees that were kicked over only a few days ago, you'll remember?" She sighed. "*And* I'm being neighborly."

"Mmm-hmm." Tansy's eyes narrowed.

"He's from Dallas or Fort Worth, isn't he?" Shelby was feeding Bea some bananas and cereal pieces. "The whole small town, in-your-business thing can be a lot for a city person. I know." She popped a piece of peach-and-honey muffin into her mouth. "I think it's sweet you're trying to make him feel welcome."

"Thank you." Astrid felt somewhat vindicated by Shelby's support.

"There's something off about the guy." Dane sat back, crossing his arms over his broad chest. "I was a city guy for a while. I've never acted like a di—jerk."

"Hmm?" Tansy smiled and batted her lashes at him. "Really? Are you sure?"

"I don't think that's it. He's just…shy. Out of his element." Astrid glanced around the table. "From the little I've learned, it seems the three of them don't have the support system we do. It's *just* the three of them. His wife died a year or so ago. They hadn't been married very long when that happened. The girls were hers but, now…well, they're his. And then his aunt dies." She paused, giving each of them a moment to digest what she'd shared. "I'm not saying he's not gruff and withdrawn and a bit socially awkward but…he sort of has a right. We should give him a break. And, maybe, a little kindness, too. I think they could all use some of both."

The whole kitchen was silent then. If they were going to try to judge Charlie's character then they needed to more fully understand the picture. Whether or not he oozed affection, Charlie wasn't a bad person.

Dane sighed. "Well, I feel like an ass."

"I'll make more cookies." Aunt Camellia stood. "We should invite them to dinner, shouldn't we?"

Aunt Magnolia had set aside her newspaper and was studying Astrid. She glanced at the basket. "You go on. And take all the cookies."

Not long after, she, Oatmeal and Pudding were walking the path to Rebecca Wallace's slightly slanted purple house. It was barely nine in the morning but the heat was thick and airless. No breeze. No movement. The buzz of cicadas, the gentle symphony of birdcalls, and the swish-swish of the dogs' tails kept rhythm as they walked the dry foliage lining the footpath.

Astrid adjusted the basket as she stepped onto the porch to knock on the front door.

"I'll get it." Halley's voice rang out seconds before she opened the door. "Hi, Astrid." She yawned. "Hi, Oatmeal. Hi, Pudding." The sight of the dogs instantly perked her up.

"Good morning." Astrid held out the basket. "I hope I didn't wake you."

"You didn't." Halley waved her in. "It's hot, though. Our air-conditioning went out last night."

As soon as the door shut, the house was an oven. Within seconds, sweat was beading along her temple and back. "Aren't you melting?"

"We camped out in the dining room." Halley led the way. "There's a window unit in there. And a big fan." She opened the door, cool air wafting out to greet them.

Astrid hurried to pull the door shut behind them.

"Astrid." Nova was up, leaving her nest of blankets and pillows, and running—full steam—into her side. "Hi. I'm in my pj's. Do you like them? Stars. All over. It's hot. We all had a slumber party here but Charlie didn't sleep and he's got a big meeting and the air commissioning men aren't coming."

"Air-conditioning," Halley corrected.

"Air co-commissioning." Nova nodded.

Astrid gave Nova a wink. Sleepless nights and no air-conditioning were bad enough. But trying to be on for a big business meeting while dealing with all the rest was…a lot. Poor Charlie.

Charlie had his phone pressed to his ear. "I understand." He wasn't happy. He leaned forward, his elbows resting on his knees, looking defeated. His hair was a mess, his white undershirt was wrinkled and snug across his broad back, and his cotton shorts showcased well-muscled thighs and calves. "Fine. Thank you."

"I'd say good morning but it sounds like we're off to a rocky start." She slid the basket of goodies onto the end of the large dining table currently serving as Charlie's desk. "I brought breakfast."

Charlie ran his fingers through his hair. "I don't suppose there's some sort of stone pig or metal cow or elephant statue Rebecca used to make the air conditioner work?"

Astrid had to smile. "Sadly, no."

His hooded eyes met hers. "I was afraid of that." His smile was lopsided and reluctant, but it was something— even if it did last less than five seconds.

Charlie was capable of smiling. Well, it was a sort-of smile.

Whatever it was, it was enough to make Astrid's heart clip along at triple time. "Have you tried giving it a good whack?" She gripped the back of the chair, pretending her heart wasn't doing odd gymnastic maneuvers in her chest. His eyes fell from hers, so it was easier for her to speak. "Rebecca was a fan of trying to beat whatever was acting up into submission. Half the time it worked."

"And the other half?" He stood and peered into the basket.

She didn't linger over how big and tall and rumpled and warm he was, this close to her. "She'd have to repair or replace it." She opened the basket more fully. "You were gifted a dozen cookies. Not exactly breakfast—"

Charlie pulled out one of the cookies. "This morning there are no rules. Cookies for breakfast." He took a big bite and sighed.

"Really?" Nova asked. "Really, really?"

"Really, really." He pointed at the basket. "You pick, Nova."

Even Halley looked surprised.

Astrid noted the open phone book on the table. "Who have you called?"

Charlie ran his finger along the ancient phone book. "Everyone but the Walsh Brothers AC. That's assuming they're still in business—this book is a few years old."

"The Walsh Brothers?" Astrid winced. "They're known for not meeting deadlines."

"Considering everyone's telling me at least a week, I'm calling." He shook his head. "We can't live like this for a week."

"No, no, of course not." She handed Halley a napkin. "Is today's meeting very important?"

He ran his fingers through his hair—meaning he was stressed. Considering how often he did it, it was surprising he didn't have a bald spot. "It is."

He'd need to concentrate—which would be easier if he wasn't preoccupied. He was still close, so she whispered, "I can take the girls back with me? We have plenty of room and air-conditioning. I'll warn you baking will likely be involved—Aunt Camellia is a consummate baker."

His gaze swiveled her way—and held. He had very nice, surprisingly warm brown eyes. Indeed, she was growing warmer by the second.

"It would be no bother. And I won't let them run free through the beehives. Not for too long, anyway." She was smiling when she finished, hoping he'd realize she was teasing. Considering his eyes narrowed the tiniest bit, she added, "That was a joke."

"I know." He swallowed, hard. "You…" He drew in a deep breath. "Thank you. I'd appreciate it. And I know they would, too."

Astrid blinked. "I was expecting to have to work harder."

"I'm not completely unreasonable." His brows rose. "Air-conditioning problems or not, they want to go. They've said so. A dozen or so times." He watched Nova shove an entire cookie into her mouth.

"Nova." Halley rolled her eyes in feigned disapproval—before falling back onto their blankets and pillows to laugh.

Astrid hadn't realized she'd placed her hand on his arm. "Everyone needs a change of scenery now and then. Plus, I have dogs. Dogs and treats… A hard-to-beat combination."

But he was staring down at her hand on his arm, his jaw muscle working.

She let go of him. "Sorry. Habit. I tend to be a toucher…"

He nodded. "Girls, Astrid has invited the two of you to her farm—"

After that, nothing was intelligible. The girls were a flurry of activity. While Nova didn't care if anything matched, Halley was far more intentional in her choices. Astrid sat and began to carefully brush the knots from Nova's hair while Halley went upstairs for more choices.

"Can you give me braids like you?" Nova asked. "I like them."

Astrid reached up to pat her braids. "Sometimes I don't even know I'm doing it, Nova. It just keeps the hair out of my face—which is quite helpful when I'm working with the bees."

"Practical." Charlie was studying her hair now.

"It's easier than carrying around clips or bands or combs." She smoothed her hand over her braids. "I... don't think about it. I just...do it."

"Do mine, Astrid, please." Nova smiled up at her.

Astrid set to work. While her hair was wavy and thick, Nova's was so curly it took effort to tame the strands into solid plaits. She put three along each side of the little girl's head and used the brightly colored bands Nova provided her to hold them in place. "Your hair is so curly, Nova. I hope the braids will stay."

"My momma had hair like me and Halley. She hated it so she cut it super short." Nova turned to look at her. "She didn't know how to braid."

"It doesn't sound like she needed to." Astrid smiled down at the little girl—who looked even more adorable with her braids and colored hair ties. "If she had short hair, she had no use for braids."

"I'm ready." Halley burst into the room red-faced and dewy but very fashionable in her ripped jeans, white canvas tennis shoes and midriff baring red T-shirt. She tugged the hem of the shirt and shot a glance Charlie's way.

From the corner of her eye, she saw Charlie run a hand over his face. His jaw was bulging and there was a noticeable tension rolling off the man, but he took a deep breath—then another, and said, "Have fun. I'll come get them when the meeting is over."

She stepped close enough that she could whisper. "Or they could spend the day with me? I'd keep them busy. And my aunts and the dogs would love the extra company. They did basically raise my sisters and I and, I think, they miss having young ones around." She resisted the urge to put her hand on his arm again. To re-assure him, not because of the undeniable urge to touch him. "How about you come get them at dinnertime? You can stay and eat and not have to cook. Unless you get someone to come fix the AC, of course." Her gaze swept over his face, lingering a hair too long on his mouth. It wasn't the first time. Her fascination with his mouth had extended beyond seeing a real smile to things she shouldn't be curious about. Namely, what it would be like to kiss Charlie. Her cheeks went so hot she was cer-tain her face was fire-engine red.

Charlie's hooded eyes bounced her way—then re-turned. He went from undecided to alarmed and... something else. Something that had him drawing in an unsteady breath and clenching his jaw. For a second, she thought he might have been equally fascinated by her mouth but then he was staring at the table. "Fine. Yes. Good." He cleared his throat. "Thank you."

Get a hold of yourself. She'd been labeled the emo-tional one her whole life. But her emotions had never run amok like this. "You're welcome, Charlie."

He was looking at her again. This time, it was the shuttered and distant look she'd come to expect.

"Are we going?" Halley's enthusiasm was edged with impatience.

"Yes." Astrid tore her gaze from Charlie and stepped

back. One step, then two, until the air wasn't so *crowded* with him. The nervous tension playing along her nerves eased with the growing distance. By the time they were walking along the footpath toward her home, the tension had been replaced by an even more distressing sensation. A hollowness. No, really, an ache. Far more distressing was accepting what was causing this new, full-body ache. Not what. But who.

HIS CONCENTRATION HAD lasted through his conference call. He'd been confident, detailed yet brief, and answered every question his client and his employer had fired his way. In short, he'd delivered. Not only had his boss scheduled a private meeting with him for the following morning but the client had been eager to extend their company's security contract for another two years.

After he'd hit Disconnect, concentrating on the lines of code, the steady influx from the team of coders he managed, or perusing the emails he'd been dodging for the last week was near impossible.

This couldn't be happening. He had cared for people before. His aunt Rebecca. Yasmina. His affection and devotion for Nova and Halley were instinctual—unshakable and more concrete than he'd thought possible. But those were familial bonds. He'd cared for them because they were his family.

Marrying Yasmina had been a relief. He had his best friend as his partner, without the pressure of any romantic complications. Yasmina's relationship with the girls' father had been so emotionally and physically combative, she'd welcomed the safety their marriage had provided. And, with Yasmina, he was getting a family of his own—something he'd never imagined possible. Yasmina's ex had been all too happy for Charlie to adopt the girls and, for a brief time, Charlie had more than he'd ever dared hope for.

Through Yasmina's patient guidance, it had become less awkward to give the girl's a hug or smiles or praise. *Something I should be doing more of.* It had been Yasmina that had put Nova on his lap—over and over—until he'd overcome his uncertainty holding the toddler.

But, none of that was…*this*.

He wasn't thinking about holding Astrid on his lap. He raked his hands through his hair and blew out a long, slow breath. Even if he did ask her to sit on his lap, he wasn't sure he'd ever get used to her. Not that the idea didn't hold a certain appeal. Why was he smiling?

He stared out the front window, sighed and checked his watch. It was almost seven. He'd worked late because he'd been so damn distracted he'd had to double- then triple-check his work…not because he wasn't having to worry over the girls, but because of Astrid.

Waiting any longer would be rude.

Par for the course.

He could do better. Halley and Nova had asked him to try—for them. It wouldn't be easy for him, but he would try. If he was being honest with himself, he had other reasons for dragging his feet. Namely: Astrid's family. He hadn't bothered to make a good impression on any of them. Now he was supposed to endure their judgment-laden stares and likely long, awkward silences after he'd taken advantage of their kindness all day? He was already dreading the evening. The sooner he got there, the sooner the whole ordeal would be over and he and the girls could come home.

The same thick heat filling his house waited to greet

him outside. There was no breeze. No movement. It was quiet. So quiet. No cars or honking, no airplanes overhead, no conversations drifting in from the upscale condominium complex he and the girls called home in Fort Worth. Instead, he was fully aware of the crunch of the river rock beneath his brown leather lace-up shoes. The sudden whir-click of a grasshopper jumping amidst the thick yellow-brown grasses. The gentle call of a dove perched in the trees overhead. Little sounds. Peaceful sounds. He slowed to take it all in. There was a calm here he welcomed.

It took a good ten minutes for Astrid's family home to come into view. When it did, he found himself chuckling. The house was straight out of one of the girls' fairytale storybooks. Two stories high, with a rounded turret window and steeply pitched roof that suggested a large attic space, too. Its pale mint green color and bright white trim blended in with the abundant shrubs and flowers overflowing from carefully tended flower beds and hanging pots. As he drew closer, he spotted the intricately carved details that covered every single one of the wraparound porch's finials. Tiny flowers and bees.

Of course.

He paused and stared up the steps at the closed front door. *Try. I can try. For the girls.* He shoved aside the anticipation of seeing Astrid—which was ridiculous—and took the stairs two at a time, crossed the wide porch and knocked. No answer.

They were home, he could hear…everything. Someone was playing the piano quite well. There were voices. Laughter. A bark? And some possible squawk? That had to be Lord Byron, the parrot.

He knocked again and rocked back on his heels. Waiting. No need to be nervous or anxious. No reason at all.

The piano kept playing and there was no discernable break in the overlapping voices from inside.

After a third knock, he opened the door and stepped inside.

If he'd thought the outside of the house was very fitting, the inside was equally fanciful. As soon as he opened the door he was transported. The scent of cinnamon hung heavily in the air. Astrid had warned him there would be baking. Lemon cleaner filled his nostrils next—faint but lingering enough to imply the house was often cleaned. The navy-and-white pin-striped walls were covered in a hodgepodge of family pictures, paintings and prints. To the left was a set of dark wood stairs. A formal sitting room was on the right. And in that formal sitting room was the piano—currently played by an older man Charlie vaguely recognized.

"Hello?" he murmured, stepping forward so the man had no choice but to see him.

"Hello." The man stood. He had a well-groomed silver-and-white mustache and beard and deep creases at the corners of his eyes. But he stood tall, fit and lean, and he had one hell of a solid handshake. "Nice to meet you. Van Kettner."

"Charles Driver." He returned the handshake, with equal pressure and vigor.

"I've heard quite a lot about you." The corner of his mouth quirked up. "Your girls are something."

The knot in his stomach tightened. "Something? Should I be concerned?"

Van chuckled. "No, no. I mean they're precocious and charming and have my Camellia and the rest of

those Bee Girls wrapped around their little fingers."
He clapped Charlie on the shoulder. "As it should be, if
you ask me. Can't spend too much time with a child."

Charlie's stomach eased. Instead of nerves, pride
welled up.

"They're all in the kitchen." Van waved him to follow. "I was getting in Camellia's way so I figured I'd
steer clear and play some tunes."

He nodded, his attention wandering along as they
walked back into the foyer and down a hallway. There
were more carvings on doorframes and built-in book-
cases. Not just carvings, though. Someone with a gentle
touch had painted bees, flowers and other hints of the
natural beauty of the region.

"First time visiting?" Van asked. "The house. I've visited more times than I can remember over the years and
I still find something new each time I'm here. Kinda like
one of those hidden object pictures for kids?"

Charlie knew exactly what the older man was talking about. Halley had loved the picture puzzles so much,
he'd subscribed to a children's magazine that offered a
new puzzle every month. It was something he and Halley could do together—but that had been a few years
back—before he and Yasmina were married. He suspected she'd roll her eyes if he showed up with one now.

The closer they got to the kitchen, the louder the chatter became. It was a constant stream of conversation.
Numerous voices, overflowing, in a harmonious stream.
He couldn't decipher the topic of conversation, but it was
being discussed with great enthusiasm.

"It's been this way all day." Van chuckled again.
"Those girls have energized the lot of them."

Charlie paused in the kitchen doorway, taking a moment to acclimate himself to his surroundings. Like everything else about the Hill house—and Astrid Hill herself—what he found was surprisingly delightful.

On the far side of the sunlit room, Nova lay propped up on what appeared to be a carpet of sleeping dogs. He couldn't tell where one dog ended and the other began, but she seemed to be reading to them. A large parrot perched on the back of a kitchen chair nearby, bobbing his head and clicking whenever she turned a page.

Halley stood between Astrid and Camellia, staring into a large pot on the stove. That was likely the source of the cinnamon.

A taller woman emerged from a door in the opposite corner of the room and came to a stop—her vivid green eyes sweeping over him before she offered a smile. "You must be the infamous Charles Driver?" She placed the bag of sugar on the counter and headed straight for him. "You don't look especially intimidating." She held out her hand. "I would know, I'm the intimidating one in the family. Magnolia Hill."

Charlie wasn't sure what the proper response was but he answered anyway. "It's not a label I strive for."

"Really?" Her thin dark red brows rose. "I adore it. It adds an air of mystery. I find mysteries fascinating. You should know, mysteries are few and far between in a town the size of Honey." She winked, hooking her arm through his.

"Charlie." Nova sat up. "Hi." She waved, eliciting the wagging of at least five tails from the pile of dogs around her.

He waved back.

"Charlie." The parrot squawked. "Charlie. Hi."

"That's Lord Byron." Nova pointed at the bird. "He is so funny."

"He'd be much funnier stuffed and mounted on the mantel, if you ask me," Magnolia murmured for his ears only. "But do watch out. If he doesn't like you, he'll let you know."

Once again, Charlie found himself at a loss for words.

"Hey, Charlie." Halley turned. Not only was her hair braided back like Nova, she was wearing a ruffled apron with Honey Makes Everything Better written on the front. "We're making creamed honey. Cinnamon."

"It smells good." He nodded, processing. A warm reception, for him, from Halley was a rare thing.

"One of our best sellers." Astrid's smile was a breath of fresh air. Free and easy and beautiful.

The tightening of his throat was instantaneous. Because of Astrid. Because of his response to her. He cleared his throat. "Looks like you've been busy."

"It's been a good day." Astrid looked at Halley for confirmation.

His daughter nodded. "I've learned so much. It's been, like, way cool."

Charlie couldn't help but note the affection in Halley's gaze as she glanced between Astrid and Camellia. "Way cool sounds good."

Camellia turned, her smile welcoming. "Your daughters are delightful young ladies."

He nodded. "A fact I should be more vocal about."

Halley's eyes widened before she turned back to the pot they'd all been watching when he came in.

"Very nice," Magnolia whispered, patting his arm before letting him go. "I hope you like lasagna, Charles."

"It's not my best meal but it's hearty and filling." Camellia wiped her hands on a bee-embroidered dish towel and walked toward him.

Van draped his arm around the woman. "Don't let her fool you, Charlie. If Camellia cooked it, it'll be melt-in-your-mouth delicious. She's magic in the kitchen."

"Says you." She patted the man's chest and smiled up at him. "You might be a tad biased."

"A tad," Magnolia echoed with real affection. "You'll have to excuse them, Charles. They have a hard time not being moony-eyed and touchy-feely with each other."

"It's 'cause they *really* like each other." Nova had gone back to reading to the dogs, but stopped long enough to announce this.

"That we do." Van hugged Camellia close against his side. "That we do."

Charlie was still too off-kilter to mind their display of affection.

"That we do!" the parrot echoed, squawking loudly.

"Oh, he's jealous." Camellia slipped free of Van's hold and hurried across the room. "Here you go, sugar." She reached into the pocket of her ruffled apron. "Momma loves you."

"That bird is getting fatter by the day." Magnolia sighed. "Dr. Abraham already told you to cut back on his food."

"I don't want him to get his feelings hurt. Birds will pluck out their feathers and strike out and do all sorts of things if they feel neglected or abused."

Charlie's gaze met Astrid's then. She shook her head as she moved to his side. "Lord Byron is spoiled by Aunt Camellia, a fact that Aunt Mags can't stand. You see, Lord Byron and Aunt Mags have more of a…love-hate relationship."

"She did mention something about the bird being stuffed and mounted on the mantel." Charlie kept his voice low.

Astrid laughed. "That sounds like Aunt Mags." Her gaze swept slowly over his face. "How was your important call? Did they give you a raise and promotion for all your hard work?"

"Actually, yes." And he wasn't sure it was a good thing. As much as he appreciated the recognition, he wasn't sure it was best for him and the girls.

"Oh, Charlie." Astrid's hand clasped his. "Really?" She lit up—as if she was happy for him or proud of him. Like his news was a big deal to her. "Congratulations."

Dammit all, his chest felt tight and achy. His lungs and heart had to work double time to keep up. She shouldn't look so happy for him.

"Always good to get a nod from the higher-ups." Van nodded.

But Charlie saw the look on Halley's face and wished he'd kept his mouth shut. She didn't have to say a word—he knew what she was thinking. Hell, he'd been thinking the same thing. Was this a good thing?

"I told them I needed some time to think about it." He spoke directly to Halley. "It's a big decision. The girls and I should decide together."

Astrid squeezed his hand.

He squeezed back—and froze. What was he doing? He wasn't the only one that noticed. Astrid did, of course. But so did Halley. And Magnolia.

Halley was wide-eyed.

Magnolia grinned.

The trembling of their joined hands caught him off guard. Not because Astrid's hand was shaking. No. Of course not. *His* hand was shaking. Like a leaf. He instantly released hers and shoved both hands into his pockets.

"Dinner will be ready in a few minutes." Camellia buzzed back to the stove, mixed the contents of the pot, then turned to Halley. "Halley, Nova, will you girls help Astrid set the table?"

And just like that, the room was in motion. Charlie had never been so eager to blend into the background. He needed a moment. Hell, he needed more than a moment. The plan was to eat fast, and get out of here. After the whole natural hand-holding thing, he was rethinking staying for dinner. What was happening to him?

"It's not so bad." Van clapped him on the shoulder. "I'm not saying it's easy but… Once you find the right woman, there's not a damn thing you can do except be grateful."

Charlie resisted the urge to push back or argue. He didn't know Van and Van sure as hell didn't know him. If the man was trying to imply that Astrid…that he…

"Charlie." Camellia shot Van a look, then shoved a large basket at Charlie. "Would you mind taking the rolls to the dining room? Van, darling, you can help me with the salad."

Charlie headed toward the door Astrid and the girls had taken but he heard Camellia's voice saying, "Van Kettner, don't you push. Astrid deserves a man who sees her for the gift she is."

"You mean, like you are? For me?" Van's gruff tone left little room for misinterpretation.

"Exactly," Camellia answered. "Now kiss me and get to work on that salad."

Charlie didn't look back. Instead, he pushed through

the door and into the formal dining room of Hill house. Compared to the rest of the house, this room was stuffy and out of place. "Do you use this room often?"

Astrid was placing silverware beside each plate. "No." She paused, considering. "I can't remember the last time we used it, actually." She shrugged, her gaze darting his way before returning to her task.

"Boy bees are called drones, Charlie. Did you know that?" Nova asked, putting a bee-embroidered linen napkin beside the plates Halley arranged. "They don't do *anything*." She sighed for added effect. "When the bees get low on food, the other bees kick the drones out so they don't take it from the baby bees or the queen. They starve and die." She emphasized *die* with an extra dose of drama and paused in her napkin distribution. "All the other bees are girl bees."

"I didn't know any of that." He set the basket in the middle of the table.

"I know lots about bees now." Nova nodded.

"I bet you do." He glanced at Astrid.

"They asked." Astrid winked at Nova. "She and Halley have eager minds. So many questions."

"About bees?" He hadn't meant to sound so surprised.

"And other things." Halley shrugged.

There it was. Founded or not, a twinge of jealousy soured his stomach. Seconds later, it gave way to relief. He wasn't going to begrudge the girls someone to talk to. He sure as hell didn't have all the answers—especially when it came to things relating to girls. Astrid was more suited for that. He should be grateful to her.

He glanced at Astrid only to find her studying him. Openly. As if he was a puzzle she couldn't quite work out.

I know the feeling.

It wasn't the first time he found his gaze exploring every detail of her face. Then, lower, to the arch of her throat. Which reminded him. "How is your sting?"

She blinked. "What sting?"

He touched the back of his neck. "Your sting. From the great bee rescue."

Her smile was blinding. "Oh, I like that. The great bee rescue. That sounds like a book title." She tucked a strand of long hair behind her ear and touched the back of her neck. "I'd forgotten. All healed. Thank you for asking." Her cheeks darkened pink and…yes, she *was* staring at his mouth.

It was enough to have Charlie gripping the back of one of the dining room chairs. He shouldn't be reacting this way. He shouldn't notice things like that or worry over her bee sting or go warm and breathless from one of her sweet smiles. And yet, there was no stopping it. If only there was some sort of suit, like Astrid's beekeeping suit, that could protect him from whatever was happening. Unfortunately, he suspected the damage she would leave him with would take more than ointment and time to recover from. If he let her, that is. He wouldn't. He couldn't. There was no way he'd be foolish enough to let that happen.

CHAPTER EIGHT

Astrid wasn't sure but she had the distinct feeling the evening was a success. At least, her family made a point of being especially courteous and including Charlie throughout dinner. Which, possibly, might have been more stressful than leaving him alone.

Poor Charlie.

"What do you think of our tiny town, Charles?" Every time Aunt Mags addressed him, she called him Charles. Nova thought this was hilarious and giggled each and every time. Like now.

"It's nice." His attention bounced between the massive serving of lasagna Aunt Camellia had put on his plate, the saltshaker in front of him and Aunt Mags herself.

"I like the café place." Nova held her fork in one hand and her knife in the other. "I especially like their pancakes."

"If you like their pancakes, you should try some of the aunts' pancakes." Tansy was sitting beside Nova.

"Ants?" Nova looked distressed. "The ants make pancakes? And you eat them? The ants back home don't do that."

"The aunts." Halley sat on Nova's other side and leaned over to nudge her. "Aunt Camellia and Aunt Magnolia."

Nova's eyes widened. "Oh, that makes more sense." She glanced at Scorpio, propped beside her on her chair. "Scorpio was confused."

"Where else have you gone?" Aunt Mags redirected the conversation.

Halley and Nova both turned to look at Charlie.

That was answer enough for Astrid. *Poor Charlie.*

"Well…" Charlie cleared his throat, looking acutely uncomfortable. "Where would you recommend?"

One of Aunt Mags's finely shaped red eyebrows rose. "I'm sure they'd love the river. And the lake. There's a lovely little painting shop that just opened up on Main Street." She glanced at the girls. "And, of course, there will be fireworks and a parade for Labor Day."

But Charlie wanted to get back to Fort Worth as soon as possible. They probably wouldn't be here in September.

"You can't miss that," Dane agreed. "With the dry weather, there's a burn ban so the city has decided to set the fireworks off out on the lake, near by a place locals call goose island."

"What's goose island?" Halley asked.

"It's a tiny island in the middle of the lake where geese have been known to rest mid-migration." Van offered Nova another biscuit from the basket.

"Are there lots of geese there?" Nova asked around a mouthful of roll.

"Nova," Charlie murmured.

She covered her mouth. "Sorry. Are there lots of geese there?"

"Sometimes." Astrid nodded. "But I don't know about now. It's so hot, they might have flown off in search of a cooler option."

"Won't the fireworks scare them?" Nova asked.

"I'll ask my friend, Everett. He works for the parks department. Knowing Everett, he wouldn't do a thing that would upset any wildlife." Dane scooped himself a second large portion of lasagna.

"You mentioned Delaney's earlier... I heard they received a substantial offer on the restaurant." Aunt Camellia sat back in her chair.

"From the same company trying to buy our shop?" Astrid found herself looking Charlie's way.

Aunt Camellia sighed. "Yes."

"It's like they're trying to buy up the whole town." Aunt Camellia's distress was sincere.

"No one has accepted, have they?" Tansy set her silverware aside. "I can't imagine any true Honey resident selling to some...some developer trying to change our town."

Charlie squirmed in his chair, his gaze fixed on his plate.

"I don't think so." Aunt Camellia fiddled with the edge of her linen napkin. "Though Willadeene was carrying on about what a windfall it would be if Nicole would just up and sell the beauty parlor."

Tansy glanced her way.

Astrid understood the look. Shelby had told her to consider the offer. Until now, she hadn't thought about how accepting the offer would impact the town. Honey was a mom-and-pop community. They'd pushed back on most large chain stores and had managed to keep too many large-scale developers from coming in and building subdivisions.

"All it takes is one person. One shop. Selling could

change the landscape of Main Street and Honey forever." Aunt Camellia's smile was strained.

"Let's not worry about something that hasn't happened yet, Camellia. It's not good for your blood pressure," Aunt Mags soothed.

Van instantly reached over to take Camellia's hand. Astrid loved that about them. The little touches and reassurances they constantly made. It seemed without thought—almost instinctual.

"For all Willadeene's blustering, she won't sell," Aunt Mags continued. "If she didn't have Nicole to badger and prod on a daily basis, the woman wouldn't know what to do with herself."

It was sad, but true. Astrid loved Nicole—she was a best friend and an extra sister all rolled into one. The idea of Nicole having to continue to put up with her mother's antics was enough for Astrid to see the wisdom in Shelby's advice, albeit reluctantly. What if the offer was good enough to get Nicole out from under her mother and get her a shop of her own? Her friend deserved happiness. Everyone deserved happiness.

The thought made her acutely aware of the man sitting opposite her. Bit by bit, truths about this wary, broken man were coming out. The more she learned, the more she wanted to know. She wouldn't deny that he occupied far more of her thoughts than he should. Or that, when he was near, it was a challenge to stop herself from stealing glances that tended to morph into much longer, tingle-inducing stares. So far, she'd managed to control herself. If she didn't, he'd leave and she'd be forced to listen to the unsolicited opinions and speculation from everyone at the table. But that didn't mean she wasn't tempted. Very tempted.

Don't look at him. With her fork, she pushed a lone cherry tomato around on her plate. She lasted a full minute.

Charlie was watching her. Somber. Intense. Reserved. Yet…not. If only she could see inside that head of his and know what he was thinking. Was she simply a nuisance to him or, maybe, he wasn't as immune to her as he acted? Maybe, and it was a gigantic maybe, he was struggling with some of the same simultaneously bewildering and exhilarating roller-coaster ride of sensations she experienced whenever he was near.

Wanting something didn't make it reality.

Wait… She swallowed against the sudden lump lodged in her throat. Is that what she *wanted*? The lump seemed to grow. Did she want Charlie to be the…opposite of unaffected by her? Her throat felt too tight. And, if that was true—which she was fairly certain it was— what, exactly, did the opposite of unaffected mean? She cleared her throat but it didn't help.

His dark gaze never wavered.

Even though his singular attention had her insides a melting jumbled mess, she managed to smile. It was what she did. Smile. She was a smiley sort of person. It was, she thought, why people liked her. People normally liked smiles. Except for Charlie.

But then, for the briefest of moments, the corner of his beautiful mouth quirked up and Astrid couldn't think or breathe or remember what she should or shouldn't do or say or feel or—

"Haven't we, Astrid?" Tansy asked, almost laughing. "Astrid?"

"What?" She was so startled, she poked the cherry tomato with such force that it shot across the table and smacked Charlie in the chest—spattering juice all over his impeccably clean and pressed button-down oxford shirt.

There was an audible intake of breath from the entire group.

Charlie looked down at his shirt to assess the blood-like spatter stain seeping into the fine cotton shirt.

"Uh-oh." Nova's eyes were round as saucers.

Uh-oh is right. "Oh, no." Astrid was up.

Charlie slid his chair back. "I can spot treat it later—"

"If you wait, it'll set." Aunt Magnolia was up, too. "A little dish detergent and hydrogen peroxide will take care of it."

"It looks like you shot him." Dane pointed at the spot. From the grin on his face, he was enjoying this far too much. It didn't help that Tansy kept elbowing him in the side.

Astrid's mortification doubled.

Charlie eyed the stain again. "It does. Good aim."

"I'm so sorry." Astrid glared at Dane—which only made him laugh.

"He has a lot of shirts," Nova offered. "It's okay, isn't it, Charlie?"

Charlie nodded. "Accidents happen."

"If it was an accident," Dane mumbled, still smiling. Tansy's elbow slammed into his ribs with added force.

"Come with me." Aunt Magnolia waved Charlie to follow.

And, to his credit, he followed.

Astrid debated going after them but decided against it. The fact that all eyes were on her might have played a role in that decision. "What was the question?" she asked, taking a deep breath.

"I was telling Nova that chickens can be very helpful to the bees and that we've set up a few backyard hives close to the chicken coops." Tansy propped her elbow on the table and rested her chin on her hand.

"Yes." Astrid had no idea when the conversation had turned back to bees but she was grateful. Bees were a safe topic—and had nothing to do with Charlie Driver.

"The bees don't sting the chickens?" Nova asked.

"Very rarely." Tansy was studying Astrid closely. Too closely.

"Can you have chickens for a pet?" Nova asked.

"I don't see why not." Astrid went back to her seat.

"There's this chicken on TikTok that has, like, a million followers," Halley said. "Probably more now. Not that I can check. My phone has no reception and sometimes it doesn't work. Like, at all."

Dane held out his hand. "I'm pretty handy with smartphones."

"Leif taught you well." Tansy's grin was all mischief. "Maybe hold on to your phone and ask Leif, Halley."

Halley gave Tansy a thumbs up.

Dane didn't take the bait. "Yeah, yeah. You're hilarious."

Nova giggled. "I think you're both funny."

"I think so, too." Van had scooted his chair closer to Aunt Camellia's so it was easier for him to hold her hand.

As always, their attentiveness had Astrid smiling.

"We can help clean up," Halley offered.

"Well, now, you two have already been such a help." Aunt Camellia beamed at the two girls. "But Dane and Van have cleanup duty tonight. We girls can sit on the porch and have some cookies for dessert." She led the girls out of the dining room and down the hall, the telltale click-click of Aunt Camellia's dog pack following seconds later.

Neither Van nor Dane argued. Instead, they started clearing the table.

"I'll get the cookies." Astrid barely looked at Tansy. She was more concerned about Charlie. Hopefully, Aunt Mags hadn't terrified him so that he'd bolted from the house. The girls might be at ease here but she couldn't shake the feeling that tonight had been an utter failure as far as Charlie went. Pelting him in the chest with a cherry-tomato projectile hadn't exactly helped.

"Stop frowning," Tansy whispered. "You've got nothing to worry about."

"What are you talking about?"

"Him. Charlie." Tansy rolled her eyes. "You. Astrid."

"What? He ate dinner. That's it." She kept frowning. "What does that mean?"

"Right. Okay. Sure." Tansy sighed. "But the only thing that man is really interested in is you." She shook her head. "I'm going to need extra cookies tonight so bring lots."

Astrid was frozen in place as Tansy and Aunt Camellia escorted the girls out onto the porch. But deep down, a tiny flicker of hope took root. Astrid was still smiling when she carried the piled-high cookie plate out to the front porch.

"You remind me of someone." Magnolia Hill held up his now spot-treated shirt to the light. "My uncle. He was a man of few words, too. He said people talked too much and thought too little. You strike me as quite the thinker." She tossed his shirt into the washer. "A quick rinse should do."

"Thank you." Charlie was on the same page as Nova. He would have been content to throw the damn shirt away when he got home.

"For the character assessment or the shirt?" Magnolia put away the detergent.

He ran his hand over his white undershirt—that was also stained but he refused to remove it—and scrambled for an appropriate response.

"I thought so." She nodded. "Since Uncle Glinton preferred his own company, people decided that made him a snob." Her gaze darted his way. "In reality, he was uncertain around people. Stumbled over his words. Which got him more flustered." Magnolia walked out of the laundry room and into the kitchen, leaving him to follow.

He did.

"I always liked my uncle. When he did have something to say, he was always honest and insightful—if a little clumsy in the delivery." She poured herself a cup of tea. "Tea?"

"No, thank you." The kitchen was empty but there was a lively conversation taking place on the porch— they could hear the odd word all the way in the kitchen. He was fine staying right where he was.

"I've been told I take after my uncle Glinton. I, too, believe that people talk too much without actually saying a thing." She seemed to be waiting for his answer.

"I don't disagree."

"Good. I think I like you, Charles. I think we're going to get along just fine." Her brows rose as she nodded. "Astrid's been quite the advocate for you. She seems... invested in your little family. I'm sure you've noticed."

Charlie had noticed a lot of things when it came to Astrid—and all of it was elusive and unnerving as hell.

Not that he would say as much. He'd prefer the floor open up and swallow him whole.

"My niece is determined to keep you, I think." Once again, Magnolia seemed to be waiting for an answer.

Charlie, however, was speechless. What the hell did that mean? And now that hollowness was back, bigger and heavier than ever.

"I suppose we'll have to see what happens." She hooked arms with him. "You should have at least one of my sister's cookies before you head home this evening. It's a new recipe. Lemon raspberry cookies with a honey glaze."

He was still filtering through the woman's cryptic words after he'd wedged himself between his girls on the porch swing.

"Bees don't wear dancing shoes." Nova slumped in disappointment.

"Oh?" Had that been a possibility? He glanced around the porch—at everyone and everything except Astrid.

"The girls wear dancing shoes to their dance class," Camellia said, then sipped her tea.

Charlie couldn't argue Nova's logic. "Why wouldn't the bees?"

"I wanted to know who made the bees' shoes and Astrid said they didn't wear any." Nova sighed heavily.

"But they still dance." He nudged her. "And that's still…cool. Even without shoes."

Nova looked up at him. "It is."

"Did you just say *cool*?" Halley's shock was there, all over her face.

"Was that the wrong word? Fun? Awesome?" Charlie watched a slow smile form on her face. "Swell? Or neat?"

"Swell?" Halley laughed. "No. Nothing is *ever* swell, Charlie."

First a smile, now a laugh. He couldn't remember the last time he'd made Halley do either. Maybe tonight wasn't all bad.

"Not for the last thirty years, anyway." Tansy laughed, too.

"*Cool* is good, Charlie." Nova patted his knee.

Charlie was surprisingly relaxed—considering he was only wearing his stained undershirt in front of a group of mostly strangers.

"What's wrong with *swell*?" Van had his arm draped around Camellia's shoulder. "I used it when I was about your age, Halley."

"Exactly, dear." Camellia leaned into the man. "And I'm sure you sounded cool saying it. You were probably quite the hipster."

That made everyone laugh.

"Cookie?" Astrid held the plate forward.

"Thank you." Charlie took one, careful not to touch her or look her way.

"They're really good, Charlie," Nova whispered. "I ate two."

"You did?"

"Yummy." She nodded. "Everything here was good."

"Thank you, Nova. And thank you for all your help today." Camellia smiled. "She helped zest lemons and squeeze the juice. She sifted flour and washed the bowls. And she tested the batter a time or two." The woman winked at his little girl.

"I was a soup chef." Nova beamed with pride.

"Sous-chef," Halley corrected.

"Yep. That." Nova nodded. "Halley, too. She helped cook for the bees."

"For the bees?" Charlie did look at Astrid then—for clarification. But once their eyes locked, he went a little hazy on what he was hoping to clarify. How did she do that?

"The drought is hard on the bees. Things can't bloom so the bees can't eat. Astrid and Tansy make pollen patties so they don't starve." Halley paused. "Is that right?"

"I couldn't have said it better myself." Astrid gave her a thumbs-up.

"Charlie, the Hills are famous," Nova not-whispered in true Nova fashion.

"They are. They've been on television." Halley leaned forward, her face animated. "And magazines and podcasts, too."

Now would be the time to start talking and acting like a somewhat normal person.

"Not famous," Tansy said.

"Maybe a little famous." Dane chuckled. "In the bee world, at least."

Finally, Charlie managed to untangle his gaze from hers. Breathe. Calm. Speak. "It's a whole other world." He wasn't sure if he was talking about the bee world or the one he'd discovered here. Not just in Honey but on the Hills' front porch—with everyone watching and smiling at him as if having him here brought something more than awkwardness.

"Charlie," Halley whispered, her knee nudging his. "Staring."

Which stopped the staring immediately. He was oh so grateful it was Halley and not Nova that made this announcement. Something told him the rest of the Hills might have thoughts on his and Astrid's charged looks that lingered far longer than necessary. It wasn't normal. It wasn't rational. While he'd yet to determine the cause of his overabundance of fascination with Astrid, it was undeniably real. That didn't mean he wanted everyone knowing, and speculating and, likely, judging on whatever it was that was happening.

He didn't add much to the constant flow of conversation, but he didn't mind it as much as he'd thought he would. That wasn't the only surprise that remained for the evening. One, he found the small, one-eyed Chihuahua that wedged itself between him and Nova charming. Butters the dog sighed, rested his head on Charlie's knee and fell right to sleep. Charlie could do low maintenance. The next was Camellia's cookies. They were good. Unexpectedly good. Before he knew it, he'd inhaled four.

"I'll make sure Camellia makes a batch just for you, Charles." Magnolia Hill insisted he take another cookie. "We'll just add it on to tomorrow's baking list."

"Yay." Nova clapped her hands, earning a disapproving look from the dog. "Oops, sorry, Butters." She patted the dog's back and he went back to snoozing on Charlie's leg. "Can we come back tomorrow, Charlie?"

"You're not supposed to ask in public." Halley leaned around him to talk to her sister. "It makes everyone uncomfortable because they feel like they have to say yes."

"Oh." Nova glanced around the porch. "Never mind."

"Don't you fret about that. I hope you two will come back—whenever you like." Camellia nodded. "It's been a long time since I've had so much help in the kitchen."

"Without any air-conditioning, it must be miserable in the house," Magnolia added. "You're likely to melt inside or outside when the heat is like this."

"It is hot," Nova agreed, glancing up at him.

He knew he should protest. He'd already taken advantage of the Hills' hospitality once; it felt like an outright imposition to ask for more.

"It's up to you, of course, Charlie." That was Astrid. Her voice seemed to tug on some invisible thread tying him to her. That was how it felt. He'd been caught, by her, in some intangible trap. Only he didn't feel trapped. Slightly panicked, yes. And so much more... But now was not the time to dwell on that. He focused all of his attention on Butters. "I appreciate it. I know the girls do, too." Thankfully, he didn't sound conflicted.

"Excellent." Camellia was all smiles. "I'll have to make you pancakes in the morning."

"We're going swimming this weekend. Sunday." Dane glanced his way. "There are a bunch of places to picnic and hang out. You and the girls should come."

Charlie felt both of the girls staring up at him, expectant. Considering Nova wasn't a fan of swimming, he was surprised by their interest. Almost as surprised by Dane's invitation. "Sunday?" It was Thursday.

Dane nodded.

"That sounds good." Charlie smiled at Nova's squeal and Halley's "Yes."

"Not to beat a dead horse but *swell* would have worked just fine there," Van said, making everyone laugh.

Everyone except Nova. "A dead horse?" She was horrified.

"It's an expression, Nova." Astrid was quick to add. "There aren't any dead horses."

"You're sure?" Nova looked to Astrid for reassurance—not him.

"I'm one hundred percent certain." Astrid's smile had his heart twisted in knots.

"We should go. It's late." He stood, dislodging Butters and making the swing wobble.

"Yes, yes, I suppose it is." Van pressed a kiss to Camellia's cheek. "I can give your little crew a ride home, if you like? It's probably not the best idea to go tromping home in the dark. And it's on my way."

Charlie nodded his thanks and stood aside while the girls said their goodbyes. All the hugging seemed a little unnecessary but no one was hugging him so he let it go. With any luck, he'd get out of there without any further incident.

No such luck.

"I'm sorry about your shirt." Astrid stood, waiting for him. "It was an accident."

"That's a relief." He wished she wouldn't smile at him like that. No, that wasn't true. He liked her smile. He especially liked it when she was smiling at him. *Dammit.*

"It will be clean when you come to dinner tomorrow." She pulled her hair over one shoulder, drawing him in.

Had he agreed to that? Coming back? Putting himself in the same predicament all over again? "I'm coming to dinner?"

"I hope so." It was a whisper.

The strangest sensation rose up inside. Not pain. More like warmth. Not the smothering panic-attack clammy warmth he was all too familiar with. This was different. Almost buoyant. He was warm—all of him. Because of her.

"Good night, Charlie." Her words ran together.

"Night." He cleared his throat. "Good night, Astrid.

Thank you." Just when he thought her smile couldn't get any brighter, he was wrong.

He didn't say a word on the drive home. While he gave Nova her bath, he let her chatter on about her day and how they needed a dog and the Hills were wonderful. He was trying to make sense of the evening. Magnolia had said Astrid wanted to keep him. It had been a strange thing to say. What did it mean, exactly? Even when he was lying on his makeshift bed in the dining room, with Nova and Halley snoring soundly on their mattresses, the words taunted him. Eventually, the steady whir of the small window air-conditioning unit lulled him into a restless, Astrid-filled dream.

CHAPTER NINE

ASTRID KNOCKED. It was almost nine but there were no noises coming from inside the house. "I hope we're not waking them up." Which wasn't likely. Knowing Charlie, he'd been working for hours.

Oatmeal wagged his tail.

She adjusted the basket on her arm and waited.

Oatmeal whimpered.

"I think we should wait a minute longer before we knock—"

"Astrid." Halley opened the door, all smiles. "Come in. Ooh, what's in the basket?"

"Breakfast and lunch for Charlie. Aunt Camellia is making pancake batter right now." After the girls had gone on about the yummy pancakes at Delaney's, Aunt Camellia was determined to show them what *real* homemade pancakes were like. Food was definitely Aunt Camellia's love language.

"She is?" Halley stepped back. "I'm dressed. Nova's getting ready now."

Astrid followed Halley across the stifling entry hall to the closed doors of the dining room. "How's your morning going?"

"Pretty good." Halley opened the door.

The room was a mess. Blankets, sheets and pillows were in piles. Several stuffed animals and books scattered around. And Charlie—sound asleep on his make-shift bed on the floor.

"Charlie. Astrid is here." Nova knelt beside him on his bed, shaking his arm. "Charlie, wake up."

Poor Charlie. "Maybe we should let him sleep?" she whispered.

"His phone's been pinging all morning." Halley shook her head. "I don't know what's wrong with him. He never—ever—sleeps this late."

"I normally don't have a tiny ninja in bed with me, either." His eyes slowly opened and he ran a hand over his face. "Morning."

"Is that me? Am I the tiny ninja?" Nova smiled down at him. "You were sleeping loud, Charlie." She imitated what sounded like a bear growling. "Like that. Over and over."

Astrid giggled.

Charlie sat up and stretched. "I'm not sure I was really sleeping."

"Astrid is here," Halley pointed out. "And someone's trying to reach you on your phone."

"Morning." He gave Astrid a long, assessing look. "Is that more food? I blame all the food for my dreams last night."

Astrid slid the basket on the table. "It's breakfast and lunch." She shrugged. "You don't have to it eat, though."

"Were they bad dreams?" Nova asked. "Were there rat monsters in it?"

"No." His expression softened. "Thankfully. I know I wouldn't have slept, then."

"They are scary." Nova nodded.

It wasn't the first time she had mentioned this rat monster. Clearly, it was something that troubled the little girl. Maybe today she could try to get more information about this invisible threat.

Charlie reached for his phone. He blinked, held it closer, then blinked again. "Is it really nine?" He stood and headed around the table, turning on his computer and lamp. His hair was mussed and his shirt and shorts rumpled, and he was generally frazzled.

Astrid wasn't sure which she preferred, starched Charlie or rumpled Charlie. They were both handsome. Then again, she'd yet to find Charlie anything but handsome.

"Uh-oh." Nova frowned. "You late for work?"

Charlie muttered something under his breath.

"Get ready, Nova. Then we can go with Astrid and Charlie can work." Halley took her little sister's hand and tugged her up and off Charlie's bed. "I'll help."

Seconds later, the dining room door slammed, and they could hear the stomping of the girls' feet on the stairs.

He rubbed the back of his neck, avoiding eye contact. "I appreciate you—and your family—taking care of the girls. It's very kind."

Astrid pushed the basket closer to him. "There's breakfast and lunch for you. I know you liked the cookies so there's a few extra." She paused. "We'll see you for dinner again. Unless you've got a repairman coming today?"

"They're saying next week." He glanced at her, the muscles of his jaw working. "I can't impose on your family for a week."

She hoped he would. Last night had been lovely. Other than her pelting him with a cherry tomato. Even then, she thought he'd enjoyed himself. She hoped he had.

He was the reason she'd put a little more effort into getting ready this morning. A sundress that she thought was especially flowy and soft. She'd brushed her hair and had yet to put any braids in it. She'd even put on some lip gloss which he must have noticed since he kept looking at her mouth.

"What color is your hair?" His question was abrupt.

"My hair?" She pushed her hair from her shoulder. "Auburn? Or strawberry blond?" What a strange question.

He frowned, staring at her hair.

"Charlie." Astrid fiddled with the basket handle. He was so hard to read. What was he frowning over—her lip gloss or her hair? And why? Instead, she asked, "Did you have bad dreams?"

"I don't normally dream." He shrugged, flipping through a notebook on the table. "Your beekeepers can come here." He ran his fingers through his hair. "If that was what Rebecca wanted, I won't stop it."

Astrid blinked rapidly. "Really?" This was a surprise. She was smiling like a fool as she hurried around the table—but she caught herself. She stopped short of reaching for him. She wrapped her arms around her waist and swayed where she stood. "Thank you."

His frown deepened. With an impatient groan, he took one step closer. Then another one.

Astrid froze.

He stopped mere inches from her. Yes, he was still frowning but his eyes… "Astrid."

Every inch of her responded to him as she leaned closer. One more step and he would hear her breathe. Unsteady. Wavering. He was close enough for her to put her hand on his arm now. Or for him to reach out for her—

"We're ready." Nova burst into the room, the warm air trailing in after her.

Charlie took several steps back and almost tripped over his makeshift bed.

"Nova," Halley whispered, grabbing her little sister's arm before facing him. "Is everything okay?"

"Yes." He answered quickly. "Fine."

"What are we cooking today?" Nova skipped across the room to take Astrid's hand.

Cooking? She shook her head, still lost in a fog of Charlie. What would have happened if the girls hadn't come in? But the girls *had* come in. And Nova was waiting for an answer. Astrid smiled. "First, pancakes."

"Yay!" Nova's excitement was contagious.

Charlie cleared his throat. "You look pretty, Halley."

Astrid noticed the sundress the girl wore—so different from the too-adult clothes the teen normally favored. *Pretty* was the exact right word.

But Halley was staring at Charlie. Her shock would have been comical if it wasn't so sad.

"You do," he pushed. Poor Charlie, he wanted Halley to believe him. "I'll see you at dinner." His glance darted her way. "Thank you. Again."

It was hard not to hug him then. He was trying. Which, for Charlie, was a lot. "Of course." She swung Nova's arm. "Oatmeal wanted me to come even earlier but I didn't want to wake you up."

"He did?" Nova bounced on her toes, then began tugging her to the door. "Bye, Charlie."

"Have fun," he murmured.

Neither one of the girls heard him, but Astrid did. She turned back and smiled. "Have a good day, Charlie."

His dark eyes were pinned on her face. He didn't frown or smile, he just stood there.

"Let's go." Halley pulled the door shut. "Man, it is hot."

"It is." Astrid opened the front door. "Here they are, Oatmeal."

The walk home was eventful. Nova decided to hop from stone to stone all the way back to her house. She hopped, Oatmeal bounding along beside her, while Halley told Astrid about the kind of music she liked. It was almost enough to keep Astrid from thinking about the way Charlie had looked at her when she'd left—almost like he didn't want her to go. *Wishful thinking.*

The cold, hard truth was she wanted Charlie Driver to... No, that was it. She wanted him. She wanted his time and his smiles and whatever else he'd give her. She wanted it—him—very much.

"At least I can listen to music on my phone." Halley paused, pointing. "Who's here?"

Astrid's gaze swept over the small group of vehicles. "Dane, of course. Probably Leif and Benji. You'll like Benji. He's about your age—super sweet. Maybe Felix. There's always some Junior Beekeepers underfoot." The kitchen table was pretty crowded for breakfast.

"Dane's brother, Leif?" Halley perked up at this.

"Yep. His girlfriend, Kerrielynn, might be here. Where there is one, the other's not far behind." Astrid approved.

"I know how that is." Halley sighed. "I miss Sean."

"Who is Sean?" This was the first Astrid had heard of Sean.

"He's my…friend." Halley glanced up at her. "Charlie freaked out over him."

"'Cause you were kissing." Nova had hopped back and was standing on one leg.

"We were not." Halley shook her head. "We weren't. He was hugging me."

Astrid was beginning to understand Charlie's freakout. "And Charlie didn't approve?"

Halley's look said it all. "Charlie doesn't get it. He's not… He's weird. He's not into hugging and touching and holding hands or stuff."

"Mommy said Charlie didn't grow up with lots of 'fection so that stuff is hard for him." Nova hopped to her other leg. "It's not his fault, Halley."

"Affection," Halley murmured.

Astrid's heart hurt over this newest revelation. Poor Charlie. "Did you tell Charlie that you and Sean are just friends?"

Halley's cheeks went a little pink. "I guess we're sort of more than friends."

"Sean has a car." Nova took a huge leap over one of the flat flagstones. "A big, loud car. And a teeny-tiny mustache."

Mustache aside, the car meant Sean was a bit older than Halley. That, alone, wasn't reason enough to condemn Halley's relationship. Something told her there was more to this story.

A chorus of whimpers and barks and a stampede of wagging tails greeted them halfway across the front yard.

"Good morning." Nova set about giving each dog a pat and smile. "Good morning. I'll play with you in a minute. I'm hungry."

"I hope so." Astrid led them up the porch steps. "Aunt Camellia was making enough for an army."

The girls went inside but Astrid lingered. There, off on the horizon, was a streak of gray. It wasn't much to look at but it was enough. Rain. Finally. The earth needed a good, quenching drink. The bees would be thankful. It should also cool things down a few degrees. That was something they could all be thankful for.

"Expecting someone?" Tansy asked, leaning out the door.

"No." She went inside.

"I wasn't sure if lover boy was joining us this morning?" Tansy nudged her. "It wouldn't be so bad. Last night, he was sort of normal."

"Sort of?" Astrid thought he'd been perfectly charming—if a little shy.

"Not all of us are as swoony over him the way you are." Tansy batted her eyes. "Oh, Charlie, tell me about your all-important code and I'll throw food at you."

Astrid was laughing then.

"Just promise me you won't actually fall for him, Astrid. He doesn't strike me as someone who'd be okay living in Honey. And I can't imagine you ever leaving home." She hugged Astrid close. "Bottom line, I don't want you to get hurt."

Astrid hugged her sister back. It was hard to imagine him here permanently. And Honey was everything to her. But she couldn't promise her sister she wouldn't fall for Charlie—it was too late.

CHARLIE HAD HIS phone on speaker, the tinny on-hold music spilling out into the otherwise quiet dining room. He was pacing—it helped keep his anxiety attack at bay.

Speaking to either of his sisters took focus and effort. Even a brief conversation triggered the inadequacies and insecurities of his youth. But there was no helping it. He had the feeling his sister Lindsay and her husband, Theodore Stinson III, were up to something and he didn't want to be blindsided.

Lindsay and her husband owned Stinson Properties. Wheeling and dealing and raking in the dough. According to Lindsay, that is. They had three teen boys who excelled in sports. It was important that everyone knew she and Theo were successful and had a perfect family.

Blair, the eldest sibling, was a plastic surgeon—like their father. Unlike their father, she didn't spend *all* of her time and money on herself. She had a successful clinic in California with a rich and famous clientele but she also did charity work. Last he'd heard, she was doing reconstructive surgeries for children who were victims in conflict areas.

His sisters were competitive to the point of ridiculousness. If Blair was happy, Lindsay was not. And vice versa. His father had encouraged them, believing healthy competition provided the incentive to work harder. As a result, Charlie's childhood soundtrack was mostly his sisters yelling and screaming and fighting—which was how most of their family holidays still ended.

"Charlie? What a surprise. I don't think you've ever called me before." Lindsay always sounded like she was selling something.

"Did your man go to the hospital?" He saw no reason to beat around the bush. "The one that was trespassing."

She didn't sound the least bit upset. "We don't know who owns what so, *technically*, I have just as much a right to be there as you do."

Charlie wasn't going to get pulled into a debate with her. "Did he go to the hospital?"

"He did. It turns out that many bee stings can be quite dangerous." She sighed. "I'm surprised you're letting those pests stay on the property. Heather and Natalie could get hurt."

She knew the girls' names but insisted on getting them wrong just to get under his skin. "What's Stinson Properties' sudden interest in Honey? A little off the beaten path for you and Theo, isn't it?"

"We go where the money is, Charlie. Do you have any idea how much Rebecca's property is worth? Or what a gem that little town is? Rebecca's neighbors are sort of famous, you know. Which makes the property and town even more valuable. It could be the next Fredericksburg—if it's developed the right way."

Initially, he'd been fine selling to Lindsay. But now he didn't like the idea of his sister and Theo getting their hands on any part of Honey. "How's that going?"

"Oh, you know me. It'll take a little persuasion, but it'll happen." She sighed. "Theo and I will be there next Friday. The reading of the will is still the following Saturday?"

"Yes." At least he had a week to prepare.

"Excellent. I have a feeling we'll have a lot to talk about after that."

He and Lindsay had never had a lot to talk about. Rebecca's will and the sale of her property wouldn't change that.

"The air-conditioning is out. You'll have to stay in town." Even if it was repaired by then, he couldn't have them staying here.

"Oh, we were planning on it." She paused. "Is there anything else?"

"Any word on Blair?" Blair was slightly more tolerable than Lindsay.

"Why would I know what Blair is doing, Charlie?" She wasn't happy. "I don't see why she'd come but you can ask her yourself, if you want to know. Talk later." And she disconnected.

He sat, rested his head in his hands and took a deep breath. That was done and over. Now he had work to do.

There was the faint rumble of thunder when he was on his second conference call. The lights dimmed and flickered but the power stayed on. Today's view from the window differed from every other day since they'd arrived. Surprisingly ominous looking clouds were crowding in to smother the normally blue sky. Thunder rolled again—louder this time. A lightning strike hit a little too close for comfort. The lights of the house flickered again.

He was just about to double-check he'd used a surge protector power strip when a flash of white drew his attention back to the window. There, walking along the path to his house, was Astrid. The wind whipped around her, tossing her hair this way and that while her white skirts caught and held—like a sail on a sailboat.

A crack of thunder shook the house but Astrid didn't seem to notice. When the sky opened up and big, rapid-fire drops began pelting the ground, she tilted her head back and spread her arms wide.

Lightning spider-webbed across the darkening sky. Its long, spindly fingers were too sinister to ignore. It wasn't safe. She wasn't safe.

That realization squeezed every bit of air from his

lungs and forced his heart into a slow, shuddering rhythm. He was walking down the porch steps before he made the conscious decision. He had to get her to safety.

The rain grew heavier with each passing second. Thick, torrential sheets roaring down from the heavens to crash into the ground with surprising force. The roar of the downpour was deafening so he didn't realize Astrid was laughing until he stood before her.

She wiped the water, and several rain-plastered curls, from her face. "It's raining." The joyful smile on her face was a stark contrast to the ever-darkening sky. "Isn't it wonderful?"

It was that smile that broke something loose inside him. That free, blinding, simple expression of unguarded pleasure loosened the vise compressing his chest. A new warmth settled in his stomach. It wasn't normal to feel a sense of…contentment when he was standing in a rainstorm. But he was beginning to accept that his reaction to Astrid was never normal. While he'd never felt anything like what she was currently reveling in, he might be experiencing something close. Because of Astrid.

"We needed this so much." She was oblivious to the thunder and lightning and the fact that her flowy dress was now soaking wet and clinging.

Charlie, on the other hand, did not miss the clinging. Or the impact it was having on him. It…she…all of this was dizzying, in fact. Breathing was a challenge. It was likely the lack of oxygen that had him aching to reach for her. He, the man who avoided touch whenever possible, wanted to touch her. Desperately. His brain wasn't fully functioning. That was the only explanation he had for such an uncharacteristic action.

If a clap of thunder hadn't shaken the ground beneath

them, he had no idea what he would have done. Maybe
he would have made a complete ass out of himself and
reached for her. He'd never know. The ripple of air and
bolt of lightning set him in motion.

Dammit. She wasn't safe. That was not acceptable.

He took her hand and pulled her, splashing through
newly formed puddles, after him. The rain continued
to pound down on them until they reached the shelter
of the porch.

The moment they were safely inside the dining room,
he let go of her hand. There was no reason to hold on—
even if he wanted to. And he wanted to. There was nothing he wanted more than to touch Astrid. The realization
had him reeling.

He should step back, put space between them and get
a grip, but he didn't move.

Astrid's words were a rush. "I didn't mean to…inter-
rupt you." She was studying him, a deep furrow between
her brows. "Or irritate you."

Irritate him? She didn't irritate him. Frustrate him.
Confuse him. Definitely. Make him ache, apparently.
But not irritate. If he was irritated, he was irritated at
himself. At his ineptitude at being fully functional when
it came to communicating and experiencing human emotions. It took every ounce of courage he could muster
to look her in the eye. He was afraid. He was afraid of
the effect she had on him. That she had any effect on
him made her different. Special. *Not* irritating. He had
to say something.

Words. The *right* words.

"Astrid, you don't…irritate me." His voice was gruffer
than he'd intended. "I…I don't know…" He broke off. *I
don't know how to do this. Or what to say.*

Astrid was staring up at him but the furrow between her brows smoothed when her gaze settled on his mouth.

Whatever words he'd planned to say turned into a groan. He was done. He was done fighting—he didn't want to. He wanted... He swallowed. With one hand, he grabbed her skirt and tugged her close. So close he could breathe her in and feel the warmth rolling off her. *Astrid.* He ran his nose along the side of her face, the last bit of resistance slipping away.

His lips found hers. The taste of her almost brought him to his knees. A full-body shudder wracked her. He groaned, pulling her closer still. He wanted more. Needed more. More of Astrid. The sweetness of her mouth. The brush of her breath against his cheek. The feel of her arms, tight, around his waist. And her hands pressing his back. He was drowning in her and he welcomed it.

She was so soft, so damn soft. The cling of her lips was heaven. Every touch fed this new hunger raging inside of him.

Did she feel this, too? Did she want this? It was enough to make him freeze.

He broke away, shaking. "I'm sorry." His breathing was ragged.

"I'm not." She shook her head, her hands gripping his shirtfront.

Charlie looked at her then, exploring every inch of her beautiful face. "You're not?"

"No." She let out a long, unsteady breath. "I'm not."

He rested his forehead against hers. Relief came first. Then something better, sweeter. It was what he wanted to hear. Until now, he hadn't realized just how much he'd wanted to hear it.

She slid her arms up and rested her hands behind his neck, trembling.

"Astrid," he murmured, adrift in an ocean of new-found sensation. Keeping his distance had always ensured he'd never be vulnerable or hurt. But it was painfully clear that he couldn't keep his distance from her. The need she stirred flooded his veins. This new sweetness was tempered with a new fear.

Her lips were light against his. She was kissing him now. Gently. Tentatively.

His heart tripped over itself, stopped, then launched into an irregular rhythm. The way she melted into him had him shoving all fear and doubt aside. Right or wrong, this was what he wanted. Each kiss was longer than the last. Each grew more frantic and urgent. Her hands slid up to grip the back of his head. Her fingers twined in his hair. He closed his eyes, his nerves electrified by her touch.

When her lips parted beneath his, instinct took over. His tongue traced the soft swell of her lower lip. The shudder that wracked her body was all the encouragement he needed. His mouth sealed with hers as his tongue continued to explore. He liked the way her hands plucked at his shirt. The way she gasped against his mouth made him want to do more. He liked that he was responsible for each of her gasps and shivers. He wanted to make her feel. He wanted to give her pleasure.

And it terrified him. She terrified him.

Astrid's phone began to chime. Over and over. She didn't seem interested in answering it—or ending their kisses.

As tempted as he was to ignore it, too, he was hard-wired to always answer. "Should you get that?" he murmured against her lips. *Don't answer it.*

The chiming continued.

"Astrid." His voice was thick.

"Okay," she whispered. "Hello?"

He missed her mouth instantly, too frazzled to hear who said what.

She rested her head against his chest so her voice was somewhat muffled. "I'm fine."

Camellia Hill's voice was loud enough for Charlie to hear. "We wanted to make sure you made it before the rain started."

"I'm here." Astrid paused. "But I didn't miss the rain—I'm a soggy mess."

Charlie's hand stroked up and down her back. He didn't mind the wet.

"Please wait it out there, won't you?" Camellia asked. "I don't like the idea of you walking about with all that thunder and lightning carrying on."

Charlie nodded.

"I'll wait it out." This time, he thought he heard a smile in Astrid's voice.

"Can I speak to Astrid?" It was Halley.

"Of course," Camellia said, followed by a rustling.

Charlie braced himself.

"Astrid? It's Halley." She took a deep breath. "Don't worry, Nova said she doesn't want you and Scorpio out in the storm so take your time."

"Oh, good." A slight shudder ran down Astrid's back. "I'll bring Scorpio as soon as it stops."

"There's something else." Halley's voice dipped. "It's about Charlie." She paused. "But, if he… Maybe I should talk to him?"

"I can get him," Astrid offered, peering up at him.

Charlie swallowed down a groan. Halley, however, didn't bother hiding hers. He wasn't sure whether he should be offended or amused.

"Or I can relay a message?" Astrid was grinning from ear to ear.

"Yeah, okay. It's just…" Halley took a deep breath. "Tell him not to be weird. That's all. Tell him the message is from me *and* Nova."

"I'll tell him." Astrid nodded, still grinning.

"Okay." Halley sighed. "Here's Aunt Camellia again."

"Don't you worry about a thing. We're having a grand time here." Camellia sounded sincere. "Be safe. Love you."

"Love you, too." Astrid ended the call and tucked her phone back into the soaking pocket of her dress. Her arms slipped back around his waist as if it was perfectly normal.

He drew in an unsteady breath. Normal, it wasn't. But it was pleasant. Very pleasant.

"I'm sure you heard but Nova and Halley asked me to tell you not to be weird." Her chin rested in the middle of his chest.

"Too late," he murmured, pushing a long strand of wet hair from her shoulder.

"Oh?" Astrid waited.

"This." He could stare into her eyes for hours. "This is weird."

"Is it?" She smiled. "I think it's lovely."

There was an ache inside of him. Something else new. It wasn't hollow, though. It was alive and fluid and entirely based upon the woman shivering in his arms.

"You're cold." He gripped her shoulders and eased

her away from him. It wasn't pleasant. He didn't like the space between them. The air was colder.

"Only a little." She was wide-eyed and flushed as she said, "You were warming me up."

Breathing was once more a challenge. "Dry clothes." But that meant completely letting her go, which he didn't want to do.

"I'm not that cold." She stared up at him. "I'd rather stay as we are for a bit longer?"

No. She was cold and wet. Instead, he said, "I... Yes." Enough talking. He'd make a mess of it if he kept trying. Instead, he drew her against him. He wanted to savor every second with her. Her breath hitched as he ran his nose along her neck and he was burning for her.

She shivered, her hands gripping the soaked fabric of his shirt.

He gave in. When his lips met hers, he didn't give a damn about the cold or the wet. Thunder rolled and shook the house. Lightning continued to crack and shoot long, spindly fingers across the purple velvet sky. Massive raindrops pelted the world around them. But Charlie held Astrid close and nothing else mattered.

CHAPTER TEN

KISSING CHARLIE WASN'T anything like she'd imagined. She'd pictured a sort of halting, uncertain—perhaps a bit awkward—kiss.

She was wrong.

His kiss was strong. Fierce. Almost desperate. He was delightfully relentless in his exploration of every dip and curve of her lips. Dizzyingly so. First, whisper-light brushes at the corners of her mouth, followed by a slow, lingering kiss that had her gripping his sodden shirtfront, then sucking her lower lip inside his mouth. His broken groan had a toe-curling, bone-melting effect.

Her heart would likely erupt from her chest at any second and she didn't care. Breathing no longer seemed important—unless, of course, she was breathing in Charlie. Drawing in great, gulping lungfuls of his minty eucalyptus aftershave was more delicious than...well, anything.

One large hand rested at the base of her skull, his fingers twining in her wet hair as he continued his exploration. He was quite thorough. His hands moved with purpose, cradling her head, then cupping her cheek. His fingers left a fiery trail along her neck. The stroke of his thumb along the seam of her lips left her gasping.

It was too much. Charlie was too much. And she hoped he'd never stop.

At some point, she wrapped her arms around his neck to prevent herself from sliding into a quivering, boneless puddle at his feet. Instead of being held upright, the two of them melted together. She was only vaguely aware that he sat on the table's edge with her between his legs—she was too distracted by Charlie's mouth brushing the edge of her ear.

"Astrid." Charlie's gruff whisper set the hair along the back of her neck on end.

She didn't bother opening her eyes. Instead, she tugged his face back to hers so she could kiss him.

"Astrid," he murmured, between kisses.

"Shh." She pressed against him. "I'm kissing you. I need to concentrate."

Then Charlie did something Astrid had never heard him do before. He laughed.

She knew he was laughing because she could feel him smiling against her mouth. That was enough to make her let go.

Charlie was smiling? And laughing. And, oh, my, so manly and beautiful she had no choice but to stare. He was breathing hard, his hair a tousled mess and his shirt plastered to his broad chest. All lovely things. But his smile. His laugh. Like his kiss, they were so much better than anything she could ever have imagined.

"That's my favorite smile." Her fingertips traced the arc. "You should laugh more often."

Red flooded his cheeks. Was he embarrassed? He cleared his throat, twice, then said, "You surprised me."

"I will now attempt to surprise you at least once a day." Now that she'd seen his smile, she couldn't bear the thought of not seeing it again. Soon. Regularly.

"Believe me, you do." If he was having a hard time holding her gaze, he hid it well.

"Really?" She loved the warmth in his dark brown eyes. "You have a lovely smile, Charlie. If I were having a terrible day, that smile—right there—would make it better."

He didn't say anything or move. One dark brow rose but he didn't speak.

She waited, but he stayed quiet. "What are you thinking?" she whispered.

"I'm...processing."

"Oh." Today had been a lot to process. "Good. You're not regretting this..." Where had that come from? Why had she said it out loud? If he did, and said so, it would crush her.

"No." He took a slow, steady breath and repeated, "No."

Whew. "Then we should go back to kissing. Don't you think?" she whispered. She was more than willing to pick right up where they left off. Eager, was more like it.

His smile was back.

The ground seemed to wobble beneath her feet. Her hold on his shirt tightened. "Or not."

But he was staring at her mouth now so she hoped a kiss was imminent. Until his phone rang. He reached around and grabbed for his phone.

"Work?" It was business hours. Instead of turning her world upside down, he might have important work to do.

He shook his head as he stared at the screen and held the phone to his ear. "Halley. Hello?" He stared at the floor by his feet but one arm still held her against him.

"Charlie." Nova's voice rang out sweet and true. "I stole Halley's phone. Don't tell, okay?"

"Okay." He was frowning. "Is everything all right?"

"It's a bad, bad rainstorm." And Nova was clearly terrified.

Poor Nova. Astrid wanted to give the little girl a hug. A big one.

"We are okay, Nova." Charlie's voice was low and soothing. "You are okay, too."

"Astrid… Astrid can borrow Scorpio if she gets scared." Nova didn't sound convinced.

He stared down at Astrid, the corner of his mouth quirked up. "Astrid, huh? What about me?"

"You don't get scared, Charlie." Nova giggled. "You're silly." She lowered her voice. "Can you come to Astrid's house? I…I want you and Scorpio and Astrid to come *here*. We can all be safe *here*. Together."

Astrid's heart ached for the little girl. It was a loud and intense storm. Thunder boomed. Lightning lit up the sky. Rain continued to slam down with substantial impact. And the power was flickering. Scary stuff, especially for a five-year-old in a big, strange house with mostly strangers.

"Please?" Nova's little voice was trembling. "Please, Charlie?"

Astrid didn't want to interfere but Nova's near-frantic pitch had her ready to run into the storm and back home.

Charlie glanced at the large window and the ominously dark sky, his jaw muscle tightening. "We're coming."

"Thank you. Thank you, Charlie," Nova gushed. "Hurry. Be safe, but hurry. And don't tell Halley I called. Or that I used her phone. Bye."

He frowned. "She sounds scared. She is scared." He

slid his phone into his pocket and ran his fingers through his hair.

"Then let's go." It took effort to step back and put space between them, but it was the right thing to do. If she didn't let go, they'd never leave and Nova needed them.

He pushed off the table, grabbed his keys and his laptop, and looked at her. A long, hard-to-distinguish look.

"What does that look mean?" She tried to imitate his expression. Rather, the lack of expression.

"I'm going to grab some dry clothes." He left the dining room, leaving the door open behind him.

She blinked. She could still feel the imprint of his lips on her mouth while he was back to being... Charlie. If she hadn't felt the urgency in his hands and the fierceness of his kiss, it'd be easy to think what had happened between them was a daydream. A wonderful, fiery, passionate daydream. She drew in a shuddering breath. Lucky for her, his reaction was seared into her mind and skin.

A clap of thunder shook the house. *Poor Nova.*

Which reminded her. She spun, searching the three pallets on the floor until she found Scorpio. The plush blue star peered over the edge of one of Rebecca's quilts, his stitched smile fraying and his white-mitten gloved hands a bit dingy. She scooped it up, plucking lint from the embroidered wide-eyed and smiling toy. "There you are." She smiled back at Scorpio. "Nova is missing you."

The seconds creeped along and the fact that she was wet and cold grew harder to ignore. The last thirty minutes had, for her, inexplicably changed things. It was more than her reaction to Charlie's touch—as overwhelmingly delicious as that was. Her heart. Charlie had taken a very firm hold of her heart. The question was, did he want it? It was a real question. One she had no answer for. They'd been so caught up in a bubble of euphoria, so tangled up in the newness of exploring one another, that she hadn't cared about much else. But now that Charlie wasn't within reach to cloud her mind and distract her from overthinking, the uncertainty was hard to ignore. The longer the silence held, the tighter her nerves were stretched.

That was why she jumped at his sudden reappearance in the doorway.

Charlie paused, his dark brows furrowing. "You all right?"

She nodded, Scorpio clutched to her chest. As soon as her eyes met his, her heart took off at an alarming rate. "Found him." She held out Nova's beloved toy.

He was studying her in that unreadable way of his.

With those gorgeous, brooding eyes. She drew in a steadying breath. "Ready?"

He blinked, turned on his heel and headed for the front door.

"Okay," she murmured, following.

"Here." He took Scorpio, put the toy inside his waterproof athletic bag and zipped it shut before pulling open the front door. With a howl, the wind blew the door wide to slam into the wall.

The sky flashed, alternating cracks of lightning and the deafening boom of thunder making Charlie pause. He glanced at her, his jaw clenching. Rebecca's car wasn't far—a quick dash across the front lawn and out the side gate.

"Let's make a run for it." Astrid offered up a smile.

Yes, they'd get wet but they were both already soaked through so what difference would it make?

"Be careful," he grumbled.

She nodded, then dashed out the door. She didn't mind the rain. They needed it, desperately. She did, however, hope it tapered off a bit. Flash flooding was a thing in the Hill Country. And while they needed the rain, too much, too soon presented a whole new set of problems.

She reached the passenger door of Rebecca's old tank of a car and pulled the heavy door wide. She sat and slid onto the vinyl seat, then turned for the grip on the door. The wind fought her, holding the door wide with a brutal force.

Charlie, however, waved her back and slammed the door.

Astrid was still wiping the rain from her face when he got into the car.

"Here." He unzipped the gym bag and handed her a towel.

"Thank you." She dried her face, rung out her hair and blotted at her dress—but it was a lost cause.

Charlie drove carefully. Rebecca's car was big and solid so there was no worry about getting blown off the road but the rain made visibility limited and, by the time they reached Astrid's house, they were both tense. He turned off the ignition and looked at her. He didn't look happy.

She waited, bracing herself.

"No," he murmured softly.

She swallowed, her throat going tight. "No?" she whispered.

He cleared his throat. "What…what happens now?"

"We get soaked, again, and give Nova Scorpio and—"

"What happens next here." He cleared his throat again, harder this time. "With…us?"

"Oh." *Us. He said* us. She was ridiculously happy as she slid across the bench seat of the old car. Her hands cupped his face as she leaned forward to give him a gentle kiss.

Charlie mumbled something unintelligible, then grabbed her to him. His hands pressed against her back until there was no room between them. His kiss wasn't gentle. It was everything. Hungry and fierce and desperate.

Her hands slid down to rest on his chest. Under her palm, his heart beat. It was no more controlled than his kiss. It thundered away, broken and frantic. Just like hers. Hope rolled over her. Maybe, just maybe, there was a place in Charlie Driver's heart for her.

THIS WAS IRRATIONAL. All of it. Knowing that didn't stop him from kissing her. He couldn't seem to stop kissing her. He should. Now. They were parked in front of her house—chances were her entire family were peering out the window wondering what the hell was going on. And yet, he kept right on kissing her.

It had taken him less than five minutes to put a bag of dry clothes together but he'd forced himself to take longer. Once he cleared his head, he'd be fine. But that hadn't happened. He'd sat on the edge of his bed, fighting the need to go back to her. And, dammit, it was *need*. To see her. To be near her. To hold her and kiss her and breathe her in. It was beyond reason or explanation but true. The pull to get back to her had won out in the end. He'd hurried down the stairs to stand, desperate, for some sign that she might be feeling something similar to whatever sweet hell this was.

When she hadn't instantly reached for him, he'd been kicking himself. He was losing it. This was all him. It wasn't entirely his fault. He didn't have much of a frame of reference for this. Who was he kidding, he had no frame of reference for this. He didn't date. After a hand-ful of bad experiences, Charlie had gotten the message loud and clear. He'd decided he'd rather be single than face continual rejections. If he and Yasmina's long-term friendship hadn't led to their arrangement, he'd have stayed single. As a result, he clearly had no idea what was going on.

But now it was better. She was holding on to him and he could breathe again.

Until it stopped.

"Charlie." Astrid's husky whisper set the hair on the back of his neck upright.

He had a new word for Astrid. *Sexy.* No, *sexy* was cliché. And trite. She was more than that. *Stimulating.* That fit. Everything about her stimulated everything about him. "Hmm," he murmured, kissing her with re-newed enthusiasm.

Even her laugh was husky. And shaky. "Charlie." She braced a hand against his chest. "We're here."

He groaned, his forehead resting against hers. "I know." How the hell was he supposed to do this? To let her go and go inside like his entire world hadn't been knocked off its axis. It had. That was a fact. He hadn't known something—someone—could feel so good. No, not someone. He wasn't that naive. This was all because of her.

"Nova—"

"I know." Slowly, his hold eased. He wasn't ready to let her go, but she slid away before he could argue. Then, she was opening the door and climbing out of the car. He was gripping the steering wheel with both hands as she sprinted through the rain to the front porch of the massive old house.

It took him a minute to peel his fingers off the steering wheel. It took him another minute to grab the bag and muster enough courage to leave the car and run to the porch—where she was waiting.

"Ready?" she asked, dripping wet.

He shook his head. But she was shivering so he pushed the door open, his hand resting on her lower back and steering her inside.

"Charlie!" Nova was a running blur that slammed into him. "You're here! You're here!" Her arms wound tight around his knees and her face rested against his thighs.

Charlie stared down at her crooked ponytail, his heart so full it hurt. "I'm here, Nova." He patted her back. "It's okay."

She beamed up at him. "It is now."

The lump in his throat caught him by surprise. She was so happy to see him. *Him.* What had he done to earn that look? That confidence? He didn't deserve it, that was for certain.

Nova was hugging him again.

And Astrid was smiling at them. There was a sheen in her eyes that made the lump in his throat double in size. What was happening? Where was all this coming from? And what the hell was he supposed to do with it?

"Charlie?" Halley was staring at him, in shock. "Astrid? What are you guys doing here? Ohmygosh. Like, you guys are soaked."

"I thought I saw headlights." Camellia Hill was bustling their way, towels hanging from both hands. "Good gracious. You are drenched, aren't you?" She handed off the towels. "Astrid, go put on some dry clothes before you catch pneumonia."

Astrid was drying her hair with the towel but there was a puddle forming beneath her feet.

He should have made her change into something warm at his place. If she got sick... He silently cursed himself. He'd been worried about her getting struck by lightning but had no qualms about her getting sick.

"I hope you have dry clothes in that bag, Charles?" Magnolia Hill followed, shaking her head. "I'll make some hot tea for you both."

"Go change, too, Charlie." Nova let him go. "I don't want you or Astrid to get sick. That'd be bad."

"Don't worry, Nova." Not about him, anyway. Astrid? That was another story. "You should listen to your aunt." He glanced at Astrid, resisting the urge to reach for her. He shoved his hands into his pockets.

"Yes, please." Nova nodded. "No knee-money-uh."

"Pneumonia," Halley murmured.

"'Xactly." Nova nodded again.

"You heard them." Magnolia nodded. "Now, scoot." She waved Astrid toward the stairs before heading into the kitchen. "You, too, Charles."

"Yeah, Charlie. You, too." Nova pointed at the stairs.

"Yes, ma'am." He forced himself to smile down at her. "Scorpio is inside the bag."

Nova let go of him, dropped to her knees and unzipped the bag. With a squeal, she pulled the toy free and hugged it against her chest. "Scorpio!"

"There." Camellia crouched beside Nova. "All better. You've got your Charlie and your Scorpio." Camellia regarded him with affection.

That damn lump in his throat was three times the size now.

"Charlie." Even Halley was looking at him with something other than frustration. "You should go change."

"There's a bathroom at the top of the stairs on the right. A shower, too, if you'd like." Camellia stood. "Come on, girls. Let's get a nice warm snack ready for them."

"Okay." Nova, holding one of Scorpio's hands, dashed down the hall without a backward glance.

Camellia followed, chuckling.

"It's cool," Halley said, shrugging. "You coming here. For Nova, I mean."

He nodded, wishing he knew what to say to her.

"She was worried about you." Halley broke off. "We both were." She spun and walked rapidly down the hall to the kitchen.

He stared after her, reeling. Halley had made it perfectly clear how she felt about him. And none of it was good. She was worried about him?

"You coming?" Astrid called down from the top of the stairs.

He grabbed the bag and took the stairs, two at a time, until he was at the top. It took effort, but he didn't reach for her. "You didn't change." He stepped closer, frowning down at her.

"I'm about to." She shook her head. "Don't frown like that." She pressed her fingers to his forehead and rubbed until he relaxed. "Better."

He caught her wrist. "Please, get changed." She was

warm. Her skin was so soft. His thumb ran along the edge of her palm.

She shuddered.

Dammit. There it was, that ache. The need for her—more of her. Now was not the time or the place. He knew that. And yet, he wasn't so sure he cared. If he leaned forward, an inch was all, he could kiss her temple. Another inch, he could kiss her mouth.

She stared up at him, her breath fast and shallow.

"Um…" Tansy's voice had them both jumping. "Yeah. Hi."

He glanced from Tansy, to Astrid, to the open door of the room that should be the bathroom. Without another word, he headed straight for it. Once the door was shut, he dropped his bag and braced himself against the sink.

"What was that?" Tansy was laughing.

"Nothing." Astrid's voice was high and unsteady.

He closed his eyes, imagining her full-body shudder. A shudder he'd stirred.

"That wasn't nothing," Tansy said.

Tansy Hill was right. It wasn't nothing. He shook his head, wishing the walls and the door were thick enough to stop him from hearing what was being said.

"You're so loud." Astrid wasn't laughing.

"I'm always loud. It doesn't normally bother you."

"Tansy… Don't tease, okay? This…" Astrid broke off.

Charlie held his breath. He shouldn't be listening. This was none of his business. He should respect their privacy.

"This is special. Okay?" Astrid's voice was gentle yet pleading.

Special. That was good. Or was it? His sisters used

to call him special and it had been their attempt at a clever insult.

"I know." Tansy's tone was different now. Less teasing. "I see that. You could feel the spark between you. I honestly thought you two were going to get naked and have sex right here on the landing."

Charlie swallowed hard. Sex. It was made up of everything he avoided. Rejection. Awkwardness. Losing control. Not being proficient. Sex meant touching. Lots of intimate touching. It was exposing body parts and being vulnerable in a way that made him physically recoil.

But he'd felt that way about kissing until Astrid. He'd never been so happy to be proven wrong. And the idea of Astrid naked didn't make him recoil. More like the opposite. Astrid was beautiful. Her body would be, too. Would he enjoy exploring her body as much as he'd enjoyed exploring her mouth?

What the hell is wrong with me?

"Tansy," Astrid groaned. "I didn't mean *sex*."

Astrid didn't want to have sex with him? He shouldn't be disappointed. But he was. *There is* definitely *something wrong with me.*

"Uh-huh, sure. You're telling me I read the vibe wrong?" She made a snorting sound. "I don't think so. Hey, I think it's great. Go for it. Kiss a lot of frogs, remember? Have fun and all that. Just remember he is leaving, Astrid. I don't want you to get hurt."

"Tansy, I'm fine—"

"I'm stopping." Tansy cut her off. "Now go get changed before you get the aunts freaked out over you getting sick."

"I'm going." Astrid sighed. "But you don't have to come with me."

"Are you kidding? Of course I'm coming. I want to hear how you made Mr. Grumpy Pants into Mr. I-Want-To-Get-In-Your-Pants."

Charlie didn't want to smile, but he did.

"I didn't do anything." But Astrid was laughing. "And you're wrong. He doesn't want to get into my—"

A door closed, blocking him from overhearing the rest of their conversation.

It's probably a good thing.

He leaned against the bathroom counter, exhausted. Today had been one of those days that would remain etched into his brain. One of a handful of days. Only this one was good—a rarity.

Kiss a lot of frogs? He wasn't stupid. Nova and Halley had plenty of books with fairy tales about princesses. The princess kisses the frog and the frog turns into the prince—and for some reason that's a happy ending. He never understood why that was the goal of the story or enough to make the princess happy, but Yasmina said he was overthinking it. She said the message was about getting beyond appearances to get to know the person inside.

Obviously, I'm the frog.

It was also obvious Tansy didn't consider him prince material—and she was right. The chances of anyone liking who he was—with all his quirks and eccentricities—was slim. He'd come to accept that years ago; he wasn't foolish enough to think a few kisses would make Astrid feel different. No matter how incredible the kisses had been. For him.

He stared at his reflection. *Really?* Enough about Astrid and the vortex of unfathomable *feelings* she'd un-leashed inside of him.

Nova had been happy to see him. Truly happy. She'd hugged him with as much gusto as she hugged Scorpio. That *was* special. That he would treasure.

And Halley. She hadn't run to hug him, but she'd worried about him. It was a start. Maybe. He didn't want the girls to hate him. He wanted to be there for them—to be some sort of parent. Today gave him hope that he wasn't an absolute failure.

An especially loud clap of thunder had him shrugging off his wet clothes. He took a quick, icy shower to freeze the lingering effects of Astrid's touch, then dressed. His khaki slacks and button-down shirt provided the sense of normalcy that had been so lacking most of the day. He put on socks and shoes, combed his hair, and put the wet clothes in his bag.

Downstairs, he followed the chorus of conversation to the large family kitchen. He'd heard the term "heart of the home" but, until now, he'd never understood what the term actually meant.

It wasn't just his girls, Magnolia and Camellia, Tansy and Dane, either. The two women from the café were here. And the baby. There were also three teens huddled around the massive kitchen table. It looked like Halley and the as-yet-unknown teens were playing a board game. One teen girl and two teenage boys. His internal warning alarm instantly triggered. *Great.*

"Feeling better, Charles?" Magnolia waved him toward the table. "I've made some tea. The girls made some honey ginger scones. They're still warm, so help yourself. Oh, and there are some more of those cookies you like, too."

Charlie crossed the room, his gaze pinned on Halley and the two boys. One was undeniably Dane's younger brother. A good-looking kid. Exactly the sort of boy Halley didn't need right now.

"Charlie, this is Leif and Benji and Kerrielynn." Tansy introduced him. "These fine young people are part of the Junior Beekeepers and will be coming out to replace the older hives on the back of Rebecca's property."

Of course they were. Charlie managed not to sigh. To his surprise, Leif and Benji both rose and Benji shook his hand.

"It's nice to meet you, sir." Benji nodded. "Thank you for supporting our program."

"Welcome to Honey, Mr. Driver." Leif had a firm handshake.

"Kerrielynn is the Hill Country Honey Queen, Charlie." Halley said this as if it was a big deal—and that he should know what a Hill Country Honey Queen was.

"Oh, well. That sounds like quite an accomplishment." He hoped that was an acceptable thing to say.

"Thank you." The girl made eye contact and offered a smile.

"She worked hard to get it." Leif sounded proud—which gave Charlie pause.

The way Leif Knudson was staring at the Hill Country Honey Queen set Charlie's mind at ease. The boy was smitten. And, from the way the girl was flushed and smiling back at Leif, the feeling was mutual. *Crisis averted.*

He sat in the chair at the far end of the table, eyeing the game board the four of them were gathered around. "What are you playing?"

"Settlers of Catan." Halley scanned the board, shaking the dice in her hand.

"It's for big kids." Nova came to stand by his chair, her hand resting along the chair's arm. "I can't play."

"You can be on my team," the boy Benji offered. "I can use all the help I can get."

But Nova shook her head. "Can you read to me, Charlie?" She looked at him, jumping when another boom of thunder shook the house.

Charlie scooped her up and put her on his lap. "Sure. What are we reading?"

She beamed up at him. "I don't know." She relaxed against him with a sigh.

He took a deep breath, smoothing her hair from her face. She was always so happy, like her mother, that it was easy for him to forget she was so young and vulnerable. He shouldn't. Protecting her shouldn't only be about keeping her physically safe, but emotionally, too. His childhood should have taught him that. He didn't want his girls to feel as alone and lost as he'd been. Everything and everyone had seemed against him then; he'd been so scared of the world. Halley and Nova shouldn't feel that way. *I'll do better, Nova. I promise, Halley. I'll do better.*

He tucked an arm around his little girl. His laptop could wait. Phone calls could wait. Right now, this was more important. It was a privilege that he could ease Nova's—and possibly Halley's—fear. A privilege that, starting now, he wouldn't take for granted.

I KNEW YOU'D COME. I knew it.

Halley said Charlie didn't want to be with them but that was wrong. "I told you," Nova whispered to Scorpio. *He loves us. He is our dad.* And now she and Scorpio were cuddled up on his lap.

"What did you tell Scorpio?" Charlie asked.

"That you would come." She smiled up at Charlie. "And you did."

He nodded.

"You should try the lemonade, Charlie. Nova made it." Halley took a sip from her tall glass. "Nova *and* Aunt Camellia made it."

"They didn't add salt. They used lots of sugar and honey. Aunt Camellia puts honey in everything. That's what Tansy said." Nova didn't want Charlie to think the lemonade was nasty.

"I thought you were going to wait to come over until it stopped raining," Halley said.

Nova wrinkled up her nose. *Don't tell, Charlie.* Halley would be so, so mad if she knew Nova had taken her phone.

"I changed my mind." Charlie glanced down at her and smiled.

Because we have a secret. She smiled back and gave him a thumbs-up.

"And if we hadn't come home, we'd have missed out on all of this." Astrid was back and she wasn't dripping wet anymore. Her hair was dry again.

She and Halley agreed that Astrid was the prettiest person they'd ever seen in real life and not on the television or in the movies. After Mommy.

"You *were* all wet and drippy. But you're not sick?" Nova asked. "No knee-money-yuh?"

"Nope." Astrid sat in the chair next to Charlie's. "Ooh, did you make these?" She reached for a scone.

"Yep." Nova nodded, yawning. "They are yummy."

"Everything made in this kitchen is yummy." Benji laughed.

"It is," Miss Nicole, Benji's mom, said. She had green hair. Not all of it, some of it. She got to do that because that was her job. Charlie would never let Nova have green hair. But, if Nova were going to color her hair, she'd rather have blue or pink or purple. Not green.

"Mom." Benji leaned away from his mom. She liked to mess up his hair. She did that a lot. Benji said he didn't like it but it made him smile so Nova figured he was pretending. Like Halley. To be cool. Halley liked to act cool.

Nova didn't like that. Being cool meant not being able to dress up or talk about dinosaurs or crawl on the floor and pretend she was one of Aunt Camellia's puppy dogs. Cool was boring.

"Want more tea?" Astrid would be a good mommy. She liked taking care of people.

Halley said she thought Astrid liked Charlie. *Like* liked him. If that was true, then maybe Charlie would marry Astrid and they'd be able to stay here with all the dogs and cats and Astrid's family. Nova liked having aunts and she loved all the cookies and treats and laughing, too. The laughing was her favorite.

"I'm fine. Thank you, Astrid." Charlie didn't sound grumpy when he talked to Astrid. He did still act weird around her, though. Halley said it was because Astrid made Charlie nervous. But if he liked her, why was he nervous? As far as Nova was concerned, grown-ups were weird.

"You're welcome, Charlie." Astrid's smile was *so* pretty. And she didn't even have to wear lipstick. Halley said it was cool that Astrid could be so pretty and not wear lipstick and Halley loved lipstick so Astrid must be *really* cool.

Cool couldn't be all bad if Astrid was cool.

Nova shrugged. Her eyes were feeling heavy. Even with the loud thunder booming, Charlie was here and it would all be okay. She hugged Scorpio against her and turned into Charlie.

"Tired?" Astrid whispered. "I have a big, comfy bed upstairs, if you want to nap."

Nova did want to nap but she didn't want to do it upstairs. "Charlie is comfy."

Charlie laughed *and* he hugged her.

We can sleep, Scorpio. Charlie will keep us safe.

CHAPTER ELEVEN

A STRID ROLLED THE DICE. "Ha, ten spaces." She hugged Nova against her side. "See."

"You are the bestest teammate ever." Nova sat up on her knees, watching their game piece move around the board. "We passed the Go." She clapped her hands together.

"Another two hundred dollars." Charlie counted out the bills and slid them to Nova.

"You landed on Chance." Halley pointed at their game piece.

Astrid saw Nova frown. "Chance is bad." Nova sighed. "It takes *all* your money away." She gave a thumbs-down.

"Maybe not." Astrid took the Chance card Benji offered her. "Oh, Nova, you're right. It does take money. But not ours. Every player must pay *us* twenty dollars."

Nova clapped her hands again. Her enthusiasm was contagious.

"We should give up." Halley sat back in her chair, but she was smiling. "Astrid and Nova are totally kicking butt."

"Halley," Charlie murmured.

She rolled her eyes. "Astrid and Nova are totally *winning.*"

For all the eye rolling, there was no edge to Halley's

words. Astrid suspected she was having a good time. It probably helped that she was interacting with people close to her own age.

"Never give up." Benji handed over his twenty dollars and reached for the dice. "Underdogs have their day. Every once in a while."

"You're not under a dog, Benji." Nova laughed. "That's just silly."

"You're right, squirt." Halley laughed, too. "He's not."

"It's an expression." Charlie leaned forward, reaching across the game board for a cookie. "Underdog. It means someone who isn't likely to win but keeps fighting."

"It was also a movie." Benji looked like he'd tasted something awful. "It was really bad, though."

"Your face." Nova laughed.

Benji was good at making faces. He made another over-the-top expression, and both Nova and Halley were laughing.

Charlie stirred then, his gaze bouncing back and forth between Halley and Benji. Astrid could almost hear the wheels turning inside his head. The slight thinning of his mouth had Astrid wanting to reassure Charlie that it was okay. Benji was a good kid. He was responsible, funny and not girl-crazy.

"Benji is our resident film expert." Kerrielynn hugged Benji. "He knows everything about movies."

"Because he watches too many of them." Leif shook his head.

"Can you watch too many movies?" Benji shrugged.

"Yes." Nova sounded off. "Charlie says you can rot your brains out if you watch too many." She looked gravely concerned. "Are your brains okay, Benji?"

Astrid glanced Charlie's way. He was having a hard time not smiling.

Benji managed to cover his laugh. "I think so."

"Are they? Are they, though?" Leif scratched his chin.

"Be nice." Kerrielynn frowned. "Also, let me remind you he has, like, the highest GPA in the whole school. Which means his brain is great, Nova. Don't you worry."

"Whew." Nova took a deep breath. "I'm glad. You know brains are important."

"He knows, Nova." Halley shook her head. "What's your favorite movie?"

"I don't have *one*." But Benji sat back, contemplating the question.

"He has many." Nicole looked up from the knitting pattern she'd spread out on the side table. Shelby and Nicole were determined to learn how to knit. And since knitting was something Aunt Camellia could do with her eyes closed, she'd offered to help teach them. "I can tell you which ones he's watched over and over." She stared at the knot of yarn hanging off one of her knitting needles.

"Oh, dear." Camellia eyed the knot. "How did that happen?"

"Natural talent, I guess." Nicole handed over the knitting needle.

"Which mo*vies*?" Halley emphasized the plural.

Nicole started rattling off a list of movies but Astrid was distracted by the way Charlie propped his arm on the table. Resting along her arm. There were so many of them squished in, tight, around the table it wouldn't necessarily be obvious to anyone watching. But it was to Astrid. Charlie didn't touch, even accidentally. Unless he wanted to.

She glanced his way—to find him studying her arm. His expression was unreadable. True Charlie. He seemed transfixed, his gaze leisurely running down the inside of her arm to her wrist. Then he glanced her way. His eyes gave him away. The hunger, the fire, was for her. And it was exhilarating.

"We saw that at the movie theater, didn't we, Astrid?" Tansy asked.

"What movie?" Astrid scrambled. There were other people in the room. A whole lot of other people, actually. That Charlie was looking at her, like that, with such an audience was more than a little surprising. And delightful.

Tansy was smiling from ear to ear. "The last Thor movie."

Dane shot her a look. "How do you always manage to slip Thor into every conversation?"

"Not every conversation. But, if I do, it's because he looks like you." She leaned against Dane's well-muscled shoulder. "Remember, Astrid? The one where Dane won the Thor lookalike contest—even though he didn't enter." She fluttered her eyes. "My big, hunky superhero."

Dane kissed the tip of her nose. "That's me."

"Gag." Leif made a series of choking noises. "Get a room."

"I guess the rain has put a wrinkle in your weekend getaway to Weaver Bee Farm?" Astrid knew Tansy had been looking forward to it. A lot.

"There are other weekends." Dane draped an arm along the back of Tansy's chair, his hand resting on her shoulder.

"What happens when it rains? For the bees, I mean?" Charlie asked, drawing all eyes his way.

Was he really curious or was he being polite? Astrid was so excited, her words floundered.

"They take shelter," Dane started. "They're really good at sensing a weather change so, on days like today, they're prepared."

"What if a bee gets stuck outside the hive?" Halley moved her token and counted out money to buy the property she'd landed on.

"They'll take shelter somewhere and wait it out." Astrid glanced at the window. "But Dane's right. Most honey bees stay close to home when a big front rolls."

"Astrid has a sixth sense about bees." Tansy smiled. "We call her the Bee Whisperer."

"Do you whisper to the bees?" Nova used her not-so-soft whisper voice.

"She does. And she uses her manners, too." Tansy leaned forward, her face animated. "Last time we collected a hive—"

"From the barbecue thingie?" Nova asked.

"Yes, that." Tansy nodded. "We tried and tried to find the queen. I was ready to give up and try again later, but Astrid is stubborn."

"Determined," Astrid cut in.

"Potayto-potahto, whatever." Tansy waved her aside.

"Without the queen, the bees don't want to leave the hive." Benji jumped in, speaking directly to Nova.

"How did you find her?" Halley waited, her money in her hands. "The queen?"

"Astrid talked to her." Tansy paused for affect. "She was sweet and complimentary and calm, explaining that we were trying to help them and that we'd never hurt them. It coaxed the queen into walking right out so Astrid could put her into her little condo clip until we could get them moved and settled."

"Condo clip?" Dane chuckled.

"I was telling a story. I thought it sounded better than just *clip*." Tansy shrugged.

"I've seen her do it." Leif sat back in his chair. "Talk to the bees. Seriously."

"Me, too." Aunt Magnolia looked up from her crossword puzzle.

"And find a swarm." Aunt Camellia was still trying to fix Nicole's mess of yarn. "And she was so mad at herself for not splitting the hive before it happened. You are too hard on yourself, Astrid."

Astrid shot her aunt a smile.

"You want to find a swarm?" Halley glanced at Benji. "That sounds like a bad thing."

"It isn't great." Astrid did feel bad for not saving the bees the hassle. She'd known they were going to swarm, but she'd thought she'd had more time. "Bees normally swarm when they're overcrowded. They go out like a big cloud with the queen safe inside the very middle. Scout bees go out to try to find a new home but, if you're a keeper, you do it for them."

"You find the swarm, get the queen bee into a new hive box and the bees will follow." Leif explained, reaching for the dice.

"How did you know where to find the swarms?" Nova was staring up at her with big eyes. "Is it magic?"

"No." Astrid shook her head, smiling.

"Maybe," Tansy cut in. "I sure didn't know."

"Astrid does have a…connection with the bees." Aunt Camellia handed the knitting needles back to Nicole.

"Poppa Tom, my father and Astrid's grandfather, said she had the touch. And Poppa Tom was magic when it came to bees."

"Wow." Nova was still staring at her now.

"It's not magic, Nova." Astrid gave her another hug. "I'm just a really good listener. That's all. Bees, like people, can tell us things without using words. You just have to be patient and watch."

"But people don't sting you." Nova said this very matter-of-factly.

"I don't know about that." Dane chuckled, earning an eye roll from Tansy.

"People can do far worse," Nicole muttered.

Poor Nicole. Astrid couldn't imagine having a mother like Willadeene. She couldn't imagine not having the love and support of the people right here in this room. To grow up with something less was unfathomable.

"Mom." Benji shook his head. "Way to read the room and keep things light."

That made everyone laugh.

Everyone except Charlie. He was staring out the window at the dark sky. She didn't know much about his family. How had he grown up? Rebecca implied he hadn't had the best childhood but she'd never said much more than that. The older woman had loved Charlie, that much she knew for sure.

The rain was still pounding the roof but no one seemed to care. Astrid wasn't sure what was making her happier: how much Halley and Nova were enjoying themselves or how relaxed Charlie appeared to be. The game wrapped up almost an hour later.

"We won, we won." Nova was ecstatic. "I've never won Monopoly before, Astrid."

A clap of thunder startled the room into silence.

The pitter-patter of rain went back to a heavy downpour, earning an "Oh, dear" from Aunt Camellia. "I'd best go check the attic. Make sure that patch is holding and there's no leak."

"I'll go." Astrid hopped up.

Aunt Camellia's last doctor's appointment had revealed high blood pressure—alarming the entire family. While she and Van took long walks each and every day, Astrid didn't like the idea of her aunt tripping over one of the trunks or boxes filling the space in order to patch the roof.

"If it is leaking, it's not a one-person job." Aunt Magnolia spoke up. "Charles, why don't you lend a hand?" She didn't look up from her book this time.

Dane's chuckle was cut short when Tansy smacked him on the arm.

"Oh, I can do it." Astrid was beyond mortified. Not only was her family trying to set her up, they weren't even bothering to be subtle about it.

"I don't mind." Charlie stood, seemingly unaware of the not-so-subtle maneuvering happening around them. Instead, he listened as Aunt Mags led him to one of the many cabinets.

"You'll need duct tape. A bucket. Oh, good, we have tar paper." Aunt Magnolia dropped each item into the bucket she'd given Charlie.

What are you up to? Astrid mouthed at her sister.

Tansy had the gall to shrug. Dane, however, laughed and kept laughing even after Tansy smacked his shoulder again.

"You help me put away the Monopoly, Nova." Halley

took her sister's hand. "And when that's done, if Charlie says it's okay, Benji is going to play a movie for us."

"Not a scary movie?" Nova glanced at Halley.

"Nope." She shook her head. "Not scary."

"Okay." Nova shrugged. "Can we watch a movie, Charlie?"

He nodded. "As long as it's age appropriate."

"It's a cartoon movie about superhero pets." Benji waited.

Nova's sharp inhalation was followed by her whole body tensing up and then bouncing on the balls of her feet. "Superhero pets?" she squeaked.

"Fine." The corner of Charlie's mouth quirking up as Nova sped from the room.

"Guess I'll put the game away." Halley smiled her thanks as Kerrielynn helped out.

Astrid couldn't be sure but she thought she saw Halley and Aunt Camellia exchange a wink as the girls, Leif and Benji headed for the family room. Was everyone in on this? Did Charlie really not pick up on what was happening? Her cheeks were on fire.

"Everyone is settled?" Aunt Camellia took in the mostly empty kitchen and tied on her apron. "I'll start dinner. I'm not sure Van will make it, with the storm and all, but it looks like we'll have a full house, regardless."

"Your favorite kind." Aunt Mags stood and joined her, sliding an apron on and coming to her sister's side. "What can I do?"

Astrid was very aware of Charlie at her shoulder. "Okay, then." She didn't look at him; she couldn't. Tansy was watching her like a hawk. "Let's go."

Charlie followed her back up the stairs to the second floor and down the hall, past her bedroom, to the end of the hallway. The farther away from the kitchen and the family room and everyone else in the house, the harder it was not to turn around and throw herself at Charlie. "Attic." She opened the door that led to the attic stairs.

"I can probably do this on my own." He flipped a switch on the wall and the attic light turned on.

"I don't think that's what Aunt Magnolia had in mind," she murmured. Or the rest of her family, for that matter. "It's a big space. I'll show you." But the truth was she didn't need her sister or aunts or anyone maneuvering for her. She was exactly where she wanted to be. She wasn't going to walk away from some alone time with Charlie—even if it was in a dark, dusty, cobweb-laden, musty-smelling attic.

SINCE HE'D FIRST pulled Astrid into his arms, Charlie had been in a constant state of flux. Part of him had never been happier. The other part was lost and terrified. Today had triggered something troubling—something beyond his control. If she was close, he had to touch her. Had to. At the table, if his arm wasn't against hers, his knee was. If they weren't touching, he was looking at her. The slightest contact and he was fine. Without it, he felt off-balance. He didn't know how to undo it. He'd agreed to come help purely for the opportunity to kiss Astrid again. It was all too much, too fast.

"So." Even with the space between them, the pull was magnetic. He ran a hand over his face. "Where is the patch in the roof?" He made the mistake of glancing her way. "Astrid?" If she kept looking at him like that, his self-control would go out the window.

She blinked, visibly shook herself and walked around him. "Back here."

Instead of staring at her back and watching the way the skirt of her pale blue dress swayed when she walked, he forced his attention to his surroundings. Old steamer trunks, suitcases and aged brown boxes lined the walls and created mazelike partitions throughout the space. There were overflowing bookshelves, a mannequin, several metal racks packed full with plastic-covered clothing, and a coat tree with a dozen or more hats. "What is all this?"

"Bits and pieces of my family's history. After we lost our parents, my sisters and I came to live here with the aunts and my grandparents. This was one of our favorite places to play. Most of the time. Once, the mannequin fell over on Rosemary and she screamed so loud Poppa Tom said he'd leaped over the kitchen table to get here. He had a Santa belly, so the imagery had Rosemary laughing away her fears. We put a quilt over the mannequin until she forgot about it. Let's be honest, mannequins can be scary." Astrid smiled back at him.

He glanced at the faceless figure and nodded. Nova would probably have a similar reaction.

"Sometimes Aunt Mags would come up with us. She liked to organize little plays or fashion shows." Astrid ran her hand along the top of a scarred chest of drawers.

"What about her daughter, Shelby?" There was no denying Shelby was Magnolia's daughter. From the deep red hair to the probing nature of their dark green gaze, they were both slightly intimidating.

"Oh, Shelby wasn't here." Astrid tucked a strand of hair behind her ear, her face shadowing. "We didn't know Shelby existed until a few months ago. Mags was very young when she had Shelby so she gave her baby up for adoption—hoping she'd have two loving parents and a family that could better care for her."

"I didn't know. You all seem at ease with one another." Aunt Rebecca was the only person he'd ever been that close to. But he'd been a child then. As an adult, his letters took the place of his visits.

"Dane said the Hills make you part of the family, whether you like it or not." Astrid smiled. "I guess that's true. Mags says the family of our heart will always find us. I guess that's true, too."

He had a hard time picturing Magnolia Hill saying such a flowery, sentimental statement. But, then again, he couldn't picture her playing up here with her nieces. He had no problem imagining little Astrid and little Tansy donning hats and spinning in front of the large mirror propped against the far wall. He could imagine Nova and Halley doing the same.

"On bad weather days, we'd spend hours playing dress-up." Astrid patted one of the chests. "Clothing and gloves, fascinators and jewelry. Every little girl wants a dress-up box. We had that, plus some."

"Bad weather only?" It was such an odd thing to say that he needed clarification.

"If the weather was good, we were outside." Astrid squeezed between an antique wardrobe and a grandfather clock. "With the bees."

"With the bees." He shook his head. "Even when you were little?" He couldn't forget what her precious bees were capable of.

"Our bees are gentle. Sadly, you've yet to see that, but it's true." She dusted her hands off on one another. "Poppa Tom had zero tolerance for a hot hive."

"Am I supposed to know what that means?" Beekeeping was a whole other world. But if Astrid loved it, there had to be some good in it.

She smiled at him. "No. It just means bad-tempered."

"Are the Hill bees sent to some sort of etiquette school?" He was terrible at jokes so it was a surprise to hear her laugh.

"No." She was still laughing. "You're funny."

"I'm really not." Her laughter caused a series of physical reactions. Palms sweaty, throat tight, the urgent need to put his hands on her. He flexed his hands and shoved them into his pockets.

"That was funny," she argued. "Etiquette school." She shook her head. "No, you requeen a hive with a docile, laying queen and she'll take care of the rest."

He was too busy trying to breathe and get a hold of himself to keep the conversation going.

The thunder sounded especially loud in the cavernous space. Through the dormer windows in the wall, the flicker of lightning cast long shadows across the wooden floor. It was the sudden surge in rain that reminded him why they were there. He looked up, scanning the ceiling for any spots or discoloration.

"It was really bad over here—the repair is on Aunt Mags to-do list." Astrid climbed over an especially large trunk and stopped. "No sign of water." She pushed her hair from her shoulders and nodded. "Thankfully."

Astrid's hair fascinated him. The way the light revealed different shades of red, gold and copper. It moved with an almost fluid grace.

"I guess we're done up here. Unless you want to dress up?" She was smiling until her eyes met his. Then she froze. She swallowed and drew in a deep, unsteady breath.

"I overheard you and you sister." The words came out far gruffer than he'd intended. "Earlier. Talking about kissing frogs."

Her cheeks went scarlet.

"I…" He hadn't meant to say a thing but, somehow, words were still coming. "You might have plenty of frogs in your past but I…I don't." These weren't good words. "I don't."

"No. I don't have a lot of frogs in my past, Charlie." Astrid swallowed again.

"I mean, none." He forced the words out and braced himself. He was a grown man. Grown men didn't choose to be celibate. But, for him, the alternative held no appeal.

Astrid blinked. "Kissing?"

"Like today?" He shook his head. "I don't know what the hell this is. I don't know what I'm supposed to do. And, to be frank, I'm not sure this is a good idea."

Astrid drew in an unsteady breath.

He waited, hoping she'd argue or say something that would prevent all his locked-up childhood insecurities and self-loathing from getting out. Anything.

"I understand." She hugged herself.

"No, you don't." He ran his fingers through his hair and started pacing.

"I want to understand." Her words were a whisper.

He stared at her. How could he explain? Did he want to? "You grew up with all this. Your aunts, your grandparents—they supported you? Accepted you?"

She nodded. "Of course."

"That's not always the case." It was hard to go on. "I grew up knowing I was *different*." He used air quotes and added, "Special." He'd learned to hate that word.

"My family made sure of that." He cleared his throat. "I don't like groups of people. Or new people. Words… I'd rather not talk. Which translates into being rude or inconsiderate or stupid. I can't…" He broke off.

He didn't realize Astrid had moved until her hand rested on his arm.

"Eye contact." He shook his head. "Emotions. Feelings. Touch." He kept on shaking his head but took her hand. "This isn't normal for me." He stared at their hands. "But you… I want to touch you." And it scared the shit out of him. He glanced her way, hating that he'd revealed so much. He'd laid himself bare and now she could laugh at him or rip him to shreds.

"I'm so sorry, Charlie." Her hand squeezed his. "I'm sorry no one stood up for you."

He wasn't looking for pity. "Eventually, I stood up for myself." He cleared his throat. "Now I don't need anyone's approval. I don't want it. It's better that way. No one to—"

"Hurt you?" She sounded so sad.

He'd made her sad. *Dammit*. "No. Get in the way."

"Am I getting in the way?"

"Yes." He gripped her hand when she went to pull away. "No." He turned to face her. "I don't know, Astrid." What the hell was he trying to accomplish?

She was silent for a long time before she asked, "Why do you want to touch *me*, Charlie?"

His throat was too tight to answer, so he shook his head.

Her eyes were searching for something.

"You…you make me feel. Alive." The words were out, hanging between them, and all he could do was hold his breath and wait for her response.

"That's bad?" She didn't move.

He nodded. "No."

Her smile lit her up from the inside and spilled out into the room. Light and warm and all-encompassing.

He'd stand here for hours to watch her smile. It was so powerful it held all his worry and disbelief at bay. He knew this would never work. He accepted he'd be left more broken than ever when it was over. But he wasn't strong enough to resist her. Hell, he didn't want to. Whatever this was, he wanted it. He wanted her.

She squeezed his hand.

"What do you want? You're going to have to tell me or show me, Astrid. If you don't, I will screw up." He took one step, then another, stopping when her hands rested against his chest and she was staring up at him.

"You won't, Charlie." She stood on tiptoe. "But I'll show you." Her lips met his.

He caught her against him, his mouth hungry for her. Warm. Astrid was warm. Everything about her. Her lips. Her mouth. He wanted to drown in her warmth. He was free to run his fingers through her hair. It was silky soft, thick and heavy, slipping between his fingers like water. The more he kissed her, the more he wanted. How could something be fragile, yet so potent?

She clung to him, trembling, as his mouth trailed along the arch of her neck. The taste of her was intoxicating. Not just her mouth, but her skin. Her temple and cheek, chin and neck, and the hollow at the juncture of her collarbone. Astrid saturated each and every one of his senses.

But laughter from downstairs had them stepping apart.

"Shall we?" Astrid asked, steering them back to the stairs once he'd nodded.

He wasn't ready to have to explain this to Halley or Nova. Whatever *this* was. So much had changed and, at the same time, nothing had. After they'd been through so much, he didn't want to confuse things. And the facts remained the same.

He would dispose of Rebecca's property—to Lindsay. Or not.

He and the girls would go back to Fort Worth.

That was the plan. It was a good plan. Logical. So why did his stomach feel hollow and cold?

CHAPTER TWELVE

THE SUN WAS just rising over the horizon when the Honey Hill Farms van pulled down Rebecca Wallace's drive. Astrid glanced at the front porch as they passed. It was too early for anyone to be up. And besides, today was a big day for Kerrielynn and Benji—she needed to be present for it and not daydreaming about Charlie, his kisses or how delectable his touch was. Of course, reminding herself not to think about Charlie's kisses and touches had the exact opposite effect.

They took the dirt tractor path that hugged the fence line, parking when they were within walking distance of the hives they'd be working with. She climbed out of the van, closed the passenger door and waited for Tansy to unlock the back of the van.

Kerrielynn's truck parked behind them and a good portion of the Junior Beekeepers climbed out.

"Are you two ready?" Astrid asked Kerrielynn and Benji, both suiting up in the beekeeper suits.

"Can't wait." Kerrielynn's always sunny personality was in full force. "I'm so ready to take that test."

"She is. It's all she can talk about." Leif nudged her. "We all know she's going to do great."

Astrid remembered taking her Master Craftsman Beekeeper test. She'd been a little younger than Kerrielynn but confident and determined. Sitting down at that desk, amidst several older and—she thought—wiser individuals had been daunting. The test packet itself even more so. But once she'd opened the first page and shoved aside her anxiety, she'd sailed through with flying colors. She'd known she was a good beekeeper, but the test told the rest of the world she was. And she'd been so proud.

"Yep." Benji tucked his gloves into his pocket and checked his tools. "I think I've got everything."

"We've got extras of…everything, just in case. You're both going to do a great job." Astrid scanned her clipboard.

"You've done that at least ten times already, you know that, right?" Tansy leaned into the back of the van and pulled a paper bag full of burlap scraps closer. "You all right? You seem a little distracted."

"I'm good." She was more than good. She was excited. Today there was the possibility she'd catch a moment or two alone with Charlie. It had been two days since she'd kissed him. Two whole days since the rainstorm. She'd seen him several times. He'd had no luck getting the air conditioner fixed so he'd brought the girls over in the mornings and come back for dinner, forced to work through some sort of firewall breach through most of the weekend. Not once had they stolen a single moment alone together.

She hadn't thought it was possible to miss something that was so new. But she did. A little more every day. And no matter how hard it might be, she would not launch herself at him.

"Benji." Tansy handed him an empty smoker. "Can you get this going?"

"Will do." In order to take the test for the first level of his beekeeping certification, Benji had to complete a series of hands-on tasks under the supervision of a Master Beekeeper.

"Kerrielynn." Astrid handed her the other smoker.

"Got it." Kerrielynn was one level shy of testing for her Master Beekeeper certification. It was quite a fete for someone going into the senior year of high school but she'd helping out at Honey Hill Farms since before she was Halley's age. Tansy liked that she was a quick learner. Astrid liked that she was gentle and patient with the bees. Like Benji, everything she did here today would count toward the hours needed to take the written test.

"I'm going to go ahead and clear out the area." Astrid started pulling supplies together.

"Need help?" Leif offered.

"No." Tansy shook her head. "She likes to have a few minutes alone with the bees. I let her, too. Things seem to go better that way."

"Got it." Leif held up his hands.

Astrid was smiling as she took the loppers off one of the hooks installed in the van. Since it was possible they'd wind up splitting a hive, they'd need room to work. A wayward branch or a clump of cactus could make the job more challenging than it needed to be. She added the loppers and a shovel to her red wagon.

"Okay." Tansy waved. "We'll be along after I check off their suits."

Astrid pulled the red wagon through a clump of cedar and found the path to the first hive. "You look like you've recovered well." She walked around the hive boxes she and Tansy had used to rehome the bees after they'd been toppled. Bees were resilient so she wasn't too worried about them but it might be a good idea to take a look inside. After nearly twenty-four hours of solid rain, it couldn't hurt. "I'll come back."

She continued down the path. Even though it had only been two days since the monsoon-like storm, the ground had been so dry most of the moisture had already soaked in. Which was good. Heat and mud weren't exactly ideal working conditions.

She paused long enough to inspect the small pond Rebecca had installed as a water source for the bees. It had overflowed, spilling several corks onto the ground. She scooped them up and put them back into the pond, bobbing on the surface like mini-islands. They were the perfect landing spot for a thirsty bee—and essential since bees couldn't swim.

On the other side of a slight hill, were four hives that were each three boxes deep. Rebecca had taken Astrid's advice and built frames to hold her hives off the ground. The frames lifted them just enough to make working the hives back-pain free. It also helped thwart the invasion of pests like the small hive beetle.

She left her wagon in the shade of an old Spanish oak and walked around the small beeyard. It was early yet so the sunlight was soft and gentle but, far as the bees were concerned, it was time to work. "Hello." All four of the hives buzzed. "Already working hard and getting things done?" She watched as bees flitted through the small exit and set off for pollen.

"It's just me, for now." She rested a hand on the top of the first hive. "I've got some friends with me today so I figured I'd give you a heads-up." She moved on to the second one, brushing debris off the top and checking the seams between boxes for signs of water damage.

"I know things are getting a little crowded in there

so we brought you room to grow. Now that we've had so much rain, everything should perk right up and give you plenty to harvest before winter."

She scanned the space around the hives. "I'm going to do a little gardening." Armed with the shovel, she dug up two clumps of prickly pear cactus and deposited them in an empty five-gallon bucket. "I'll take those with me. A few cacti are fine, but let's not turn this into a cactus field. Don't you think?" She scanned the ground for any remnants. One cactus pad on the ground could turn into a sizable plant in no time. Satisfied, she returned the shovel to the wagon.

One of the cedars had grown so big, branches rested on top of the last hive. "That won't do." She used the loppers to trim the shrub back.

She collected the branches, pulled off the smaller shoots and leaves and put them into the wagon. "I'm going to ask you to be extra gentle with Benji, too." She'd add the branches to the pond, too. More floats for the bees. "This is his first time to do this solo. He's a good boy and he'll be an excellent beekeeper."

"They don't talk back, do they?" Charlie sounded amused.

Charlie. "No." Astrid turned. He was here. And her smile was so big her face hurt. "But Poppa Tom taught me to talk to them, so I do. I don't know if it was to soothe the bees' nerves or mine, but it's a habit now."

"A bee pep talk?"

"Sort of." He was so handsome. "How long have you been standing there?"

He shrugged.

Not handsome. *Gorgeous.* Even more so because he was wearing a bee suit. Her heart sped up. *Goodness.*

Like her, the hood of his suit was open and back so she could study his warm brown eyes for as long as she liked. "You look especially handsome."

He cocked an eyebrow. "We match."

"We do." She couldn't stop smiling.

"You weren't with your aunts when they came to get the girls this morning." He kicked at a rock.

"It was so early. And I needed to help Tansy get everything ready for today." She took a step toward him. "*And* I wasn't sure I could behave myself," she confessed, closing the distance between them. "I didn't want to tackle you in front of the girls. Or the Junior Beekeepers." Her arms twined around his neck.

His arms were tight about her waist. "I wouldn't have minded."

Which was what she'd hoped he'd say. But, to clarify, she asked, "The not behaving part or the tackling part?"

He pretended to think about it. "Either."

"Oh, good. I'll remember that." She stood on tiptoe. "Should I tackle you now?"

"Mmm." His kiss was packed with all the urgency she felt.

"I've never kissed anyone in my bee suit before," she whispered against his mouth.

"Me, neither." He smiled, she could feel it.

"See, you are funny." She leaned back so she could see his smile. "I like your smile, Charlie."

He shook his head, his cheeks going an adorable shade of pink. "What are these Junior Beekeepers doing today? Besides bee fighting."

"Beekeeping." She patted his chest.

"So far, Nova's description fits." He smoothed her

hair back, twining one long strand between and around his fingers.

"I guess that means I'll have to show you, then." She stepped out of his arms and marched over to the closest beehive. "In Texas, becoming a beekeeper is a lengthy process. Which is good. A person should have a real understanding of the importance of this work. Today, Benji is working toward his first-level beekeeping test. Kerrielynn is ready to take the test for the Master Bee-keeper's exam."

"You and Tansy are Master Beekeepers?"

She nodded. "I'm a Master Craftsman Beekeeper. So is Rosemary, my other sister. But Tansy and both of my aunts are Master Beekeepers." She shrugged. "It makes sense, being a family business and all." She gave him a head-to-toe once-over. She really couldn't get over it. Charlie, in a beekeeper suit. That fit. Which meant it wasn't the one she'd left for him. "Where did you get that suit? It fits you."

"Magnolia brought it this morning. She thought I'd help out today." He shook his head. "That got the girls excited. Halley expects me to record everything so she and Nova can watch later." He surveyed the suit. "I think I did it right? There are a lot of zippers."

She'd never thought of a beekeeping suit as an espe-cially attractive look, but Charlie made it almost sexy. "I'll double-check all your zippers," she murmured, her attention wandering to his mouth. Sexy and kissable.

He cleared his throat, pulling her gaze upward. His face was red and he stared at her long enough for her to realize that what she'd said sounded rather suggestive. That, with the way she'd been devouring him with her eyes, had him obviously rattled.

"Your bee suit. I mean." She was a little rattled herself. With Charlie, it didn't take much. "Where were we?"

He ran a hand over his face. "Bees. Testing."

"There are four levels in Texas. An Apprentice Beekeeper. An Advanced Beekeeper. Master Beekeeper. And Master Craftsman Beekeeper. You have to advance from level to level—no skipping ahead. Each test gauges your knowledge *and* skill set. Only Kerrielynn and Benji are testing, but the others can observe and help and count these hours toward their eligibility."

"What sort of things are on the test?" Charlie circled the hive, wary of the bees flying back and forth.

"It starts with knowing the parts of a hive—"

"Which are?" He stepped closer to the hive.

He was curious. She could see the concentration on his face. And his curiosity had her bursting with excitement. "This is a Langstroth hive. It's the most common because it's easy to work. It comes apart." She pointed at the seams between the hive boxes. "You can add boxes or take them away."

"These sections or boxes make up the hive as a whole?" He waited for her to nod. "Why are there different size boxes?"

"Each serves a different purpose." She moved from hive to hive, pointing out the three different depths. "Honey supers are the smaller ones. The medium size boxes are called a honey super, too, sometimes. We use something called a 'queen excluder' to keep the queen in the larger, lower box to lay all the eggs there. The rest of the boxes will be all honey."

Charlie nodded, taking it all in.

"The larger bottom boxes are normally the brood box.

It's where all the baby bees are fed and groomed until they're ready to work." She didn't want to overwhelm him with information, but he kept asking questions so she kept answering.

By the time Tansy arrived with the Junior Beekeepers, she'd given him a rundown on the internal parts of a hive and the jobs and life cycles of the bees.

"Hey, Charlie." Tansy waved. "Fancy seeing you here."

"Everyone, this is Charles Driver. He's been kind enough to have us here for our project. When we're done, I'd like there to be no trace that we've been here." Astrid waited for them all to nod. "Charlie, you've met Benji, Kerrielynn and Leif. This is Grace, Felix, Crissy and Oren."

Charlie nodded.

"We're all taped up and ready to go." Tansy gave Astrid a thumbs-up. "Kerrielynn, how about you go first."

"Okay." Kerrielynn approached the hive and clicked the smoker, releasing a cloud of white-gray smoke.

"What's that?" Charlie asked.

Astrid grabbed the tape from Tansy's pocket and walked to Charlie's side. "It's a smoker. The smoke interrupts the bees' alarm signals and helps keep them calm." She held up the roll of tape. "Extra security."

He glanced at the young beekeepers, then Tansy. "You don't have any," he whispered so as not to interrupt Kerrielynn's running dialogue.

"I'm the bee whisperer." She winked.

He shook his head but stood still while she circled him, securing the multitude of zippers and adding a strip of tape over any potential spots the bees could sneak in. Not that Astrid was worried. She knew these bees well.

They'd been requeened until all four of the hives were sweet-tempered and high-yield honey producers.

She pulled Charlie's hood forward and zipped it shut. Even with the mesh, he was frowning.

"Stop frowning, watch and listen," she whispered. "Kerrielynn has to explain as she goes, it's required. She'll probably answer most of your questions."

"I will, once your hood is on." He sighed. "Bee whisperer or not, you did get stung."

Astrid was smiling as she pulled her hood up and zipped it closed. For all his frowning and snipped tone, he wasn't angry. She was beginning to figure Charlie Driver out. It was a slow process but, the more she knew, the more it made sense. Words weren't his thing. Actions were. He was worried about her. And, if he worried about her, it could only mean one thing. One big, wonderful thing that filled Astrid with excitement and hope. Charlie Driver, this big, broken, gentle and uncertain beautiful man, might care about her.

As soon as Kerrielynn had the hive lid open, the sound of buzzing increased exponentially. Charlie waited for a cloud of angry bees to rise and attack. He grabbed the back of Astrid's suit so he could pull her along with him, just in case.

But the bees stayed calm, flitting around the hive and going about their business.

He watched as Kerrielynn moved slowly, her voice steady and even as she continued to narrate her process.

"Slow and precise movements help," Astrid whispered. "Tone of voice, too. Like any living creature, bees will pick up on stress and respond to it."

"I remember." That was why he was here, ready to whisk her away—whether she liked it or not.

By the time Kerrielynn and Benji had finished, Charlie was impressed by both young people. He might not be able to understand the motivation but he could appreciate their focus and ability.

It was when Astrid took over that Charlie began to see beekeeping differently. Astrid was graceful in everything she did. That included working with bees. Her movements were fluid and slow. Her voice was coaxing and affectionate. More than that, she was wholly engrossed in what she was doing.

The more he watched and listened, the more interesting beekeeping became.

If his damn phone hadn't vibrated, he would have forgotten it was a Monday. Work existed. Always. They wouldn't care he'd worked through the weekend to prevent a major breach. That was done. There was more work to be done today. And, if he wanted to stay employed, he'd do well to remember that.

He pulled his phone from his pocket. Not work. *Lindsay.* His stomach twisted.

Arriving Thursday night to explore the town. Don't worry, we won't bother you. I didn't want to run into one another and trigger one of your episodes.

Charlie read and reread the message. *One of your episodes.* He hadn't seen Lindsay in years—intentionally.

His phone started ringing then, startling him so that he almost dropped it. "Sorry." He froze, hoping the phone wouldn't send the bees on a rampage. He glanced at Astrid, whose smile was barely detectable through the layers of mesh covering her face, and took a deep breath. She was fine. She'd been doing this for years.

But Yasmina had been a cyclist for years.

The cold, hard truth of that turned his stomach to lead. He stared at Astrid, still happily working. He couldn't leave. He couldn't. He silenced his phone and shoved it into his pocket.

Whoever was calling was insistent. The damn phone kept vibrating and vibrating. It could be the girls. It could be work. *Dammit*. He took several steps away from the beeyard—Astrid called it an apiary—and pulled his phone out and pressed it against his ear. He turned back to ensure he could still see her. "Hello?"

"Mr. Driver? This is Calvin Walsh from Walsh Brothers Air-Conditioning." His voice was muffled by the bee suit's hood, but Charlie could still understand well enough. "We had a cancelation today so we can come check out your unit in, oh, about ten minutes?" The man waited.

Ten minutes. He glanced at Astrid. She was waving all the Junior Beekeepers closer so they could see something on the frame she was holding. There was a whole other hive to inspect. That would take longer than ten minutes.

"Mr. Driver?" Calvin Walsh was waiting for his answer.

"Yes." He knew he was overreacting. Astrid was an adult and more than capable of doing her job. She'd been doing it for years before he'd arrived and she'd be doing it for years long after he left. He swallowed. Where the hell had that come from? And why the hell did it feel like he'd been kicked in the gut? Leaving hadn't been something he'd contemplated much the last few days but…

It had only been days. Days. That was all. Nothing had changed. Not really. "That sounds good."

"See you then." The phone went dead.

First, Lindsay's comment. Then, Astrid's safety. Now this arbitrary reminder that they were leaving. Not leaving. Going home—where they belonged. Back to their real lives. Where life was scheduled and organized and familiar...

Where Astrid didn't exist.

Hot tension bubbled up. Calming breaths. Deep and even.

The burning pressure expanded slowly, pushing up and out against his ribs and compressing his stomach.

He kept breathing but it was more gasping now. Ever so slowly, the world was shrinking, closing in on him. *Dammit.* He looked overhead, at the wide-open sky. It didn't help.

Sweat beaded along his upper lip and trickled down his back. His pulse was accelerating. Soon he'd be shaking. No, dammit, he'd get it together. Walk it off. But, just in case, he didn't want to be here if that happened.

He turned on his heel and headed down the path back to the house. The tape over the hood sticker wouldn't give. He tried once, then again, but his fingers were so slick with sweat he couldn't get a grip on the fabric. He wiped his hands on the front of his suit but the multilayers of flexible fabric were coarse and abrasive against his fingers. There was tape over all the zippers. Keeping him safe—keeping him trapped.

Suddenly, the suit was sweltering. His skin was raw and itchy. He tried to steady his breathing, but the rising panic gripped him by the throat and made it damn near impossible.

When the house came into view, he zeroed in on it and only it. He was so close. Each step was weighted and the ground shifted but he'd get there. He had to get there.

The porch railing helped him pull himself up the steps. He braced a hand against the wall until he'd reached the door. Inside, the house was like an oven. He forced the dining room door wide and stumbled inside, gasping for breath.

Even with the cool darkness of the room, Charlie was baking.

He sat on the edge of the table, shaking, and gripped its edge with both hands. *Breathe, dammit.* Tears stung his eyes. *Get it together.* He pressed his eyes shut. *Get it together.*

"Charlie?" Astrid's voice. Astrid's hands on his shoulders. "Are you okay? Was it a bad phone call?"

Speaking wasn't an option. Hell, if he let go of the table, he'd fall to the floor. She couldn't see that. She shouldn't see *any* of this.

"Did you get overheated?" Astrid tugged the tape loose, unzipped the hood and pushed it back.

Cool air flooded his lungs and soothed his scorched skin but he still couldn't say a word.

"You're soaking." Astrid was fanning him.

He couldn't open his eyes—couldn't look at her. He couldn't bear to see her realize the truth. If she knew what was happening, what he fought against, she'd see him for who he was. Broken. Emotionally damaged. Unworthy.

"Charlie?" Her fingers smoothed through his sweat-soaked hair. "Is everything okay?"

He resisted leaning into the hand she pressed to his cheek. Instead, he pulled her between his legs and against him. If she couldn't see him, maybe he could hide the truth from her for a little bit longer. He buried his face against her chest and breathed her in. Deep, strong breaths that fed his starving lungs with her scent. Comfort. Safety. His hold tightened, until there was nothing separating them.

He felt her stiffen in his hold and braced himself.

"Charlie," she whispered, cradling his head against her. With a sigh, she relaxed. The rapid beat of her heart echoed beneath his ear. Over and over, she smoothed his hair with slow, even strokes.

He hated the need that shook him. Hated that her touch soothed him.

A real man kept his shit together. He deals—without making an ass out of himself. A real man isn't weak. That had been his father's response after he'd witnessed one of Charlie's panic attacks. He'd been packed off for military school the next week.

He had learned to deal, for the most part. Panic attacks like this were a rarity. But they were a part of who he was. He'd seen enough doctors and therapists to know there was no cure. Managing was the best he could do.

"I think Kerrielynn did a great job today. I think, once she graduates from college, she'll be an asset to Texas Viking Honey. That's Dane's family's honey farm. If, of course, she and Leif are still together." She kept up the same steady, reassuring touch. "I'd like to think they'll make it. I know they're young but I don't think that matters when it comes to love. Real love, anyway."

He should tell her love didn't exist.

"Poor Leif went through some dark times—and not all that long ago, either. But Kerrielynn has helped with that. With her, he seems more confident. And happy."

She paused. "Before I forget, I set aside some fresh honeycomb for you and the girls. It's a treat. I think that's why Aunt Camellia's cooking is so delicious. She uses honey in everything. And I mean *everything*."

He realized he'd stopped shaking.

"That's a Hill family thing, though. We have a book full of generations' worth of recipes and anecdotes. Aunt Camellia and Aunt Magnolia keep it up now, though Tansy and I have added a note or two. Shelby, too, now that she's here." She paused again a bit.

"Are you okay?" She hugged him. "That's the only question I'll ask. I promise."

He shook his head again. He'd acted like this and she wasn't expecting an explanation? He had never met anyone like Astrid. *Because there is no one else like Astrid.* "I will be."

"Okay." She went back to stroking his hair. "You have lovely hair, Charlie. It's so thick. Nicole said she wanted to cut it a little, but I like it just like it is. Besides, if you let Nicole cut it, you might end up with a pink or blue stripe. Nicole doesn't shy away from making bold statements with her hair. But, as she likes to point out, it's just hair." She laughed. "Nova did ask how she could get a stripe in her hair."

"Oh?" Slowly, he eased his hold on her.

"I told her there were clips with all sorts of different colors of hair attached and that would be best so she could change it out herself. She seemed content with that."

"Thank you." His arms relaxed a bit more. "She adores you."

"And I adore her. What's this rat monster she's talking about, Charlie? She's really scared about it. Halley said it was just a nightmare but Nova swears it's not."

"She didn't dream about it before we got here." With a deep breath, he sat up. He took another deep breath and managed to meet Astrid's gaze. "But she hasn't had an easy time sleeping since Yasmina's death."

"That's understandable." Her smile was gentle. And beautiful. As always. Her hair was a tangle of braids and her bee suit was streaked with who-knows-what, but her eyes were full of life. When she looked at him, he wanted to see the world through those eyes.

"You're beautiful, Astrid." His voice was husky. "You're a beautiful person." He reached up to cradle her face between his hands.

"Are you going to kiss me?" she whispered. "I've been wanting to kiss you for two days so I really hope you're going to kiss me."

He'd just had a panic attack and now she was making him smile? "You could always kiss me—"

"Okay." Her mouth brushed his, light as a feather. Then again, firmer and longer. Her breath wavered and, finally, her lips sealed with his.

He wanted to get lost in her. Wanted to feel… And, with Astrid, there was no shortage of feeling. He smiled at the sound of tape ripping free and opened his eyes to find her unzipping her suit.

"It's hot." She shoved the suit around her waist. The black fabric of the tank top she wore was painted on her, one of the straps hanging off her bare shoulder.

He stared at her shoulder. Then the strap. Then her shoulder. Slowly, he rested his hand there and ran his thumb along the ridge of her collarbone. Her skin, like the rest of her, was soft and warm. She shivered, the slight hitch of her breath drawing his eyes back to hers.

The doorbell rang.

"Was that a doorbell?" He frowned. "I didn't know this house had a doorbell."

Astrid laughed. "That's because the only visitor you have is rude and makes herself at home." She stepped back, twisting her hair into a knot at the back of her head.

Why had he ever resisted her visits? He didn't know then what he knew now. Astrid was... What? He swallowed. What was she to him?

"Are you expecting someone?" She pulled the strap onto her shoulder but it slid back down.

He shook his head, far too distracted by that damn strap and her shoulder. He wasn't done exploring. Then he remembered. "Yes." He stood. "Walsh Brothers Air-Conditioning."

"That's fantastic." She pulled her suit back up but left the zipper open. "I'll leave you to it. Tansy's probably wondering where I am, anyway." She paused. "Or, I can stay?"

She didn't outright say it, but she was asking if he needed her to stay. As tempting as it was to say yes, he shook his head. "Go, see your bees." But he stopped her when she reached the front door. "Astrid."

She turned and waited, her gaze searching his.

He cleared his throat, words rushing up to stick and clog his windpipe. He only managed to say, "I'm sorry, for earlier. And thank you."

"I don't know why you're apologizing or what I did but... I'm here, Charlie." Her smile was radiant. And, with a little wave, she opened the door for the Walsh brothers and let herself out.

Once the Walsh brothers were pulling apart the air-conditioning unit, Charlie went upstairs to take an ice-cold shower. The panic attack was over but his brain was still recovering. There were a few things he was going to have to deal with. One, his sister was coming. Other than the reading of the will, there was no need for them to interact. He'd make sure they didn't. Two, was going back to their old life what he wanted—or was he second-guessing things because of Astrid? When and why had she become relevant to his decision-making process?

It had taken him years to learn how to navigate life alone. He'd been good at it. Now he had Halley and Nova and he was struggling. But they were his, nonnegotiable. Did he really want to bring anyone else into their lives? Could he relinquish what little control he had left? That's what would happen if he let Astrid in. Chaos. She was the opposite of control. She was… She… He closed his eyes. She'd been there to steady him when he'd been free-falling. Her heartbeat. Her touch. Her scent. Letting her in worried him. But, letting her go? That was truly terrifying.

CHAPTER THIRTEEN

ASTRID WHISKED THE melted chocolate into the butter and sugar but her mind was elsewhere. She'd replayed the morning over and over, looking for something that might explain what had happened. Charlie. Her chest hurt. Finding him in the dining room—gasping for breath, shaking and clinging to the table—she had panicked. Her first thought was he'd been stung and was having an allergic reaction. But once the suit hood was off and she could see his beautiful face, she knew it was something else. There'd been no trace of the controlled and emotionless mask Charlie wore so often. There'd been anguish. Bone-deep and all-encompassing. It had ripped her heart wide-open.

Even hours later, she could still feel the desperation of his touch. He'd held her against him with such ferocity she'd been stunned into silence. What did he need? What could she do?

He'd admitted he liked her touch, so slow, soothing caresses made sense. The inane chatter was to distract him from whatever internal torment he was battling. She had no idea what she'd said—that part wasn't important. What mattered was that, in time, his shaking stopped and his desperation eased.

"Don't forget the eggs." Aunt Camellia placed a hand on her arm.

Astrid smiled her thanks. She whisked in the eggs and flour and poured the batter into a greased sheet cake pan, her mind returning to Charlie. He'd seemed himself when she'd left but she couldn't entirely shake off her concern. Dinner was soon and he'd be here. And since Halley had mentioned he liked brownies, there would be homemade brownies waiting for him.

"I'll wash up." Camellia took the whisk and bowl.

"I'll prewash that spoon." Nicole reached for the wooden spoon covered in brownie batter.

"There are uncooked eggs in that, Nicole." Aunt Camellia shook her head as Nicole took a big lick. "Don't blame me if you get a stomachache."

"I won't." She smiled. "But, yum, it'll be worth it."

"What is it?" Nova's question had them all glancing across the kitchen. For the last hour, Nova and Ginger, Nicole's six-year-old cousin, had been quietly coloring in one of Nova's dinosaur coloring books. Now Van Kettner lowered himself onto the kitchen floor between the girls—a box in his hands. "We got this in our shipment today and I thought you might have some fun with them. It's a whole set of jungle animals." He opened the box.

Nova and Ginger gathered around him to ooh and aah over the contents of the box.

"Isn't he the most precious man?" Aunt Camellia leaned closer to Astrid, hugging the unwashed whisk to her chest. "I love him, dearly."

"I know. You're pretty precious, too, Aunt Camellia. You two were made for one another." Astrid pointed at her aunt's apron.

Aunt Camellia glanced down at the brownie-batter-whisk imprint on her apron. "Land sakes." She laughed. "Oh, well, that's what aprons are for."

"It's really delicious, Astrid." Nicole sat on the opposite kitchen counter, licking the last of the brownie batter off the spoon. "And thanks, again, for letting me bring Ginger over." She whispered, "I don't know what to do with her."

"She and Nova are fast becoming two peas in a pod." Astrid grinned as Van arranged the animals in a line.

Nova took the two lions and handed one to Ginger. "Rawr!" Nova moved the plastic lion across the sunlit patch of tile floor. "Like that, Ginger."

Ginger held the other plastic lion toy. She was about Nova's age but shy. Astrid suspected the little girl was likely struggling with her new surroundings, too. "Rawr?"

"But louder." Nova nodded. "'Cause lions are the king of the jungle."

"Rawr!" Ginger tried again.

Nova nodded. "I bet Beeswax and Jammie will want to play with them." She hopped up. "Come on."

Ginger stood. "Who are Beeswax and Jammie?"

"The cats. Lions are cats, too." She took Ginger's hand and led her from the room.

"Be nice to my kitties," Aunt Camellia called after them.

"Promise, Aunt Camellia," Nova called back.

"That Nova is a cutie." Aunt Camellia slid the pan of brownies into the oven, then went to offer her hand to Van. "And you. You are the sweetest man to bring them new toys."

He stood and dropped a kiss on her forehead. "It's nothing."

"It's not nothing. It's thoughtful. *You* are thoughtful." She patted his chest.

"Everywhere I turn, it's a lovefest. Tansy and Dane. Your aunt and Van. Leif and Kerrielynn." Nicole stopped and looked pointedly at her. "You and..."

"Nicole." Astrid shook her head.

"What, I was going to say this brownie batter." Nicole pointed at her with the wooden spoon. "Let me guess, you thought I was going to say you and your moody neighbor?"

Astrid laughed, then scrambled to redirect the conversation. "How long will Ginger be staying with you?"

"Ugh. I have no idea." Nicole sighed. "I mean, I'm happy she's here. I am. But having Child Protective Services show up on my front porch bright and early with her was kind of a major surprise."

"I can imagine." Astrid squeezed her friend's hand. "I'm sure your cousin appreciates it."

"I am better than a foster home." Nicole shrugged. "I can't imagine, you know? Poor thing was scared enough. It's been so long since we've seen each other, she barely remembers me. And Benji's been such a help."

"You've raised a fine young man, Nicole." Van pulled a Dutch oven from one of the lower cabinets and started collecting spices.

"I can't thank you enough for sponsoring him, Van. I have to hug you." She slipped off the counter to hug him. "When he learned he could go to camp, he was over the moon. I've never seen him that excited. Not even on Christmas morning."

"My pleasure." Van patted her back, then turned to the spice cabinet. "He's earned it."

Nicole nodded. "He is a hard worker, that's for sure."

"Like his momma." Aunt Camellia watched Van pull spice jars out with a growing smile. "Now, Van, are you sure you don't need my help with dinner? You've been on your feet working all day."

"I imagine you've been doing the same, Camellia Ann." He winked at her. "I wouldn't have offered if I didn't want to. But I'll let you keep me company."

"If you think I'm leaving you alone in my kitchen, you've got another think coming." Aunt Camellia giggled when Van pulled her into an embrace.

"That's our cue to vacate the premises." Astrid grabbed her and Nicole's glasses of lemonade. "Porch?"

"Lead the way." Nicole followed her out onto the wide, wrap-around porch. They sat side by side on the bench swing, arranging the pile of pillows until they were both comfortable.

"I need to thank Shelby again for that whole sponsorship idea." Nicole took a sip of her lemonade. "She's pretty cool. Things still good there?"

Astrid nodded, her gaze sweeping the property. "Great, really." It was nice to see how the grass and trees had perked up from the rain. Bits of green speckled the otherwise waving wheat-colored grasses.

"Has Rosemary met her yet?" Nicole pulled her knees up.

"Online—Facetime and that sort of thing." Astrid lifted her arm so Jammie the cat could jump into her lap. "Hopefully, Rosemary will get a chance to visit. Soon." She missed her sister so much.

"I'm sure she misses you." Nicole patted her leg. "And wants you to be happy. I can only imagine how nice that must be." She rolled her eyes. "I don't want to bring the mood down but… Astrid, I just don't get Willadeene."

"What did she do now?" Astrid braced herself.

"Besides telling me that Ginger would be better off in foster care?"

"Nicole." Astrid shook her head, horrified. "That's just mean."

"She's mad. And when she's mad, she gets mean. I have a feeling she's going to keep it up until I agree to sell the shop." She tucked a strand of her lime-green hair back behind her ear.

Astrid stroked along Jammie's back. "Surely, she can understand why you're conflicted about selling. It was your grandmother's shop. Her own mother's shop."

"You'd think, wouldn't you? I've tried to explain that to her. Several times." Nicole sat forward, propping her elbows on her knees. "But it *is* a good offer. Like, a lot of money. I didn't want to look but… I did. Even split, it's a lot. I've got to give it to them, these Stinson Properties folk aren't playing games."

"They're persistent. Aunt Camellia has thrown a dozen or more of their business cards and notes in the trash. She says they're just harassing us at this point." Astrid shook her head. "Do you know what they want to do with the place? I know they've been making offers all over town." Ever since those men had stumbled onto Rebecca's property, Stinson Properties had left a bad taste in her mouth.

"No." Nicole sighed. "That's the only reason I'm not jumping on the offer. I don't want some General Dollar or Express Grocer's chain store going in."

"I'm pretty sure city council wouldn't let that happen, Nic." But, then again, if Stinson Properties had really deep pockets, there was no guarantee. "Take time and really think about it. I don't want you to have any regrets."

"Exactly." Nicole smiled.

About then, the loud rumble of Rebecca Wallace's car could be heard. Charlie was coming. Astrid glanced toward the long drive. No car yet.

"Is Charlie here?" Nova peeked around the screen door. "I thought I heard his car."

Astrid leaned forward and shielded her eyes. "Not yet."

"Okay." She disappeared.

"Speaking of regrets. Tansy says you're officially crushing on Mr. Tall Dark and Moody."

Astrid blinked. "What? I'm not crushing on anyone." Which wasn't true. "What did Tansy say?"

"Only that she's never seen you like this with a man before." Nicole shrugged.

That was true.

"I guess I'll have to judge for myself at dinner. Aunt Camellia invited us to stay." She grinned. "He's been having dinner here since his AC died, right?"

"It's being repaired right now." Did that mean there'd be no more dinners together? No more time with Nova and Halley? "And how did we get here from regrets? You said, 'speaking of regrets.'"

"You know, you might regret it if you don't jump his bones." Nicole cocked her head to one side.

"Nicole." Astrid could only stare at her. "I mean… Nicole." She was not having this conversation with her.

Nicole couldn't stop laughing. "Oh, your face." She laughed even harder when Charlie's car came around the bend. "Look who's here."

Nicole was her dear friend but she wasn't averse to a good piece of gossip now and then. As much as she'd like to think Nicole would never spread gossip about her, she didn't want to risk it. Especially since Charlie was as…skittish as he was.

"Charlie." Nova ran onto the front porch, Ginger trailing behind her.

"Who's that?" Ginger asked, standing behind one of the large wicker porch chairs.

"Charlie is my dad." Nova was bouncing on the balls of her feet. "He's kinda grumpy but he's really sad."

Astrid watched as Charlie parked the car, got out and headed their way. He wore his usual, pressed slacks and a crisply ironed button-down shirt. Beekeeper's suit or business attire, he took her breath away.

"Why is he sad?" Nicole asked, glancing at Astrid.

"He gets sad lots—since Momma died." Nova's little face almost broke Astrid's heart. "Me, too."

"I know you miss her, Nova." Astrid moved the cat into Nicole's lap and slid off the swing. She held her arms out and Nova ran into them, hugging her tightly. "I miss my mom, too. I bet we always will. When I get really sad, I try to remember all the people around me that love me and want me to be happy."

Nova smiled up at her. "Now I have lots of those. Like you. You and Aunt Camellilla and Aunt Mags and Tansy and *everyone*."

"That's right." Astrid nodded. "Everyone."

"What's wrong?" Charlie asked as he came up the porch steps. He glanced from Nova to her and back again.

"Hi, Charlie." Nova skipped over to him and took his hand. "We were talking about Momma. Astrid misses her mom, too."

Charlie hesitated, then nodded. "It's good to talk

about her." He scooped her up. "She loves you. And she's watching over you."

"In the stars." Nova hugged Scorpio close.

Charlie nodded.

"Oh, Charlie, Charlie." She wriggled until he put her down. "I have a new friend." She spun around, searching.

Ginger was crouching behind the chair.

"Ginger." Nova marched over, took the girl's hand and dragged her back to Charlie. "This is Charlie."

Ginger used Nova as a shield. "Hi, Nova's dad."

"Hello, Ginger." Charlie waved.

"We're gonna go play." Nova tugged Ginger back into the house, the screen door slamming behind them.

"And who is Ginger?" Charlie asked, his hands shoved into his pockets.

"My niece." Nicole shook her head. "Well, she's actually my cousin's daughter but it's easier to just say niece."

"She's staying with Nicole and Benji for a while." Astrid waffled between returning to the swing with Nicole or sitting on the empty love seat in the hopes he'd sit beside her.

"What's Halley up to?" He shifted from foot to foot, looking everywhere but at her.

"She went on a walk with Benji." Nicole scratched Jammie's head, oblivious to Charlie's reaction.

He went rigid, the muscle in his jaw working. "When?"

"They headed out with Aunt Mags, Shelby and Bea about an hour ago." Astrid knew how protective he was of the girls and hoped having adults along would put his mind at ease. "She really adores baby Bea." She sat on the love seat.

Charlie's posture was still stiff but he didn't look ready to leap off the porch and hunt them down.

"Miss Nicole." Nova peered around the screen door. "Ginger is crying."

Nicole popped up. "I'll check on her. Thank you, sweetie." She disappeared inside.

Nova ran across the porch and sat on the love seat beside Astrid. "Ginger was really sad. Do you think she's missing her mom, too?"

"Maybe. I'm sure Nicole can cheer her up." At least, Astrid hoped she could. Without knowing the specifics of Ginger's homelife, it was hard to know what the little girl was dealing with. At the very least, she would be homesick.

Charlie sat beside his daughter. "Have a good day?"

Nova bounced her feet against the love seat. "Yep. Van brought animal toys." She pulled a plastic zebra from her pocket. "And I went with Aunt Mags and Aunt Camelllila to feed the donkeys. One is itty-bitty." She held up her thumb and forefinger. "Like this."

"That small?" Charlie held up her hand for a closer look.

"Maybe." Nova giggled. "They like crunchy carrots. I do, too."

"Next time, take some apples. They love apples." Astrid held her hand out with the palm up. "Did you feed them like this?"

"I didn't. I watched. Can you come, Charlie? They're so cute." Nova waited for his nod. "And Astrid can bring the apples so they will really like you."

"I can use all the help I can get." Charlie sighed, shooting a look Astrid's way.

She shook her head and smiled at him. "I'm sure they'll like you, apples or no apples." He might not see the progress he was making with his girls, but she did. And, more importantly, the girls did. "What's the news on the air-conditioning? Good news, I hope?"

"They fixed it." Charlie draped an arm along the back of the love seat, his hand resting at the base of her neck. The brush of his fingers on her skin sent a toe-curling shudder down her back.

"Are you cold, Astrid?" Nova handed Charlie the zebra and slipped her arms around her. "I'll hug you till you're warm."

"Oh, thank you." Astrid hugged her back. "You give such good hugs."

Nova stayed against her, her little arms twined around her. "If the air 'ditioner is fixed, do we have to sleep in our rooms again?"

Astrid picked up on the little girl's apprehension and, from the look on Charlie's face, he did, too.

"You don't want to be back in a real bed?" Charlie made the zebra run down Nova's arm.

She shook her head.

"Why not?" Astrid asked. As always, Nova's ponytail was off-center. Astrid slid the hair tie free and finger-combed the riot of curls back into place. She double-twisted the ponytail to secure it—and looked up to find Charlie watching her.

Every inch of Astrid went warm and tingly.

"The rat monster didn't come to Charlie's office." Nova leaned further into Astrid. "Only in my room." She buried her face in Astrid's side. "It's scary."

Astrid hugged her even tighter. Nova was truly scared. "When I was little, my sister Rosemary had a gerbil named Mr. Fluff. It's sort of like a rat—only cute. One night, he got out of his cage. I didn't know that he was out so when I woke up to scratching under my bed, I was too scared to do anything but hide under my covers."

"You didn't get help?" Nova was wide-eyed. "Aunt Magnolia would save you." She looked around the porch then whispered, "She's sorta scary, too."

"She can be." Astrid laughed. "But I was too scared to get out of my bed. I didn't know what was underneath it and Aunt Magnolia's and Aunt Camellia's rooms were all the way at the other end of the hall. I didn't wake up my sisters because I didn't want them to be scared, too." She shrugged. "I waited all night and didn't get a wink of sleep. The next morning, Rosemary came into my room crying. She couldn't find Mr. Fluff anywhere. And then I realized who was under my bed. I leaned over, lifted up the quilt, and Mr. Fluff came scurrying out. I guess he was scared, too, and wanted to hide until Rosemary could find him."

"Poor Mr. Fluff." Nova shook her head. "Do you think my rat monster is a gerbrill?"

"Gerbil," Charlie murmured.

Nova nodded. "A grebirl."

"Probably not." Astrid shook her head. "But I don't think it's a monster."

"But it comes at night. Monsters come at night." Nova glanced up at her. "It's real dark and scratches on the sky window. Like this." She scratched on one of the pillows. "Over and over." She sat up then. "Astrid, you should come and see. It's real. It's really real. You can sleep in my bed and it won't be as scary."

Astrid was more than willing to solve the rat monster problem. Spending the night with the girls was an added perk. But it was Charlie's call and she'd respect his decision.

"Astrid, would you be available to help us with our rat monster problem?" Charlie asked, his smile absolutely devastating.

"Please, please, please." Nova bounced on the love seat.

"I am available. I'll make sure to bring my rat monster hunting gear. And pajamas." She gave Nova a high five.

"I'm going to tell Ginger." Nova leaped off the love seat and ran inside.

Without Nova between them, Astrid found herself scooching just a tiny bit closer to Charlie. He did the same—until his thigh rested against hers. She drew in a deep breath. He sighed. As tempted as she was to rest her head on his shoulder, she was content to be as they were. Together. Enjoying the sunset, his fingers running through her hair, in long, even strokes. "Charlie?" she murmured.

"Hmm?" His eyes were warm upon her.

"Hi." She smiled up at him.

He chuckled, then shook his head.

"What?" Oh, how she loved his laugh.

A crease formed between his brows as his gaze drifted across her face. "Nothing."

"I'm not sure I believe that. But I'll let it go, for now." It was impossible not to look at his mouth.

"For now." He grinned, but the warmth in those brown eyes ratcheted up several notches.

The longer he stared at her, the more molten her insides became. She'd never had someone look at her the way Charlie did. He made her feel desirable and beautiful and ache with yearning. Not just her body, her heart. Maybe it was finding him so broken. Maybe it was watching him with Nova or how protective he was with Halley. Maybe it was how adorable he was when he'd been soaking up information about the bees. It was probably all of that and more. Whatever it was, her heart was no longer her own.

CHARLIE CARRIED A stack of plates into the kitchen. "Where do these go?"

Astrid nodded at the counter by the sink. "Right there."

He eyed the mountain of dishes. "Need help?" She wore yellow gloves and an apron and was up to her elbows in soapsuds. She looked beautiful.

"It's mostly just rinsing and loading the dishwasher. You can go and enjoy yourself with the others."

He set the dishes down on the counter. He was adjusting to the overlap of conversations and general loudness that accompanied every Hill family meal, but he didn't necessarily enjoy them. It was easier when Astrid was close. She seemed to know when he needed an encouraging smile or, if she was nearby, a touch of reassurance. Without her, everyone was louder and bigger.

Besides, Halley and Nova had happily commandeered his phone and were watching the video he'd taken of this morning's bee happenings. There was no reason for him to return to the dining room when what he wanted was here, in the kitchen.

"There are more brownies, if you want some." She nodded at the pan.

"I'm full. I've never been this full." After a meal

of roasted chicken, new potatoes and fresh-from-the-garden green beans, he'd had two massive helpings of brownies à la mode. If he was going to keep eating like this, he needed to start running again. Delicious home-made food was never in short supply in the Hill house. Which reminded him. "Halley said you made the brownies for me."

Astrid paused for a split second, then went back to washing. "She might have mentioned that you liked them so…" She shrugged.

He stood beside her, resisting the urge to touch her. "You made them for me?"

"I…did. Yes." Her mossy green gaze met his. "I hope you liked them."

Dammit. She'd made him brownies and it made him… happy. It was that simple. How had this happened? How had he gotten *here*? He didn't understand it. But he liked it. "I did. Thank you."

"You're welcome." She smiled and went back to washing dishes. "Can I ask you something?"

He braced himself. After this morning, she'd have questions. But he wasn't sure he was ready to answer.

She glanced at him. "About Halley, really."

Halley? He wasn't sure he was qualified to answer questions about Halley. He had plenty of his own. "Sure." He scraped the plates into the trash and stacked them within her reach.

"You were upset when you learned she'd gone on a walk. Was it because she'd gone walking with a boy? Or that they might have gone walking without adult supervision?"

She'd picked up on that? "Both." He continued scraping plates. "She was too attached to a boy back home.

I caught them…" He broke off. "It was good I came home from work when I did. Coming here was to get Rebecca's affairs settled—and for distance."

"I see." She started loading the dishwasher. "That makes sense. Benji is a good kid. In case you were wondering."

After watching Benji in action, Charlie had been impressed. The boy had been polite and respectful, he'd listened to everything Astrid and Tansy had said, and, so far, he'd treated Halley as a friend—only. While he was still wary, Halley deserved friends. Yasmina had told him, over and over, that no man was an island. It was only recently that he'd begun to get a basic understanding of what that truly meant.

He realized she was watching him so he added, "I do prefer the girls to have adult supervision. I realize it's a false sense of security." He wasn't sure she could understand but, surprisingly, he hoped she would. "But it's what I need to focus and get work done."

"You'd mentioned something about a promotion?" Astrid finished loading the dishwasher, tugged off her gloves and wiped her hands on a kitchen towel. "Have you made a decision?"

"I haven't." He hadn't given it much thought. Which was unlike him. Between Astrid and trying to connect with the girls, he'd been preoccupied. It wasn't something he could put off forever.

"Dessert plates," Nicole announced as she entered the kitchen, balancing way too many dishes. "I got them all."

"Be careful." Astrid winced as she set the stack on the counter.

"I'm always careful." Nicole grinned. "Look at you two being all domesticated."

Charlie wasn't sure if he liked Nicole yet. Benji was her son, so that was a mark in her favor, but there was something about her that put him on guard.

"Nova's telling everyone you're having a sleepover tonight?" Nicole glanced between them.

"I'm spending the night with the girls, yes." Astrid's inflection on *the girls* was pointed.

"Uh-huh." Nicole grabbed a piece of brownie and headed back into the dining room.

Charlie frowned after her. Maybe tonight was a bad idea? He hadn't stopped to consider any possible repercussions. Nova might not be old enough to understand the looks and smiles undoubtedly going around the dinner table but Halley was.

"What are you thinking?" Astrid asked, pulling the dishwasher open and fitting the dessert plates into whatever spot she could make.

Watching her set his teeth on edge. The plates were every which way. No organization—just clutter. And it didn't bother her. She finished, then closed the dishwasher, looking at him like she had no cares in the world.

"I have no idea what I'm doing." He leaned against the counter, gripped its edge and stared at the closed dishwasher. "Sometimes, I think coming here with the girls was a huge mistake." He ran his fingers through his hair. "I didn't plan on any of this happening. Now I don't know how to undo it. Or incorporate it."

"What is *it* exactly?" Astrid leaned against the opposite counter.

You. This. "Change." He pushed off the counter and opened the dishwasher. "I don't handle change well." He started with the cups. "I plan. Schedule. Map things out so I have a clear path forward." He pushed the top drawer in and started straightening plates. "I try to leave room for unexpected detours but I make sure I have an understanding of all the variables at play. That way I can manage them, do damage control before there is any real damage." Now that everything was in its place, he could relax. He closed the dishwasher and turned.

"Wow." Astrid was watching him with wide eyes. "From now on, you're in charge of the dishwasher."

He blew out a deep breath. "Deal."

"Everything you said makes sense in business, Charlie. But with people, there's no way to know all the variables. Free will, spontaneity, emotions—human nature—those aren't things you can manage. Those are the very qualities that make people, people. People are flawed and complicated."

"And why I don't, generally, like people." He glanced at the dining room.

"I suppose there have been a few unexpected detours here."

A few? He chuckled at that. Since he'd arrived in Honey, nothing had gone as he'd expected.

"Now that your air conditioner is fixed, things should quiet down." As much as she tried to infuse her normal enthusiasm into her voice, it didn't work. He'd hurt her and he hated himself for it. "And I'll make sure to give you a heads-up before coming over."

But if she did that, he'd find an excuse to stop her. "No." He didn't want that. Whether he liked it or not, there was no ignoring the truth. He liked spending time with Astrid. Holding her. Kissing her. Sitting across the table from her. Apparently, even standing in the kitchen and reloading the dishwasher made him oddly content. "You don't have to do that."

Her head cocked to one side. "You are a mystery, Charlie Driver."

Did he want to be a mystery to her? He was over-thinking. And oversharing. Enough. He shook his head. "I'm talking too much."

"No, you aren't." Her hand rested on his arm. "I happen to like it when you talk."

He shook his head. No one had ever liked hearing him talk. That's why he rarely did it.

"Yes, I do." She paused. "Shake your head all you want, it's true."

"Astrid." Nova came running into the kitchen, Halley trailing after her. "It's getting dark."

"Are you really spending the night with us?" Halley's gaze darted to his arm—where Astrid's hand rested.

"I promised Nova I'd help her with her rat monster problem." Astrid's hand lifted from his arm to push the hair from her forehead. "Whatever it is, we'll figure it out."

"See." Nova pointed at Astrid. "I told you she was."

"That's really awesome, Astrid." Halley shrugged. "Sorry I didn't believe you, Nova."

"It's okay." Nova was bouncing up and down, ecstatic. "You can sleep in my bed, Astrid."

"I can bring my sleeping bag," Astrid offered.

"Nova has the biggest bed in the house. I don't know why since she's so small." Halley smiled. "I bet we could all fit in it."

"We can share." Nova nodded. "Halley and Charlie, too." She looked at her sister, who nodded, then his way.

That brought Charlie up short. There was no way that was going to happen. "The bed isn't that big." When-ever Nova climbed into his bed at night, he was aware of her every sound and move. Add Halley and Astrid to that and he'd be exhausted.

"You have to." Nova's lower lip flipped out. "You have to keep us safe, Charlie." Her big eyes filled with tears.

Tears. He didn't do tears. "Nova."

"Come on, Charlie." Halley put her arm around her sister. "You could sleep on the floor. Or in the rocking chair?"

"Yeah." Nova sniffed, wiping the back of her arm across her face. "Please."

"Fine." He'd rather sleep on the floor than have Nova sobbing. That was unbearable. "Before we go, let's say thank you for dinner." He steered the girls back to the dining room. Manners were important. After tonight, he wouldn't have to impose on the Hills' generosity anymore. Even with all the noise and chaos that was part of any Hill family meal, he was disappointed. But there was no delaying the inevitable.

This weekend was the reading of Rebecca's will. Once he'd made sure his aunt's wishes were honored, he and the girls would go home. Just the three of them. Life would get back to normal.

CHAPTER FOURTEEN

THE WHOLE RIDE to Charlie's place, Astrid was smiling. Kerrielynn had done a makeover on Halley after dinner, so she was in high spirits. Nova was excited over her new friend, Ginger, and Astrid's sleepover. By the time they were pulling down the drive, even Charlie was relaxed. Astrid's heart almost beat out of her chest when he reached over and gave her hand a squeeze.

"Bath time." Nova ran into the house and up the stairs. "You coming, Astrid? I can show you my room first."

Astrid laughed. "I'm coming."

"Wow, Charlie, it's, like, way cold in here." Halley hugged herself.

"At least we know they fixed the AC." Charlie closed the door behind them.

"That's for sure." Halley shrugged. "Can Kerrielynn come over tomorrow night? She wanted to introduce me to some of her friends. So, it would be Kerrielynn and her friends. Don't answer right now, okay? Just think about it." She climbed up four steps. "Please."

Charlie nodded. "I'll think about it."

"Okay." She smiled and ran up the stairs.

Once she'd reached the top of the stairs, Charlie ran his fingers through his hair. "I have to do this, don't I?"

"You don't have to. But she's asking them to come here, so you could keep an eye on them. And you've met Kerrielynn. I can vouch for the others." She smiled when he looked her way.

"Can you really see me with a house full of teenage girls?" The face he made was priceless.

Astrid burst into laughter.

"It's not funny." He sighed but then he smiled his beautiful smile.

"Your expression was." She kept laughing. "If you're that worried, you can call in backup."

His brows rose. "And that would be?"

She pointed at herself. "Or Tansy."

"Astrid," Nova called down. "Where are you?"

"I'm coming." She headed to the stairs. "On my way." She looked back, but Charlie was nowhere to be seen.

After bath time, Astrid lay between the girls on Nova's big bed, reading. "That's beautiful. Like a firework in outer space." Astrid pointed at the picture on the page, the big book propped against her knees.

"That's a comet." Nova traced the long tail of the picture. "Halley was named after Halley's Comet."

"It only appears in our sky every seventy-six years and you can see it in the sky for six months. Did you know that?" Halley adjusted her pillow. "Mom saw it when she was little and that's why she became an astronomer."

"Mom loved stars." Nova held Scorpio up. "Wanna look out her telescope?"

"It's late, Nova." Charlie came into the room, wearing a T-shirt and athletic shorts. He sat in the rocking chair and stretched his long legs out in front of him. "Maybe next time."

"Yay!" Nova made Scorpio do a little dance. "Next time!"

Astrid was trying not to ogle this version of Charlie. Sporty Charlie was equally as handsome as beekeeper-suit-wearing Charlie or business attire Charlie.

"Did you hear that, Astrid? Next time." Nova scooted closer to her, her head against Astrid's shoulder.

"I did." She hoped there would be a next time. "Where were we?" She turned the page. "The black hole is a point in space where the gravity pulls so much, even light can't escape."

"Like a big vacuum." Nova made an impressively loud whooshing sound.

Halley laughed. "I bet it sounds just like that."

"There's no sound in space." Charlie sat forward, his elbows on his knees.

"We know," Halley and Nova said in unison.

"Right." Charlie smiled, smothering a yawn. "What was I thinking?"

"It was a joke, Charlie." Nova shrugged, like it was the most obvious thing in the world.

Halley started laughing then. "Good one, Nova."

Nova lit up. "I know."

Astrid smiled. "You're both funny. And so smart. I didn't know anything about Halley's Comet or black holes or that one million earths could fit inside the sun." She set the book aside.

"Mom taught us." Halley rolled onto her side to face Astrid. "She loved space. She said, when she was little, she wanted to be an astronaut more than anything. She would talk about it for hours."

"Halley and Charlie tell me what Mom said 'cause I don't 'member lots." Nova hugged Scorpio and yawned.

Astrid wondered which was harder—having memories to hold on to or not. She had so many treasured moments with her parents. Time had taken the edge off their loss but, every once in a while, the grief inside overpowered all else. Not that she'd give up those memories. They kept her parents' love for her alive. She knew how much they'd loved her and how much she'd loved them. It was up to Charlie and Halley to make sure Nova knew how loved she'd been, too.

"I like talking about her." Halley's voice was low and thick. "It's like she's still here. I mean, I know she's not. It helps, sometimes, is all."

Astrid caught the girl's hand in hers. "I'd love to hear about her, Halley. She was your mom. And Nova's mom. That tells me she was an amazing woman."

Halley smiled. "She had the funniest laugh. Like a snort, but really high-pitched. It made everyone that heard it laugh."

Charlie chuckled.

"She loved oatmeal and headbands, like me, and opera music. I never understood the words but some of it sounded way intense." Halley kept a hold of Astrid's hand. "Do you like opera music?"

"I never have before but now I feel like I've missed out."

"Astrid," Nova whispered. "It's really dark now." She pointed up at the skylight.

"Right." Astrid stared up at the window and the brilliant view of the stars. So far, there'd been no scratching or rat monster appearance. "Everyone else is ready for bed. I guess I should change into my pj's." She sat up and scooched off the end of the mattress. "I can finish the book when I get back."

"Okay." Nova gave a thumbs-up.

She carried her bag to the bathroom that connected

the girls' bedrooms, took a quick shower and put on her bee-print nightgown. After brushing her teeth, she headed back into the bedroom. The overhead light was off but Nova's night-light was surprisingly bright. She tiptoed across the room to the bed. Halley had rolled onto her side. Little Nova had pressed herself against Halley's back and was snoring softly.

Astrid moved to the other side of the bed. Charlie's sleeping bag was there—with Charlie on top of it—with mere inches between where he lay and the bed. From his position, he'd have a good view of the skylight overhead and the mysterious rat monster, when it finally made an appearance.

He didn't move or acknowledge her presence, so she tiptoed along the edge of the bed, pulled back the thick fleece star-covered blanket and slid between the sheets. She lay on her back and stared up at the skylight. A moth flew by. A beetle hit the glass and walked across the pane. No rat monster.

Other than the ebb and flow of the crickets' nightly concert, she could hear Halley's deep and even breathing. Nova's soft snore made her smile.

Charlie was absolutely silent.

She was very aware of Charlie's silence. Was he even breathing? He was too quiet. She was tempted to lean over and make sure he was still breathing.

Instead, she tried to relax and not think about the fact that he was lying inches away.

She took a deep breath and stretched, then adjusted her pillow. She pushed back the too-warm fluffy blanket—jumping at the touch of Charlie's hand. His fingers threaded with hers. Astrid's eyes squeezed shut, smiling so broadly her cheeks hurt. He'd sought out her touch.

He wanted to hold her hand. And it filled her heart with hope and love.

Because she loved Charlie.

She rolled onto her side and peered onto the floor. He, too, was on his side, facing the bed. He stayed silent and so did she. But her thoughts were shouting the truth. *I love you, Charlie Driver. I love you so much.*

She was on the edge of sleep when she heard the noise. It was, as Nova described it, a rapid scratching. It stopped, then started again.

Astrid let go of Charlie's hand and rolled onto her back to stare up at the skylight. At first, all she could make out was a shadow. A hairy shadow. It disappeared for a moment, the sounds of claws on the roof tracking back and forth until the shadow reappeared. This time, it covered the top portion of the skylight.

"You see it?" Nova whispered, grabbing Astrid's hand in both of hers.

"I do." Astrid squeezed her hands.

"I told you it was real." Nova's whisper was insistent.

Astrid watched the animal. It wasn't a raccoon. This was slower, more sluggish. From the back and forth, it was clear it was eating. Bugs, most likely. "You always sleep with your night-light on, right?"

"She does." Halley sat up, yawning. "What's going on?"

"It's here." Nova let go of Astrid, stood on the bed and pointed up. "See? See."

Astrid flipped on the lamp on the bedside table.

"Ohmygosh." Halley rubbed her eyes. "What *is* that?"

The rat monster ran over the skylight, giving Astrid a good look at the animal's tail. "It's a possum." She sat up, smiling. The mystery wasn't such a mystery after all.

Charlie sat on the side of the bed, staring up at the skylight. "I'm sorry I didn't believe you, Nova."

She climbed into his lap, her gaze glued to the skylight. "It's okay, Charlie." She patted his leg.

Charlie smiled down at her. It was such a tender smile, Astrid's heart tripped over itself.

"What's a possum?" Nova turned to Astrid. "Are they bad? Will it hurt us? Is it trying to get into the house to chew us up?"

Astrid managed not to laugh at Nova's earnest questions.

Charlie, however, did laugh. It was a wonderful sound. From the smiles on both the girls' faces, she wasn't the only one that thought so.

"No, no." Astrid was quick to reassure her. "They might look a little creepy but they're actually very helpful animals."

Nova shook her head. "But he's trying to get into the house."

"Possums are pretty shy. They eat bugs and lizards and frogs." Astrid pointed at the night-light. "Light attracts them. At night, it's very dark in the country. I bet the night-light is giving him an all-you-can-eat bug buffet."

"I'm feeding the possum?" Nova stared back up at the night-light.

"Yes." Astrid glanced at Charlie, marveling at how smart Nova was. He shrugged in answer but there was no missing the pride on his face. "We can turn off the night-light?" Astrid suggested. "If I'm right, then he'll go away."

"We could try that, Nova?" Charlie's hair was rumpled and he looked sleepy and delicious. She tore her gaze from his and forced her attention back to Nova.

She was thinking, her little face scrunching up as she considered Astrid's suggestion. "But then he wouldn't have food?"

"And he wouldn't scratch on the roof." Halley flopped back on her pillow. "And you could sleep."

"He is a wild animal, Nova. I'm sure he'd be able to find plenty of food on his own." Charlie pointed up, the possum's head clearly visible now. "Do you feel better now that you know it's not a monster?"

Nova nodded. "He's kinda cute."

"Mystery solved." Halley yawned. "Since you've got Astrid and Charlie, I'm going to sleep in my room."

"Okay." Nova waved. "Night, Halley. I love you."

Halley kicked off the blankets. "I love you, too." She waved as she left.

Astrid chose that moment to look at Charlie. He loved his girls, it was there on his face. She only wished he could say it out loud. When it came to words, he didn't trust himself.

"It's late." Charlie smoothed Nova's hair back. "And, now that we know the rat monster isn't a rat monster, we should try to get some sleep."

Nova nodded. "I think we should leave the night-light on."

"You do?" Astrid waited for her to lie down beside her, then covered her with the blanket.

"He's hungry." She shrugged. "You can sleep in the bed now, Charlie." She patted the space beside her. "There's room."

He stared at the bed. "I need to sleep here? Even though we know there's no monster?"

"It's a sleepover, Charlie. You can't leave, too." Nova frowned at him, leaning closer to whisper in her not-so-whispery voice, "It'll hurt Astrid's feelings."

Charlie grinned. "It will? Then I guess I have to stay."

"I knew you'd fix it, Astrid." Nova's eyes closed the second her head hit the pillow.

Once the lamp was turned off and Nova was tucked in between them, Astrid couldn't sleep. She watched the possum running back and forth across the skylight while Nova snored peacefully beside her.

"I guess there's nothing to fear now?" Charlie's voice was low. "You saved the…night."

Astrid turned her head on the pillow. He lay on his side, facing her. "I'm glad it was such a simple fix." She rolled to face him. "You should tell them you love them, Charlie. I know you want to. And I know that it would mean the world to them."

He frowned. "It would?" He didn't sound convinced.

"Oh, Charlie." Was that what he was afraid of? That they didn't want his love? Or love him in return? "I know that words are hard but… Telling them you love them gives them permission to show you they love you. Especially Halley. I think, sometimes, we forget to tell people how important they are to us. We shouldn't. Family can be complicated but you can't give up on them. They're family."

He stared at her for a long time. "What if you're wrong?" He swallowed, his voice thick and gruff. "I'm…" He closed his eyes. "I'm not easy to love." The last word was tainted with bitterness.

Normally, Astrid didn't get angry. But, right now, she was angry at whoever had made Charlie believe this. And hurting. Who could look into those eyes and not see the tender soul inside? What hard-hearted person had led him to believe *he* was the problem? "Yes, you are." She reached out to smooth the hair from his forehead. "I love you, Charlie."

Charlie's eyes opened and his muscles flexed tight.

"And your girls love you, too," she hurried on. "Trust me." She managed a smile, then turned onto her back. She'd put her heart out there with no expectation from him. He needed to know he was worthy of love *and* was loved. She loved him—even if he didn't reciprocate.

HE COULD FEEL sunlight on his face but he wasn't ready to wake up.

Soft hair tickled his nose. An arm draped across his chest. In his dreams, he'd been with Astrid. His arm tightened around her. *Astrid?* He was still dreaming.

Her sigh had his eyes pop open.

He lay perfectly still. He was still in Nova's bedroom, in Nova's bed—but there was no Nova separating him and Astrid.

He wasn't dreaming. His heart picked up speed as he assessed the situation. Astrid was using his chest for a pillow. She was on her side, so close there was no space between them. Her arm draped across him and her hand had somehow managed to slide beneath his shirt. Her hand was warm against his stomach. Her leg was hooked, her thigh resting atop his. His arm, wrapped around her, rested against bare skin.

His hand moved slowly. *Dammit.* Her nightgown was twisted up and around her waist. He lifted his hand. It didn't feel right to touch her when she was sound asleep. He couldn't do it without her being fully present and wanting his touch.

"Astrid." His whisper was gruff.

"Hmm?" She stretched into him.

He sucked in a deep breath, acutely aware of every flex and shudder as she stirred against him.

"Astrid," he hissed again, his hand hovering over her.

She went perfectly still then. "Charlie?"

"Yep." He concentrated on breathing.

"Nova's gone?" Slowly, she lifted her head to look at him.

"Yep." *Breathing. Keep breathing.* He didn't look at her. But when she tried to move, his arm tightened. "Sorry." His arm dropped. As awkward as this was, he liked having Astrid close.

She relaxed against him. "I thought… This is… This is a lot of touching."

That's why he was struggling to breathe. So far, panic hadn't kicked in. His heart was hammering away and his chest felt tight, but it wasn't panic. "It's…different." This was more like anticipation.

She rested her chin in the middle of his chest. "Different bad or different good?" Her eyes searched his.

"Good." It was enough but it was all he could manage to get out. He ran his hand over her silky hair.

She leaned into his touch and smiled.

Her smile lit a fire inside him. He wanted to kiss her. He'd never wanted anything more in his whole life. And, from the way she was looking at him, she wanted him to kiss her. Until the thundering of footsteps on the stairs had them jumping apart.

"I want to go first, Halley." Nova's voice. "It's my room."

"Charlie?" There was a knock on the door. It was Halley. "Are you guys awake?"

He was up and out of the bed before the door opened. "Yes."

"Hey, Astrid." Halley walked in, all smiles. "I love your nightgown."

Nova ran in and jumped onto the bed. "It's got bitty bees on it. You really love bees, don't you, Astrid?"

He was pleased to find Astrid's nightgown was no longer twisted around her waist.

"I certainly do." Astrid hugged Nova to her. "Good morning."

"Charlie, you snore." Nova bounced up and down on the bed. "Really loud."

He'd barely slept. How had he done any snoring?

"That's why Mom and Charlie had separate bedrooms, Nova." Halley adjusted her pale pink headband. "We made you breakfast. It's ready."

"That was very thoughtful of you." Astrid pushed back the blankets. "I'm hungry. Let me get dressed and I'll be right down."

"Okay, but hurry." Nova kept bouncing on the bed. "Get dressed, too, Charlie."

It was disconcerting how normal this felt. All of it. "Will do." He made a hasty exit and headed for his room.

Astrid and the girls were sitting around the table when he reached the kitchen. The table had been set and there was a sizable stack of pancakes on a platter, waiting.

"You made these?" He eyed the counter and tried not to wince at the mess. An empty pancake box lay on its side next to eggshells and a mostly empty milk container.

"We did." Nova was so proud. "I tasted one, too, and they're yummy."

He sat with the clutter behind him, determined not to let it ruin their gesture. "Let's eat."

The food was good and the company was even better. With Astrid around, the girls were more willing to talk. It seemed they both had a lot to say that morning. He was finishing his second helping of pancakes when his phone vibrated.

"Work?" Halley frowned.

"But we're not done with breakfast." Nova stopped chewing her pancakes.

He held up his finger and answered the phone, fully intending to tell them he'd call later.

"Charlie?" It wasn't work. It was Lindsay. "I thought I'd touch base. Theo can't wait check out the town. You know him, always looking for new opportunities."

He didn't really know Lindsay's husband and he didn't want to.

"But that's why we're one of the top real estate developers in the state."

He stared at his pancakes, taking slow, deep breaths. "What does this have to do with me?"

"You are my brother, Charlie. Something Dad was keen to remind me. And since he and Mom are coming, too, we should arrange some sort of family thing." She sighed. "I mean, we should catch up with the girls."

Absolutely not. Alarm bells were going off now. His parents were coming? His mother and Rebecca hadn't spoken in years. There was no reason for them to come to the will reading. Or had Rebecca wanted them there? It seemed unlikely.

He glanced up, to find everyone at the table watching him. "That's not necessary." It was starting, he could feel it. The tension, burning the back of his throat. *You can't give up on family...* Astrid's gentle reminder flitted through his head. Right or wrong, he couldn't face them. "Let's stick to the plan. I'll see you in the lawyer's office."

"Mom and Dad, too." Lindsay was enjoying this.

He took a deep breath, pulling at the collar of his shirt. His father. He couldn't remember the last time he'd seen his father. Most memories concerning his father were boxed up, chained closed and buried deep away for his mental health's sake. "Is Blair coming, too?"

"How the hell would I know what she's doing?" Lindsay sighed. "Whatever. Don't be surprised if Mom or Dad call you, though."

That would be a surprise. The last time his parents had called was to offer their condolences after Yasmina's death. The whole conversation lasted maybe five minutes. "Anything else?" His chest was tight and the pressure kept building.

"I guess not. As usual, you're all about the warm fuzzies, aren't you?" She sighed.

"Goodbye, Lindsay." He ended the call and tucked his phone back into his pocket. He couldn't face the sympathy on Astrid's face or the urge to draw her close. "Excuse me a minute." His palms were clammy but he wasn't drenched in sweat—yet. He rubbed his hands along the top of his thighs and stood. The back of his chair steadied him but he needed to stop this before it got any worse. With a deep breath, he headed for the downstairs bathroom.

He turned on the faucet and leaned forward to splash water on his face. It helped.

This wasn't going to happen. Lindsay wasn't part of his life. He'd made that choice. Why the hell would he let her into his head? She only had power if he gave it to her. There was no way in hell that was going to happen.

What the hell is wrong with you? His father's words echoed, along with a host of others. *Toughen up.*

I'm ashamed to call you my son.

There's no changing or fixing you, is there? It was harder to lock away his father's words. He'd grown up with them, heard them until he believed them. *Keep being this way and you'll wind up alone.*

He leaned forward and submerged his head in the cold water.

Your girls love you. Astrid's voice echoed in his head.

He gripped the sink's edge.

I love you, Charlie. Trust me. He wanted to believe it, to trust her.

There was a soft knock on the door. "Charlie?" It was Halley. "Everyone wanted me to check on you. Nova thinks you need a hug."

A lump settled in his throat.

Another knock. "Charlie?"

He took a deep breath and opened the door. "I'm okay."

Halley looked at him for a second, then shook her head. "No, you're not. It's okay to need a hug." She stepped forward and put her arms around his waist.

His eyes were burning as he hugged Halley close. "You're right. I do need a hug."

She hugged him tighter. "I give good hugs. Mom always said so."

"Your mother was right about pretty much everything." He held on until the pressure in his chest eased. "Thank you."

Halley smiled.

He smiled back. "I have some pancakes to finish."

When they got back to the kitchen, Nova was standing on a stool wiping off the counter. Astrid had braided her hair back and was washing dishes. Halley warmed up his pancakes in the microwave and Charlie ate every last bite, letting the gentle camaraderie in the kitchen soothe him. He knew he needed to check in at work—he had a meeting in less than an hour—but he didn't want to cut this time short.

"I think that should do it." Astrid wiped her hands on the dish towel as she surveyed the newly tidied kitchen.

"Everything is clean as a whistle." Nova gave Charlie a thumbs-up. "That's what Aunt Camellilla says when she's done cleaning."

"It is one of her favorite sayings." Astrid tapped Nova on the nose. "I had a lot of fun at our sleepover. I'm glad we discovered your rat monster wasn't a monster after all."

"Me, too." Nova jumped off the stool and took Astrid's hand. "You can stay again, if you want?"

"It's weird not going to your place this morning." Halley slumped in her chair at the table. "I mean, there's always something going on or someone to talk to," she said without any accusation or sarcasm. She was just being honest—until the Hills had stepped in, life had been quiet. Maybe too quiet.

"You and Nova and Charlie are welcome anytime." Astrid glanced his way. "Even when your air conditioner is working." She smoothed her braid from her shoulder. "I'll go get my bag."

The minute she left the kitchen, it went silent.

"Charlie." Halley leaned forward. "Nova and I want you to know that we like Astrid."

"I know you do." He grinned. "You've told me. Many times."

"Now you have to like Astrid." Nova climbed onto the chair beside him. "Please, Charlie."

"I do." He frowned, glancing back and forth between them.

"Like her, like her." Nova's not-so-whispery whisper seemed especially loud.

"What Nova means is we think it would be cool if you two, you know—"

"Were boyfriend and girlfriend," Nova finished.

This was the last thing Charlie had expected them to say. It took a minute for him to process this announcement. "We'll be going home soon, girls."

Nova's smile vanished, almost surprised.

Halley didn't say anything, but she didn't look happy, either.

"That was always the plan." He frowned, astonished by their reaction. "Don't you miss your friends? What about swim team and dance and school?"

"If they were really my friends, they'd try to text me or call me or something. But they haven't." She shrugged. "I've made some new friends here. Kerrielynn wants me to meet Grace and Crissy—they're both around my age."

Charlie felt a twinge of guilt then. If he hadn't changed the settings on her phone, would she have heard from her friends? The girls Halley had gravitated toward had been toxic and competitive. Would text exchanges and DMs have been a good thing? There was no way of knowing. While he'd meant to protect Halley, he was beginning to realize that a lot of his protecting was really controlling. That, after growing up in the household he had, made his blood run cold. He ran his hands through his hair, truly hating himself.

"Everyone's been nice. Like, everyone." Halley's smile was sweet. "Kerrielynn has been so nice."

These were the girls Halley wanted to have over—four teens under his roof. For Halley. "I can order pizza for tonight?" he offered. "If you still want them to come over?"

Halley stared at him in shock. "Seriously?"

He nodded, swallowing hard.

"Charlie." Halley jumped up out of her chair and hugged him. "That would be so, *so* great. Thank you. I'll go call her now." She ran from the room.

"Wow." Nova shook her head. "Halley was excited."

He nodded again, trying to determine what was the best course of action: telling Halley what he'd done or fixing her phone? He'd messed up. He'd messed up and he didn't know what to do. Either way, it wasn't going to go well.

The excited murmur of voices told him that Halley was probably filling Astrid in on this new development. He wondered if Astrid had meant it when she'd offered to be his backup. *No.* The more time he spent with Astrid, the more muddled he got. He was thirty-four years old. He was too old to become someone else—someone worthy of Astrid. That was why leaving was the best option for them all. He'd rather wake up without her than spend every day knowing she deserved better.

CHAPTER FIFTEEN

WHEN ASTRID CAME back downstairs, Charlie was on a business call and Nova was coloring in her dinosaur book. She lingered, hoping he'd ask her to come that evening to help out. Instead, he'd nodded at her and closed himself in the dining room.

She tried to convince herself he was in work mode—that it had nothing to do with her blurted declaration of love. But, the whole walk home, she worried it had been too much for him. Then, waking up in the comfort of his arms. His heartbeat. His hand against her side. His thigh between hers. When he'd looked at her, there was hunger burning in his eyes.

But wanting wasn't loving.

As soon as Astrid walked through the door, Aunt Camellia asked if Charlie and the girls would be coming by for a visit.

Over coffee on that day, Aunt Mags had asked if they should expect the Drivers for dinner.

On Wednesday, Tansy pointed out that it was awfully quiet without the girls around—and then Camellia asked if they were coming over.

Each time, Astrid had told them the truth. She didn't know.

On Thursday, no one asked.

Halley had sent her a handful of texts. She'd had fun

with Kerrielynn and really liked Crissy, who was her age. Another was all about how Charlie had taken them on a bike ride around the lake. And that Nova had made it down the drive without her training wheels before falling over. And each and every text ended with how much she and Nova missed her. Astrid had replied to them all, sending words of encouragement and strings of happy emojis. She was genuinely happy that Charlie was making time for the girls—she wanted him to have a strong relationship with them.

But it hurt that Charlie didn't reach out.

She didn't regret telling him how she felt. She did love him. She loved him and she missed his beautiful reluctant smiles and his frequent *accidental* touches.

"Is that right?" Aunt Magnolia asked, stooped behind the glass front counter of the Hill Honey Boutique.

"Move the skep a little bit forward." The case showcased tools of the trade from the previous Hills. An old cone basket, called a skep, that was once used to keep hives. There was one metal pot and one ceramic pot, peppered with holes, and a bellows pump. All three items served as smokers of the past. Her great-grandpa Norman's pair of elbow-length calfskin gloves and canvas smock with a mesh hood were also on display. Both Mags and Camellia treated each and every item with special care. She waited until her aunt had moved the old beehive basket. "Perfect."

"Thank you." Magnolia closed the case and came around front to inspect her handiwork.

Astrid glanced at the almost empty basket in front of her, then the digital inventory list on her tablet. How many times had she lost her place? The plan was to stay so busy, she wouldn't have time to think about Charlie. The plan didn't seem to be working.

"Astrid." Aunt Magnolia tapped the duster handle on the countertop until Astrid looked her way. "Are you okay?"

Astrid forced a smile. "Of course." She went back to scanning the tablet in her arms. "We need to order more bee buttons. And we need to start thinking about winter items. Are we going to do mail-order holiday-themed gift baskets this year?"

Aunt Magnolia and Aunt Camellia exchanged looks.

"We're still discussing." Aunt Magnolia wasn't a fan of taking risks. She preferred sticking with what worked.

"I don't think there's much left to discuss." Aunt Camellia was unloading the cardboard box of decorative pot holders onto a display rack. "Tansy is going to be on *Wake Up, America*. She's got them coming here to take a tour of the Hill Honey Boutique. I say we strike while the iron is hot."

"We'd have to hire extra manpower to assemble the baskets. And cover postage. I'm not certain we'd break even, let alone come out ahead." Aunt Magnolia stopped dusting the contents of the glass cabinet.

"If we don't see a profit, then we know not to do it again." Aunt Camellia carried the now-empty box behind the counter.

Astrid watched the conversation volley back and forth between her aunts. When it came to business, they both had strong opinions but Astrid had faith they'd work it out. Her aunts never fought, they discussed. Even if they disagreed, they remained respectful and kind. Astrid and her sisters had taken their example to heart and tried to do the same.

"We have time." She scanned the order. "Unless you can think of anything else, I think we can go ahead and place our order."

"I'm sure you've thought of everything." Aunt Camellia glanced at the large clock on the wall. "Time to open."

Thursday was the beginning of the shopping weekend. And with the long, hot days of the Texas summer dragging on, families and tourists were trying to fit in one more holiday before the break was over.

Honey, Texas, had always been a Hill Country tourist destination but having Wholesome Foods sponsoring the last Honey Festival had brought national attention to the town—and the honey that made the region so famous. The Hill Honey Boutique had benefitted greatly. People wanted to buy their blue-ribbon honey and meet one of the all-female Hill beekeepers.

Aunt Magnolia stowed away the cleaning supplies while Aunt Camellia unlocked the front door.

"Good morning." The door swung open the minute Camellia had unlocked it. "Oh, Theo, isn't this the cutest shop?" The woman, tall and blonde and very well put together, clasped her hands—showing off extra-long manicured nails that sparkled. "Look, bees everywhere."

"It's something." Theo trailed after her. He was shorter than the woman, balding, and wore a neon-orange golf shirt and khaki cargo shorts.

"Welcome." Aunt Camellia was all smiles. "First time visiting Honey?"

"It is." The woman nodded. "I've read up on it, though. Your little town is all over the internet, but I guess you know that since so much of it is about the famous Hill family. What a charming place." She was scanning the boutique. "I'm Lindsay. This is my husband, Theodore. You might know my brother, Charlie."

Astrid's head popped up. Lindsay? Lindsay as in Charlie's sister. Astrid hadn't meant to eavesdrop on Charlie's phone conversation, but the woman had been so loud the entire kitchen had heard. While it was clear the siblings weren't close, it hadn't been what was said that worried her. It'd been Charlie's reaction.

"I believe he's your neighbor—for the time being." Lindsay turned her dazzling smile on Aunt Magnolia, then Astrid.

"Charlie is your brother?" Camellia, being Camellia, hugged the woman. "That makes you almost family."

"Oh?" Lindsay blinked rapidly, looking confused. "Does it?"

"He's a dear boy. And his girls are just precious." Aunt Camellia glanced Astrid's way. "They've gotten quite close to our Astrid."

"Charles didn't mention he was having company." Aunt Mags looked to Astrid for confirmation.

Even Lindsay was looking at her. Her thorough head-to-toe inspection wasn't exactly polite. And, unlike Charlie, Lindsay didn't have a poker face. The woman's smile had an edge to it—Astrid didn't like it.

"I think this calls for a family dinner." Camellia was too sweet for her own good. "We'd love to have you join us this evening. Astrid can get Charlie and the girls to join us."

"You can?" Lindsay's tone was sharp but her smile was dazzling once more. "Would you? That would be lovely."

Charlie had made it perfectly clear he didn't want to see his sister. Astrid knew it. Lindsay knew it. If he didn't want to see her, he'd have a good reason. All eyes remained on her, waiting, so she said the first thing that came to mind. "I think he was taking the girls to... Alpine Springs. Tonight." Her cheeks went hot—no doubt she was red-faced. She'd always been a terrible liar.

"Alpine Springs?" Aunt Camellia frowned. "But—"

Aunt Magnolia took one look at Astrid and nodded. "Yes, that's right. Alpine Springs."

Thank you, Aunt Mags. She took a deep breath.

"Perhaps tomorrow night?" Lindsay's smile was still in place but it didn't reach her eyes.

"Tomorrow is perfect." Camellia was delighted. "The girls are going bowling with friends but Charlie should be free."

Halley had texted her to tell her the good news. Nicole was chaperoning the group and bringing Ginger—which meant Nova would have a friend, too. She'd been so happy that Charlie was letting the girls go. Now Astrid regretted sharing Halley's text with them.

"We can't answer for him, Camellia." Thankfully, Aunt Magnolia seemed to have picked up on Astrid's distress. "He might have made plans."

"You're right, of course." Lindsay sighed. "That was presumptuous of me."

Astrid was relieved when the door to the boutique opened—eager to end this increasingly awkward conversation. But her relief vanished when Charlie walked inside.

"Look who's here." Camellia, bless her, wore such a hopeful smile.

"Charlie." It was Theo that moved first. He stepped forward, clasped Charlie's hand and gave it several solid shakes. "Good to see you."

"Why do you look so surprised? I told you we were coming into town today." Lindsay made no move to hug him. If anything, she stiffened—her head angled in an almost defiant manner. "And here we are."

"So I see." Charlie's voice was flat and his face was blank.

This was the Charlie she'd met weeks ago. Stiff and withdrawn. *To protect himself.* This was one of the people that had hurt him. His sister? A vise grip tightened around her heart. There was no reason for her to go to him. None.

Charlie beat her to it. He took several large steps and stopped beside her. It was odd but he offered no explanation and made no apologies.

"I wanted to invite your family for dinner tomorrow night." Aunt Camellia gushed a little less. "We'd love to have you and get to know your family."

Astrid could feel the tension rolling off him in waves.

"I said we'd love to." Lindsay was watching the two of them, eyes narrowed—but still smiling. "We have so much to catch up on."

Did his sister know how upset he was? If so, why was she pushing this? Why not go and leave Charlie in peace?

"But it will just be us. Sadly, Mom and Dad couldn't get away after all." Lindsay was watching him like a hawk.

That's what Lindsay looked like. A hawk, circling her prey. Charlie was the prey?

He cleared his throat. "That's asking too much, Camellia." His tone was much gentler now. "We couldn't impose—"

"You know I love a full house. We've missed you and the girls these last few nights." Aunt Camellia broke off, her smile faltering. "But, of course, I understand if you've got other plans."

"It will be fun, Charlie. Tell him, Theo." Lindsay slid her arm through her husband's. Theo didn't say a word. "When was the last time we were all together?"

"Two years ago." Charlie ran his fingers through his hair—then looked at Astrid. He was searching for something. "Family is family." Beads of sweat were forming along his upper lip but his gaze held hers. "Tomorrow works."

"Lovely." Lindsay sighed. "What time is best?"

Charlie's jaw flexed so tight, Astrid worried he'd crack a tooth.

"Six o'clock," Aunt Camellia said.

"We'll see you then. I can't wait." Lindsay left, her husband following, but Astrid never took her eyes off Charlie.

The door closed and she took his hand. "Come with me," she whispered, leading him into the storage room. Watching him struggle tore a hole in her heart. "Would you like a moment alone?" She didn't want to leave him but whatever he needed, she wanted him to have it.

He shook his head, his hand tightening on hers.

"Breathe," she whispered.

He took a deep breath, then another one, forcefully exhaling each time. He'd close his eyes, then open them, focusing on her.

"If I'd known that she…that your family…" Astrid shook her head. "You don't have to do this, Charlie."

"I'll have to face them alone at the reading of the will on Saturday." He took another deep breath, exhaling loudly. "I might as well have backup the first go-round." His hand squeezed hers, still breathing—still intently focused on her.

She nodded. "Are you okay?"

"I will be." He rolled his shoulders, took another deep breath and blew it out.

"What can I do?"

"Nothing. This is up to me." He shook his head. "There are two ways to deal with your inner demons. One method is facing them head-on, the other is removing them from your life. I've removed them, but this still happens." He was breathing easier now. "I guess it's time to confront them."

"You won't be alone Saturday. I'll be there, too." She had no idea why Rebecca had left her in her will, but she was glad to be going now. No matter what happened, Charlie wouldn't be alone.

He pulled her into his arms. "Good."

Astrid clung to him, fighting against the tears that burned her eyes. He didn't need her tears. He needed her strength. He wanted her strength. He had it. No matter what happened, he wouldn't be alone.

CHARLIE WANTED TO throw up. He had for the last twenty-four hours. Why the hell had he agreed to this?

While he was relieved his parents weren't coming, he didn't want to see Lindsay. Part of him suspected she'd said they were coming just to mess with him. He wouldn't put it past her. Bottom line, he didn't want his family to take up any more space. Family or not, he didn't need or want them in his life.

But he did want to show them they were wrong.

He wasn't worthless; he was capable of taking care of himself and his girls. He'd found a family that had accepted him. He'd found a woman that saw that he was broken but, so far, she hadn't laughed at him or left him.

I love you, Charlie.

The last three days, those four words had given him purpose. He wanted to be worthy of love. Not just Astrid's, but his daughters. Every day, he'd carved out time to spend with them. Astrid had opened his eyes to what he'd been missing but it was up to him to build a relationship with each of his girls. It was important that he do this on his own. That he was capable.

But he'd missed Astrid every damn day.

He'd come to the boutique because he couldn't take it anymore. Astrid was important to him. When she wasn't near him, the world wasn't as bright. She'd brought that brightness into his life and, even though he didn't want to let it go, he wanted what was best for her. That was why he felt it was important for her to know at least twenty reasons she shouldn't settle for him. She needed to have as much information as possible to understand that he wasn't good for her. She'd changed his life for the better, but it would crush him if he changed her life for the worse. He'd pored over the list and added them to the carefully crafted speech he'd written on index cards and tucked into his wallet. He'd never get the words out on his own.

But the speech had been forgotten the minute he'd walked into the boutique.

Now he was driving to Astrid's place doing his best to keep it together.

If history repeated itself and he couldn't keep his panic at bay, it would be bad. Surprisingly, he didn't give a damn about what his family would say and do. It was the Hills he was concerned about. Dane and Van, men he'd come to respect. And Astrid. Always Astrid. He didn't want to humiliate himself in front of them.

He parked, grabbed the flowers off the passenger seat and headed for the front door. Before he could knock, Astrid pulled it open.

"Hi." She was beautiful.

"Hi." He shook his head.

"What?" Her smile soothed the unease churning his stomach.

"You're beautiful." He held out the bouquet.

Her eyes went wide. "Thank you." She took the flowers. "Come in. Come in." She waved him forward. "The troops have rallied. I should tell you, Aunt Camellia feels horrible."

"Troops?" He followed her into the kitchen. "Oh, the troops."

"Charlie, I am so sorry." Camellia stopped short of hugging him, but the look on her face tugged at his heart. "If I'd known it would cause you any distress I never, ever would have issued the invitation."

He took a deep breath and gave her a quick, one-armed hug. "I know. You've all been nothing but kind to me." He cleared his throat. "My family isn't quite as…" He stared around the room. Van Kettner. Dane and Tansy and Magnolia.

"Big?" Dane suggested. "Or loud?"

"Supportive." Van cocked an eyebrow Dane's way.

"Protective." Magnolia stepped forward to stare up at him. "I'm actually excited about this evening. It's been a while since I've been able to verbally eviscerate someone and spit them out into little, tiny pieces."

"Let's not assume the worst." Astrid shook her head, but she was laughing.

"I'm not assuming. I'm preparing." Magnolia winked at him. "Come along, Charles, I'll let you approve the seating arrangement."

Charlie moved the place cards around, then gave up. "I'll leave it up to you."

"Proximity doesn't matter when it's words that are weaponized." Dane was putting silverware on all of the napkins. "If it's any consolation, my dad and I were barely speaking three months ago. It'd been that way for years."

"What happened?"

"Well, a fire took a good portion of our bees, my younger brother ran off and we almost lost our home to the bank." Dane chuckled. "It was enough to knock some sense into him. Into both of us, really."

Charlie wasn't sure what the appropriate response was for that so he stayed quiet.

"I can tell you one thing." Dane's voice lowered. "If it wasn't for Tansy and her family, I'm not sure we would have made it through. Once they decide you're part of the family, that's it. They're looking after you, whether you like it or not." He clapped a hand on Charlie's shoulder. "I hate to break it to you but…you're now a part of that family." He patted him on the back.

Charlie had a cat in his lap and was feeding oyster crackers to Lord Byron when there was a knock on the front door.

"I'll get it." Aunt Camellia went to answer it.

"You stay put." Van pointed at him. "Petting an animal can lower your blood pressure and your stress level."

"He's right." Astrid sat in the chair next to Charlie. "Why do you think we have so many animals?"

"We didn't have pets." Charlie kept petting the over-size cat.

"What a charming home." Lindsay's voice set Charlie's teeth on edge.

"Look at me." Astrid rested her hand on his arm. "We're all on your side. I'm here for you. And I love you." She stood, smoothing out her skirts, before he could respond.

Now was not the time to whip out his note cards.

He considered carrying Jammie around with him but decided against it. He set the cat in the chair and stood. Introductions were made and Charlie managed to be civil.

In a group of that size, it was easy to keep conversation flowing.

When they moved into the dining room, Charlie's sense of dread was easing.

"You're here to visit Charles?" Magnolia asked, passing around a platter of fresh-baked dinner rolls.

"Yes." Lindsay glanced his way. "And my aunt's will is being read tomorrow."

"I'm so sorry for your loss. Rebecca was a character. She and Astrid were kindred spirits." Camellia patted Astrid's arm.

"Is that so?" Lindsay was wearing her hawklike expression again. Who was she hunting this time?

"Lindsay and I have some business to do while we're here." Theo shoveled a mouthful of pot roast into his mouth.

"Theo, dear." Lindsay shot her husband a warning look.

"Oh? What do you do?" Tansy had caught the exchange, too.

"Real estate." Theo didn't seem to pick up on the panicked looks Lindsay was shooting his way. "Stinson Properties. A family business."

"Stinson Properties?" Camellia set her fork down. "My goodness."

Astrid was ramrod stiff now.

He should have said something. He should have told her about Stinson Properties and Lindsay but he didn't want to be linked to any of it. Still, learning this way wasn't right.

There was a stretch of silence before Dane asked, "I hear you've been offering to buy shops all along Main Street?"

"I think we've received some sort of communication?" Magnolia looked to Camellia for confirmation.

Camellia shrugged. "We're not interested in selling. I think you'll find most of the folk on Main Street unwilling."

"We can be pretty persistent." Lindsay was wearing her game face. Big smile, batting her eyelashes and oozing charm. "Can you blame us for wanting to be here? Honey is the sweetest little town. It's like a small-town movie. Nice people and a warm and cozy aesthetic. So much potential."

Charlie had a hard time controlling his smile. Potential? The people around this table loved their town as is. If she thought she was going to throw money at them and they'd welcome her with open arms, she was in for a shock.

"What are your plans for Honey?" Magnolia, like Dane, revealed no sign of concern or duress.

"Once we get the subdivision plans hammered out, we'll be able to reach out to woo some bigger businesses in—inject money into the community. Add more jobs." Theo stood and leaned forward, serving himself more pot roast. "Jobs are always a good thing."

"Subdivision?" Astrid glanced his way.

Charlie shook his head. He didn't know what they were talking about… Then it clicked and everything made sense. Soliciting shop owners. The survey crew on Rebecca's property. The interest in Rebecca's will. They wanted to put in a subdivision on her land? The land he'd been willing to sell to them? His stomach clenched tight. A subdivision? Next to Honey Hill Farms? Rebecca wouldn't be happy. Neither would the Hills. Or the bees.

"Let's not talk business at the dinner table." Lindsay waved his question away. "Where are your girls?"

Charlie was still processing. "Bowling with friends."

"How nice that they've made friends already." Lindsay's chuckle was forced. "Poor Charlie had a hard time making friends when he was little."

Theo laughed. "A hard time?"

"It's a good thing they take after their mother," Charlie cut them off.

The silence that flooded the room was charged with tension.

Lindsay turned to Tansy. "I read up on your big contest win. Best honey and all that." Lindsay set her utensils down, her food mostly uneaten. "But I'm confused. What does beekeeping consist of? Don't bees automatically make honey?"

"They do." Tansy propped her elbows on the table. "Our job isn't just about the honey. It's about keeping the bees healthy. Protecting them from pests. Making sure they have access to pollen and water—that sort of thing."

"Two of our employees were attacked by bees," Theo piped up. "Nasty stuff. One of them went into shock. Almost died."

"That sounds dreadful." Magnolia offered Theo the bowl of roasted potatoes. "In my experience, bees don't attack unless they're provoked. What happened?"

Theo added a heap of potatoes to his plate. "I wasn't there. I can't say."

Astrid glanced at him again. This time, there was a hint of uncertainty on her face.

"If you'll excuse me, I'm going to check on the cobbler." Camellia gave Van a quick squeeze on the shoulder before heading into the kitchen.

"Have you always wanted to be a beekeeper? You've never wanted...more?" Lindsay shrugged.

"More?" Tansy leaned back and Dane draped an arm around her. "I have everything I want right here. What more could I want?"

Dane pressed a kiss to her temple.

Charlie had to smile at the exchange. Especially when he saw the way Lindsay looked at Theo, sighed, and sat back in her chair.

"Help! Help!" Lord Byron's squawking shriek made everyone jump. "Help!"

Everything happened all at once. Van was the first one in the kitchen. "Call 911," he yelled. "Hurry."

Dane was dialing before Charlie could get his phone out of his pocket. "We need an ambulance. Honey Hill Farms."

The sight of Camellia Hill unconscious and on the floor knocked the air from Charlie's lungs.

"She's breathing." Tansy was leaning over her, relaying information to Dane. "Tell them to hurry."

Dane rested a hand on Tansy's shoulder, talking to the operator in low, clipped tones.

Astrid knelt on the ground beside her aunt. The grief on her face tore at his heart. Astrid was hurting and he felt it. Raw and crushing. He couldn't stand it. There was nothing he could do but he'd stay beside her, ready to give her whatever she needed.

Time ticked away, dragging, until, finally, the sirens were audible. Everything sped up then. Tansy started crying when the paramedics loaded Camellia onto a gurney. Astrid had a merciless grip on his hands as they followed the gurney out to the ambulance. He heard words like *stable* and *strong heart rate* but they didn't offer any real sense of comfort. How could it when Camellia was so still? It was a stark contrast to her constant motion.

Van and Mags went in the ambulance with her.

Dane, Tansy and Astrid stared after the ambulance, in shock.

He was vaguely aware of his sister and Theo leaving, mumbling something on their way out—but they weren't important.

"I'll drive." Charlie waited for his words to register before placing his hand on Astrid's waist and steering her to his car. It was hard not to remember the morning he'd lost Yasmina. After the accident, there was no expectation she'd make it. And yet, he'd fought against the crushing terror and hoped that, somehow, someway, she'd survive. It was only after the ER doctor sat him down to officially announce her death that he'd accepted it and the ground beneath him had fallen away. If he was being honest with himself, he was only now finding his footing again.

It was hard to wrap his mind around the sudden turn

tonight had taken. Just like with Yasmina, one minute all had been well and the next had gone horribly wrong. But unlike Yasmina's accident, Astrid would *never* be alone. He'd make sure of that. For now, that was all he could do.

CHAPTER SIXTEEN

ASTRID WAS COLD. So cold. Charlie had her wrapped up against him, but she couldn't stop shivering. The nurse had given her a warm blanket but it wasn't enough. Charlie alternated rubbing his hands up and down her arms and holding her tightly against him—all the while whispering encouragement. "Camellia is strong. She's tough."

He was right. Camellia was vital and young and had so much to live for. She had to hold on to that. "She'll fight for Van."

"She'll fight for all of you." He smoothed the hair from her forehead.

She buried her face against him, breathing him deep into her lungs. It helped. Having him close made her feel less adrift. While the world around her pitched and turned, he was her anchor.

She rested her head against his chest and stared around the silent waiting room at the anguished faces of her loved ones. Tansy was curled up in Dane's lap. Magnolia was pacing to and fro, while Shelby sat nearby, rocking a sleeping Bea in her arms.

Van sat apart, his elbows resting on his knees, and stared at the floor. He looked so alone.

Oh, Van. She crossed the waiting room, digging deep for strength. Camellia would want her to be strong for him, so she'd try. She sat beside the man her aunt adored and rested her hand on his back. "Van."

He cleared his throat. "She'll be fine, Astrid."

They all wanted to believe that. "I know." Maybe if they said it enough, it would be true.

"She has to be." He shook his head, choking on his words. "She has to."

Astrid draped her arm across his back and rested her head on his shoulder. Her heart hurt for Van—for them all. Camellia was too important. They all relied on her. Not just her sunny disposition and endless love, but her constancy. She was always there for you—a rock.

What was happening right now? Was she awake? Scared or hurting?

When the doctor emerged, they all jumped up.

"I'm Dr. Edwards. You're Camellia Hill's family?"

"I'm her sister. Her nieces and their significant others. And Van...her partner." Magnolia crossed her arms over her chest, blinking rapidly. "How is she?"

"She's stable," he assured them, holding his hands up.

There was a collective sigh in the small space.

"From the electrocardiogram, we can determine she suffered a mild heart attack. We've given her a thrombolytic—which will help dissolve the clot and get the blood flowing." He checked his watch. "I'm scheduling a coronary angiogram now. It will identify any narrowing or blockages in the arteries and give us a better idea of what's going on. Depending on what the tests show, there is a chance we might need to fly her to Austin."

Astrid reached up to cover Charlie's hand on her shoulder.

"She'll have to be sedated for the angiogram so I thought a few of you might like to see her first? She's awake, but groggy. We need to limit it to five minutes." He paused. "Any questions?"

"She's safe?" Van asked. "She's going to be okay?"

"She is out of danger. The tests will help us determine what we need to do to make sure this doesn't happen again."

Van nodded. "Why Austin?"

"They have more specialized equipment. But I will let you know if that's what needs to happen. Anything else?"

"Yes." It was hard to see their indomitable Aunt Mags so rattled. But she was. They all were. "If she doesn't go to Austin, what then?"

"She'll get a room. Whether she stays here or goes to Austin, she won't be leaving for several days." He waited.

Astrid was still processing what he'd said. A heart attack. Tests. It would be exhausting for her aunt—and scary if she had to face it all alone. "If she gets a room, can she have visitors?"

"Two at a time." He glanced at his watch again. "I'll show whoever is going back."

"Go." Charlie squeezed her shoulders. "Give her my best. I'll be here when you get back."

She and Tansy, Van and Magnolia followed Dr. Edwards through the emergency room doors and past several curtained-off stations.

"Remember, she's tired. Keep it short." Dr. Edwards pulled the curtain back.

"There you are." Camellia's smile was small and her voice was thick, but she was alive and breathing.

Van reached her first. "Camellia Ann, you've given my

heart a fright." He bent low, pressing a kiss against her forehead. "Don't you ever do that again, you hear me?"

"I hear you." She smiled up at him. "You sweet man."

He caught her hand in his and pressed a kiss to her knuckles.

Mags took her place on the other side of Camellia. She pressed her hand to Camellia's cheek but couldn't speak. Instead, her lips trembled and she blinked rapidly, taking the handkerchief Van offered her.

Astrid and Tansy stood at the foot of the bed. Since Aunt Camellia didn't have a free hand, they each held on to one of her feet.

"Sweet girls." Camellia smiled. "I'm sorry to have caused such a fuss this evening."

"No, ma'am." Tansy shook her head. "You are not going to apologize for having a health crisis. It's not like you planned it, Aunt Camellia." She paused. "Did you?"

That earned a chuckle from Van and a smile from Camellia.

"It's so good to see your smile." Astrid gave Camellia's toes a squeeze. "Your smile makes everything better, don't you know?"

"That it does." Van cradled her hand against his chest.

"My goodness, what a fuss." Camellia's eyelids were heavy. "I'll be right as rain in the morning."

"We know." Tansy patted her foot.

"But you have to rest, Camellia." Magnolia finally spoke. "You don't have to be right as rain in the morning. You have to rest and heal and listen to what your doctor says. That's what matters. You, taking care of you."

"You've got a waiting room full of people that love you, Camellia Ann. It's our turn to take care of you." Van stooped and kissed her. "Please."

"Miss Hill." Dr. Edwards stepped in. "I'm going to take you for another test. Chances are you'll doze off for a bit but I'll make certain there's someone waiting for you when you come back."

"That would be lovely." Aunt Camellia smiled.

It was hard to say goodbye. Aunt Camellia was such a force of nature. She looked small and frail in that bed. Too delicate to leave all alone.

They all showered her with hugs and kisses then. Though Van stayed behind for a moment longer. Together, they headed back to the now overflowing waiting room. Leif and Kerrielynn were there with Leif and Dane's father, Harald Knudson. Dane's friend Everett Taggert and his mother, Violet, were there, along with Van's sister, Agatha, and her husband, Julian.

"How is she?" Shelby asked as soon as they came through the doors.

"She looks tired." And then Magnolia did something Astrid had never seen her do. Magnolia burst into tears.

"Hey, hey, there, Mags." Van hugged her, patting her back. "None of that now. You know as well as I do, once that woman's made up her mind, there's no stopping her. She'll get through this."

Mags continued to sob. "She better."

"She will. She'll be stronger than ever." But his voice wasn't all that steady.

Camellia's fragile condition had shaken them all to the core.

Questions were coming from all over, but Astrid let Tansy and Van do the talking. Her throat was tight and her eyes were stinging. If she tried, she'd wind up sobbing like Mags. What she needed was... Charlie. She glanced around the room. He'd been at her side the whole, horrible night, but now he was gone. She drew in a wavering breath and hugged herself.

It was late. Charlie had the girls to take care of.

She'd manage just fine.

"Astrid, come sit." Violet patted the vinyl chair beside her. "Rest a bit."

Astrid didn't want to sit. She needed a moment alone or she'd fall apart. Mags didn't need that. Van didn't need that. "I'll be right back." She walked down the hall, found a family bathroom, closed and locked the door, and turned on the cold water.

Someone knocked on the door but she ignored it.

She splashed cold water on her face.

The knocking continued.

"Someone's in here." Her throat was so tight it hurt to get the words out.

"I know." It was Charlie.

She unlocked the door and pulled it wide. "You're here." She frantically wiped at the tears falling.

He nodded, a cup of coffee in each hand. "I thought someone might need this."

He was so thoughtful. "But... What a-about the g-girls?" She tried to stop crying.

With his foot, he pushed the door closed behind him. "They're fine." He set the coffee cups on the counter.

The tears kept coming. "But y-you need to...to go—"

"Astrid." He tilted her face back, a deep furrow settling between his brows as he stared down at her. "I'm where I need to be." He spoke with such tenderness.

That did it. She stopped fighting the tears and stepped into his arms. Her world had been knocked off its axis and there was no knowing the outcome. "She's the heart of our family. We all need her, Charlie. She can't...she can't…" She wasn't going to say it out loud. "I can't lose her."

"I'm sorry you're hurting." His arms tightened. "What can I do?"

She buried her head against his chest. "This…just… don't let go."

CHARLIE LEFT THE hospital feeling lighter. Exhausted, but hopeful.

"I'm so relieved." Astrid held his hand. She was smiling again. It was a tired smile, but happy.

After hours of waiting and fearing the worst, the doctor had delivered good news. Camellia's heart showed no signs of further clots or blockages or anything else concerning. She wouldn't be going to Austin, but she would be staying at the hospital for at least three more nights. Astrid had wanted to stay until Camellia had a room—making them the last to leave.

"I'm so glad Van and Aunt Mags can be with her." Astrid smiled as he held the car door open for her. "Thank you."

Once he'd started the car, he glanced her way. She'd cried so much he'd begun to worry. Her grief was so deep and endless. And he'd been helpless to ease it. They knew things were going to be okay, but she had to be exhausted. He was—but he wasn't worried about himself. "You need some sleep."

She nodded, yawning. "What about the girls?"

"Nicole is having a big slumber party." He wasn't going to think about it. They would be fine.

"Are you okay with that?" She rested her head on the seat. "If you're worried, we can get them."

He shook his head. After all the hell she'd been

through, she was asking if he was okay. He still hadn't accepted that she could care about him. Didn't she see that she deserved so much better?

"I don't mind, Charlie."

"I'm sure they're asleep." He hoped they were asleep. "I'll get them in the morning."

"Okay." She yawned.

He was tired, so the drive home felt longer than usual. The highways were lit up but once he turned onto the farm-to-market road, he forced himself to perk up and concentrate. It was pitch-black. No streetlights. No house lights. Just country. When they'd first arrived, it had been unnerving. Now he didn't mind. The view of the stars overhead was like nothing he'd ever seen.

"Charlie?" Astrid's voice was soft. "Shelby is probably already asleep and Tansy is staying with Dane and I don't want to be alone. Could you stay with me tonight?"

He glanced her way. He didn't want her to be alone, either. "If that's what you want."

She nodded.

When he parked, she was asleep. He managed to scoop her up and carry her to the house. The door was unlocked,

All of the downstairs lights were on, but the house was quiet.

Until a stampede of dogs came clicking down the wooden floor. A chorus of whimpers and whines woke Astrid.

"Are we home?" Astrid murmured, looking down. "It's okay. She's going to be okay."

Charlie set her down. "Do I need to feed them? Let them out?"

"They have food." She crouched, giving each of the

six dogs a pat and scratch. "And a doggie door. But I'm sure they know something's up. The house is never this empty." She stood and hugged herself. "It's too quiet." She smiled at him.

"Is someone crying?" Charlie stared down the hall.

"Oh." Astrid hurried down the hall. "Lord Byron." She moved to the perch where the bird sat. His head was tucked under his wing and he was making a pitiful sound. "Hey, pretty boy. Camellia is okay."

Lord Byron sat up. "Camellia? Camellia?" he squawked.

"She will be home soon," she assured him.

"Does he understand?" His knowledge of birds was limited.

"I think so." She nodded. "Don't you? Camellia is okay, pretty boy." She ran a hand over his head, speaking with a low, soothing tone. "It's okay. She will be home soon." She reached into a small basket on the counter and fed the bird. "Camellia will be home." Astrid's voice cracked. She glanced back at him. "Sorry."

"Don't be." It hurt to see her cry but if that's what she needed, he'd deal with it. "You can cry. It's been a hell of a day." He took the hand she offered him. "You need sleep."

"You're right." She nodded, letting him tug her along behind him.

She led him up the stairs and down the hall. "My room." She opened the door and pulled him inside after her. She sat on the edge of the bed and he squatted, pulling off her shoes.

"I'll be downstairs on the couch." He stood.

"It will be less crowded up here with me." She yawned and patted the bed beside her.

"Less crowded?"

"The dogs will want to sleep with you. All of them." She lay back on her pillow. "I promise, I won't bite." She smiled up at him.

He chuckled and went around to the other side of the bed. He unbuttoned his shirt and draped it over the chair by her vanity, followed by his slacks, and joined Astrid in the bed.

"I feel overdressed," she murmured.

It was only then that he realized he'd undressed. "Force of habit." He sighed. "Want me to—"

"Get in the bed, Charlie." She waited for him to lie down beside her before covering them both with the extra quilt from the foot of her bed.

He lay flat on his back, staring up at the ceiling.

"Charlie?" She rolled onto her side, draped her arm across his waist and rested her head against his chest. "Is this okay?"

He let out a deep breath, his arm slipping beneath her to come around her waist. "Yes." It was better than okay. He rested his cheek against the top of her head and closed his eyes. With her close, things were better.

It was wrong to need someone this way but he didn't know how to stop it. She felt so good against him and he was so tired, he could barely keep his eyes open.

His dreams were disorienting. One minute he was back in the condo in Fort Worth and the girls were solemn-faced and ready for school. The next he was standing in Rebecca's kitchen with Halley, Nova and Astrid chatting and laughing and waiting for him to make breakfast. Back in the condo, he was going room by room but they were all empty. No Halley. No Nova. No Astrid. The more doors he opened, the more appeared.

Nothing was there. He called out for them but there was no answer. Emptiness and white walls. He was alone—running down tunnel-like halls only to find another door.

He woke up suddenly, breathing hard. Lost.

"Charlie?" Astrid glanced back at him, her eyes puffy from sleep.

He lay on his side, spooning Astrid. She was so soft. So real. "I'm sorry." He panted, burying his nose at the base of her neck.

"Bad dream?" She hugged his arms against her stomach.

"Hmm." He didn't want to talk about it. This reality was better than any dream.

Her breathing evened out and she relaxed in his hold, but he couldn't sleep. He didn't know how long they stayed that way but he was perfectly content. Eventually, the front door opened and voices echoed up the stairs.

Nova, he recognized her laugh.

He smiled, carefully sliding his arms from around Astrid. She needed sleep. He needed to check on his girls. He left the lights off, dressing in the semi-dark and tiptoeing from the room—with his shoes in his hand.

He heard Halley say "Where is everyone?" on his way to the kitchen.

"Morning," he said, stifling a yawn. "How was your night?"

Halley stared at him, her expression unreadable. Was she upset? Did she know about Camellia? Or was she angry with him?

"We had so much fun, Charlie." Nova skipped around the kitchen. "We had s'mores and pizza and watched movies and ate popcorn."

Nicole sat at the table, sipping a cup of coffee. "We watched every princess movie I own."

"Princesses are pretty." Ginger said this, her smile shy.

"I guess. Not as cool as dinosaurs, though." Nova hopped up and down. "And, guess what, Charlie, my eyes didn't rot out."

"I'm glad to hear it." He risked another look Halley's way. She was angry with him. First things, first. "I appreciate last night, Nicole." He took a deep breath. "Girls, I want to start by saying that everything will be okay. That's the important part."

Nova stopped hopping.

Halley sank into a chair at the kitchen table.

"Aunt Camellia is in the hospital." He went to sit between them at the table.

"What happened?" Nova's chin crumpled and she clutched Scorpio to her chest. "Did she fall? Did she get hurt?"

"But she's okay?" Halley asked, staring at him. "You're not just saying that?"

"She's not going to die?" Nova had big, fat tears rolling down her cheeks.

It was a logical conclusion. The only time the girls had gone to the hospital was after Yasmina's accident. They'd come home without their mother.

"She's not going to die." He wiped at Nova's tears.

"Then why is she still in the hospital?" Halley was watching him closely.

"They need to keep an eye on her for a few days. When they think she's ready, she'll come home." He took a deep breath. "Everyone will get to pitch in and take care of her for a while. Until she's better."

"Will we still be here, Charlie?" Nova sniffed. "I want to take care of her, too."

Charlie didn't have an answer for that.

"You're lying." Halley glared at him.

"I'm not." He shook his head. "Why would you—"

"Because you're a liar." She slid her phone onto the table. "Benji fixed it. My phone wasn't broken, you blocked everyone—turned everything off." She stood and stomped out of the room.

He glanced up to see Shelby and Nicole wide-eyed. "I'll be back."

"You're not lying, are you?" Nova grabbed his hand. "Aunt Camellilla isn't dying?"

"I'm not lying." He'd brought this on himself. "Can you stay here while I go talk to Halley?"

"How about you help me feed Bea?" Shelby asked.

"I love babies." Ginger hurried to Bea's high chair.

"Okay." Nova sniffed, wiping her nose with the back of her hand. "I guess."

"I'll be back." He nodded his thanks at Shelby and headed outside.

Halley was across the yard. She sat on the ground with her knees drawn up and her head down. He couldn't tell if she was crying and he didn't know what to say, but he sat on the ground beside her.

"I'm mad at you." Halley's voice shook. "I don't want to talk to you."

"You can be mad at me." He plucked at the grass beside him, way outside his comfort zone. "I messed up. You should be mad at me."

Halley didn't move.

"I'm not good at this dad thing." He heard her muttered "No duh," but kept on going. "I worry about you and Nova all the time."

"You're not worrying about me. You hate me." She spat the words out. "I know you do."

Charlie was momentarily speechless. "Halley, I've never hated you."

"You do." She was so angry her face went dark red. "Ever since Mom's crash. You can't look at me. All I do is mess up. Because you know it was my fault."

He was lost now. "Nothing is your fault."

"Right." She rolled her eyes. "Mom's dead because of me. It's my fault." Tears streamed down her face, every word raw. "Team A was me and Mom. Team B was you and Nova. Remember? If I'd been there, Mom wouldn't have had that crash. I could have stopped her or saved her... She wouldn't be dead." She sobbed. "But I wasn't there. She died. And you hate me for it."

He couldn't breathe. "Halley." All this time, she'd been carrying this inside of her—with no one to talk to. His heart sliced in two. "That's not true."

"It is," she yelled.

He rose onto his knees and gripped her shoulders. "I'm sorry, Halley. I'm so sorry. It's not true. If you'd been there..." His chest tightened. He couldn't think about it. Couldn't bear the pain that threatened to consume him. "I couldn't... No..." His eyes were on fire. "I could have lost you both." He cradled her face. Would he have survived that? "It wasn't your fault. I don't blame you, Halley. I would never blame you."

She was watching him with tears streaming down her face.

"I'm terrible at this." He was probably butchering everything he was trying to say. "I did lie to you about the phone. I did. It was wrong." He shook his head. "Some of the girls you were hanging around with weren't nice. You got so caught up in social media. They made you cry and picked on you and made you feel less and that was bullshit." He broke off. "Sorry." He shook his head again. "I wanted to protect you. You've been hurt too much. You deserve better friends than that. I should have talked to you but I'm not good at talking. As you can tell."

Halley stared at him for a long time.

"I could never hate you, Halley. I love you, very much. You are my daughter."

She stared crying again.

"I am sorry I haven't been here for you. I'm sorry I messed up with the phone…and pretty much everything." He didn't know what else he could say.

"You don't hate me?"

Dammit. He sat and pulled her into his lap, rocking her back and forth. All this time he'd been trying to protect her—which hurt her more than he knew. "I love you. I will always love you."

She hugged him.

Every single sob was a blow to his heart. All this pain. All these tears. He'd done this to her. He kept on rocking her. "I'm doing it all wrong. I want to be your dad."

"You *are* my dad," she murmured. "That's why it hurt that you didn't want me."

"Oh, Halley." It was his turn to cry. His father had been cruel, but Charlie had always known what his father thought of him. Charlie hadn't said enough—he'd let his little girl read all of her fears into that silence. "Please forgive me. I promise I'll try harder. I'll never stop trying. We have to be honest with each other—even when it's hard. Okay?"

She nodded against his chest.

He'd screwed this up completely. He loved Halley and he'd still hurt her. If he'd needed further confirmation that he'd never be good enough for Astrid, he had it. Instead of pulling her into his disaster of a life, he needed to focus on those that were already living it with him. Halley and Nova were all that mattered. It would hurt to let Astrid go…but he'd never had her to begin with.

CHAPTER SEVENTEEN

Astrid finished braiding Nova's hair. "All done."

Nova reached up to run her fingers along the two French braids. "Just like yours." She gave Astrid a kiss on the cheek and ran out of the kitchen.

"Benji's ready to start the movie." Nicole stepped aside as Nova ran past. "Benji brought one of his old dinosaur movies. I can't wait to hear what Nova thinks." She lowered her voice, "FYI, Charlie and Halley are in there, too."

Astrid had caught sight of the two of them outside. Whatever they'd been discussing had looked too intimate to interrupt. She hoped that, whatever it was, they'd worked it out. With Nova, all it took was some hugs and bedtime stories and a little time to make her happy. It was more difficult with Halley. Which meant it was even more difficult for Charlie.

"How are you holding up?" Shelby wiped off Bea's face and set the toddler on her play mat. "About Camellia?"

"I'm relieved. It all happened so fast, though. It still feels a little…unreal." Astrid sat with Bea on the floor. "But I know Aunt Camellia and I know she'll get better." The alternative wasn't an option.

"I agree." Shelby waved at Bea. "She has to watch you grow up and wear your first bee suit."

Bea giggled.

"How about the other thing?" Nicole asked, sipping her cup of coffee. "You know, being head over heels in love with Mr. Neighbor."

Astrid was in fact head over heels in love with her neighbor. "They're going back home soon."

"How are you doing with that?" Nicole pushed.

"Are you trying to make me cry this morning?" She shook her head. "I'm joking."

"No, you're not." Nicole sat on the floor beside her. "You weren't supposed to actually fall in love with him, Astrid."

"I didn't realize love was a choice?" Shelby carried Bea's bib and dish to the sink. "That's the problem with it."

Astrid shook one of Bea's rattles—and Jammie the cat came running over. "It's not for you, silly. It's Bea's." The baby giggled when the cat swatted the toy. "He is funny, isn't he, Bea?"

"There's no chance they'll stay?" Nicole asked.

"I don't know. I don't think so." Charlie had never mentioned considering staying in Honey. He had mentioned he didn't like change and he did like plans.

"It's a shame." Shelby joined them on the floor, stacking up Bea's blocks. "He was so…so sharp when he got here. Honey seems to have smoothed off those rough edges."

Shelby and Nicole gave her the same look.

"Oh, stop." Astrid shook her head.

Charlie came around the corner and stopped. "You're all on the floor."

"It's where the cool kids hangout." Nicole held up

one of Bea's teddy bears and squeezed it. The toy squeaked—and all six dogs came running.

Bea was delighted.

"Do you want a ride into town?" Charlie asked.

Astrid pushed up off the floor. "Yes, please. It's almost eleven, and the appointment is at Mr. Delaney's office at eleven fifteen."

"He's still practicing law?" Nicole's eyes widened. "I know his sisters are still going strong and running the café but I thought he was dead."

"Nicole." But Astrid laughed. "He did have a hip replacement and has had all sorts of physical therapy—that's why this meeting was delayed for so long."

"Still no idea what to expect from Rebecca's will?" Shelby asked.

Astrid shrugged. "No idea." She glanced at Charlie.

"No." He sighed. "I have a feeling it will be an interesting morning. Thank you, again, for keeping an eye on the girls."

"I'm planning on feeding them nothing but sugar. Other than that, we'll be fine." Nicole smiled sweetly.

"She's teasing." Astrid shot her a look.

"Or am I?" She stood and scooped up Bea. "Come on, Bea, let's go watch some dinosaurs attack," she said, carrying Bea from the room.

"Good luck." Shelby hugged her.

"I have my phone. Keep me posted on Aunt Camellia, please." Astrid hugged her back.

"Of course." Shelby nodded.

Astrid picked up on Charlie's mood a few minutes into the drive. He was quiet and tense, his hold on the steering wheel tight.

"Bea is getting so big. She's been using chairs to

pull herself up and I just know she's going to take her first steps soon." She glanced at Charlie's hands. They weren't white-knuckling the steering wheel anymore. "Aunt Mags said that Tansy didn't walk until she was about a year and a half. Then she was always on the go. I was walking by nine months because I had to follow Tansy everywhere she went. Then there was Rosemary. She has always been the overachiever. Aunt Camellia swears she skipped crawling and was walking by eight months." She paused, searching for something else to carry on about. "Tansy and Dane invited you all to the observation deck. I hoped, now that you've been here awhile and you realize how amazing bees are, you and the girls might go?" She attempted a teasing smile. "They've double- and triple-checked the screens—so there's no fear of the bees getting inside. The girls would get to see what you saw the Junior Beekeepers doing."

"They'd probably like that." Charlie sighed. "Halley has developed a sudden interest in bees."

"Is that a bad thing?" Astrid waited. "You should check out the observation deck, then. The Junior Bee-keepers are going out there tonight, around five, for their meeting. You might all learn a little something?"

"As long as she learns about safety first." He glanced her way.

She smiled. "If you weren't driving right now, I'd kiss you."

"If I didn't want to get this over with, I'd pull over and let you." His grin was short-lived.

Charlie's phone was pinging when they parked in front of Mr. Delaney's law office. He glanced at it, sighed and shoved it into his pocket.

From the twitch of his jaw, she suspected it was his

sister. "It's a nice place," she said, hoping to distract him. The office was located right off Main Street, with a dark green awning and a large pot overflowing with marigolds on either side of the door.

"I wonder if he received an offer from Stinson Properties?" Charlie held the door open for her.

"Good morning." George Delaney had a wisp of white hair on his head, hunched posture, and was relying on his cane. "You'll have to excuse me, this new hip has me stuck in first gear." He chuckled and waved them into the open conference room.

Lindsay and Theo sat on the opposite side of the table.

"Good morning. I hope your aunt is okay?" Lindsay asked. "You all disappeared and we didn't want to impose."

"I heard about dear Camellia." George Delaney shook his head. "My thoughts are with you all. I know Camellia, though. She'll be right as rain in no time."

"I hope so." Astrid nodded.

"Let's get this business over and done with, then." Mr. Delaney made his way around the table slowly, using his cane to lower himself into the high-backed leather chair. "This is all for show, you know. Texas doesn't require any sort of formal reading of the will."

Charlie paused. "It doesn't?"

"No, no. Rebecca wanted it this way." Mr. Delaney shook his head. "She seemed to think the two of you might want to hash some things out."

Astrid sat in the chair next to Charlie, puzzling over the old lawyer's words. There were things she wanted to hash out with Charlie but none of them concerned Rebecca's holdings.

"Two? Who are you referring to, Mr. Delaney?" Lindsay's smile was tight.

"As I mentioned earlier, Mrs. Stinson, Mr. Charles Driver and Miss Astrid Hill are the only two people mentioned in Rebecca's will." When George Delaney's brow furrowed, his forehead resembled an accordion. "There's no need for anyone else to be present."

Lindsay's indrawn breath was sharp. "I'm here to support my brother."

Astrid glanced Charlie's way to gauge his reaction to Lindsay's claim. His jaw was tight, but his gaze remained on George Delaney.

"Is that a fact?" Mr. Delaney chuckled. "Well, then."

Rebecca had been a woman of means. It would make sense for her to leave it all to Charlie; he was her beloved nephew. But why had she wanted Astrid here?

From the glare Lindsay was shooting her way, the woman was obviously wondering the same thing.

George Delaney sort of flopped into his chair, then proceeded to pull two sheets of paper from a manila envelope. "Rebecca kept it simple. I approve."

She and Charlie sat beside each other. She didn't know whether to hold his hand or give him his space.

Mr. Delaney scanned over the papers. "Let's skip over the rigmarole and get to the meat of it. To my dear friend, Astrid Hill, I leave $250,000 to be used for the bees as she deems fit."

Lindsay's gasp was impossible to miss.

"To my nephew, Charles Adam Driver, I leave the entirety of my wealth and investments, the house and property on Lake Champlain." He paused to look up at Charlie.

"I didn't know she still had her place on Lake Champlain." Charlie looked stunned.

But Astrid's heart was in her throat. Rebecca's gift was both unexpected and lovely.

"I also leave the four hundred acres in Honey, Texas, to Charles Adam Driver. If, however, Mr. Driver wishes to sell, the Hill family has the first right of refusal before the property can be sold." George Delaney scanned over the paper, then looked up. "Rebecca didn't want her property sold, you see."

Astrid nodded. "She loved the place."

"Sentimentality aside, it's time to be reasonable." Lindsay shook her head. "Charlie, you don't need or want the place. You said as much. What would you do with four hundred acres? And, no offense, Astrid, but can your family afford to buy the place?" She pulled a brown leather briefcase up and placed it on the table. "I've already had the papers drawn up—and an appraisal on the value of the property so you can see, Charlie, we're giving you a more than generous offer."

All Astrid could do was stare at the woman.

"You said you'd sell." Lindsay slid the manila folder across the table. "We talked about this. We agreed, remember? You and the girls will be set and Theo and I can work our magic on Honey."

Each word made the room shrink. Lindsay was right about buying the place. The money they'd won was needed for the farm as is. Adding another four hundred acres would be expensive—the purchase, the upkeep and the taxes. But...did that mean Charlie would sell Rebecca's place to Stinson Properties? Her stomach was churning so much she feared she'd be sick. She needed fresh air. And soon. She swallowed and asked, "Is there anything you need from me, Mr. Delaney?"

"I just need a signature." Mr. Delaney offered her a slight smile. "And you can be on your way."

Astrid nodded, reaching for the pen and paper he offered her.

"I'm glad you're not going to argue." Lindsay sighed. "It's not like you're walking away with nothing. I love it when everyone wins."

Astrid blindly signed the paper but couldn't look at the woman. Or Charlie. Instead, she fished her phone from her purse and sent a text to Tansy.

"I'll go make you copies." Mr. Delaney pushed himself up from his seat and inched his way from the room.

"Lindsay." Charlie cleared his throat. "We can discuss this—"

"Now," Lindsay pushed. "We have an agreement."

Astrid was on the verge of tears. "You do?" Did she really want to know the answer to that question?

Charlie looked at her then, the answer on his face. "We had discussed—"

"Agreed." Lindsay cut in. "We agreed that this was the right thing to do. Don't let a pretty face and nice people cloud your decision. I know you're not used to that, people being nice to you, but there's a reason. No one is nice without a reason. Ever. You, out of all people, know that."

Astrid's throat was so tight it hurt to breathe. The words were horrible. Lindsay was horrible. Worse, from the look on Charlie's face, he wasn't immediately dismissing what his sister was saying.

"If they haven't asked for something from you yet, they will." Lindsay shot her a look. "It doesn't even matter, though. Astrid, you can't afford the land, can you?" She waited for Astrid to shake her head. "And we have a lawyer to help tie up all the loose ends right here and now."

Astrid's phone vibrated. She read the text and took a shaky breath. "My ride is here. I'll leave you to it." She used the arms of the chair to steady herself.

"Astrid." Charlie was up. "Hold on."

She waited, blinking against the tears.

"I…" He swallowed, his jaw muscle working. "I should have told you."

A million things went round and round in her head. He wasn't staying. He'd never said otherwise. It was her foolish heart that led her to hope for something different. And the land? She swallowed and stared up into the face she loved. "She's right, Charlie. I do want something from you. And you know what it is. I've told you. You."

Lindsay's snort was grating. "And your two homes and money and, what else, the land."

"Here you go." Mr. Delaney handed her a manila envelope. "Your ride is out front."

"Thank you." She shook the older man's hand, collected her purse, then hesitated. "I don't know what's happened to make you so distrusting." She met Lindsay's narrowed gaze. "But I'm sorry for you. There are incredibly good people out there, people that honor their word or do things without ulterior motives. I'm one of them. And so is your brother." But she couldn't bring herself to look at Charlie before she left.

She headed out of the conference room, out of the lawyer's office and straight for Tansy's truck.

Tansy took one look at her. "Oh, Astrid." She grabbed her hand. "I'm sorry."

Astrid held tight to her sister's hand, her heart crumbling to dust.

CHARLIE HAD EXPECTED Lindsay's temper tantrum but her words still hurt.

"I can't believe you." Lindsay's tone was razor sharp. "I thought after all this time, you'd finally caught up or gotten better or more normal. You're just as screwed up as ever. What is wrong with you?"

"Now, Lindsay." Theo's attempt to calm her had only increased her fury. "He is your brother."

"Which means what?" Lindsay yanked her arm away from her husband. "My whole life, I've tolerated his... your weirdness. Even though it was embarrassing. Now? This? I can't believe you're going back on your word, Charlie. This is the smart business decision, you know that. And you're just going to walk away? It's idiotic." She broke off, scrambling. "Not to mention, Dad will be pissed."

When all else failed, she'd try to use their father against him. But this time it was different. He was different. "I don't care what he thinks. Or what you think." He shoved his hands into his pockets. "This isn't about getting what you want or business or money. This is about family and doing what's right. And love."

Lindsay and Theo had stared at him in shock.

"Hear! Hear!" Mr. Delaney sat in his chair, smiling.

"Charlie..." Lindsay paused. "I get that you're lonely but these people don't care about you. You can't listen to Astrid, you barely know her. She's probably been working you for the land the whole damn time. Come on, Charlie. Think. You are…you. What else makes sense?"

That she loves me. Whether or not it made sense, it was true. He accepted it, felt it, deep in his bones. The sort of love Lindsay couldn't understand. "I don't expect you to understand." He shook his head. "I'm sorry you're leaving empty-handed."

Lindsay sputtered and railed but he didn't budge. Nothing would change his mind. She was still red-faced and arguing the whole time Theo pulled her from Mr. Delaney's office.

"That was quite a show." Mr. Delaney sat forward, elbows on the table, to peer at him. "I think Rebecca would have been proud of you for standing your ground. Astrid, too."

He hoped so. "I have one thing I'd like to arrange before I leave." Charlie had taken his seat beside the older man and outlined what he had in mind.

Now, hours later, Charlie was back at home, reading emails. "School registration is coming up. Freshman year." He glanced around his computer screen at Halley. "Are you excited?"

"No." Halley shook her head. "It's a huge school. Half of my friends will go to Clark. Who knows if I'll see the friends that do go there."

Charlie and Yasmina had talked about putting Halley into a private high school. Maybe he should look into that.

"Why are we talking about school?" Nova crawled across the floor, growling loudly in her dinosaur costume. She'd hidden the jungle animals Van had given her throughout the house and had been "hunting" them all afternoon.

"Fall is coming." Charlie watched as she pounced on a couch cushion. "We're going to have to start thinking about real life." He swallowed. "We'll be heading home in a week."

Halley adjusted her headband. "It's been so long, I've almost forgotten what *home* looks like."

"It's been a month." Charlie lifted his feet as Nova crawled under his chair and out the other side. "Not that long." And yet, so much had changed he understood what she meant.

"It feels like forever." Halley's was expression puzzled. "Weird."

He agreed.

"We can't leave yet." Nova stood and took off her dinosaur helmet. "Not yet." She stared up at him. Her arms were crossed and her lower lip jutted out. She had the T. rex head under one arm and Scorpio under the other. "Summer isn't over."

"Is there something you want to do before we leave?" Charlie asked, eyeing the envelope with Astrid's name on it where it rested beside his computer.

"Not leave." Nova stomped one foot.

"Nova." He saw the distress on her face. "What's wrong?"

"I don't want to go." She sniffed. "We have friends here. It's pretty. I have a Mr. Possum. And all of Aunt Camellia's dogs love me. And her cats. And even Lord Byron." She squawked. "I love our purple house."

"It's going to be Astrid's purple house." Halley sat on the couch opposite his desk. "Charlie is going to give it to her."

"Rebecca wanted her to have it." And it was the right

thing to do. Charlie ran his fingers through his hair, trying to ignore the painful throb of his heart.

"Astrid would let us stay." Nova had her hands on her hips. "She would."

"I agree." Halley inspected her fingernails. "Why are we suddenly leaving?"

"It's not sudden. Next weekend. That's a whole week from now." A week he'd have to prepare himself for goodbyes. He hoped like hell a week would be enough. "Think about all the things you miss." If he reminded them of their previous lives, they'd remember how hard they'd fought against coming here.

"Go here, go there." Nova wiggled Scorpio. "Always go go go." She made a grumpy face.

"Dance and swim and gymnastics and piano." Halley ticked each item off on her fingers.

"You like those things." He frowned. At least, he thought they did.

"I like dance." Nova spun around. "Only dance."

"I like swim." Halley shrugged. "Mostly because of the boys, though."

"I appreciate the honesty." Charlie groaned and covered his face.

Nova and Halley laughed.

"I bet they have dance here." Nova spun around.

"We can't stay here." He sat back in his chair. "For one thing, this house isn't ours."

"Astrid would never kick us out, Charlie." Halley was frowning at him. "You want us to be honest with you. You should be honest with us."

He could do that. "We have a home, friends and a life back in Fort Worth." He wasn't going to debate this with the girls. "We have responsibilities."

"We have friends here." Nova wasn't budging. "Lots more here."

"Real friends. Not the kind that tear you down over DM." Halley held up her phone. "Honey's not so bad, Charlie. The people are awesome. And there's Astrid."

He stood, his frustration getting the best of him. "I'm not going to uproot you two and move to a place an hour from anywhere. I've let you both down, over and over. I want what's best for you, don't you understand?"

Nova went to sit beside Halley, the two of them watching as he paced back and forth.

"I don't know what their schools are like or what clubs they have—except for the bees. I know the Hills and all their friends seem to think bees are the best, but I'm not so sure. Anyway, it doesn't make sense to give up everything we know for relationships based on a couple of weeks." He kept pacing.

Halley sighed. "It does if we're happy. You want us to be happy. We want you to be happy."

"I am happy." He didn't sound remotely happy. "We *will* be happy, once we get back to our normal life. If you want to change up your extracurricular activities, we can look into that. We'll make new friends. We'll make it work. It will be good. I won't stay here just because I've fallen in love with Astrid. I don't even know what that means. I'll screw that up and then what? I'd rather leave than risk hurting or losing her…" He came to a stop, shocked at everything he'd just said.

Halley and Nova were staring at him, their mouths hanging open and their eyes round as saucers.

"No." He held up his hands. "Wait. I didn't mean to say that."

"No, you wait." Halley was up on her feet and, by the

look on her face, ready to do battle. "You did say it. You fell in love with Astrid."

"You love Astrid?" Nova was squishing Scorpio in her arms and wearing a big grin on her face. "Does that mean we'll all live here together?"

"No." He ran his fingers through his hair. "It doesn't."

"Why not?" Nova rolled her eyes. "All you have to do is tell her." She said this like it was the most obvious thing in the world. "'Cause I *know* she loves you, too."

Astrid had said as much, but he still struggled to believe it. He stopped himself from asking Nova how she knew that. She was five. She still talked to her stuffed toy. She wasn't the most reliable source when it came to the facts.

"You love her, Charlie." Halley shook her head. "Mom used to say love was the greatest gift we could give another person, remember? She said we should shower love on each other because there wasn't enough of it."

"I have you and your sister to love." He smiled at her.

"Why can't you have Astrid, too?" Halley sounded impatient. "You call me stubborn."

"You should tell her, Charlie." Nova sighed. "Even if you do mess things up, that doesn't mean she'll stop loving you."

"Yeah, Nova and I still love you and you've messed up," Halley pointed out.

"A lot." Nova used her not-so-whispery voice.

He didn't know whether to laugh or cry. He flopped onto the couch. "You two are exhausting."

"*We're* exhausting?" Halley sat beside him.

Nova hopped up on the other side of him. "Maybe, if we have Astrid, we don't need all the other stuff as much?"

   Charlie ran a hand over his face. She talked to her
toys, but she might have a point. Even if he did decide to
take the advice of his five- and thirteen-year-old daughters, he didn't know where to start.

   He shook his head. This was ridiculous. He'd made
up his mind...

   Astrid had invited them to the Junior Beekeeping
meeting at five o'clock. He glanced at the clock. It was
five now. "Get your shoes on." He didn't know what
he was going to do or say, only that he was going to
Dane's observation deck to watch bees—and find Astrid. After that, he had no idea. He grabbed the envelope
from Mr. Delaney's office and his keys. But, by the time
he had dino-Nova and Halley in the car, he was a mix
of nervous and excited. He only hoped Nova was right
and Astrid still loved him—that she could forgive him
for unwittingly being a part of his sister's development
plans. He hoped she felt even a fraction of the love he
felt for her.

CHAPTER EIGHTEEN

A FEW BEES BUZZED lazily around the honey-covered tools waiting to be washed. Texas Viking Honey had a sprawling honey house. There were stacks of used hive boxes, new hive boxes and lumber for repairs. Several large industrial-sized honey extractors ran down the middle of the room. The space between two was the perfect size for Astrid and Tansy to sit on the concrete floor, undisturbed, while Astrid poured her heart out.

"Here." Tansy handed her another tissue. "You've cried so much my head hurts."

Astrid shot her sister a look. "I can't help it."

"Love can suck." Tansy draped an arm along her shoulders. "I'm sorry he hurt you."

"That's the thing, he didn't hurt me." She sighed. "He never said he was staying. He never said he cared about me."

"Whoa." Dane came around the centrifuge and stopped, glancing between the two of them. "What's happening? Is Camellia okay?"

"She's fine." Tansy nodded. "She looked great when we peeked in on her at the hospital."

"Glad to hear it." Dane was looking at Astrid like she was a ticking time bomb. "Do I want to know? Am I going to have to go all Thor on someone?"

Astrid laughed. "You'd do that for me?"

"Defend the sister of my ladylove? Hell, yes." He pulled the band from his hair, smoothed it back and secured it.

"I love it when he has a man bun." Tansy winked up at him.

"I aim to please." He shot another glance at Astrid. "Not to intrude but the Junior Beekeepers are here." He held out a hand and pulled them to their feet. "Might want to—" he pointed at her face "—wash up or something."

"Dane." Tansy swatted his shoulder.

"No, I'm sure I look a mess." She waved them off. "I'll go pull myself together."

"You sure?" Tansy called after her.

"Yep." She moved aside the five-gallon bucket full of hive tools and frame grips, and washed her face. The idea of facing the Junior Beekeepers was too much for her, so she dumped the bucket of tools into the oversize sink and started scrubbing. It took a lot of elbow grease to make them honey-free but it was just what she needed to calm down.

She set the last 'L' hive tool aside, washed her hands and took her time walking outside.

"Just remember, this will give you service hours," Dane was saying to the group. "How many of you are working toward your Apprentice test?"

Three hands popped up.

"This is a good place to start."

Astrid headed for the observation deck. Tonight was an invite-only audience. Most of the guests were Junior Beekeeper parents. This was a time for their kids to show off their knowledge base and get time working with the bees. As far as she was concerned, nothing could compare to hands-on experience.

"Hey, Astrid." Crissy Abraham waved. "I was wondering if Halley was coming?"

Nicole said the two became instant best friends at the sleepover. Which was exactly what Halley needed.

"I'm not sure." Astrid managed a smile. "I did invite them." Part of her hoped they wouldn't come. She knew her meltdown wasn't entirely due to Charlie. She was tired and worried about Camellia—Charlie leaving was the cherry on top of her emotion-laden sundae.

"I hope so." Crissy crossed her fingers.

"Me, too." She was almost to the observation deck when she heard Nova calling her name. The little girl was running straight at her, Scorpio bouncing and jiggling from one hand. "Hello, Nova." She caught her, lifted her up and braced the little girl against her hip. "Did you and Scorpio come to see the bees?"

"We did." She grinned widely. "Where are they?"

Astrid pointed at the cluster of hive boxes on the far side of the observation deck. "They're still inside. We should go in before they open up the hives."

Halley waved but headed straight for Crissy.

"Sorry we're late." Charlie looked as beautiful as ever.

"Lucky for you, they're running behind." His smile melted her insides and had her heart shuddering. "Let's go."

"It's more like a screened-in gazebo, isn't it?" Charlie gave the structure a once-over. The screen would keep the observers safe while being able to hear everything they were being told. "Only bigger."

"Pretty much. Dane and Tansy are hoping to branch into agritourism. Honey tastings and hive experiences, that sort of thing." Astrid put Nova down but held her hand. "There's a lot of interest in beekeeping. The more interest, the better. Doing something like this can only help."

"Because bees are important," Nova said, swinging their arms.

"They sure are," Astrid agreed. "Without bees, we wouldn't have any almonds."

"Really?" Charlie looked at her.

"It's true. They pollinate lots of fruits and flowers and vegetables, but almonds are pollinated exclusively by bees."

"Did you learn something?" Nova asked Charlie.

"I did." He chuckled.

"Astrid is supersmart." Nova grinned up at her.

"I do know a lot about bees." She gave Nova's hand a squeeze. The observation deck was surprisingly crowded but Astrid managed to get them up front so Nova could see.

"This is so cool." Halley pressed in beside them. "I would so be freaking out if I were them."

"You think so?" Astrid laughed.

"Um, I know so." Halley's expression was of mock terror.

The first thing in the demonstration was lighting the smoker. It wasn't hard, but making sure to keep the kindling burning was key. "There's nothing worse than working with a hot hive or doing a bee removal and having your smoker run out." Tansy held up one of the smokers and pumped the bellows twice. Clean white smoke billowed out.

They moved on from the smoker to the tools.

"That's the scary thing," Nova said, pointing at the frame grip.

Tansy laughed. "Let me show you what it's for, Nova."

Benji used the L hook to break the seal on the hive. Kerrielynn puffed some smoke into the open box and Tansy reached inside with the frame grip. A wiggle and the frame came out.

"Oh, I get it." Nova gave Tansy a thumbs-up. "It's not scary."

Astrid shifted from one foot to the other, trying to put more space between Charlie and herself. There was no help for it. With so many people vying to see, she was pinned between him and Nova. There was no way to ignore his scent or the brush of his breath against her neck. When he laughed, her insides went molten. It took everything she had not to lean into him. He was right there.

The exhibition dragged on and her patience was wearing thinner by the minute.

Nova and Halley were both mesmerized when Benji carried one of the frames close. Bees scurried back and forth and covered the wooden frame. The hum was audible. Nova covered her ears. But Halley leaned forward to get a closer look.

When Astrid moved to give Nova space, she wound up stepping on Charlie's foot. "Sorry," she murmured, jumping and onto his other foot. "Oh, sorry."

He laughed, one hand resting against her back. "As long as it was an accident, it's okay."

He was teasing her? She glanced over her shoulder at him. Why wouldn't he tease her, nothing had changed—for him. She couldn't deny the appeal of his smile. She loved his smile. His gaze was all intensity and heat. The current between them was as strong as ever, holding her in place, staring up at him, wanting so much more than he was willing to give her.

He swallowed hard, his gaze falling to her lips.

Oh, Charlie. Her heart took off, doing its best to thunder its way out of her chest. *No, wait.* It was actual thunder. She stared at the clouds on the horizon.

"Looks like we're finishing right on time." Dane shielded his eyes. "Tansy and I will take it from here. Thanks for coming out tonight."

"Astrid." Nova clung to her hand. "Is it going to be a bad storm?"

Astrid scooped her up, again. "I don't think so. We need the rain. The bees need it, too." She gave the little girl a big smile. "Poppa Tom used to tell me that thunder was when the clouds went bowling."

Nova giggled. "Clouds can bowl?"

"I don't know." Astrid shrugged. "But it does sort of sound like it." She carried Nova to their car. "In you go."

A gentle rain started. "Can I drive you home?" Charlie's smile hurt to look at.

She stared up at the sky. "I should help Tansy and Dane."

Charlie looked over her shoulder. "It looks like they're done." His shirt was getting wet, and water dripped off the end of his hair.

She tore her gaze from his and looked back. The hives were closed and there was no sign of her sister or Dane. "I guess so."

He opened the passenger door. What was she doing? She wanted to go with him. She wanted him to smile at her and kiss her and hold her like she was everything to him. If Nova and Halley weren't in the back seat, she'd be kissing him. Instead of losing one second of the time with him, she should make the most of it. She'd deal with her heartbreak once he was gone.

THE WINDSHIELD WIPERS squeaked as they slid back and forth across the glass. Charlie was struggling with the beginnings of a panic attack. And the rain was picking up.

"That's really annoying," Halley sounded off from the back seat.

Nova imitated the sound of the windshield wipers.

"You sound just like it," Halley laughed. "I wonder if making funny sounds is, like, a job? If so, you'll be a millionaire."

"I'll get everyone a tiny donkey. Like Chickwy." Nova started laughing.

"Chicory?" Halley asked.

"Yep." Nova sighed.

From the corner of his eye, he saw Astrid smile—before it faltered. She was still worried about Camellia. "How did the visit with Camellia go?"

"She was happy to see me." She turned, smiling at the girls. "Eager to come home, of course. But she's made friends with all the nurses and doctors, of course. Oh, and she told me she'd made a special raspberry and honey tart, just for you girls. And to tell you to pet the dogs and cats for her."

"Do we need to feed Chockry and Dandelion, too?" Nova asked.

"Chicory," Halley mumbled.

"That."

"No, we don't. But, once the rain clears, we can go visit them." Astrid glanced his way. "If you're free to stay for a bit?"

He took a deep breath. "We are." At least now he

didn't have to come up with an excuse to stay. Not that it helped with the tension tightening his throat. He tugged at the collar of his shirt.

"Are you okay?" Astrid whispered.

He nodded but kept his eyes on the drive leading to Astrid's home. He concentrated on the rain. Light and steady. When he parked, he turned to tell the girls to wait—only to find them both out of the car and running for the porch.

"I guess they really want to try that tart." Astrid's smile didn't reach her eyes.

"I guess so." He took a deep breath. "Umbrella?"

She shook her head and made a mad dash through the rain to the porch.

He took another deep breath and followed.

"Would you like a slice of tart?" Astrid was asking Shelby.

"No, thank you." Shelby was sitting on the front porch with a book in her lap. "Nothing better than a sleeping baby and a good book on a rainy day."

"We'll leave you alone." Astrid smiled and waved the girls inside. "Enjoy."

Shelby took one look at him and frowned. "You look like you're going to be sick."

"I'm fine." He was trying to be fine, anyway. The girls had left wet footprints along the wooden floor. He followed the trail to the kitchen.

Enough is enough. There was no point in dragging this out. If he waited much longer, he'd be doubled over and dripping sweat—not the best way to woo someone. Not that he had any experience with wooing. Or women.

He stepped into the kitchen and his mind went completely blank.

Astrid was rifling through the refrigerator while his girls waited, asking her questions.

"Who painted the bees on the walls?" Nova asked.

"My great-grandmother, grandmother, aunt and my sister Rosemary. Rosemary is such a talented artist, she's done the illustrations for an entomology book."

"What's in-to-mawlowgy?" Nova did try.

"It's the study of bugs," Astrid said. "Found it."

He took a deep breath. "Girls." He exhaled forcefully. "Go watch TV."

Astrid turned, confused, with a foil-covered pan in her hand.

"Can we have some tart, please?" Nova used her best manners.

Charlie took the tray from Astrid's hand and handed it to Halley. "Go."

Halley grabbed Nova's hand and tugged her from the kitchen.

Astrid stepped closer. "Charlie, what's wrong?" She pressed a hand to his temple.

"Nothing." He was not going to let a panic attack ruin this. "Here." He held out the envelope.

Astrid took it and opened it slowly, her gaze never leaving his face. "What is it?"

"Read it." He cleared his throat.

She did. Frowned. Then read it again. "You're going to sell me Rebecca's property? For…for six dollars?" She stared at him, her mouth open.

"A dollar for each Bee Girl." He nodded. "Legally, Mr. Delaney figured selling it would keep anyone—my sister—from questioning the legality of it…" He shrugged. "If you want it?"

"Of course I do. But, are you sure?" She clutched the paper to her chest.

"You were meant to have it. It's yours." He swallowed, knowing there was more to be said. This was too important. She was too important. He took her hand. "Astrid, I—"

The sudden wailing of Bea flooded the kitchen, causing two of the dogs to jump up from their spot on the floor and howl along.

"I'm coming," Shelby called out, the screen door slamming behind her.

He waited, hearing every footfall on the stairs as Shelby made her way to her screaming child. The dogs kept baying until Bea's cries stopped.

He opened his mouth—

"Oh, my, look at that diaper." Shelby's voice echoed off the walls. "Oh, Bea, honey, that's toxic."

Charlie closed his eyes and shook his head. He spun around, until he found the baby monitor.

"You poor, *poor* thing." Shelby kept going. "Oh, whew, that is so gross—"

Charlie turned off the monitor. Deep breath in, strong breath out. He turned and headed back to Astrid. Looking into her eyes helped. "I have to tell you—"

"You're wrong." The screen door creaked open, then slammed shut. "I told you the whole thing lasted four nights." Leif came into the kitchen, followed by Benji. "Hey," he said, heading straight for the cookie jar. "What's up?"

"Did the girls like the exhibition, Mr. D?" Benji asked.

"They're in the living room." Charlie ran a hand along the back of his neck, his nerves on end. "They have a tart."

"We need forks," Halley called out from the other room.

"On it." Benji grabbed a handful of forks ran out of the kitchen.

"Food." Leif carried the cookie jar with him. "I'm starving."

Before Charlie could get a word out, Tansy's shriek of laughter reverberated down the hall.

Seconds later, Dane arrived with Tansy over his shoulder. Shelby trailed behind, a much quieter Bea in her arms.

"Is that everyone?" Charlie's patience was nonexistent now. "Anyone else coming?"

"What's wrong?" Tansy asked as Dane set her down. "Is it Aunt Camellia?"

"I talked to her not ten minutes ago." Shelby hugged Tansy. "Don't worry."

Dane was frowning. "Then what happened?" He took one look at him and shook his head. "You look like hell, Charlie."

"I'm fine. I'm trying to tell Astrid that I love her. I was hoping to have a moment alone—to make it special. Instead—"

Astrid threw her arms around him. "You love me?"

He frowned. "I love you."

Suddenly the room was empty.

"Stop frowning." She was grinning.

"I had a speech. It lists off all the reasons you should probably not decide to be with me." He pulled the cards from his back pocket.

"It does?" She took the cards from him and ripped them in half.

"Astrid." He tried to get the cards back. "I don't want you to make a decision you're going to regret."

"What decision?" She tossed the cards over her shoulder. "I love you. There's no decision to be made."

"You can love a person and not act on it." She had to understand.

"Why?" Her arms slid back around his neck. "This is the happiest day of my life, Charlie Driver. My heart is so full. You can try to change my mind all you want—it won't work."

"It won't?" His arms circled her waist. "You're certain? There's nothing I can do or say to change your mind?"

"No." She rested her hand against his cheek.

He had to be sure. "If you do—"

"Charlie." She pressed a kiss to his lips. "I promise you. I love you. That will never change."

He crumpled against her, relief washing over him.

She tilted his head back. "I'll show you, every day, so you'll never doubt it."

He crushed her against him. "You'll teach me? How to love that way."

"Oh, Charlie, you already do. I know it. Don't be afraid to let the rest of our family know it, too." She kissed one cheek, then the next.

He kissed her gently. He knew it wouldn't be easy but, with Astrid by his side, it would be worth it. "I will never stop trying to deserve you." His fingers ran through her hair.

Her smile was the most beautiful thing in the world. "I love you."

"I love you." He kissed her again. "And I always will."

EPILOGUE

"I THINK IT'S PERFECT." Astrid held up the whisk, the chocolate brownie batter smooth as silk.

Nova peered into the bowl. She'd helped Astrid with each and every step and was quite proud of herself. "Looks good. Charlie?"

Charlie stopped loading the dishwasher long enough to take a quick look. "It looks right."

Charlie doing the dishes was one of the many things Astrid found desirable about her new husband. His handiness in the kitchen was nothing compared to his exuberance in the bedroom. Astrid couldn't wait to go to bed every night. "You have to taste it, Charlie." Astrid held the whisk out. "That's the only way to be sure."

"Why do I feel like you're up to something?" He cocked an eyebrow, but leaned in.

She pushed the whisk forward, leaving a big chocolate dollop on the end of his nose.

Nova shrieked with laughter. "Charlie, you have chocolate on your face."

"What?" Halley looked up from her phone. "Ohmygosh." She snapped a picture.

"You think you're funny?" Charlie stepped closer, pinning Astrid against the counter. "Let me share." He leaned forward and ran his nose across her forehead.

"Charlie." Nova kept laughing.

Astrid held the bowl forward. "This could get messy."

"Wait, wait." Halley jumped up. "I promised Crissy I'd have brownies. Can you maybe have a food fight with something else?"

There was a knock on the door.

"I'll get it," Nova and Halley said in unison, running for the door.

Charlie took the bowl from her. "You look delicious."

"I was just about to say the same thing about you." She leaned forward to kiss him. "Chocolate-flavored Charlie kisses. Yum."

"I told you. Newlyweds." Halley stood in the doorway, Benji, Crissy, Leif and Kerrielynn gathered around her. "They are like this all the time."

"Not with brownie batter," Charlie said.

Astrid was so surprised, she couldn't stop laughing.

"Ick. Do you need me to put that into the oven?" Halley asked.

"Do we want to eat those brownies?" Leif murmured.

That had Astrid laughing all over again. Which made Charlie laugh.

"We'll get it." She wiped the chocolate from his face. "You need anything else?"

"Nova asked for juice boxes for her and Ginger." Benji crept into the kitchen. "I can get them."

Juice boxes secured, the two of them had the kitchen to themselves.

"Have I told you how much I love you today, Mrs. Driver?"

Astrid pretended to think. "No, I don't think you have, Mr. Driver."

"Well, I do." He pulled her close. "I love you. Very much."

* * * * *

Must Love Bees Recipes

Honey Ginger Scones

Ingredients:

2 cups unbleached, all-purpose flour
1 tbsp baking powder
½ tsp ground ginger
3 tbsp sugar
½ tsp salt
5 tbsp chilled unsalted butter, cut into ¼ inch cubes
2 oz chopped crystalized ginger
1 ¼ cup heavy cream
¼ cup honey

1. Combine flour, baking powder, ground ginger, sugar and salt in a large bowl and whisk together until well combined.

2. Cut the butter into the flour mixture with a fork or pastry cutter until it resembles coarse meal. Stir in crystalized ginger.

3. Whisk 1 cup of the heavy cream and honey together.

4. With fork or rubber spatula, stir cream mixture in with dry ingredients until the dough begins to come together.

5. On a lightly floured surface, knead dough together until it's a rough sticky ball.

6. Divide the dough and form two small rounds about 3/4-inch thick.

7. Cut each round into 8 triangles and place triangles onto prepared parchment-covered baking sheet. Brush each triangle with remaining heavy cream.

8. Bake for 8–10 minutes in a 425°F oven until just golden.

9. Let cool on pan for 5 minutes and transfer to a cooling rack.

Honey Apple Muffins

Ingredients:

1 small apple, grated
1 egg
½ cup plain Greek yogurt
3 tbsp honey
1 tsp vanilla extract
½ tsp cinnamon
2 tsp baking powder
1 ½ cup rolled oats
½ cup milk

1. Grate apple and set aside.

2. Combine egg, yogurt, honey, vanilla, cinnamon and baking powder in bowl.

3. Add oats and stir well. Add apple and mix. Add milk and combine.

4. Spoon into lined or sprayed muffin pan and place into preheated 350°F oven.

5. Place onto wire rack until cool.

Honey-Glazed Roasted Chicken

Ingredients:

1 whole chicken—4 lbs
1 cup lemon juice
2 tsp kosher salt, plus more for seasoning
1 tsp extra virgin olive oil
freshly ground black pepper
sprigs fresh thyme
½ fresh lemon, cut into wedges
½ cup honey, warmed

Preheat oven to 400°F and place the rack in bottom third of the oven.

1. Rub exterior of chicken with about 2 teaspoons of kosher salt and lemon juice. Put the whole chicken in a resealable plastic bag, seal, and move/shake so the lemon juice coats the chicken. (Place the bagged chicken in a bowl, so there are no leaks.)

2. Chill 2 hours or overnight. Turn the chicken occasionally so it stays coated with the lemon juice.

3. Remove the chicken from the refrigerator, remove from bag, and discard bag and marinade.

4. Use kitchen towels to pat the chicken dry, then rub olive oil all over the exterior of the chicken. Sprinkle all over with salt and pepper, including the cavity. Place thyme sprigs and lemon wedges into the empty cavity.

5. Put chicken in oversize, shallow roasting pan. Roast for 20 minutes at 400°F, then lower the heat to 350°F and roast for another 45 minutes.

6. While the chicken is roasting, heat the honey to make it easier to brush.

7. After the chicken has roasted for the full 65 minutes, use a pastry brush to generously brush honey on the entirety of the chicken.

8. Return to oven and roast for another 10 to 15 minutes at 350°F until meat thermometer reads 160°F for the breast and 170°F for the thigh, or when the breast and thigh releases juices that run clear, not pink.

9. Watch the chicken so the skin doesn't get too dark, loosely tent the chicken with a piece of aluminum foil. Brush the chicken with honey one more time before taking it out of the oven.

10. Remove chicken from oven, transfer to a cutting board and tent with foil to rest for 15 minutes.

11. Scrape up the drippings from the roasting pan with a metal spatula. Pour the pan juices and drippings

into a small saucepan. If there are blackened bits from burnt honey, remove them. Spoon off all but a tablespoon of fat.

(To create gravy, thicken the juices with a teaspoon of cornstarch or flour and a tablespoon of water. Add to the drippings, heat and stir until thickened. Season to taste with salt and pepper.)

12. Serve the chicken with pan juices or thickened gravy.

Honey Cinnamon Roll-Ups

Ingredients:

2 cups ground walnuts
¼ cup sugar
2 tsp cinnamon
12 sheets frozen phyllo, thawed
½ cup salted butter, melted

Syrup:

½ cup honey
½ cup sugar
½ cup water
1 tbsp lemon juice

1. Preheat the oven to 350°F.

2. Combine walnuts, sugar and cinnamon.

3. On a 15x12-inch sheet of waxed paper, place 1 sheet of phyllo flat and brush with butter.

4. Add second phyllo sheet on top, brush with butter.

   (To prevent drying out, keep remaining phyllo covered with damp towel.)

5. Sprinkle ¼ cup of the walnut mixture.

6. Using waxed paper, starting with the long side, roll up tightly jelly-roll style and slice into 4 smaller rolls.

7. Place rolls on 13x9-inch greased baking dish.

8. Repeat until all phyllo and walnut mixture is used.

9. Bake 14–16 minutes—or until light brown.

10. Cool on wire rack.

Syrup:

1. Combine all ingredients in saucepan over medium heat until a rolling boil.

2. Set aside to cool.

3. Use immediately.

Buttermilk Honey Pancakes

Ingredients:

1 egg, beaten
2 tbsp honey
1 cup flour
¼ tsp salt
1 tsp baking powder
½ tsp baking soda
1 cup buttermilk
toppings of choice

1. Beat egg, stir in the honey, and set aside.

2. In a medium bowl, whisk together the flour, salt, baking powder and baking soda.

3. Stir egg mixture and buttermilk into dry ingredients. Don't over stir, just until all dry ingredients are moistened.

4. Scoop batter onto a greased hot skillet or griddle—approximately a ⅓ cup.

5. Flip once the edges are browning and the top is bubbling.

6. Cook other side until pancake is fully cooked.

7. Serve with simple honey syrup, maple syrup or your topping of choice.

Honey Simple Syrup

Ingredients:

honey
hot water

1. Heat to simmer 2 parts honey to 1 part hot water over medium-low heat in a saucepan.

2. Can infuse with fruit, spices, vanilla bean, etc. while simmering, if desired.

3. Remove from heat and cool. If any additional ingredients have been infused, strain the mixture before cooling.

4. Store at room temperature or refrigerate as desired. (Can be refridgerated for up to four weeks.)

Brownies With Honey

Ingredients:

½ cup butter
½ cup cocoa powder
2 oz unsweetened chocolate
¾ cup fresh honey
1 tsp vanilla
½ tsp salt
2 eggs
¼ cup all-purpose flour

1. Preheat the oven to 350°F.

2. Melt butter, cocoa and chocolate over low heat in saucepan. When melted, remove from heat and whisk in honey, vanilla, salt and eggs.

3. Stir in flour and spoon into an 8x8 greased and floured baking dish.

4. Place in a 350°F preheated oven and bake 15 minutes, then cool.

Frosted Oatmeal Cookies

Ingredients:

1 cup rolled oats
1 cup all-purpose flour
¼ tsp kosher salt
½ cup sugar
¼ cup brown sugar
1 large egg
2 tsp pumpkin pie spice or cinnamon
1 tsp vanilla
½ tsp baking soda
4 tbsp unsalted butter, melted
¾ cup powdered sugar
5 tsp milk (or more)

1. Combine the oats, flour and salt in a bowl.

2. In a separate bowl, mix both sugars with the egg, cinnamon, vanilla and baking soda on high speed, scraping the bowl as needed, until glossy, pale and thick, a full 2 minutes. Reduce the speed to medium.

3. Melt butter and slowly drizzle in and whisk until incorporated.

4. Add the oat mixture and gently fold with wooden spoon or rubber spatula until incorporated. Be careful not to overmix.

5. Drop 15 scoops of dough onto a parchment-lined sheet pan, 2 inches apart.

6. Bake in a 350°F preheated oven for 12–14 minutes or until the edges are set and lightly golden brown, but the center is still gooey.

7. Remove from the oven, tap cookie sheet on the counter a couple of times to flatten the cookies a little more, and cool on the sheet for 5 minutes.

Frosting:

1. In a bowl, use a fork to mix the powdered sugar and milk until the icing is smooth and thick.

2. Dip only the tops of the cookies into the bowl of icing, then flip the cookies over and return them to the cookie sheet to allow the icing to harden, 10–15 minutes.

Honey-Lemon Sugar Cookies

Ingredients:

2 cups all-purpose flour
1 ½ tsp baking soda
½ cup honey
⅓ cup butter, softened
¼ cup sugar
1 tsp finely grated lemon zest
1 egg
1 cup powdered sugar
2 tbsp lemon juice

1. In a small bowl, combine flour and baking soda.

2. Beat honey, butter, sugar and lemon zest with an electric mixer, in a large bowl, until creamy.

3. Add egg and beat until smooth. Reduce speed to low and gradually stir in flour mixture until blended.

4. Drop spoonfuls of dough 2 inches apart on nonstick or lightly greased cookie sheets.

5. Bake in 350°F preheated oven for 7–8 minutes or

until lightly browned. Cool completely on wire racks.

6. While cookies cool, blend powdered sugar and lemon juice until smooth. Drizzle over cooled cookies.

Honey Vinaigrette Salad Dressing

Ingredients:

½ cup olive oil
¼ cup white wine vinegar
1 lemon, zest and juice
1 tbsp Dijon mustard
¼ cup honey
salt and pepper to taste

1. Put all ingredients into Mason jar or salad shaker.

2. Shake until completely blended.

3. Pour over favorite salad.

4. Keep sealed in an airtight container in the refrigerator for 3–5 days. Shake well before use.

Honey Streusel Coffee Cake

Ingredients:

½ cup unsalted butter, softened
1 cup granulated sugar
2 large eggs
1 tsp vanilla
2 cups all-purpose flour
1 tsp baking powder
½ tsp salt
1 tsp ground cinnamon
⅔ cup honey
⅔ cup buttermilk

Topping:

6 tbsp unsalted butter, cut into cubes
1 cup packed brown sugar
¼ cup flour

1. Cream butter and sugar together.

2. Add eggs and vanilla and blend.

3. In a different bowl, mix the flour, baking powder, salt and cinnamon.

4. Alternating with honey and buttermilk, add some of the dry ingredients to the butter mixture and continue until all of the flour has been added and the batter is smooth and shiny.

5. Pour into 9-inch parchment-lined or greased and lightly floured pan.

6. Make topping: crumble together butter, sugar and flour until it resembles chunky breadcrumbs.

7. Sprinkle topping over the surface of the cake batter and place in a 350°F preheated oven for about 45–50 minutes or until middle of the cake is springy when gently prodded.

Honey-Glazed Roasted Carrots

Ingredients:

Salt
1 lb baby carrots
2 tbsp butter
2 tbsp honey
1 tbsp lemon juice
freshly ground black pepper
¼ cup chopped parsley

1. In a medium saucepan, bring water to a boil.

2. Add salt and then carrots and cook until tender, 5–6 minutes.

3. Drain the carrots and add back to pan with butter, honey and lemon juice.

4. Cook until a glaze coats the carrots, 5 minutes.

5. Season with salt and pepper and garnish with parsley.

Spiced Honey Pear Pie

Ingredients:

*1 refrigerated piecrust or homemade piecrust of
your choice
5 ripe Anjou pears
½ cup raisins, or raisin/dried cranberry combination
¼ cup honey
¼ tsp ground cinnamon
¼ tsp grated nutmeg
⅛ tsp ground ginger
⅛ tsp allspice
⅛ tsp ground cardamom
⅛ tsp salt
⅓ cup cornstarch*

Brown Sugar Crumble Topping:

*1 cup all-purpose flour
½ cup unsalted butter, cold/cubed
½ cup brown sugar*

1. Preheat oven to 350°F.

2. Combine flour and brown sugar in a bowl. Cut in
   butter until crumbly. Set in refrigerator until ready
   to use.

3. Unroll piecrust or press homemade pie dough into pie pan.

4. In medium mixing bowl add peeled, cored and thickly sliced pears. Add raisins and spices.

5. Distribute honey and spices over fruit with spatula. Sprinkle with cornstarch and stir to combine.

6. Pour fruit and honey mixture into piecrust.

7. Top with flour, brown sugar and butter mixture.

8. Bake 45 minutes or until pie is golden and bubbly. Let cool before serving.

Honey Brown Sugar Shortbread Cookies

Ingredients:

1 ½ cup softened butter
¾ cup packed light brown sugar
¼ cup honey
½ tsp kosher salt
¼ tsp baking powder
3 cups all-purpose flour
¾ cup cornstarch
turbinado or sugar crystals for sprinkling on top

1. Line 2 sheet pans with parchment paper and set aside.

2. Stir softened butter until smooth and creamy. Then stir in brown sugar and honey.

3. Sprinkle the salt and baking powder over the top and stir to combine. Add the flour and cornstarch.

4. Slowly stir in the flour until dough is stiff.

5. Place dough onto lightly floured surface and form a ball. Knead until smooth. Form second ball and press into a flat disk.

6. Roll out dough to a ¼-inch thickness.

7. Cut desired shapes and place on prepared pans. Use all the dough.

8. Place cutouts in the refrigerator for at least 1 hour or up to 24 hours.

9. When ready to bake, preheat oven to 350°F.

10. Remove cookies from the refrigerator. Sprinkle with coarse or regular sugar.

11. Bake for 9–12 minutes or until golden brown all over. (Cookies thicker than ¼-inch will take more time.) Rotate pans halfway through for even browning.

12. Cool completely on a wire cooling rack before serving.

Honey Citrus Iced Tea

Ingredients:

7 bags of black tea (Lipton or the like)
½ cup honey
2 key limes or 1 lime, sliced into rounds
1 lemon, sliced into rounds
fresh mint leaves for garnish
4 kumquats, sliced into rounds (optional)

1. Bring 4 cups water to a simmer in a saucepan.

2. Remove from the heat and add the tea bags. Steep for 8 minutes.

3. Remove tea bags and stir in honey. Let cool.

4. Add the sweetened tea to a pitcher with 2 cups ice and an additional 4 cups water, then stir.

5. Add key limes and lemon and, if using, the sliced kumquats.

6. Pour into glasses over ice, garnish with mint and enjoy.

HONEY EVER AFTER

CHAPTER ONE

MAGNOLIA HILL WATCHED her sister, Camellia, slowly turn the four-tier wedding cake. Her sister was likely ensuring that every nook and cranny of the domed cake was dusted with just the right amount of powdered sugar. Small sugar honey bee confections glistened amidst the delicate spun pale pink camellia sugar flowers, as if they were going about their business and gathering pollen for honey. As far as Mags was concerned, the cake was perfect. And Mags wasn't the type to use the word *perfect*.

"You've outdone yourself, Aunt Camellia." Their niece, Astrid, stopped flipping pancakes. "It's beautiful."

"I can't believe you made your own wedding cake." Tansy, another niece, shook her head and went back to setting the kitchen table. "But it's your best cake ever."

"I knew what I wanted, is all." Camellia stepped back and nodded. "It'll do." She pressed her hands against her apron.

Mags crossed her arms over her chest. "It'll do?" Leave it to Camellia to downplay her gifts. Her sister's humility was as charming as it was sincere. "It's one of the most elegant desserts I've laid eyes on. It'll do."

"It's too pretty to eat." Shelby, Mag's daughter, sat on the floor keeping an eye on her baby girl. Tiny Bea scooched and wriggled on the brightly colored playmat— making happy noises and being as adorable as ever. Until the arrival of Beatrix Amelia, Mags hadn't been a baby person. She still wasn't. But she was a shameless Bea person. The first time Bea had smiled up at her, Mags was smitten. She'd do anything for Bea. "Seriously, Aunt Camellia. It's a…a work of art." Bea made an extra loud happy sound and clapped her hands. "See, Bea agrees."

Mags smiled at the baby. "Well, if Bea says so then it's true. She is a genius after all. She is my granddaughter."

The others laughed but Camellia was still inspecting the cake. "You think Van will like it?"

Mags heard the wobble in her sister's voice. Camellia was nervous. As the maid of honor and sister of the bride, it was up to her to calm Camellia's nerves. Nerves were to be expected on a day like today, weren't they? Mags had no frame of reference—but she'd heard it so often that she assumed it was true. It was still hard to accept what was happening. Today was the day. Everything would change. Again. *Today is my sister's wedding day.*

Today, Camellia needed her to be the rock. A role Camellia normally played.

Tansy, Shelby and Astrid were all looking at Camellia, wearing the same smile.

"Of course, he will like it. He'll love it. He'd love a store-bought cake as long as he got you at the end of the day." Magnolia smiled at Camellia's look of horror. Store bought cakes were unacceptable. If it wasn't made from scratch, it wasn't made with love. And without love, food wouldn't nourish the body and soul. This was one of the many words of wisdom their grandmother had passed to them when they were young girls. Camellia remembered them all. Mags didn't need to remember them all because she had Camellia.

Not after today.

Mags slid an arm around her sister's waist and offered a reassuring squeeze. "That man thinks you walk
on water. Anything you offered him would please him,
Camellia Ann. I'm not sure he'll even see the cake once
he sets his eyes on you." She leaned to rest her head on
Camellia's. "As it should be." It was true. As hard as
Mags tried, she could find no fault with the man her
sister was marrying. Van Kettner was kind and gentle,
giving and supportive, and he lit up with pride every
time he laid eyes on Camellia. More importantly, Camellia loved Van.

"He is a wonderful man." Camellia sighed—a sigh
Mags wasn't sure what to make of.

"Is that a question?" Magnolia lifted her head and
met Camellia's gaze. "Have you changed your mind? If
you have, you don't have to worry about a thing. I have
no problem telling him you've changed your mind and
sending everyone away. None at all."

Camellia's eyes went round. "I thought you liked
Van?"

"I do. But I like you more." She swallowed at the
lump on blocking her throat. "You're my sister and the
queen bee of Honey Hill Farms. We're all just worker
bees, following your lead. I plan on reminding Van of
how special you are, regularly."

"I'm sure you will." Camellia took both of Mags's
hands in hers. "And while I appreciate you making the
offer, I haven't changed my mind. I can't wait to be Van's
wife. Remember he'll be family now, too. Your family.
It would mean the world to me if you'd welcome him
with open arms, Mags."

"Camellia, I rarely welcome *anyone* with open arms.

As you know." Mags saw the pleading look on her sister's face. "Fine. I'll try."

"Poor Uncle Van." Tansy shook her head but she was smiling broadly. "He's not just getting the woman of his dreams, he's getting her super protective, opinionated and free-speaking older sister, to boot."

Astrid and Shelby laughed.

Mags ignored the teasing to ask, "*Uncle* Van?"

The three young women exchanged amused looks.

Why was this funny?

"He will be their uncle, Mags." Even with her hair in curlers, wearing her daisy-print housedress and bee slippers, Camellia looked lovely. She was happy and that was all that Mags wanted for her—for all of Poppa Tom's Bee Girls.

"If Poppa were here today, his buttons would be bursting with pride." Mags could picture him, standing there, praising Camellia's cake, his booming laughter filling the kitchen. "He'd known Van and liked him. I think he'd approve." Knowing that was comforting.

"I think so, too." Camellia's big eyes had an extra sheen to them now.

Mags didn't resist when Camellia pulled her in for another hug—even though one of Camellia's curlers squished her nose.

"Pancakes are ready." Astrid's hand rested on Mag's back. "Wait a minute." She set the spatula aside and slid her arms around Mags.

Second later, Tansy and Shelby and baby Bea were all squished together in a huddle.

"All right. All right." Camellia sniffed. "Enough hugging, time for brunch."

Mags sat, watching as everyone took a seat and

Shelby buckled Bea into her high chair. This was the best view. Her favorite people, gathered together, enjoying a quiet moment in life together. From new faces to new families, and the expansion on the honey farm, every day was a new normal. So much had changed the last year.

Tansy and Dane had gone from enemies to significant others. They never talked about getting married because they were happy as is. They'd get around to it when they were ready, and Mags respected that.

Astrid was married. She'd tried to draw out the quiet, brooding, wounded man who'd moved in next store and wound up falling head-over-heals in love with him *and* his two sweet daughters.

Then there was her Shelby. Every night, Mags went to bed thankful her daughter had pushed to find her birth mother. She'd had a hole in her heart since the day she'd given Shelby up for adoption. But Shelby had arrived, with a daughter of her own, and Mags's life and heart were complete.

And now her own sister was in love with a longtime friend and was getting married.

As happy as she was for her sister, Mags considered herself a cautious woman—with good reason. Since Camellia's birth fifty-two years ago, it had been the two of them against the world. A team, best friends and sisters. Camellia was the yin to her yang, the good cop to her bad cop. Camellia was the one to smooth all the feathers Mags ruffled and the person who'd stood by her through everything...

Now she was going to be Van's wife. It wasn't that she begrudged her sister love and happiness, she didn't. She did worry about how lonely her own life would become.

"Charlie's almost here." Astrid held up her phone. "With the girls. They're so excited for their pancake brunch—it's their favorite."

"And the only thing I can make from memory," Tansy added, winking at Astrid who winked back.

What was all the winking about? Astrid and Tansy were up to something. But what? Mags was already walking an emotional tightrope, she wasn't sure how she'd handle a surprise.

"The girls are *so* excited to be your flower girl and junior bridesmaid." Astrid stood and came around the table. "I'm sure they'll be extra bouncy today. Especially Nova."

"I love Nova's bounces. So does Bea." Shelby put a few more pieces of cut up pancake on the high chair tray. "Don't you, little Bea?"

"It's a family wedding after all." Camellia took this part seriously. She wanted every member of the family involved in the wedding—Mags was walking her down the aisle. "And little Bea will be the most precious ring-bearer ever."

"She will." Mags was quick to agree. But then, she was biased when it came to her granddaughter.

"It will be a wonderful wedding." Tansy reached across to squeeze Camellia's hand. "A magical, joyous occasion."

The front door of the old house opened, followed by rapid footfalls, and the appearance of young Nova. "We're here, we're here." She was out of breath, like she'd run the whole way. With a quick wave, she made a beeline to Astrid. She wound her arms around Astrid's knees and hugged her tight.

"Good morning." Camellia smiled as Nova ran over and planted a kiss on her cheek.

Halley, Nova's big sister, came into the kitchen and froze. "Holy wow, is that the cake, Aunt Camellia?"

"It is." Tansy winked.

"Halley?" Astrid smiled at the girl. "Anything else?"

"Oh, right." Halley stepped aside, bouncing on her toes with excitement. "We brought an early present."

Mags held her breath, hoping it wasn't a string quartet or baskets of doves or butterflies or... It was Rosemary. Mags blinked, then looked again. She was here. Standing in the doorway of the kitchen. Rosemary, her youngest niece. She'd come home. Mags and Camellia were up, as one, running toward the new arrival—equal parts laughing and crying.

"You're here." Camellia hugged Rosemary close. "You're really truly here."

"Oh, darling girl." Mags hugged Rosemary next. "What a wonderful surprise. I can't believe everyone managed to keep this a secret."

"It wasn't easy," Nova chimed in. "I had to keep my lips locked." She mimed locking her lips and throwing the key over her shoulder.

"And you did great." Astrid held Nova's hand.

"I can't believe it." Camellia's gaze wandered around the women in the kitchen. "We're all here. All of Poppa Tom's Bee Girls—under one roof at the same time. This is truly the best day of my life."

Mags's throat was too tight to speak.

"I wouldn't miss this for the world." Rosemary wrapped an arm around both Camellia and Mags and pulled them back in for another hug. Her words were soft and muffled but not so much that Mags didn't hear the heartache. "It's good to be home. To be here. I've missed you both so much. And your hugs—" Her words broke off and she took a deep, unsteady breath.

Rosemary's tone set the hair on the back of Mags's neck upright. Something was wrong. She could feel it but she had to be sure. Behind Rose's head, Mags shot Camellia a worried glance—the same look Camellia was sending her. It wasn't just her then.

Mags patted her niece's back. "You're home now. We're here." And, together, they could work through anything. Together, the Bee Girls were unstoppable.

CHAPTER TWO

"I KEEP LOOKING to make sure you're all really here. Rose especially. And I see you all but..." Camellia sat on the velvet topped stool before her vanity table. "It's like a dream."

"I can pinch you, if that helps?" Mags rested a hand on her sister's shoulder, her eyes locking with Camellia's in the large vanity mirror. "To ensure you're awake."

"While I appreciate the gesture, no, thank you." Camellia waved her hand.

"You can count on me. However, you have to stop looking around so I can get your hair right. *Or* I might have to resort to pinching." Mags wasn't one to gush or go on about her feelings, but she was just as thrilled to have Rosemary home. To have Camellia's bedroom filled with those nearest and dearest to her heart made this day near perfect.

"I can't believe I'm here, either, Aunt Camellia. You have no idea how many times I've visited—in my dreams." Rosemary's smile was genuine, any hint of her earlier sadness gone. "It's been so long—"

"Too long." Tansy hugged Rosemary. "We have to promise never to let that happen again. Astrid and I have missed you."

Astrid joined in the hug then, the three of them a

tangle of arms and varying shades of red and gold hair. "I agree."

"Me, too." Rosemary's voice was muffled. "I promise."

Mags watched the sisters. They'd grown up so close—just like she and Camellia. Being apart for so long... Well, Mags couldn't imagine it. She was having a hard time with the idea of Camellia moving across town to Van's home. She didn't want to think about coming downstairs each morning and not seeing Camellia. Every morning was the same. Camellia, sitting in her chair at the table, tea in hand, and her menagerie of adopted pets sprawling on the floor at her feet.

Mags shook off the image. She had things to do. Thinking that way was the surest way to fall apart. Her mother had taught them to keep a smile on your face through anything. Be polite and social without getting too familiar. Their mother hadn't taken kindly to women that cried or carried on or caused a scene for attention. She said it was disgraceful. Keeping one's personal business private was the only way to keep a family's name clean and respectable. Mags tried to do the same. Honey, Texas, had too many town scuttlebutts—like Willadeene Svoboda and her entourage of bored silver-haired ladies—constantly sniffing around and stirring up drama.

Today would be an exercise in patience, manners and self-control. Since her sister was the kind, big-hearted woman that she was, most of Honey would be in attendance today. Meaning, the gossip-loving Willadeene and her cronies would be there. Mags had voiced her concerns but Camellia assured her everyone would be on their best behavior. Mags, of course, knew better. Weddings were just the sort of place to stir up trouble and create a spectacle or plant the seeds for nefarious rumors. Mags had already spoken to her nieces and her daughter and they agreed to keep today's focus on Camellia's wedding.

"We've got plenty of time for hugging later." Mags was gentle, but the women needed to get a move on. "*After* your Aunt Camellia gets married."

The three sisters ended their group hug, all three of them a little flushed and teary-eyed.

"That's right. I'm getting married." Camellia's nervous giggle had them all laughing with her. "I'll try to behave and not move, Mags. I promise."

"Good. I wouldn't want to make a mess of your hair." Mags gave her sister a sly smile in the vanity mirror.

"You wouldn't." Camellia blew her a little kiss.

There was a general commotion as nine females of varying age began to ready themselves for the afternoon's festivities.

"More?" Astrid walked around Nova, taking in her stepdaughter's flowered wreath circlet and the fresh flowers she'd woven through the little girl's braided updo.

"Any more and the bees might get a little too excited." Tansy used a daisy as a pointer.

Rosemary, who sat on the bed, chuckled softly.

"She's perfect." Shelby was helping Halley button up her junior bridesmaid dress. "And so are you." She placed her hands on Halley's shoulders and turned the teen to see her reflection.

"Wow." Halley smiled. "I feel so…wow."

"Well, you look wow, too." Tansy tapped Halley on the nose with the daisy.

Mags used the large vanity mirror to keep an eye on

everything, removing the rollers from Camellia's hair one at a time. It had been so long since she'd felt this content. Like all was right with the world. And she wanted to keep it that way.

"Oh dear." Camellia's exclamation was soft but Mags heard it all the same.

"Oh dear, what?" Mags met her sister's gaze in the mirror.

"I'm a bit poofy, don't you think?" Camellia pointed at the rather large bump on the top of her head. "I knew better than to put a roller there. What was I thinking?"

Mags pressed against the curl but it popped back up. "You'll be wearing a flower circlet, Camellia."

"It looks like a tidal wave. Cresting. Right there." She poked the curl, which wiggled in a rather wave-like fashion.

Mags giggled. "I'm sorry." She covered her mouth.

But Camellia started giggling, too, making the curl bounce and shimmy—which had them both laughing even harder.

"What did we miss?" Astrid, along with the rest of them, were watching them.

"My hair." Camellia poked the curl again, swallowing back another giggle. "It's horrible."

But an hour later, Mags had managed to tame the curl, helped Camellia slip into her vintage lace garden-party wedding dress, and made sure her sister felt and looked every bit the glowing bride she was. Mags could hardly wait to see Van's reaction.

Since the wisteria was in full bloom, Camellia had decided to embrace the color and beauty that surrounded them for her celebration. The nieces and Shelby wore matching tea-length cream dresses covered in an elegant wisteria print. Nova, Halley and Bea wore solid pale lavender dresses. Mags, the maid of honor, wore a plum colored tea-length dress with a low V-neck and wide shoulders straps of the same color. All of them wore the same flower circlets in their hair with long thin plum and lavender ribbons hanging down their backs.

"Pictures." Shelby scooped Bea up. "You smile for Auntie Camellia."

Bea nodded and clapped her hands.

"Good girl." Shelby patted Bea's back, glancing Mags's way. "Do you want to go to your Mimi?"

Bea leaned forward with outstretched arms. And Mags's heart melted. "You know I'll never pass up a chance to cuddle my baby bee." She rested Bea on her hip, loving the baby girl's smile and the way she rested her head on Mags's shoulder. "You can cuddle Mimi any time you want." She pressed a kiss to the top of the baby girl's head.

"Let's go." Astrid held open Camellia's bedroom door and waved them outside. "The photographer wanted to get a few bridal party pictures before the wedding."

"Van isn't here." Mags was quick to assure Camellia, bouncing Bea on her hip. "He's just as superstitious as you are." That was something else Mags appreciated about her soon-to-be brother-in-law. He, like Camellia, wanted this to last. If it meant not seeing one another for twenty-four hours before the wedding, so be it. It was no small sacrifice considering her sister and Van hadn't been apart for that length of time since their first date.

They took the hall, went down the wooden stairs— the swish of skirts and excited whispers of the younger girls pulling Mags back in time.

Young Mags and an even younger Camellia had loved

playing dress up in the attic, where Great Grandma Hill's clothes were stored. Great Grandma Sybil Hill may have been a beekeeper's wife, but she'd been socialite Sybil Graham from Boston first. According to their father, Sybil had met Norman Hill at the Texas State Fair and never went back to Boston. She had, however, insisted on having all of her fancy things brought to her. For the girls, Great Grandma Sybil's things were a glimpse into another world. So many full skirts, evening gowns, petticoats, big sparkly broaches and beaded necklaces, and fancy hats. Camellia and Mags would spend hours going through the steamer trunks. From ballerina slippers to an elegant tea set to fancy evening wear and elbow length gloves, there was always a new adventure to have or imaginary world to visit.

There were no elbow length gloves or ballerina slippers in use today. Today was the start of a brand-new adventure for Camellia.

"Mimi." Bea pressed her hand to Mags's cheek.

"Yes, baby bee?" She smiled, giving her granddaughter a bunny-nose rub. "I was just thinking of how much fun we'll have when you're a little older."

Bea smiled widely.

"You and I will have all sorts of adventures together." She made a silly face and Bea's laughter rang out.

For the first fifty years of her life, Mags had waged war against wrinkles. She'd managed to train her facial features to maintain a somewhat blank, therefore wrinkleless, expression. But having her daughter and granddaughter restored to her changed everything. With Shelby and Bea here, smiling and laughing and making silly faces had become a regular part of her daily life. If she was going to wind up with wrinkles, she couldn't think of a better way to earn them.

"Charlie said the photographer is setting up outside." Astrid led the way, holding Nova's hand while the little girl skipped along beside her.

Mags shifted Bea to her other hip, then paused at one of the dozens of yellow blooming lantana buds to show Bea a butterfly. "Butterfly," Mags said. "Isn't he pretty. He's like the bees. Collecting pollen."

Bea nodded as if she understood every word.

Rosemary and Halley walked past them, in deep conversation. Halley was a curious child—she questioned everything.

"You work in a bee research lab in California?" Halley asked Rosemary. "My mom was a researcher, too. Only she studied atmospheric sciences and astronomy."

"That sounds fascinating." Rosemary slowed her pace to match Halley's.

"It was. It is. I want to be like her, someday." Halley reached up to straighten the floral circlet on her head. "We have telescopes all over the place so I practice a lot."

"That's the best way to become an expert. Practice and making mistakes. No one likes to mess up, but sometimes it's the most effective teaching tool." Rosemary stopped to help adjust the pin in Halley's hair.

"Thank you. I never thought about it that way. You can come look through one of our telescopes, if you want?" Halley waited.

"I'd love to. I've always been curious about space and stars—especially black holes." Rosemary's voice lowered. "I remember watching a scary movie I wasn't supposed to, when I was younger, that had a black hole in it. It sucked up spaceships like a vacuum. I've always wondered if that's how they work."

Mags bounced Bea. "Your Auntie Rosemary's brain never stops working, Bea. She and Halley should get along just fine."

"Blah-uh." Bea paused, then babbled some more and waved her hands around for emphasis.

"You don't say?" Mags was certain Bea was saying something in all her gibberish. Likely, something genius because Bea was, of course, a prodigy. "What else?"

"Dog." Bea pointed. "Dog dog. Mimi."

"Yes." Mags glanced at the herd of dogs Camellia had brought into their home through the years. She couldn't be sure, but she suspected Camellia had added another one—or two—when Mags wasn't paying attention. "Lots and lots of dogs." And beside the dogs, walking toward her, was Shelby and a rather well-dressed man. "I bet that's our photographer, Bea."

"Mags." Shelby fidgeted, clasping and unclasping her hands. She was nervous? Her gaze darted to the man, then to Bea, then back to Mags.

"Momma." Bea leaned forward for her mother.

"Hi, baby bee." Shelby took her daughter from Mags, facing her outward so Bea could see everything.

Bea clapped her hands with glee and said, "Hi."

"Hi, Beatrix." The man waved at Bea. From the look on his face, he was no stranger. He was looking at Bea with pure adoration.

Mags had a sinking feeling in the pit of her stomach. Who was he? Surely, he wasn't Bea's father? Shelby never talked about him. But this man was Mags's age, at least. Slightly older.

"Mags, this is my father, Roman Dunholm." Shelby smiled up at the man by her side.

Her initial reaction was to grab Bea, take Shelby's hand and run into the house… But that was ridiculous. Shelby was a grown adult, perfectly capable of making her own decisions. Shelby hadn't mentioned his visit or any changes in their current living situation. She had to hope this man's arrival was because he was missing Shelby and Bea, not that he was taking Shelby and Bea back with him.

"Mr. Dunholm." She held her hand out. *Breathe. Stay calm.*

"Miss Hill." He shook her hand, his gaze locking with hers. "Finally, we meet."

He was curious about her, his dark eyes returning to her again and again. She stood her ground, refusing to be intimidated by him. She knew nothing about the man who'd adopted her daughter—except what Shelby had told her. He was the one who'd read Shelby bedtime stories, kissed her scrapes and bruises away, watched her first steps and watched her walk the graduation stage. He'd been with Shelby every step of the way. Shelby was a delight, and Mags gave him partial credit for that and was grateful to him.

But Roman Dunholm was also the one who'd been against Shelby's search for her birth mother. Now that he was done with his inspection, Mags felt it was within her rights to use her most intimidating expression as she sized the man up.

Mr. Dunholm was shorter than her by an inch. He was trim and fit—he seemed to take care of himself. He had thick black and silver hair, a close-cropped salt-and-pepper beard and mustache, and was impeccably dressed.

From his wire-rimmed glasses, starched coffee-colored slacks, a white button-up shirt, to his casual leather lace up shoes, he was well put together.

"I picked a bad day to visit." He shoved his hands into his pockets. "It looks like some sort of celebration?"

"My sister is getting married." She turned, waving at the preparations all around them.

Dane, Tansy's beau, and his little brother, Leif, were stringing up strand after strand of white fairy lights. They'd already secured the crystal chandelier over the dance floor for the reception. Charlie, Astrid's husband, was straightening the rows of white wooden folding chairs. Nicole Svoboda, a friend of Astrid, Tansy and Rosemary, was placing flower arrangements beside the honeysuckle wrapped arch and around the dance floor. Mags paused, her gaze bouncing back to Nicole. *My goodness.* Nicole, normally one to sport outrageous makeup and hair color and display her tattoos, wore a simple blue sundress and muted makeup. Mags adored the added pale lavender streaks Nicole had added to light brown hair. She looked lovely.

"I've never seen anything like it." Roman scratched his chin. "It's something."

What did that mean?

"It's just like you described." Roman's gaze swept over the family home before he turned to Shelby, sliding an arm around her shoulders.

"Isn't it beautiful?" Shelby asked. "I can't quite explain it, Dad. It's like… I fit here. I belong. I've never felt so… Well, this is home."

Mags saw Roman's smile falter and felt a twinge of sympathy. He'd been a good father to Shelby and now his daughter was referring to Honey Hill Farms as her home.

"And the bees. Oh, you have to meet them." Shelby sighed. "It's crazy, really, how amazing these little creatures are. I've learned so much—"

"Aunt Mags?" Astrid called out. "Shelby?" She waved them over.

"Picture time." Shelby shrugged. "For the bridal party."

Roman gave Shelby's shoulder a squeeze before letting her go.

As much as Mags wanted to ignore the disappointment on the man's face, she couldn't. He adjusted the wire glasses on his nose. "I should probably go—"

"You are welcome to stay." Mags couldn't believe the words were coming out of her mouth. "I'm sure Shelby would like having you here. There's plenty of room and you'll have more of a chance to get to know Shelby's other family."

He studied her for a long moment. "I couldn't impose—"

"It's no imposition." Mags held out her hands and took Bea. "You get to come to Mimi."

"Mimi!" Bea squealed, giving her a big kiss on the cheek.

"My goodness." Mags laughed, carrying Bea to the bridal party patiently waiting on them. "Sorry."

"It's okay. The photographer is taking pics of Aunt Camellia alone first, anyway." Rosemary gestured with her bouquet.

Sure enough, Camellia stood before an explosion of wisteria smiling sweetly at the photographer.

"Who is that man?" Astrid asked, fanning herself, staring pointedly at Roman.

"He looks like that actor. In all the reruns of that

show?" Nicole had joined the group and was glancing across the field at Roman like the rest of them. "You know the one? It was funny. Steve Carell? On television. Not young Steve Carell. Older, silver fox Steve Carell."

"Who's that?" Mags didn't watch television.

"Never mind." Tansy waved the question aside. "Who is he, really?"

"His name is Roman Dunholm." Mags bounced Bea as she spoke. "He's Shelby's adoptive father."

CHAPTER THREE

THERE WAS MOMENT of absolute silence—as if her announcement had stupefied them. Which was exactly how she'd felt as Shelby had made the introductions.

"I'm sorry? Who?" Tansy's brows rose.

Nicole was still staring at the man with interest. "Was she expecting him?"

"I don't think so. If she was, she'd never mentioned it to me." Mags felt certain Shelby would have told her. "I think he wanted to surprise her."

"Well… What… Is he staying?" Astrid was studying the man in question.

"I'm sorry, I'm still processing how good looking he is." Nicole fanned herself. "I never thought I was into older guys but Mr. Silver Fox…" She practically purred the man's name. "Roman Dunholm might be the exception."

"Nicole." Astrid was both amused and horrified by this.

"You're all staring at what?" Dane approached them—turning his head to look in the same direction they were.

"Don't stare." Tansy tugged at his arm.

"Well, hello there." Dane pulled Tansy into a close embrace. "Why would I stare at anything or anyone that wasn't you?" He bent his head to kiss her and kiss her and kiss her.

Mags was fairly certain her mother would not have approved of this public display of passionate affection.

"Blech." Leif made a series of gagging noises.

Mags laughed—so did the rest of them.

"Do you hear something?" Dane lifted his head from Tansy's. "Oh look. There are other people here."

Tansy leaned against him, smiling blissfully.

"Who's the dude with Shelby?" Leif asked. "The one you're all staring at."

"That *dude* is Shelby's dad." Tansy ruffled Leif's overlong curls.

"Like bio-dad or adoptive dad?" He glanced from face-to-face.

"Adoptive." Astrid reached over to take Mags's hand.

Shelby wasn't the product of a willing, love-filled entanglement—a fact her nieces knew. They'd never asked for details and she'd never offered them up. What happened had been horrible but, over time, she'd learned not to let the event rule her. She'd been so young and her family had been struggling with drought, loss of bees and her mother's failing health. Giving up her baby had been the best option. Shelby had gone to the Dunholms and, every day, Mags had grieved for her baby girl.

"He's not sticking around, is he?" Dane played with one of the flowers in Tansy's hair. "Or is he crashing Camellia's wedding?"

"I hope not." Astrid squeezed her hand.

"I hope so." Nicole smiled, biting her lower lip and fluttering her eyelashes.

"Nicole." Tansy rolled her eyes. "He's just the sort of *development* Willadeene will jump on."

Mags took a deep breath. Tansy was right. Roman would be a distraction—the very thing Mags had hoped to prevent for Camellia's big day. She was kicking herself as she admitted, "Well, actually, I…might have invited him to stay for the wedding."

All eyes swiveled her way.

"That's…sweet of you." But Astrid's owl-like eyes were shocked.

"Aunt Mags…" Tansy opened her mouth but nothing more came out.

"I can't believe Willadeene is still wreaking such havoc." Rosemary frowned. Her hands on her hips. "Why doesn't someone put the woman in her place." She shot Nicole an apologetic look. "I'm sorry, Nic, I know she's your mom—"

"Oh, no. I totally agree. Willadeene and I aren't close. Like, at all." Nicole held up her hand to stop Rose. "Mom or not, I have no illusions about the woman."

"The Wicked Witch of the—" But Leif broke off when Dane flicked him, hard, on the ear. "Oww."

"Dane." Mags chastised, shooting him her most disapproving look. "Be nice to your little brother."

Dane let go of Tansy to take her hand. "Come on, Magnolia. You, of all people, know how it is to be the oldest sibling. He was about to make a grievous error. It's my duty to stop that from happening." His smile was rather devastating. If it wasn't for poor Leif still rubbing his ear and red-faced, she might have been swayed.

Mags's brows rose but she managed not to smile in return. "You're wasting your charm on me, Dane Knudson. Now, apologize to poor Leif while we go take pictures." She extricated her hand from Dane's grasp and waved the others forward.

She noticed Dane grab Leif in a headlock. Seconds later, Dane was tickling Leif until the teen was laughing and trying to pull away.

"They're two little boys trapped in six foot plus size bodies." And Tansy didn't sound the least bit upset about it.

Mags didn't argue.

The pictures went well. The photographer was a bit jumpy over the bees and Bea smiled only when the photographer *wasn't* taking pictures so Camellia called in reinforcements. Bea adored Camellia's canine menagerie. The baby girl was so excited when Camellia called them over, she smiled for the next ten minutes straight.

"Now you have all your mutts in your bridal pictures." Mags suspected her sister calling her beloved fur babies over wasn't purely to soothe baby Bea. They were, as Camellia pointed out, the only children she'd have.

Camellia crouched, giving pats and scratches and adoring words to whatever dog stepped close. "They're family, too."

"Don't I know it." Mags wondered how many brides would kneel in the grass, in their wedding dress, to shower her dogs with unbridled affection. It was such a… Camellia thing to do.

"You look lovely." Charlie Driver, Astrid's husband, was solemn-faced as ever.

"Thank you, Charles." Mags hooked her arm through his. "Flattery will get you everywhere."

He chuckled.

"Your daughters look like fairy-princesses." Mags pointed at Nova, spinning around and around on the dance floor, while staring up at the crystal chandelier.

Halley stood close to the wisteria with Astrid, peering at some of the blooms. "Your wife looks beautiful."

"She does." He nodded, a smile on his face. "But she's always beautiful."

"How right you are." Mags patted his arm. "Did you meet Rosemary?"

He nodded.

"We are all so excited she's home." Mags glanced up at him. "Your Halley reminds me of Rosemary. Always thinking. Always asking questions."

"That's Halley, all right." Charlie's gaze drifted to his eldest daughter. "Is there anything else can I do?"

Mags stopped to take in the farm's transformation. Camellia's hope chest had been brimming with color samples, bits of ribbon and lace, postcards and pictures from weddings past. Bits of whimsy with a very vintage feel—that's how Camellia had described it. And everything brought in for the day had been arranged as she wanted it.

Today it seemed as if the family home's flower beds, surrounding bushes, and blooming vines and vegetation had put on their best colors for the big day. The tubular flower of Blue Giant Hyssop. Black-eyed Susan swaying in the breeze, their golden daisy like petals and dark center cones instantly recognizable. Interspersed with the abundant vines of wisteria were the yellow flowers of the Lantana. Clumps of white-petaled Rock Daisies, bright white beneath the spring sun. Bluebeard, Texas bluebonnets, prairie asters and foxgloves added Impressionist-style strokes of deep blues, purples, to the palest of lavender, to the mix.

"I can't think of a single thing." Mags took her time, going over every detail at least twice—and spied Roman

Dunholm unrolling a strand of twinkle lights and feeding them up to Dane. "Excuse me, Charles." She patted his arm and hurried to the ladder Dane was using to wind more lights around the tree.

"I've already re-wrapped them." Dane sighed. "I know they might not be exactly two inches apart—"

"They look fine." Mags interrupted. "Mr. Dunholm, you are under no obligation to help."

"Call me Roman, please." He glanced at the lights in his hand and then up at Dane. "I'd rather help than stand around. If that's all right with you, Magnolia?"

Mags wasn't sure she liked his reserved smile or that there was a hint of condescension to his voice.

"Thanks for letting Dad stay." Shelby hugged her. "It's weird to see you side-by-side but I like it." She rested her head on Mags's shoulder. "I'm so happy." She reached out and took Roman's hand.

Mags hugged her daughter. "If you're happy, then I'm happy."

"The minister is here." Tansy stood by the gate, waving.

"Is it time already?" Mags stared at the lights. "Finish what you can and get cleaned up, Dane. I can't believe it's almost time." She took a deep breath as her nieces and daughter circled around her. "I might wind up locking Willadeene Svoboda and her friends in the old honey house before the night is through. Whatever it takes for Camellia to have her special day."

"Dane said he'd dance with her," Tansy said. "And he's going to force Leif and his father, too."

Mags grinned at the idea of that peacock of a man, Harald Knudson, tangling with Willadeene. "That will be a sight."

"Charlie, too." Astrid grimaced and added, "Not that he's happy about it."

"I wouldn't be either." Nicole sighed. "If I had a guy to throw at her, I totally would. Benji's terrified of her so I'm not even going there."

"But... Benji's her grandson?" Rosemary shook her head. "That's awful."

"It is. I won't ask it of the poor boy." Mags straightened her back. "None of us are magicians so we'll have to take it as it comes, I suppose. I'm going to get Camellia some tea and have her sit and be quiet." Mags turned to go. "Mr. Dunholm."

"Is there something wrong with this woman? This Willadeene?" His brow was furrowed.

"Yes." Mags cocked a brow. "Am I to assume you were eavesdropping?"

"I was standing here when you started talking." He adjusted his glasses. "Does that count as eavesdropping?"

"I believe it would, in polite society." She brushed past him and headed into the house. "Camellia?"

"In the kitchen."

Sure enough, Camellia was in her chair, sipping her tea, looking calm and lovelier than ever—even with all of her pets covering the better part of the floor.

"I was coming to make you some tea." Mags peered into the tea kettle, put an orange-honey tea bag into a cup, and filled it with steaming water. "Are you pleased with everything? Is there anything else that needs to be done?"

"It's perfect." Camellia sipped her tea, her gaze darting to the large clock on the wall. "Not too much longer." Her tea cup was shaking.

Mags took a deep breath. "Camellia Ann, it's time we had an important talk."

Camellia set her cup down. "What is it? Is everything all right?"

"It should be, but you need to be prepared." Mags took her sister's hand. "You see, when a man and a woman love each other very much and marry, like you and Van are about to do, there are certain expectations."

"Are you giving me *the* talk?" Camellia blinked, a slow smile growing.

"I thought it was only fair to warn you." Mags sipped her tea, grinning ear-to-ear. "Unless you and your soon-to-be husband have already started the honeymoon?"

Camellia giggled. "He's old-fashioned, Mags." She couldn't stop giggling.

"Not too old-fashioned, I hope. You're a young, passionate woman with needs he needs to fulfill." She paused, enjoying her sister's laughter. "Perhaps I should speak to him about his husbandly duties."

Camellia broke into a full laughing fit then. "I can see his face." She snorted. "Poor Van." She kept laughing. "Do not do any such thing."

There was a thump and the front door closing, then footsteps running down the hall to the kitchen.

"What's going on in here?" Leif came in, hopping on one foot as he tugged on his boot.

"Never you mind." Camellia's laughter slowed and she dabbed her cheeks with a handkerchief.

"You look beautiful." Leif blushed as he said it.

"And you look especially handsome." Camellia stood, smoothed the boy's shirt and adjusted his collar. "I'm sure Kerrielynn will approve."

Leif turned a brilliant red. "She should be here by

now." He thundered out of the kitchen, the front door slamming behind him.

The sisters' winced, then went back to their tea—only to have Charlie walk in.

"I'm looking for Astrid." He did a quick search of the kitchen, Astrid's purse clutched in his hands.

"She's not here, Charles. Last time I saw her, she and Halley were exploring the flowers."

Charlie frowned and nodded then walked out the back door.

Camella shot her a questioning look. Mags shrugged. They sipped on their tea, the voices of guests reaching them. Camellia reached for Mags at the same time Mags reached for her. They held hands, held tight.

The front door opened and, this time, Dane stepped into the kitchen. "This might not be the right time but I know you and Van will be gone for a bit and I wanted to make sure I did this the right way." He smiled. "You both look beautiful. Camellia, Van is a lucky man." He cleared his throat and started pacing.

Mags and Camellia exchanged another questioning look before Mags asked, "What is it, Dane? Should we be worried?"

"No." He stopped and held up his hands. "It's just... Well, my family—my father doesn't have the best track record with marriage. I hope you won't hold that against me as I want to ask Tansy to marry me." He cleared his throat. "With your permission, of course."

Camellia jumped up and hugged him. "Of course, sweet boy. My heart is full to bursting."

Mags stood. "I might need to think about it."

Dane's smile melted away, but he nodded. "If you—"

"Mags, behave." Camellia huffed, rolling her eyes. "This is no time to torture him."

"Fine." Mags smiled. "Did you really think I would say no?"

"I hoped you wouldn't." Dane hugged her close. "But I didn't want to take it for granted that you'd both be happy about it."

Mags smiled up at him. "And that, Dane Knudson, is why I heartly give you my blessing."

"Thank you. You know I love her more than anything." Dane's jaw clenched. "I love you both, too."

Mags felt a surprising sting in the corner of her eye.

"We love you, too." Camellia squeezed his arm. "So much excitement."

"The best is yet to come." Mags slid an arm around her sister's waist. "I imagine your groom is on the way."

"He was parking when I came in. I'll go back and see if we're ready." Dane was all smiles when he left.

"It sounds like it's time to take our places." Mags circled around Camellia, smoothing and flouncing until she was satisfied. "You've never looked more beautiful." Her throat went tight and her eyes were full of tears but she managed to smile.

"Thank you. I know you're worried about my marrying Van but it's going to be wonderful. It won't be a big adjustment, you'll see." She took Mags's hands in hers. "You're my sister. My best friend. I love you dearly. Nothing and no one will ever change that."

Mags drew her sister into her arms and hugged her. She wasn't worried; she was terrified. Not about Van and Camellia or how happy they would be. But about being lonely, missing Camellia and growing old alone. *Such cheerful thoughts.*

The front door opened again and Nova came bouncing in. "It's time, it's time. Everyone is here and they're all waiting for you."

Mags tucked Camellia's arm through hers. "Let's not keep him waiting."

CHAPTER FOUR

Mags KEPT HER eyes straight ahead. She had Camellia's arm hooked through hers and they kept giving each other supportive squeezes but she knew one look at her sister might break her calm exterior. Ahead of her were the people who gave her life meaning. The three adored nieces she and Camellia had raised, her precious Shelby, Halley, Nova, and Bea. Dane and Charlie looked so handsome and proud as they watched her and Camellia advance. They were standing up with Van, along with Van's brother-in-law Julian and Van's nephew Oren. While Mags prided herself on being a rational person, even she felt the excitement and love for Van and Camellia.

They were almost to the honeysuckle and wisteria draped arch when Mags finally glanced at the groom. The look on Van's face as he waited for Camellia took her breath away. She'd never questioned Van loved her sister, but she'd never fully grasped just how much until now. That look gave Mags instant comfort. She would never need to worry about Camellia because Van would take good care of her. For the first time, Mags was truly happy for her sister. A tear, or two, slipped down her cheeks and there was nothing she could do to stop them.

Van reached his hand out, Camellia took it and let Mags go.

She didn't falter or try to keep a hold of her sister. People were watching. It was possible her mother and grandmother were looking down on them. If that was the case, they wouldn't approve of any emotional outburst. She took her place by Tansy and kept her eyes on the happy couple.

It was a short service, with traditional vows, and a surprisingly passionate kiss. The guests applauded and Van and Camellia walked back down the aisle as husband and wife.

"They're just precious," Tansy whispered.

"And so happy," Astrid agreed. "They're practically glowing."

"I've never seen anything so romantic." Shelby bounced Bea in her arms. "I'm so happy for them."

Mags nodded. Everything the girls said was true. "Let's head over for more pictures." She took Van's brother-in-law's arm and headed down the aisle, the rest of the bridal party following.

"The photographer's over here," Nicole called to them, offering a glass to Astrid. "Ginger ale?"

"Oh, thank you." Astrid took the cup.

"Your Charles was looking for you earlier. But it looks like he found you." Her gaze bounced between Astrid and her husband. "Is everything all right?"

"Yes," Charlie answered, giving Astrid a gentle smile and taking her hand in his.

"Everything is fine." Astrid patted her arm. "I promise."

But Astrid looked anything but fine. Her color was off and she was dewy with sweat. Astrid was never sick. Not ever. And even though she was probably overreacting, Mags grabbed her niece's hand. "Are you sick?" As far as she could remember, Astrid had been fine this morning. Or had she? Mags had been so preoccupied, she might have missed something. "Is there something I can do?"

Astrid glanced at Charlie, who shrugged. "We didn't want to tell anyone until after the wedding but—"

"We're going to have a baby." Charlie slid his arm around Astrid and pulled her against his side. "She's tired. Nauseated. The girls and I are trying to make sure she rests and takes care of herself."

Mags laughed. "Astrid, how wonderful. Charles, congratulations. What a day." She wiped at the tear that spilled onto her cheek. "You must tell your aunt. She will be overjoyed for you both—and for all of us." She wiped another tear aside. "Happy news is always welcome."

"I agree." Charlie tucked one of Astrid's long curls behind her ear.

"What's the hold up?" Tansy called. "Picture time."

"You two go on, I need just a minute." Mags sought a moment's refuge between two tall bushes. She took several deep breaths, patted her cheeks dry, and smiled up at the sky overhead. What a day. She took another deep breath and turned.

"Magnolia?" Roman Dunholm stood, with Bea in his arms, watching her.

"Roman." She stepped out from between the bushes. "You move very stealthily."

"I do?" He shrugged. "Shelby asked me to find you." He nodded at the altar. "For pictures."

"Thank you." She had no choice but to lean in and coo for Bea.

"Actually, I wanted to thank you." He cleared his throat. "It was generous of you to let me stay. Shelby loves being here—she loves you. I wanted to see it all for myself. So, I could picture where she was, if that makes sense?"

Mags nodded.

"I want her to be happy but I don't want to lose her." He nodded, his dark eyes shifting to Shelby. "She is all I have, Magnolia. And… I miss her. I miss Bea. I want to be a part of her life. Whether it's here or…wherever."

Mags nodded. "You should know, I'm not especially easy to get along with. I have strong opinions, particular tastes and no tolerance for drama. Most importantly, I love my family above all else… Which I believe we have in common."

"We do. My late wife was the same." Roman looked her directly in the eyes. "And I respect your honesty."

"I will never prevent you from seeing Shelby or Bea. You're her father and for that, you are part of this family." Mags took the baby.

"Then you wouldn't mind if I found a bed and breakfast and stayed for a while?" He adjusted his glasses.

"Why would I mind?" She smiled as Bea ran her tiny fingers over the pearls of her necklace.

He seemed to consider this. "I…I don't know."

She gave him an assessing gaze. She was torn. On the one hand, playing nice with Roman would make Shelby happy. On the other hand, he'd been against Shelby trying to find her so playing nice wouldn't be easy. In the end, Shelby's happiness was what mattered most. "I suppose, since Camellia is married and will be off on her honeymoon, we might be able to find a room here." She turned as Tansy was calling her name.

Roman blinked.

"You can think about it while I go take pictures." She

smiled at Bea and headed to the altar without a backward glance. "Your grampa is a strange man." Bea giggled. "My thoughts exactly."

Bea gave her an open-mouth kiss on the cheek.

"Thank you." She kissed Bea back. "Do you think he'll stay?" It was more practical. It would also be more private. Either way, Roman Dunholm staying would definitely get people talking. She gave Bea a bunny-nose rub. "First tears, now scandal, your Mimi is breaking all the rules."

Mags felt certain they posed for a hundred pictures—maybe more. The cake was brought out and another hundred pictures were taken of it, the cake cutting, and Van and Camellia feeding one another. The band from the local Veteran's Hall played big band and jazz and the dancing began. Van was a surprisingly good dancer, spinning Camellia out then reeling her back in. When he dropped a kiss on her lips, there were plenty of whistles and clapping from the guests.

Things started to slow a few hours later—not that Van and Camellia noticed. They danced until the sky was dark and the guests were saying their goodbyes.

Mags was profoundly relieved and the slightest bit proud of herself. She'd managed to go the whole day without exchanging anything more than pleasantries with the wedding guests. She'd been warm and polite, every bit a Hill hostess. If Willadeene Svoboda or Harald Knudson appeared in her line of vision, she'd turned and headed the opposite way.

Mostly, she kept an eye on everything—especially the happy couple. She was bound and determined to make this a perfect day. She did have one dance with Van and another with Bea, but she preferred to stand apart and watch or help as the need arose. Like making sure Astrid stayed hydrated and nibbling on the crackers Charlie had stowed in her purse. Nova and Halley kept Charlie on the dance floor while poor Astrid watched and cheered them on. Dear Astrid was too big hearted to complain or leave early—for fear of missing anything.

Tansy and Dane rarely had eyes for anyone else.

Leif had his sweetheart, Kerrielynn, on his arm the whole afternoon but the two of them wandered off somewhere around twilight.

Rosemary and Shelby sat at one of the white linen draped tables, laughing and talking like they were best of friends, while Roman Dunholm sat listening in and sipping his cup of punch.

As Van and Camellia made the rounds amongst the remaining tables, Mags cut a massive slice of cake. It was a long-standing tradition for their family to let the bees know when a big life change happened. Births, weddings, deaths—that sort of thing. They'd take cake to the apiary, tell the bees the news and leave the cake so their winged family could take part in the celebration.

She turned, saw Camellia sitting with Astrid, and carried the cake plate to their table.

"You're green, Astrid." Camellia was saying, taking her niece's hand. "You're never ill, Astrid, not ever."

"Are you sick, Astrid?" Rosemary stood and came around the table.

"What going on?" Tansy asked, tugging Dane to the table. "What's wrong?"

Charlie's hands rested on Astrid's shoulders and he leaned forward to whisper something in her ear.

Astrid smiled up at him. "Charlie wanted to tell you

all. So did Aunt Mags." She leaned closer to Camellia. "But I didn't want to detract from your big day."

"Sweet girl." Camellia glanced at Van. "If something is going on, we'll stay put until everything is right as rain."

"Of course, we will." Van nodded, looking almost as concerned as Camellia.

"No, you will not." Astrid shook her head. "I'm pregnant. You will not delay your honeymoon or spend another second worrying about me."

There was a general commotion then. Lots of hugs and kisses and laughter. The three sisters held on to each other the longest, just like they'd done when they were little. So much had changed over the years—while remaining the same.

Mags pressed a hand to her heart and smiled.

"A baby." Camellia squealed, grabbing Mags's arm. "Can you believe it?"

"The more, the merrier." Van hugged Camellia with one arm and offered his hand to Charlie. "Congratulations."

Charlie shook the man's hand and nodded, wearing his sweet awkward smile.

"Mags?" Shelby tugged her arm, her voice so low only Mags could hear her. "Are you sure about Dad staying here? You're really okay with it?"

Right. Her impulsive, sympathy offer. She'd never thought Roman Dunholm would agree. She answered truthfully. "I'd rather he stays here than have you and Bea leave."

"Why would we leave?" Shelby rested her head on Mags's shoulder. "Unless we need to move on?"

"No. Don't be silly." She took Shelby's hand. "I'd choose for you stay here forever but I know that may not be what's best for you." She turned so Shelby faced her. "This is your home, Shelby. You and Bea are Bee Girls now. You're welcome here as long as you like. And if you want your father here, then he's welcome, too."

Shelby hugged her tight. "Oh, thank you, Mags. You'll like him, I promise. You'll see."

Mags caught sight of Roman Dunholm. The man was sitting, bouncing Bea, and making the most hideously amusing faces she'd ever seen. Bea loved it—giggling and clapping her hands until he did it again. He appeared completely at ease with making a fool out of himself for the baby. Mags had to, reluctantly, respect his single-minded devotion. But like him? The man that hadn't wanted Shelby to find her? She wasn't so sure.

"What about the bees?" Charlie asked. It hadn't been all that long ago that he and Astrid had shared their cake with one of the apiaries.

"They're waiting." Mags offered up the giant piece of cake. "For the bees. I thought, between your marriage, Rosemary's homecoming, and Astrid and Charlie's announcement, the bees deserved a hefty slice."

Camellia smiled as she took the cake plate. "I couldn't agree more. Shall we, husband?"

"We shall." Van offered his arm to Camellia. "Let's go tell the bees all the good news, my beautiful wife." As soon as Van declared he wanted to repair some of the damage to the Fairy-Tale apiary hives, he'd found his place at the farm. The Fairy-Tale bees would have a feast tonight.

Mags stared up at the darkening sky. Tomorrow

would be a brand-new chapter for the inhabitants of Honey Hill Farms. But the bees, the family and the love shared amongst them would remain. Knowing that was all Mags needed to be happy. And she was.

* * * * *

Do you love romance books?

JOIN

on Facebook by scanning the code below:

A group dedicated to book recommendations, author exclusives, SWOONING and all things romance! A community made for romance readers by romance readers.

Facebook.com/groups/readloverepeat